WEAKEST LYNX

THE LYNX SERIES

FIONA QUINN

WEAKEST

Lynx

Fiona Quinn

THE WORLD OF INIQUUS

Ubicumque, Quoties. Quidquid

Iniquus - /i'ni/kwus/ our strength is unequalled, our tactics unfair – we stretch the law to its breaking point. We do whatever is necessary to bring the enemy down.

THE LYNX SERIES
Weakest Lynx

Missing Lynx

Chain Lynx

Cuff Lynx

Gulf Lynx

Hyper Lynx

MARRIAGE LYNX

STRIKE FORCE
In Too DEEP

JACK Be Quick

InstiGATOR

Uncommon Enemies

Wasp

Relic

Deadlock

Thorn

FBI Joint Task Force

Open Secret

Cold Red

Even Odds

Kate Hamilton Mysteries

Mine

Yours

Ours

Cerberus Tactical K9 Team Alpha

Survival Instinct

Protective Instinct

Defender's Instinct

Delta Force Echo

Danger Signs

Danger Zone

Danger Close

This list was created in 2021. For an up-to-date list, please visit FionaQuinnBooks.com

If you prefer to read the Iniquus World in chronological order you will find a full list at the end

of this book.

For my husband, Todd

And our children
~ my life's most amazing teachers.

1

The black BMW powered straight toward me. Heart pounding, I stomped my brake pedal flush to the floorboard. My chest slammed into the seat belt, snapping my head forward. There wasn't time to blast the horn, but the scream from my tires was deafening. I gasped in a breath as the BMW idiot threw me a nonchalant wave—his right hand off the wheel—with his left hand pressed to his ear, still chatting on his cell phone. Diplomatic license plates. *Figures.*

Yeah, I didn't really need an extra shot of adrenaline—like a caffeine IV running straight to my artery—I was already amped.

"Focus, Lexi," I whispered under my breath, pressing down on the gas. "Follow the plan. Give the letter to Dave. Let him figure this out." I sent a quick glance down to my purse where a corner of the cream-colored envelope jutted out, then veered my Camry back into the noonday DC gridlock, weaving past the graffitied storefronts. I recognized that the near-miss with the BMW guy probably wasn't his fault. I couldn't remember the last ten minutes of drive time.

I watched my review mirror as a bike messenger laced

between the moving cars on his mission to get the parcel in his bag to the right guy at the right time. Once he handed over his package, he'd be done—lucky him. Even though I was handing my letter off to Dave, the truth was that wouldn't be my endpoint. I wasn't clear about what an endpoint would even look like. Safe. It might look like I was safe, that I had my feet back under me. But that thought seemed like it was far out on the horizon, and right now, I was just looking for something to grab on to, to keep me afloat.

When I finally parked in front of Dave Murphy's mid-century brick row house, I sat for a minute, trying to regain my composure. I'd pushed this whole mess to the back burner for as long as I could but after last night's nightmare... Well, better to get a detective's opinion. Dave had handled enough crackpots over his time with the DCPD that he'd have a better grasp of the threat level. Right now, even with all my training, I was scared out of my mind.

I glanced down at my hands. The tremor in them sent the afternoon sunlight dancing off my brand-new engagement and wedding rings. I felt like an imposter wearing them—like a little girl dressed up in her mother's clothes. *I'm too young to be dealing with all this crap,* I thought as I shoved my keys into my purse. I pulled my hair into a quick ponytail and stepped out into the February cold. Casting anxious glances up and down the street, I jogged up the stairs to bang on Dave's front door.

The screen squeaked open almost immediately as if he'd been standing there waiting for my knock. "Hey, Baby Girl," he said, stepping out of the way to let me in. Dave had been calling me Baby Girl since I was born because my parents couldn't decide on my name, and that was how I was listed on my hospital ankle tag.

"Glad I found you at home." I walked in and plopped down

on the blue gingham couch. It had been here since I could remember. The fabric was threadbare and juice stained by his five-year-old twins. On a cop's salary, fine furnishings ranked low in priority. Right now—edgy and confused—I appreciated the comfort of familiarity.

Dave shifted into detective mode—hands on hips, eyes scanning me. "Long time, no see."

"Where are Cathy and the kids?" I asked.

"They've got dentist appointments. Did you come to tell us your news?" He lifted his chin to indicate my left hand and settled at the other end of the couch, swiveling until we were face to face.

"Uhm, no." I twisted my rings, suddenly feeling drained and bereft. What wouldn't I give to have my husband Angel here? The corners of my mouth tugged down. I willed myself to stay focused on the reason for the visit. My immediate safety had to take priority over my grief.

Dave raised a questioning brow, waiting for me to continue.

"Angel and I got married Wednesday. I'm Lexi Sobado now." My voice hitched, and tears pressed against my lids. I lowered my lashes, so Dave wouldn't see. But his eyes had locked onto mine, and he never missed much.

"Married? At your age? No introduction? No wedding invitation? Why isn't he here with you now?" Dave angled his head to the side and crossed his arms over his middle-aged paunch. "I'd like to meet the guy," he all but snarled.

Dave probably thought I'd come here because my husband screwed things up already. I pulled the pillow from behind my back and hugged it to me like a shield. "I'm sorry. I should have let you and Cathy know what was going on—I was caught up, and I just..." I stopped to clear my throat. "Angel and I got married at the courthouse, and no one came with us. Not even Abuela Rosa."

"Angel Sobado. He's kin to Rosa, then?"

I gave the slightest tip of a nod. "Angel is her great-nephew. I couldn't bring him with me today because he deployed with the Rangers to the Middle East Thursday. That's why everything happened so fast. He was leaving." The last word stuck in my throat and choked me.

Dave leaned forward to rest his elbows on his knees. Lacing his fingers, he tapped his thumbs together. "Huh. That's a helluva short honeymoon. Married Wednesday. Gone Thursday." Dave's tone had dropped an octave and gained a fringe of fatherly concern.

His compassion gave me permission to break down. But those Angel-emotions were mine. Private. Right now, I needed to hold myself in check long enough to get through my mission of handing off the letter. I shifted my feet back and forth over the rug as I glared at my purse.

"Might even explain the expression on your face," Dave said, narrowing his eyes. He slouched against the arm of the over-stuffed couch.

Stalling wasn't going to make this any easier. I reached a hesitant hand into my bag, pulled out a plastic Zip-loc holding the envelope, and held it up for Dave. "The expression is because of this," I said.

Dave took the bag. After a brief glance, he hefted himself to his feet. Over at his desk, he pulled on a pair of Nitrile gloves, then carefully removed the letter.

Dearest India Alexis,
   O my Luve's like the melodie

That's sweetly play'd in tune!
As fair thou art, my bonnie lass,
So deep in love, am I:
And I will love thee still, my dear,
Till a' your bones are white and dry:
Till a' your veins gang dry, my dear,
And your skin melt with the sun;
I will luve thee until your heart is still my dear
When the sands of your life shall no more run.
And fare thee weel, my only Luve,
And fare thee weel a while!
And I will come again, my Luve, so I can watch
you die.

Dave read the words aloud then stared at me hard; his brows pulled in tight enough that the skin on his forehead accordioned. "What the—"

"Someone shoved the poem under the door to my room, and it's scaring the bejeezus out of me." I gripped the pillow tighter.

Dave peered over the top of his reading glasses. "Last night? This morning?"

"Wednesday morning." I braced when I said it, knowing it would tick Dave off that I didn't bring this to him immediately. Ever since my dad died, his buddies had stepped in and tried to take over the fathering job, even though I'd be turning twenty in a few days.

True to my expectations, Dave was red-faced and bellowing. "*Wednesday?* You waited two whole days to tell me you've gotten a friggin death threat?"

Yup, this was exactly the response Dad would have given me.

Dave jumped up, pacing across the room. Obviously, he didn't think this was someone's idea of a joke. Fear tightened my chest at his confirmation. I had hoped he'd say, "No worries—someone is having fun pranking you," and then I could go on about my life without the major case of heebie-jeebies that tingled my skin and made me want to run and hide.

"It was our wedding day." I worked to modulate my voice to sound soft and reasonable. "I only had a few short hours before Angel had to take off. So yeah, I decided to focus on us instead of this." I motioned toward the paper in his hand.

Dave took in a deep breath, making his nostrils flare. "Okay." I could almost see his brain shifting gears. "When you first picked up the letter, did you get any vibes?"

"You mean, ESP-wise?"

He nodded stiffly, his eyes hard on me.

Vibes. That wasn't the word I would have chosen to explain my sensations. "I didn't hear anything. It was more like an oily substance oozing over me." I tucked my nose into the soft cloth of the pillow and breathed in the scent of cinnamon fabric freshener. "I vomited." My voice dropped to a whisper. "It felt like evil and craziness, and I can still smell that stench." A shiver raced down my spine.

Dave's lips sealed tightly; he was probably trying to hold back a litany of expletives. Finally, he asked, "That's all?"

"Yes."

"Did any of your neighbors notice anyone unusual lurking around? Did you check with management and run through the security tapes?"

"Dave, didn't you hear? My apartment building burned to the ground three weeks ago. I assumed you knew. It was on the news."

Dave's eyebrows shot straight up.

"I've been living in a motel the Red Cross rented out for all the families displaced by the fire. But to answer your question, no, nobody saw anything, and there were no cameras trained on my motel corridor." I curled my lips in to keep them from trembling. I was used to holding my emotions in check. I trained myself to present a sweet exterior, a costume of sorts, but right now, I was filled to overflowing, and my mask kept slipping out of place.

"Shit." Dave ran a hand over his face. "I had no idea. I'm letting your parents down. Apartment burned, married, husband gone, and now a death threat." His eyes narrowed on me. "Do you think that about covers all of your surprises for me today?"

I paused for a beat. "Yeah, Dave, I think that's it for today." Okay, even if he was like family, the way Dave was talking pissed me off. I was frightened. I wanted a hug and his reassurance. What I was getting was... Dave's brand of love. He wouldn't be this red-faced and agitated if he wasn't worried about me. Tears prickled behind my eyelids, blurring my vision.

"Hey, now. Stop. We'll get to the bottom of this. Did you already let Spyder McGraw know what's going on?"

I wiped my nose with the back of my wrist. "Spyder's still off-grid. I have no idea when he'll get home."

"Were you assigned a different partner while he's gone?"

"No, sir. I only ever worked for Spyder—he sort of wanted to keep me a secret." I still couldn't believe Mom had sat Dave down and told him all about my apprenticeship with Spyder McGraw. Under Spyder's tutelage, I was following my dream of becoming an Intelligence Officer, learning to out-think and out-maneuver the bad guys trying to hurt American interests. And like anyone heading toward a life in the intelligence community, my skills needed to go under the radar. Now that my mom had died, only four people—Spyder, the Millers, and

Dave—knew that side of my life. I would prefer Dave didn't know.

"Still, did you consider bringing this to Spyder's commander? Iniquus would probably give him a heads up. Get a message to him."

"Iniquus is my last resort. Sure, Spyder told me to talk to them if I ever found myself in trouble." I sucked in a deep breath of air. "Bottom line? He never wanted them to know I worked for him, well, for them. Safety in anonymity and all that." My fingers kneaded the stuffing in the pillow. "Besides, I guess I was hoping this would all just go away."

Dave's eyes were hard on me. "You know better. Once some psycho's caught you on his radar, you're stuck there until someone wins."

"Okay, so I make sure it's me who wins."

"Exactly right." He considered me for a minute before he asked, "You've kept up with your martial arts training?"

"I have a sparring partner who's pretty good. We rent time at a Do Jang twice a week."

Dave lowered his head to read over the poem again. He put the letter and envelope back in the Zip-loc and placed it on his mantle. Pulling off his gloves with a snap, he looked down at them. "I hate these things. They give me a rash. Look, I'm going to take this down to the station and open a file. If you get anything else, I want you to bring it to me right away. Understood?"

"Yes, sir."

"This is the only poem, letter, communication of any kind you've gotten?"

I nodded. For the first time since I walked into Dave's house, I became aware of sounds other than our conversation and the thrumming blood behind my eardrums. A football game played on TV. I glanced over as the announcer yelled some gibberish about a first down, then moved my gaze back to Dave. "You must have taken graveyard shift last night," I said.

He picked up a remote, zapped off the TV, and sent me a raised eyebrow.

"It doesn't take a psychic. You look like an unmade bed."

Dave ran a hand over his dark hair, thick on the sides, sparse on top. He hadn't used a comb today or bothered to shave. He was hanging-out-at-home comfy in jeans and beat-to-hell tennis shoes. It looked like the only thing I was interrupting was the game re-run.

"Double homicide. Turned into a long night up to my ankles in sewage."

"Yum." I tried on a smile, but it was plastic and contrived.

Dave narrowed his eyes. "We need to move you. Pronto. It's priority one. You need to be someplace secure where I can keep better tabs on you."

"I've been looking since the fire, but I haven't found anything."

"Would you consider buying?" he asked.

"Yes, actually—I'm looking for a low-cost fixer-upper I can work on to help me get through this year without Angel." I followed Dave into the hallway. "Diversion, and all that."

"How about here, in my neighborhood? I could keep a better eye on you—and you won't be showing up at my door with a suitcase full of surprises." He grabbed his coat from the closet and shrugged it on. "I'm taking you over to meet my neighbor. She has the other half of her duplex on the market." He looked over his shoulder at me. "You shouldn't be running around without a jacket." He handed me an oversized wool parka that smelled like raking leaves. He kicked a Tonka truck out of the way, and we moved out the front door.

On the front porch, I slid into the shadows and took in the length of the road—no cars, no barking dogs, everything quiet.

Dave glanced back. "Coast is clear."

I tucked the coat hood up over my ponytail. Screened by Dave's broad back, I started across the street. Down the road, a car motor revved. I reached under my shirt and pulled out my gun.

2

A rusty "For Sale by Owner" sign swung from the porch rail. Bare wood peeked through the curling paint. I rocked back on my heels as my skeptical eye took in the turn-of-the-century duplex. "A big snow storm's heading this way in a few days. You think the roof will hold?" I asked.

Dave gazed up at the roofline. "It's not in the best of shapes," he conceded. "But of the houses for sale around here, this one might fit your budget."

"It's been on the market awhile?"

"Two-years. So the price tag is bottom-basement."

"Okay." I kicked at the sidewalk. "I'm keeping an open mind."

Dave turned, his gaze following my arm to where I held the Ruger under the fold of my coat. He gripped my shoulders, pushed me toward the ancient oak leaning precariously in front of the house, and scanned up and down the street. His attention back on me, Dave wagged a stern finger. "I didn't see that. What's more, you're going to make damned sure no one else sees that, or you'll end up in a jail cell."

I nodded my understanding.

"You been up to the shooting range with Stan lately?" he asked.

"I'm still going once a week with him, as usual," I said. Stan worked for the DCPD with Dave and had been one of my dad's poker buddies before Dad was killed in the car accident.

"Good." He scanned the neighborhood again. "Wait here."

As Dave clomped up the rickety steps, I holstered the gun. He banged on the door, and a tiny woman with a stooped back pushed open the screen. Her translucent skin, stippled with age spots, creased as she smiled up at Dave.

"Hello, David. What a lovely surprise." She held the door wide. "Won't you come in for a cup of tea?"

"I brought a friend to meet you." Dave gestured toward me, and I climbed the stairs to stand beside him in her living room. She might have been all of five-feet tall. At five-six, I towered over her.

I gently shook her hand, barely clasping her fingers for fear I would break her. She reminded me of my mom's eggshell porcelain teacups that used to sit on our mantle back at the apartment.

"Mrs. Nelson, Lexi's interested in seeing the house you have for sale next door," Dave spoke loudly using staccato, over-enunciated words.

"Oh, wonderful, dear." Mrs. Nelson turned to retrieve a keychain from a basket on her upright piano.

A book of hymns lay open to "Nothing but the Blood." An omen? A warning? Paranoia, I concluded, taking in a deep breath. Mrs. Nelson reached for her coat on the hall tree, and Dave helped her shrug it on.

"I didn't like the couple who lived there last," Mrs. Nelson said, pushing the screen closed behind us and stepping cautiously down the steps with Dave's protective hand under her elbow. "They left their trash on the porch for the neighborhood dogs to get into. What a mess, and it smelled gosh-awful. I was relieved when they moved." In a moment, we stood in front of the fixer-upper, making up the other side of the duplex. Mrs. Nelson unlocked the door, then turned faded blue eyes on me. "You're awfully young." She flipped the switch, flooding the room with light. "Are you married?"

"A newlywed," I said, though it felt like a lie. I needed more time to get used to the idea. "My husband's in Afghanistan right now."

"Oh." Mrs. Nelson touched my arm and raised her other hand to her heart. "How lonely for you."

I bristled. Pity didn't sit well with me.

She shook her head, making her tightly curled hair bob. "I don't know then—this house might need a man. The last family left the place in quite a shamble. Lots of repairs to be made. Lots."

The front door opened into the living room. The space would be a comfortable size with furniture; it seemed overly large, standing empty. Dated, cranberry wallpaper rolled at the seams. I wrinkled my nose as the smell of wet dog rose from the heavily stained, brown, wall-to-wall carpeting.

My breath hung like a cloud in the air. It wasn't much warmer than outside. The furnace rumbled, but the temperature had been set low—just enough to keep pipes from freezing, I guessed. I shoved my hands deep in my pockets and hunched my shoulders as we passed silently through an arched doorway into the dining room. The design mimicked the living room with a fireplace centered on the right wall, flanked on either side by large windows. Wouldn't it be wonderful to have a fire crackling on a wintery night, and a table full of friends enjoying pumpkin soup with sage butter and homemade bread? I imagined the scene, warm and inviting, full of laughter. I pictured Angel stoking the fire and sending me a smile.

Mrs. Nelson patted my arm. "Go ahead and look around upstairs, dear. I'll wait down here."

"Sure, thanks," I said, turning, happy to get out of the room. Thoughts of Angel bubbled my emotions too close to the surface.

I toured the second floor, looking into the closets. It was funny how my body just seemed to fit into this space. Like I'd been here before. Like I belonged. I moved over to the front window and watched a car drive down the street and pictured myself living here, waking up to this view. I turned to take in the whole room. I'd like to paint my bedroom something warm and happy, maybe buttery yellow. My domestic thoughts suddenly exploded with a *BANG!* outside.

My shriek surprised me as I crouched low, clutching at the sill with one hand and my Ruger with the other.

"Lexi?" Dave's feet hammered up the stairs. "Where are you?"

"Front bedroom." It felt like all my blood had drained from my face and pooled in my feet.

Dave paused in the doorway. He had his hand on his hip, where he usually wore his gun, and worked his way around the room, sliding his left shoulder along the walls. He peered past the molding of the curtain-less window. I lifted my head to peek out, too. An old Ford pickup chugged down the road. Two more backfires shot out of the tailpipe before the truck disappeared in a cloud of blue smoke.

I stood, feeling stupid. "I thought—" I waved my hand vaguely.

"I know what you thought." He stared down at me. "I've never seen you wound so tight."

"I…" Swiping at angry tears, I scowled.

"It's okay." Dave wrapped me into a bear hug. "One step at a time. Let's start here. How about the house?"

"Yes." I nodded against his shoulder.

He released me and pulled back so he could study my face.

"Inspections first, obviously," I said, adjusting my shirt and smoothing over the bulge from my belly holster.

"And the bank. Is Angel as young as you are?"

"A couple of months older. I don't think we can get a loan, though. We don't have much credit history."

"So?" Dave leaned into the wall. "What's your Plan B?"

"Money from Dad's life insurance. I have almost all my inheritance still in the bank, so I can write a check. I have enough to cover the house and some minor repairs."

"Would you be okay? We're talking about a big chunk to hand over all at once. What about your college?"

"I still have Mom's life insurance."

Dave's face slacked. A frown made deep wrinkles at the corners of his mouth. When he reached out and stroked a hand down my arm, I breathed in sharply and pulled away. The pain of Mom's death still stabbed at me, but if Dave treated me like I was fragile, I'd fall apart. I couldn't crumble now. I needed to act as brave as Angel did when he got on the bus with the other Army Rangers.

I moved toward the door. "So I guess everything depends on how bad things are here structurally—especially the roof."

I turned to find Dave's self-satisfied smile. *"One problem solved."* I could almost hear him thinking. *Maybe.* But where I laid my head at night wasn't nearly as important to me as the fact that my head was still attached and functional. Dave couldn't smell the putrid scent filling my nostrils ever since I read the poem. He didn't wear it, as cloying as ambergris, on his skin like I did. And he wasn't living this unrelenting anxiety.

3

By three o'clock, I was back at my motel. Circling the parking lot twice, I vigilantly scanned for anything out of place—someone lurking in the line of trees separating the building from the road or scrunched down in one of the cars. Nothing. But still, I couldn't force myself to pull into a parking spot.

It isn't safe.

That thought took up almost all of my mental space, growing rigid and unyielding, pushing me until I aimed back toward the street. I steered onto I-395 North. My foot steady on the pedal, I kept a watchful eye on the highway in my rearview mirror, changing lanes frequently, taking off-ramps, then turning to head back north. No one was following me, and I had no idea where I was heading. Away seemed good enough.

The muscles in my jaw and neck tensed as a car zoomed up behind me, inches from my bumper. Flicking on my signal, I slid to the right-hand lane and let out a rush of air as the Audi blew on by.

Panic will kill you, Lexi. It makes you unable in mind and body. I heard the voice of my mentor, Spyder McGraw, in my head.

Yeah, yeah, Spyder, I know that intellectually, but it's hard not to panic when my whole damned world is falling apart, piece by piece.

I thought back to the hug Dave gave me as I'd left his house this afternoon. He volunteered to get his buddy to handle the building inspection then pulled a promise from me that I'd be careful. I patted my pocket where I'd tucked the business card of the lawyer he and Cathy used. Dave's myriad contacts—very helpful. I could manage all the new house stuff by phone and fax —no real pressing need for me to hang out in D.C.

Out of town might be good. I tapped nervous fingers on my steering wheel and looked down at my backpack. Along with my purse, I had a laptop and a banana. I wouldn't get very far without supplies. Should I go pack up my things and check out? No, that would be a big waving flag saying, "Follow me."

I held the slim hope that out of sight would put me out of mind. Maybe the unknown poet would find something else to do with his time. Dave was right, though; getting caught up in someone's instability was like stepping into quicksand. Once it sucked you in, it was hell to get out. And the very worst possible response was to flail around. I needed to lay still, get my bearings, get a plan together. And that was hard to do looking over my shoulder in DC.

I hit the steering wheel with the heel of my hand. "What a freaking waste of money," I yelled toward the man singing about his broken heart on the radio. Reaching out, I fiddled with the knob until I came to a news channel. The newscaster's words "Strike Force" caught my ears. I tuned in and turned up the sound to listen to the report that an Iniquus team had rescued

Graham Chasm, President of CBN Oil, along with his wife and children, from a Mexican drug cartel.

The team was now en route from Texas to New York to deliver the family safely home.

New York?

Maybe heading up to New York City was a good idea—I could find a high-security hotel where I could hole up. And Strike Force would be there. Which meant Striker, their team leader, would be there. Striker was Spyder McGraw's golden boy. If anyone knew how to contact Spyder, it would be him. Should I try to reach Spyder—just to run this crazy letter situation past him and get some ideas? That wouldn't hurt anything, would it?

As I drove north, my head filled with Striker thoughts. He was legendary. When Striker was still a Special Forces Operator, Spyder had lent Iniquus contacts and regional expertise to Striker's SEAL team on various operations. Spyder was there in Iraq when Striker earned a Bronze Star for valor and was with him again in Africa with the UN when Striker earned a Silver Star for heroism and a Purple Heart.

Spyder loved to recount their exploits. As a teen, I ate those Striker stories like manna. Hungrily. Greedily. I was starving for a hero to come and fight the dragons in my life. Mainly, I needed to fend off my depression when Dad died in the car accident, especially knowing my mom's illness meant she'd be dying soon after, and I'd be left with no family. I remembered how desperate I was for Striker to be mine, though, at that point, he was just a fairy tale—like Arthur or Prince Charming.

Soon after, I met Striker in person, after he left the military and signed on to an Iniquus Team here in DC. The introduction made everything worse. I was so desperately lonely and overwhelmed, and Striker was so damned *perfect.* So unattainable and accomplished.

I shook my head to clear away those ideas. I hadn't thought about Striker since the second I laid eyes on Angel. And that was how I wanted it. But still, New York.

My stomach growled, and I realized all I'd had to eat in the last 24 hours was a few bites of a doughnut and my coffee. I pulled in at the next truck stop, taking my laptop into the restaurant, and got myself a sandwich.

I bit into my chicken salad as I booted up my computer to search for somewhere to stay. With all of my things still back at the motel, I'd have to run by a store someplace and pick up necessities—clothes and some food. It looked like PB and J until I could get back home, I thought as I scrolled through the search site.

Score!

A secure hotel—right in the middle of the city for a great price.

"More than I had to spend, though," I grumbled under my breath as I hit ENTER. It seemed a little cowardly, doing a vanishing act. Cowardly wasn't how I normally viewed myself. Well, a hidden enemy was a dangerous enemy; probably even Spyder would agree this was a smart tactical move.

Without any strategic planning, I found myself pulling into a parking space at LaGuardia Airport, where the radio news anchor had said the Chasm family would land. I checked my watch. They were still twenty-five minutes out.

I still hadn't made up my mind about approaching Striker. Right now, I'd wing it.

I walked around to my trunk and took out a baseball cap. Pulling the bill low over my brows, I dashed up to the news team from Channel 11 and followed behind like I belonged—they would know where to go. As the doors to the terminal slid open automatically, my heart quickened. What was I thinking? I couldn't talk to Striker privately here, especially in front of all these reporters. Besides, I chastised myself. It would be wrong to mention Spyder McGraw in public. And if I did, Striker would be suspicious of my approach. Why would he tell me, a stranger, where a fellow Iniquus agent went after disappearing from my life a year ago? Would Striker even have contact? Iniquus only meted out information on a need-to-know basis.

Still, I moved along as if I had a plan.

No one questioned me as I scrambled behind News 11 into the bay that was set aside for the news conference. The excitement was palpable. The extended Chasm family huddled in front of the dais, with tear-stained faces, while various report teams claimed turf and filmed teasers. I worked my way over to where I thought Strike Force would exit. I'd wing it based on how Striker positioned himself. If I did get Spyder's contact information, I could make other decisions about *if* I would burden Spyder with my problem.

A shift happened in the room. Reporters raised their microphones as the on-air lights blinked above their video cameras. The well-dressed and highly polished reporters laid out the storyline; the Chasm's private jet had landed, and they were expected at the podium any second now. I crossed my fingers and willed that everything go exactly as it should. If I'm supposed to lean on Spyder, everything will go off without a hitch. But my efforts will be thwarted if it's better to do this on my own. I sent out my thought spell. Magical thinking—a sign of mental health issues. But there it was. I'd let fate figure out my dilemma for me.

The family burst jubilantly through the door. Their bright grins were dichotomic to the black circles under their eyes. I stared at the door. Why was the family alone? Maybe Strike Force didn't want their images broadcast in order to preserve their anonymity. I slid along the wall to get to the door the family had entered. Hopefully, Strike Force was just on the other side, and I would find Striker away from this circus.

Just as I pushed through the door, a reporter asked about the rescue team. Graham Chasm said, "An assignment came up. As soon as the team delivered us safely home, they were wheels-up on another assignment. We wish them Godspeed."

They were already gone.

I spun in place. Well, thanks, fate. Looks like I'm on my own.

No Spyder.

No Iniquus.

Alone.

4

The sky was a deep violet when I stepped out of my car onto the marble-paved turnabout at the hotel and tipped my head up to take in the splendor. Wow, was I out of place. This was posh beyond belief—the crystal and mahogany at the valet desk, the women prancing by draped in furs and dripping jewels. I, on the other hand, stood shivering in my pink hoody and Levi's. The valet palmed the keys to my rusty Camry, and I blushed hotly as I handed him his tip. My car wheezed as she chugged away to be replaced in line by a silver Bentley.

After signing in with the front desk, I took an elevator up to the fourth floor. My room was New York small. I could barely inch past the little space between the bed and the wall to get over to see outside my one-windowed view. I peered out at the traffic and pedestrians and sighed. Nothing said anonymous like New York City.

Surely, I can safely lose myself in the crowd, I thought as I pulled my buzzing phone from my pocket. I checked the screen. *Dave.*

"Hello?" I said.

I heard panting quickly, followed by, "Holy shit!"

"Are you okay?" I asked.

"No. I am *not* okay. You gave me a friggin' heart attack. I drove over here to your motel to talk to you, and you weren't around. Not one of your apartment building neighbors has seen you since this morning."

"I was getting ready to call you in a minute, anyway." I gazed out the window at the building across the street. "I got spooked at the DC motel and drove away."

"Away where?" Dave asked.

"New York City." I clamped the phone between my ear and shoulder as I pulled my hair back into a braid.

"Spooked like a normal person gets spooked? Or did you *sense* someone out there?"

"I *am* a normal person, Dave. But yes, I had a sixth sense that hanging out in DC was going to be bad news, so now I'm here."

"How long are you planning to stay up there?" he asked.

"I don't know. Until the house is settled? I'm kind of winging it here."

He grunted, then a door slammed. "You checked your rearview mirror?"

"I did everything Spyder would want me to do. No one followed me up here. And if they did—"

"It would be a hell of a bad sign." Dave finished my sentence for me. "It's one thing to shove a letter under someone's door, and a whole different ballgame to follow someone out of state."

"Yup." I moved toward the bathroom to get a drink of water. This tiny hotel room was claustrophobic. I wanted to go out for a walk to get some air, but rain tapped against the windowpane.

"What are your plans for up there?" Dave asked.

"I need to sit tight and get through my assignments first."

"Assignments?"

"Yeah. For my classes at the community college." I turned on the water and filled my glass.

"Oh, for a second, I thought you were attached to a new partner."

I took a sip before I answered. "I told you, I'm not playing secret agent anymore."

"So, you're good?"

"Locked down under high-security. You should see this place. No one can get to me."

"All right then. I want a phone call every day. Okay? Every *single* day. I'll let you know how things are going with the house. At least the money's in escrow, so it should move forward fast enough."

"Thanks. Love you." My singsong good-bye sounded a thousand times lighter than I felt.

After a pause, Dave said, "Love you back. Please be safe."

"I promise." I hung up and set my phone back on the dresser.

Tired didn't even start to describe the hollowness in my bones. I couldn't remember ever being this kind of exhausted. The stress of the day had completely wiped me out. And even though it was still pretty early, I decided to go to sleep. Let this day just slip away. I checked the locks on my door, slid out of my clothes, and pulled a T-shirt, from an earlier run to a box store, over my head.

Under the covers, I fell instantly into an aerobic and strenuous sleep.

I ran through the sandstorm, choking on the dust-caked scarf I had wrapped around my face. My gun was jammed with tiny particles of silica, and I let it dangle ineffectually from my back as I fought my way up yet another dune. The smell of charred flesh filled my nostrils and made them burn.

I jerked reflexively as a bomb blew up a truck on the road below. The move made me lose my footing. I rolled down into the enemy encampment, where they pounced on me.

"Angel!" I screamed and thrashed to escape. I woke up knotted in the sheets, my damp hair plastered against my cheeks, panting for breath. Sunlight shot through my window, and I forced myself up and away from the desperation that clung to me. Though I was dreaming about the desert, it felt like a metaphor for my threat. My two big anxieties interweaving in my dreamscape—worry for Angel's safety, worry for mine.

Climbing off the bed, I scooped my hair off my prickling neck and made my way into the bathroom. It was so small, I had to stand in the tub to shut the door. As I turned on the water, I started a mental list of the things I needed to do. Pragmatism. Linear thinking. Focus. I needed my mind on things that were completely unrelated to protecting myself from the guy with the death threat. Spyder taught me a predator wanted to disrupt his victim's life and keep them in a state of fear.

Life disrupted? Check.

Living in a state of fear? Well, I'd work hard at distracting myself. I'd finish my calculus assignment, go to the gym—burn off some stress, perhaps I'd grab lunch downstairs.

The stream of hot water soothed my nerves. I reached for the mini-bar of hotel soap. It was safe here, I rationalized. Safer than a motel in DC anyway. Yeah, but sooner or later, I was going to have to go home and deal. I massaged the lather over my stomach.

White bones, dry veins, and melted skin. Who writes crap like that?

Suddenly, my world tilted. I stretched out my hands to brace myself against the white tiles. Words illuminated my consciousness with vibrant colors and dizzying oscillations. It was a psychic "knowing." And a doozy too. I crouched down in the tub and waited for it to subside.

"Knowings" came to me frequently, since I was a little girl, but were mostly bits of useless banality. *Dave likes ice cream,* or *Dad has a cold.* Sometimes they acted as harbingers—*the ice storm will last three days.* Today's "knowing" flashed a red warning sign.

Ring-a-ring of rosies. A pocket full of poesies. Hush! Hush! Hush! Hush! You fall down!

I wrapped up in a towel and flung myself across the bed. How to interpret this information? Okay, first—not good. I pinched my nose closed and stared at the ceiling, trying to breathe deeply through my mouth, trying not to freak the hell out.

Think like Spyder's operator holding a new puzzling clue, I encouraged myself. Let's say Spyder came in with a new case and handed this to me. What would I tell him?

Anomalies. I'd start there. *Hush! Hush! Hush! Hush!* I've read something before… yes, in an antique children's anthology —that phrase was used, but not common. Hmmm. I didn't know what to do with it. Silenced, maybe? That no one would hear me if I needed help? I jumped up to pace.

A pocket full of poesies. This was clearer. Not the customary "posies" like a bouquet of flowers. "Poesies" – from old French or

Latin, meaning poems. And of course, the poem shoved under my door on my wedding day was Robert Burns' *A Red, Red Rose.* That could explain the first line, *Ring-a-ring of rosies.* I would guess the Burns adulteration was going to be the first of many poems.

Then, *You fall down.* Not "they all fall down." This was a warning specific to me. I leaned into the wall, gripping my towel tightly to me. And fought to breathe.

———

Dressed in yoga pants, I sat cross-legged on the bed and stared vacantly out my window. Storm clouds gathered. Even though I felt like Damocles with this "knowing" hanging over my head, I was trying hard to act like this was just a normal day. Keeping my mind on calculus homework wasn't working out very well, though.

A crisp knock on my door drew my attention and reanimated me. I checked the clock radio. Ten on the dot. Must be house-keeping.

Ring-a-ring of rosies... sang a childlike voice in my head as I walked cautiously toward the door.

Squinting through the peephole, I saw a liveried man holding a funeral wreath composed of deep red roses in his white-gloved hands. *Ring-a-ring of rosies...* Ah, so the first phrase was a literal freaking interpretation.

I inched open the door but left the security chain in place and cleared my throat. "May I help you?"

"Flower delivery for a Mrs. India Alexis Sobado, madam." My new legal name.

"Just the card, please," I said, lifting my hand toward the opening.

He looked at me quizzically, then plucked the tiny envelope

from the clear plastic stem and handed it to me through the chained door.

You see, my love,
> *Words have no power to impress the mind,*
> *without the exquisite horror of their reality.*

An electrical buzz from the shock of the note numbed my brain.

The man shifted his weight between his feet.

"Where did these come from?" I finally managed.

"A florist dropped them with the valet, madam."

"Thank you, I don't want them."

The man glanced down at the flowers and then down the hallway; he seemed confused about what to do. I dug a couple of dollars from my pocket and pushed them through the crack allowed by the chain. Shutting the door quietly, I slid to the floor and hugged my knees tightly.

How did he find me?

My mind searched the possibilities—all the scenarios I'd studied under Spyder's tutelage, all of the cases we had worked together for his job at Iniquus supporting the US government by cutting red tape and sometimes pushing the envelope trying to stop the bad guys from hurting our country. Still, I couldn't fathom how, apart from electronic surveillance, the Psycho could have found me. And I had checked. And checked again. How? I couldn't find a GPS device on my car. He couldn't have accessed my phone or computer, could he? Read my credit card report from where I charged this room? A hacker? But I encrypted my computer. If he was a hacker, he had access to some pretty wicked software. No, that just didn't feel right.

Huh.

When I decided to stop working as Spyder's private operator
—realizing the spy life wasn't for me—I hadn't ever imagined
I'd have these kinds of thoughts again. My operator's hat was
one I had pulled off and stuffed in the back drawer after Mom
died, and Spyder went off-grid. But here I was digging through
my chest of tricks and trade secrets, looking for an answer. I kept
coming up empty-handed. I had no explanation.

I moved over to my laptop and typed the words from the
florist's card into Google. Up popped a site for Edgar Allen Poe
—the father of creepy crap. Figures.

Leaning over, I grabbed the room phone and dialed the front
desk. While I waited for security to show up, I threw my few
belongings into my backpack. New York and its obscurity didn't
give me a sense of protection anymore. I needed to get back to
D.C., where I knew people. There, someone would care if I
suddenly went missing.

5

369 Silver Lake Road—my new address. I liked the roundness of the numbers and that they all lined up in multiples of three. I read somewhere that three in Hebrew represented limitless light, creation, and overcoming evil. Today's date was also in multiples of three—the Ides of March when Julius Caesar was attacked by his buddy Brutus. I sucked in extra air. Did I know him? Was my stalker a supposed-friend ready to stab me in the back, literally? I tried to shake off the sense of foreboding.

The day had turned out to be chilly, gray, and dreary. As I drove down the street, cranking my car heater, I decided neither the date nor the weather was going to be an omen for my new life here.

After signing the papers and getting my keys, I started hauling boxes into my house. *My* house. That thought kept a smile plastered on my face. I didn't have much to move. There were three boxes of Angel's belongings. My two boxes held my parents' journals and our photo albums—the only things I had time to grab as I ran from the burning apartment building into the freezing January night. After taking in a laundry basket filled with my clothes, I stood in the middle of the living room, hugging myself in a moment of pure joy. I glanced around. Okay, it was an empty home, but Angel and I owned it—weeds, mold, cracked ceilings and all.

I needed somewhere to sit. And somewhere to sleep. Some basics.

I climbed into Angel's truck for the short ride over to the Furniture Barn near my old apartment to pick up some cheap essentials—a bed, kitchen table set, and sofa. My plan was to hand them over to charity before Angel came back. I hoped to get everything fixed, decorated, and perfect for his homecoming.

The men loaded the make-do quality furniture into my truck while I daydreamed about the really nice things I wanted to get, eventually, when I settled on my color scheme, and the windows would shut all the way. Now that I thought about it, I wasn't sure about Angel's taste in decorating. Ours was a whirlwind romance with such a short period between hello and good-bye... Well, there were lots of holes. When he got back to his base, I'd get a chance to fill in some of the blanks.

My next stop was Wal-Mart for linens, towels, and basic kitchen and cleaning supplies. I piled my goodies into the bed of the truck, filling crevices and pockets left by the furniture boxes. Tonight was going to be my very first night in the first house of my life. A grin stretched across my face and made my cheeks ache.

But my joy imploded as I circled the front of the cab and glimpsed the cream-colored envelope tucked under the windshield wiper. Of course! Of course, he left a note on my car today. I grabbed the door handle and jerked the door wide. I reached into the glove box to get a pair of gloves from the first-aid kit Angel stored there.

When I worked with Spyder—us against the bad guy—I felt

in control. Happy, even. Dealing with the bad guy coming after me? Not so freaking happy. I grabbed the letter up, climbed in the cab, and jammed the key into the ignition. The paranormal stench assailed my nostrils—the oily ooze of something dangerous. I breathed shallowly through pursed lips and swung my head around. Was someone watching me?

I gunned the engine on Angel's black F250. Its big macho bravado gave me the sense of a protective tank. My hand juddered on the gearshift as I backed out, revving the motor to show my disdain. I was furious this day was shot to hell, just like my wedding day was.

At the red light, I took a deep, steadying breath and called over to Dave's house. His wife, Cathy, answered the phone. My tongue tripped cheerfully over my "hello, how are yous." My happy-go-lucky charade continued through chatter about the house and new marriage until I finally asked for Dave.

"He's not home yet, but I expect him any minute now," Cathy said.

"I was hoping he'd help me get some furniture into my place."

"Not a problem. Why don't you come here? We're having an early supper, and I bet you haven't turned your fridge on yet. Dave can scrounge up a few guys from the neighborhood and give you a hand."

Thirty minutes later, I parked in front of the Murphy's home. I cast my gaze over to the envelope, laying on the seat beside me. I didn't want to read the letter out here. Truth be told, I didn't want to read it at all. Using the gloves to protect any finger-prints Psycho might have left, I put the envelope in a baggie in my purse. I flipped the mirror down to make sure I had some color on my face, slapped on a make-believe smile, and jumped down from the cab.

Fletcher and Colin, the Murphy's twins, greeted me at the door. They got their auburn red hair and dusting of freckles from their mom. They looked like all-American kids in their jeans and superhero T-shirts. I walked in, and they went from curious about who came to visit to wrestling in the middle of the floor in five seconds flat. They giggled and squirmed as Cathy tried to separate them and send them upstairs to wash up for dinner.

"Dave beat you in." Cathy raised her voice over the din. "He's changing his clothes. Make yourself comfortable, and I'll go turn the heat off of the stove."

As she turned, Dave called from the stairs, "Hey, neighbor." When he saw my face, his enthusiasm evaporated. He dropped his voice. "What's up?"

I glanced toward the kitchen then whispered, "Psycho left me another note."

"You read it yet?"

"I thought we could do that together."

"Yup." He called back to the kitchen, "Hey, honey, I need a minute to talk over a police matter with Lexi—you wanna go ahead with dinner?"

Cathy came in, wiping her hands on a dishtowel. She corralled the boys to her as they stomped and jumped their way down the stairs.

Dave pulled a pair of gloves from his desk drawer, and I handed him the bag. After digging a Swiss Army knife from his front jeans' pocket, he slit the envelope across the top.

A Song for Alexis
  Monkeywrench girl, my heart's compulsion;
  The love of my life, from youth to quickened death.
  Your heart belongs to ME and to ME only;

the pain of your flesh is yours and bears my rage...

Bile slicked up the back of my throat, making me gag.

Dave fixed on the letter, skimming over the words again. "You recognize this?" His focus moved sharply to my face. "Is this another poem he's messed around with? Or do you think it's original?" Dave put the stationary back in the plastic bag.

Nothing specific popped into my mind like the Burn's poem did. I shrugged. "Look, I was driving Angel's truck today, and I drove my car in New York City. He doesn't seem to have a problem following me—no matter what I drive or where I go. He's smart. Hotel security said someone paid a courier cash to take the flower order—also paid in cash to the florist for the roses." I drummed nervous fingers on my knees. "If I had to get a loony, why couldn't he be a stupid one?" I leaned my head back onto the couch and released a huff of air. "He must know I closed on the house. The first letter crapped up my wedding, and this one drained all the happy out of my closing on the house today." I paused, focusing on the ceiling. "Who knew I was closing, though? I didn't tell anyone. Only you. Mrs. Nelson. The lawyer." I let my gaze lower to catch on Dave. He was reading over the letter, his eyes stormy.

"Do you think it's a coincidence this one starts 'My monkey-wrench girl?'" he asked.

"Could be someone I know—someone from my past, maybe from Dad's garage." My mind scanned for other possibilities. "Or someone who was watching me at the motel. Angel's truck didn't pass inspection. He and I were working on it out in the parking lot." I sighed, twisting my wedding rings back and forth. The rings held Angel-juju; I needed some of that right now. "There's always the possibility it's a random poem the nutter picked, and it happened to have significance to me."

Dave nodded. "So, what's the plan?"

"First, I'll mooch dinner off you. Then, I'm going to ask for your help getting the furniture inside my house. I'll stay at a motel again tonight. Tomorrow, I need to go get my puppies at the kennel, put new locks everywhere, and call for an emergency alarm system to go in." I ticked these off on my fingers. "Other than that, what would you suggest?"

"In general? Those are good plans. About the alarm system? I know a guy. I'll give him a call and get you hooked up."

Of course, Dave knew a guy. "Please don't tell him what's going on. I want this to stay between us, okay?"

"You're probably right about keeping this quiet. Go on back and get yourself a plate fixed up, and I'll get in touch with Boomer."

I took a step toward the kitchen then turned back to find Dave's focus honed laser-sharp on me. "Do you think you can get hold of the tapes from the Wal-Mart surveillance cameras?" I asked. "I'd like to have something concrete to work with. Maybe this guy isn't even a guy. Maybe we could get a vehicle, or better a plate, to trace."

"I'll make a call." Dave tipped his head back, making his chin jut forward. "You scared?"

I wiped sweaty palms down the sides of my jeans. "Out of my freaking mind."

"Good—then you'll be careful. Have you considered this might have something to do with your work?"

"Past work. Spyder's gone."

"Still." Dave pinched his lower lip between his thumb and index finger.

"Of course, it has," I said. "I've been chewing over every

possible scenario. I can't figure out what to do with that one."
Exasperation made my voice scale upward as I spoke.

"Talk to Iniquus Command." Dave thrust a staccato finger
at me.

"No. Let it go." I didn't want to fight this fight with Dave.
No one at Iniquus had a clue about me. Spyder and I had been so
careful. I never went into the field as "Lexi." I was always in
disguise. No one should have been able to recognize me or make
a connection. And if they had, why would they be sending me
these crazy poems?

6

Another night, another motel. I should be sleeping at my house tonight. But pragmatism told me that the alarm had to be in place first. That and I needed to go get my dogs.

Dave and Cathy had asked me to stay with them, but with two kids in the house and me not knowing anything about Psycho other than his propensity to steal other people's words and corrupt them, no, I wasn't taking a chance.

I sat down with my laptop and a copy of the letter. Running a search on the poem line by line was scraping at my already-raw nerves. Apparently, Psycho changed enough of the words that even Google was confused. Entering "Love Song for Alexis" didn't give me anything useful. I tried some permutations, and when I put in "Song for Alex," I found the original poem. *Alex.* Coincidence? Or did this person know Dad had called me Alex? Spyder did, too. I chewed on the end of my pen, staring out the window into the darkness.

Was I wrong not to go talk to Iniquus?

After logging out, I took a shower to try to wash away the miasma clinging to my thoughts. Weird how I was getting an

ESP impression through a putrid scent this time. I didn't ever remember that happening before. Visuals, yes. And auditory. Occasionally something sensate like the oozing oily crap I felt when I got the first envelope. I searched back in my memory. Well, maybe I had picked up a scent before, and I just didn't notice because it smelled normal and not like the bottom of a swamp.

I wished I'd have another "knowing." A better one than the nursery rhyme in New York. Ha! Wouldn't it be great if I woke up one morning with an address in my head? I could send the police to the psycho's door to tell him—or her—to cut it the hell out! Obscenities—the lowest form of communication, according to Mom. But they felt so good right now. My thoughts were like one long stream of expletives. Dropping my terrycloth robe to the floor, I slid under the covers and into a restless sleep.

The next morning, my cell phone buzzed as an unknown number popped up on the screen. I checked the clock—six-fifty. Apprehension prickled my skin, making me hesitate before I put the phone to my ear.

"Hello?"

"Hey, Baby Girl, I'm over at your house with Boomer."

Dave. He must be using Boomer's phone. "This early?"

"He wants to go over the system he drew up for you. He's putting off his other jobs to get this done. Can you get over here?"

I rubbed my face and threw back my covers. "I'm on my way. Tell him thanks."

I didn't bother with a shower, just brushed my teeth, pulled a comb through my tangles, and jerked yesterday's coral turtleneck over my head. On my way over to the house, I swung into Dunkin' Donuts drive-through and got us a dozen doughnuts and coffees.

I pulled up at my house, where a burly biker-type guy stood next to Dave on the sidewalk. They smiled when they saw my hands full of breakfast.

Dave reached for the drink carrier. "Not in the truck today?"

"I'm picking up Beetle and Bella. Not enough room in the pickup for such a long drive." I took a welcome sip from my latte.

Dave nodded and made the introductions.

"Glad you're here, Boomer. Thanks for bumping my project to the front of the line," I said.

"Dave said your husband's in Afghanistan, and you're afraid to stay alone." Boomer's gaze slid down to my feet, then back up to my face. "I can understand that—little girly like you."

I slit my eyes at Dave.

He gave me a shrug in return.

"Dave wants you fitted with state-of-the-art," Boomer said. "But you're renovating?"

"Right. I'll need to move the system as I upgrade my doors and windows."

"Got it. This is what I come up with." Boomer tapped his pen on the clipboard.

We moved around the first floor. I tried to focus as Boomer waxed poetic about the alarm system, complete with door and window sensors, motion detectors, and a two-way communication system. I swear, if the alarm were a girl, Boomer would be making out with her right now.

Weird.

They'd change my locks on the doors and install peepholes,

deadbolts, and window locks. It looked good to me—safe—and safe was the only thing that counted.

"A few questions. Can you put motion sensor lights on the front and back porch in protective cages? How long until the system is up and running? And what kind of cost are we talking here?"

"No problem with the lights. We'll put them on timers for you. We can start installation this morning and be done by dinner. You can say bye-bye to the motel." He gave me a macho smile—yeah, whatever, Boomer.

"This is the price." He circled the total on his clipboard—the knife-wielding skeleton tattooed on his forearm danced as his hand moved. "Dave here's calling in a favor, so it's the system itself you're paying for. Labor is gratis."

"Gratis?" I raised my eyebrows in surprise and sent a questioning look over to Dave, who offered up a conspiratorial wink.

After I signed the contract and wrote out a check, Boomer got on the phone to his office to get the parts brought over. Dave walked me to my car, where I gave him a hug.

"That was nice of you. I don't know what favor you called in, but it's appreciated."

"Oh, this isn't an act of kindness. You owe me big, and I'm planning on collecting, too." He wore a satisfied grin.

"Yeah? How exactly am I paying off this debt?" I squinted past the early morning sun at him.

"Food. I'm planning on eating lots and lots of your good cooking. Hey, but don't tell Cathy I said that. If she gets offended, it's spaghetti for a week." He shoved his hands in his pockets and sent a sheepish glance toward his house.

With a finger wave, I motored off, heading to the highway exit where I turned north toward Millers' Kennel. My puppies lived there their whole lives. Actually, they were nearly a year and a half now. I shouldn't call them puppies anymore. They were beautiful black Doberman pinschers—a gift from Spyder. Hmm, more like a reward for a job well done.

On my eighteenth birthday, Spyder said he had a task he needed help completing. The prize, he said, was pick of the litter when the Millers' breeding bitch dropped her pups.

"How dangerous is this job?" I'd asked.

"I wouldn't ask you to do it if I thought you were in danger, Lexicon. But that doesn't mean complacency. You must use your brain."

Spyder wanted me to use my sleight-of-hand skills. The job was to slip a transmitter into the pocket of a mark named Tandesco, one of the executives at Tangelsmeere Corp. That day, I dressed in a suit, bumped into the guy on the elevator, and won my prize; Spyder bought Beetle and Bella for me.

My babies stayed at the kennel while they trained as work dogs, well operator support dogs. Now that I wasn't going to be an operator anymore, I'd just use their skills for sport and for volunteering with the search and rescue crew.

I was supposed to have picked them up over a month ago, but with the fire and the motel policies, I had to put it off until there was somewhere to bring them home to.

The trip out into the country took a little over an hour. My frequent visits meant I could drive on autopilot. Thinking Psycho thoughts. Thinking. Thinking. Spyder would have tapped me on the head and said, "Come. You must use your brain, Lexicon." I'm afraid he'd hear a hollow sound when he did. I was empty of ideas.

7

When I arrived at the training ground, Mr. Miller trudged across the field toward me with my girls at his heels. I climbed out of the car and sucked in a lungful of pine-filled air. Beetle and Bella stayed at Mr. Miller's side but were squirming and whining with excitement. Mr. Miller chuckled and released them. The girls bounded over, whole bodies wagging. Ah, bliss. I rubbed their onyx fur until they calmed down.

"Hey." I greeted Mr. Miller with a smile as he ambled up on his long thin legs.

He pulled me into a hug. "Congratulations, Lexi. New home. New husband. Proud of you." He patted my back. "Come on up to the house. Judy wants to see you. She's got Spyder's dogs with her."

"You hear anything from him?" I asked with as much nonchalance as I could muster.

"I was about to ask you the same. We get a check for his dogs' care regularly, but it's from an accountant's office. We've gotten nothing from the man himself."

Bella pushed her head under my hand, and I scratched her ears. "How are my babies doing? They give you any trouble?"

"They're running the obstacle courses beautifully—working on flanking during the shooting range. Good on enemy take-downs. You need to bring them in from time to time, so we can keep their work skills up, especially scent work."

"Okay." I nodded. "I can do that."

"They still got some maturing to do." Mr. Miller's hands moved to his pockets. "You'll notice a big difference in the next six months to a year."

I paused and shielded my eyes to scan the field toward the agility course. "You have anything planned for this spring?"

Mr. Miller stopped beside me. "We're doing a paintball war. Iniquus against Omega."

"Wow. That'll be spectacular." I squinted up at him. "I want to play."

"Good. I could use your help. I'll be having some prospective clients come in for the weekend to watch the obstacle courses."

"When's this?" We started up again, moving over the uneven ground toward the house.

"Last week of May. I need you to do the demo with Spyder's pair and then with yours. It comes off different when you're on the circuit. The guys figure if a little piece of fluff can do it, they sure as hell can."

"Now I'm a little piece of fluff?"

"You're as fierce as they come, Lexi, but a guy sees you, he's not got his mind on war games. He's thinking date night."

"Hmm." I stopped.

Mr. Miller glanced back at me. "Now, don't start putting your hand on your hip with me, young lady. I got enough of that from my own house." He pointed at the figure peering out at us from behind the glass door. "I don't need you adding to the women's lib crap. You know I respect the hell out of your talent. But I'm gonna call it the way I see it. The way I see it is their thinking you're a piece of fluff is always a winning situation for you. And that's how Spyder wants it. Right?"

I pursed my lips.

Up at the house, a plump, gray-haired, motherly figure swung open the door. Her soft, comfortable body encouraged hugging. "Oh, Lexi, look at you!" She stretched out her hands to gather me in, then pushed me out to arm's length. "I can't believe Spyder's little girl is a woman, and all married!" Mrs. Miller clucked and fussed as she pulled me into the kitchen and over to a chair at the table. "Perfect timing for an early lunch. I cooked up a nice Brunswick stew, and I'm putting some in this here Tupperware for you to take home with you."

The three of us sat down at the round table. Big white pottery bowls steamed with Mrs. Miller's hearty stew. Fresh bread and apple butter rested on the cobalt-blue tablecloth.

"So, sweetie, I want you to tell me everything. Who are you partnered with while Spyder's off-grid?" Mrs. Miller unfolded her napkin and laid it in her lap.

"No one, ma'am. I'm out of the business." I ladled some stew into my bowl.

The Millers looked at each other for a minute, then back to me.

"Out altogether?" Mr. Miller pulled at his ear lobe as he locked disbelieving eyes on me. "You're not on anyone's payroll?"

"You have to remember," I said, taking a sip of water. "I worked directly for Spyder. He's the one who made the contacts. With him gone, I don't have anyone handing me cases."

"Surely someone else wants to put your skills to good use." Mrs. Miller clunked her spoon down.

"No, ma'am. I'm not in the market for a new partner. I decided to focus on school. There's only one more semester left before I finish at the community college, then I'll apply to the university and see where that takes me. Maybe I'll stay home and be a mom."

"Hard to believe, Lexi. What made you come to that decision?" Mrs. Miller considered me through squinty eyes like she couldn't quite make me out.

"I thought choosing a normal kind of life would be better for me in the long run. You know, hearth and home, raising children —no, I'm not pregnant." Both of the Millers had settled their gaze on my stomach.

"Average?" Mr. Miller asked. Then, they burst out laughing.

"*What*? WHAT? Why are you making fun of me?"

"Because water will always find level, sweet girl." Mr. Miller spooned up more stew.

I blushed. "I don't understand."

Mrs. Miller smiled. "Oh, honey, you've never lead a typical life. You don't know how to lead a typical life. Your life was cut out of a more colorful fabric."

I twisted my fingers fretfully in my lap.

"Why, Lexi, look at what happens when you try to be average," she continued. "You marry a man you've known for three weeks—met him when your apartment building caught fire, didn't you? Come on now, who does that?"

She meant it kindly, but as tightly wound as I was, it felt like an attack. My eyes hardened, and I puckered my lips to keep defensive words from jumping out of my mouth.

"You get one night of honeymoon, and he's off to war for a

year or more. You buy a house, but it's not an average house. It's going to take above-average work to even make it livable."

She wasn't stopping, was she? Couldn't she tell she was ticking me off? That this hurt? Besides, this was absolutely none of her business.

"You're just not an average person, Lexi." Mrs. Miller reached over and patted my hand.

"Maybe not, but I'm going to give it a shot anyway." I'd made my decision. I wanted to get on with my life. My new life. I didn't want Iniquus and crime puzzles to take up any of my brain space—at least not until Spyder got back home.

"Okay." Mr. Miller joggled his spoon at me. "Even though you say you're out of the business—"

"I am!" I punctuated my conviction by pounding a fist into my thigh.

Mr. Miller raised a single brow at me—I couldn't tell if it was from surprise or a warning to watch my manners. "You're still going to keep the pups' training up, right?" He tilted a questioning head to the side. "And you'll help out from time to time on the tactical side of our business?"

I glanced down at Beetle and Bella lying at my feet. They seemed so peaceful with their heads resting on their paws and their lids drooping half-mast. I loved running the courses with them. Keeping up their training couldn't hurt. "Yes, sir."

"Good. Now, if you're done with your lunch, let's get the dogs out. Run them through some trials. Find your rusty spots." At the door, he looked around at me. "You have your gun loaded?"

I took my dogs to the starting line. Mr. Miller held his binoculars and a pad of paper, ready to take notes on where I could improve my performance.

When the whistle sounded, I raced forward, running the klick to the nearest sniper's nest, diving under a bush at the first mark. There I had to wait, undetected, for my next signal to move. A bright pink paintball pellet caught my eye. I reached out my hand, wondering if this was mine from two years ago when I fought my first paintball war here on the Millers' farm.

I was just shy of eighteen, and Spyder had arranged for me to take his place on the Iniquus team. At the time, I only had a vague understanding of what Spyder's job actually entailed. I *still* only have a vague idea, I thought, tossing the paintball back under the bush.

In the paintball war, my goal was to demonstrate Master Wang's stealth technique called "shadow walking" in that particular set of conditions to Spyder. Lots of battle-hardened eyes, lots of adrenaline, and testosterone. Spyder had seen me shadow walk a lot in our training. But he hadn't been convinced, up until that paintball war, that it had a place on the battlefield. For sure, shadow walking was a much more graceful and skillful method than the one I was using now.

That day, I found myself out in the woods, prowling in my soft-soled shoes like a tiger in the jungle, Master Wang style. I became a shadow. Keeping the sun behind me, I concentrated on being one with my environment. When the enemy appeared, I nailed him full-torso with my hot pink paintball, slipping silently, seamlessly, into the brush so they couldn't track me.

Back then, I dressed in gray—baggy cargo pants, loose t-shirt, knit cap, sunglasses, and an enormous sweatshirt with the hood up, hiding the sides of my face—no one knew I had girly curves. Laying here in the mud with Beetle panting by my ear, I remembered how the Iniquus men had looked me over and discounted me right away. Took me for a little twerp. Didn't even make room for me in their huddle as they discussed strategy. I had glanced over at Spyder, and he gave me a grin. Their disinterest wouldn't last long.

The team had handed me the only paint color left. Hot pink. Some of the men laughed and slapped me on the back, making sardonic remarks. Not Striker, the team lead. He seemed concerned that not having Spyder running would leave them one man down and put them at a disadvantage, but he didn't give me any crap about it.

Maybe Striker would be in command again at the May war, and I'd get to see him and ask him where Spyder was and when he might get home. Maybe even get some contact information. As I thought that, the blush rising up my face felt like a sunburn. I remembered my huge case of hero-worship and the mad-crush I had on Striker. Who wouldn't? Striker was movie-star handsome with the build and brainpower required to be in special ops. He also had the solid, unflappability of a Zen master.

I wished Mr. Miller would signal, I'd like to put my brain on something else.

Sometimes, Mr. Miller liked to test my patience and ability to lay low by leaving me in the mud for long, cold stretches. I tried to channel a little of Striker's Zen quietude. I was out of practice with my field skills—I bet Mr. Miller was marking my scorecard with all the times I gave away my position.

I slowed my breath and forced my thoughts away from Striker to the itch on my right thigh and poor Bella's terrible case of gas. Finally, the whistle blew. I shot three bullets to hit the target's bulls-eye, then ran for the next station—my knees stiff with mud, twigs, and debris clinging to my hair. I threw myself under the rocky ledge. My girls wedged in beside me.

On signal, I shot the target with the requisite three bullets and reloaded. I ran up the hill, then down the streambed. My dogs' little tails waggled furiously. This was pretty great. I grinned broadly as I carefully leaped from rock to rock. As fun as these trials were, I'd prefer to be practicing Master Wang style. Bummer I couldn't reveal my technique to Mr. Miller, or he'd know Alex and I were the same person. Boy, would that piss Spyder off.

I finished the two-mile sprint to the obstacle. Beetle and Bella were in a down-stay behind a pile of rocks while I climbed the rope to the top of the wall, shot, and slid my way back down. Mr. Miller was waiting for me at the bottom with a grin and my scorecard. He handed me a canteen, and I bent to pour the cool water over my neck. Any Psycho stalker stress I drove in with today had worn clean away.

Done for the day, Mr. Miller and I walked toward the house where I sat on the edge of my trunk, pulled off my combat-boots and socks, and replaced them with sparkly flip-flops that matched the hot-pink polish on my toenails—back in my fluff-mode disguise. Nothing to see here, folks. Just your average everyday girl. I signaled to Beetle and Bella, and they scrambled into my back seat, then I turned to give the Millers a final hug.

With a beep of my horn and a wave out the window, I steered toward our little house. I couldn't wait to get home. *Home.* Where I'd be secure with my new, state-of-the-art alarm system. At least that was what I was telling myself.

Besides, how could anyone possibly get at me with Beetle and Bella by my side? With that thought, my skin went inexplicably cold and clammy. Goose flesh made the little hairs on my arm stand straight up. Any sense of "safe" flew out my open window.

8

The tattoo sounding at my front door could only be banged out by one person, but I pushed to my feet and peered through the peephole anyway. Precaution. After pressing the buttons to disengage the alarm, I let Dave in.

"I got your message." He sauntered past me and dropped onto the couch, the only piece of furniture in my living room.

I returned to my place on the floor, where I rested my head on Bella's belly and stared at my wall. Beetle lolled in a little stream of sunshine on the bare wood, looking peaceful.

"You've been busy redecorating," Dave said. "Interesting choice of wallpaper."

I had lined the wall with white newsprint from a roll I bought cheap at the salvage shop. The words from each of the poems I received—penned in block letters with a Sharpie—loomed above me. Variances circled in red—the correct verse to the side in blue. I just finished writing out today's new addition. I found poem number three, accompanied by a wriggling glob of night-crawlers, tucked into my newspaper after my run this morning. Oscar Wilde's adulterated "Apologia."

. . .

Is this thy will that I should wax and wane,
  Barter my soul of gold for hodden gray,
  And at thy pleasure weave a web of pain
  Whose brightest threads are your screams?
  Is this thy will,
  That your Soul's House should be a tortured spot
  Wherein, like evil paramours, must dwell
  The quenchless flame, and the worm which dieth not?...

"Do you want to explain your system?" Dave asked.

"Sure. I circled the word changes, making lists—original words, new words, beginning letters. I was looking for anagrams."

"And?"

"Nada. Then I thought there might be something in a foreign language, so I ran variations through Google Translator."

"That sounds like it took some time." Dave unbuttoned his coat and shoved his wool hat into the pocket.

"Yeah, I'm not sleeping anyway. I might as well keep my brain busy with productive thoughts."

Dave pulled the throw pillow out from behind his back and tossed it to the other end of the sofa. "I bet you got nothing in the translation direction."

"Wrong. Turns out Psycho spelled out 'I am the walrus' in Swahili."

Dave shot me a sardonic grin. "Smart aleck."

I waited while he read the newest poem on the wall.

"The letter was wrapped in my newspaper this morning." I sat up and clutched my arms around my bent knees. "I asked around. No one in the neighborhood saw anything unusual. Apparently, the only ones awake at dawn were Psycho, the newspaper carrier, and me. And you, of course. How'd the case go?"

"Blood, guts, and shotgun shells. Did you check in with the delivery kid?"

I nodded. "Pete. Twelve-year-old boy from two blocks over. He brought the paper while the girls and I ran in the park. Pete said he hadn't seen any cars drive by or anybody else up and around, no other joggers, or people heading in to work." I chewed at my cuticle. "I hate this man coming into the neighborhood. Up to my house. If he has to stalk me, I much prefer he keep his distance, leave the letters on my vehicles while I'm out."

"Did this one stink like a swamp to you?" Dave asked.

"To be honest, I wish I had a control knob on this psychic stuff. The smell is nauseating and doesn't go away. I never get a break from thinking about him."

"Has your antenna picked up anything else over the psychic network?"

I rolled my eyes. This was why I didn't like people knowing I had ESP skills. They assumed the information was easily dialed up—whatever I wanted, whenever I wanted. Which I can't. Or, I'd be playing the lottery every week.

"Dave, you love the ocean. Look around you. Do you see waves and sand? Hear gulls? Can you smell the salt air?"

"Where are you going with this?" He crossed his arms over his chest and cocked his head to the side.

"You've got five perfectly good senses, but that doesn't mean you can conjure something up when you want to."

"True." Dave's voice crackled with phlegm, and he cleared his throat.

"Same here. I can't just summon up the answers out of thin

air with my sixth-sense. I get what I get when I get it. Mostly." I pushed my hair back behind my ears.

"You located our dog easy enough when she went missing."

"That was child's play. Pets are simple. They want to be found. This guy doesn't. Right now, all I get is swamp gas filling my nostrils, and this morning—" I pursed my lips as my stomach rolled over.

Dave scooted to the edge of the couch, his elbows on his knees, looking down at me expectantly. "What did you pick up on?"

"Nothing helpful. That's for darned sure. When I got home, it felt like he contaminated my stairs and porch with a vile disease. I found myself holding my breath as I walked from the sidewalk to the front door. I didn't want to be infected with his contagion."

"You Lysoled everything down?"

I offered up a wry smile. "Hadn't thought of that." Holding my hand up to the sunlight, my diamond sprinkled rainbows across the floor. "I called Boomer and hired him to come over to install cameras with motion sensors. Maybe I can catch Psycho's image."

"Make sure Boomer angles two of the lenses to take in the road. We want a license plate. If this is someone you don't recognize, then having a face won't help much. We need a name and address so I can go after him. So that's all? Swamp gas and cooties?"

"I've got Aretha Franklin singing *Think* on endless-loop."

"Could be worse. Could be Metallica's *Bad Seed*." He stood up. "You got any coffee going?"

"Help yourself. I made a pot this morning when I came back from my visit with Pete."

Dave moved toward my kitchen as I reached out and scratched under Beetle's chin. Someone I didn't know. I feverishly hoped it wasn't someone I knew, someone who was close to me in any way. In the end, whoever this turned out to be, I didn't really think Dave or the police could control this guy to the extent I wanted them to. I read the case law; the courts would probably slap a restraining order in place and let him go. Unless, of course, he hurt me. I squeezed my eyes tightly shut to block those thoughts.

Once I had a tag on him, I *would* go to Iniquus. Their covert work fell under a different set of rules; they made sure things got handled *thoroughly*. I drummed thoughtful fingers on my knees. I'd have to wait. I wouldn't go to them with my tail tucked between my legs. Cowed. They wouldn't respect me. I'd reflect badly on Spyder, and I'd never intentionally do that.

Grinding my teeth together, tension radiated across my jaw. Iniquus and Spyder. My only contact with criminal craziness came from playing the role of secret-weapon for them. Otherwise, I had lived a pretty sheltered life. I should sit down and make a list of cases I had worked for Iniquus and the players— see if anyone jumped out at me, figuratively speaking.

Dave was banging around my kitchen, opening the fridge. I read over this morning's poem again. It sounded like Psycho thought he could outsmart me. "And let your dull failure at my unveiling."

Normally, I'd say, "Give it a go. I'm up to the challenge." I really wanted to say, "Go to hell. I'm not playing."

He planned to toy with me for a while. Should that make this better somehow? Hmm. Not so much when he said, "tortured." I didn't like the word "tortured." For sure, I didn't want my house to be a "tortured spot."

Dave came in, sipping from a magenta-pink mug that said, "I know Kung Fu—and like two other Chinese Words." A birthday gift from my sparring partner.

"Hey, I found a pile of repair estimates lying on your kitchen table." Dave handed me a ceramic smiley-face mug.

"Thanks." I reached out gratefully then burned my lips on the too-hot coffee with too little milk. "You mean you were snooping through the pile?"

"Occupational hazard. Snooping's a way of life. What's on your priority list?" he asked, hiking up his pants and taking up his habitual spot on the couch.

"The roof's about to cave, and the inspector said I can't put it off." I set my mug aside. "I wanted to have the whole house fixed and beautiful for when Angel gets home, but that's looking like a pipedream. I'm going to look for a part-time job to help pay for the contractors." I frowned. "Adding this to my school schedule won't leave me much time for DIY stuff."

"What are you looking for?" Dave asked.

"I don't know. A barista at Starbucks? Get a gig playing the guitar? I *was* going to look through the help-wanted section today, but I threw my newspaper in Mrs. Nelson's outdoor bin."

"Because?"

"It was septic with Psycho stalker germs."

Dave quirked an eyebrow, and I offered a sheepish grin in reply.

"Starbucks doesn't pay squat. Maybe you should put your skills to use," he said.

"I don't have any certifications. I can't do a stint as a P.I., or a mechanic, or anything."

"Martial arts instruction?"

"No belt ranking." I absentmindedly popped the elastic hair-band on my wrist. "I didn't train in a Kwoon."

"Iniquus would hire you in a heartbeat if they knew you were already in the field working cases with Spyder McGraw."

"What is it with you and Iniquus? You want me to tell them

about these?" I gestured toward my wall. "No laws have been broken. I don't want them to feel obligated to help me with the poems because I have a relationship with Spyder, and I don't want to work for them either."

"Give Iniquus some more thought, Lexi. Seems like a one-stop-shop to solve your problems."

I scowled by way of reply.

"I have another idea, but you're going to prefer the Iniquus option better." Dave slouched down with his mug resting on his knee. He had dark circles under his eyes, and his gaze was a little bleary. I couldn't blame him; he'd just come off a double shift.

"Okay, I'm listening."

Dave smirked. "Manny across the street."

"Hoarder House Manny?" My brow wrinkled.

"Yeah. He's new to the neighborhood too. Moved in right after Christmas."

"You're kidding. How in the heck did he just move in, and already there's crap spewing over his porch and onto the lawn like that? You'd think that kind of mess would take decades to make."

Beetle plopped against Dave's leg, and Dave reached down to scratch her ears for her, earning him a face full of wet kisses. Dave screwed his lips to the left, so he could answer me without French kissing my dog. "He inherited it from his grandparents already filled."

"How can he even get into his place, let alone live there?"

"He doesn't have much choice." Beetle lay down, and Dave swiped a flannel sleeve across his face. "His wife kicked him out and moved another guy in."

"Ouch."

"Yeah, and he's paying child support and spousal. He hasn't got a lot left over to set himself up anywhere else. Manny thought he could get his house cleaned up at least enough that the city doesn't condemn the place, and the social workers will let his kids come over and visit."

"How many kids?"

"Two. Boys."

"If it were me, I'd probably just torch the mess and use the insurance money to start over." I edged over to the wall and leaned back, stretching out my legs.

Dave drained his mug. He must have an asbestos tongue. "Manny tried, but no one will insure him. Fire hazard," he said.

"I was kidding. Jeesh. Can you imagine? Nothing like a little smoke damage to take down our real estate prices another notch." I tilted my head. "Where is this conversation leading, Dave? And if you say it's leading toward me cleaning up his catastrophe, the answer is flat-out no."

"Speaking of real estate prices, do you realize why you got this house so cheap?" he asked.

"Because it's falling apart at the seams?"

"Only partly. The other part is—houses don't sell in this neighborhood because of the hoarder house."

I tried another sip from my mug. The coffee tasted bitter, and I set it aside. "You bought here."

"I make a cop's salary. The choice was here or public housing. Anyway, Manny and I were talking, and I told him you grew up bartering stuff."

"Dave!"

"And I know how expensive it is to put in new systems and all."

"Dave!"

"He says he can get everything you need easy. Top of the line. Installed. All the warranties and guarantees."

"How?" My brows knit together. "Is he a contractor?"

"No." Dave paused before he said, "He plays poker."

My eyes widened, and my voice went up a full octave. "You're out of your mind. I'm *not* doing it." I pointed emphatically in the direction of the hoarder house. "I am *not* cleaning up a junk mountain in exchange for some guy playing poker for me."

"Think about it, Lexi. You'd get your house fixed up nice, like 'Metropolitan Home.' You could keep your own schedule, so it wouldn't interfere with your classes. And you'd raise the resale value on your house." Dave was ticking off the pros on his fingers.

"Not to mention yours," I added.

Dave winked. "And you'd be out of this house during the day."

"Yeah, across the street. I think Psycho could find me. Why doesn't Manny clean up his own mess?"

"Come on, if someone wanted to attack you, he'd probably knock ten-feet of garbage over on himself. And Manny says he's tried to clean up since he inherited the place last fall, but it was ingrained since birth—nothing gets thrown out at his grandparents' house." Dave tapped a finger to his head. "He has a mental block. Can't do it."

"He needs therapy." I took a deep breath in and let it go in one big exhale. "I probably need therapy too, because I seem to be considering this."

I stood up, walked over to my front window, and looked across the street and down one house at the early 20th-century standalone. The yellow paint was dim with accumulated pollution and mold, and it seemed to vomit junk out of every orifice. It should definitely star in a *Hoarders* TV special. No. Too big of a project. Okay, it would make a great setting for a horror flick, *Nightmare on Silver Lake*. I wouldn't be too surprised if I found a body or two lost under all the trash. Or some evil creature from the bowels of the Earth.

I turned to watch Dave closely, looking for his body language tells. I always knew when he was bluffing. "He's really that good? Poker for heating systems?" It sounded stupid when I said it aloud.

"He's got a reputation." Dave had twisted around, watching me too. "No one on the force will play with him. No one can afford to lose that bad."

"The whole thing makes no sense." I gathered our mugs and walked them to the kitchen, calling over my shoulder, "If he's so good, he should play for a professional to come take care of his problem."

Dave waited for me to come back before he answered. "Can't. If he profits from his wins, he has to declare the gains as income. It ups his support payments, and he can barely feed himself on what he has leftover now."

"You feel sorry for him."

"I feel sorry for everyone who has to look at his disaster. *And* I think everyone would win if you took this project on."

I snorted. "Saying 'this project' sounds very respectable and nothing like digging through ancient mouse poop. Look, I'll think about it." I glanced over at the poems on my wall. "Actually, dealing with someone else's crapola seems much more appealing than dealing with my own."

"Speaking of your crapola, did you finish reviewing the Wal-Mart tape I e-mailed you?"

"Yup. Male figure, just over six feet tall, dressed in oversized jeans, baseball cap, and hoodie, placed the envelope on my truck. He walked into the frame and right back out. A three-second blip."

"We got the same. Forensics wasn't able to do much with

enhancement." He changed from Uncle Dave to Detective Murphy in a nanosecond—his eyes sharp and intelligent, his jaw muscles tensed. "No facial features, not even race. At least we can tell that Psycho is a man."

"Not a lot to go on." I pulled my hair into a ponytail so I could think. "I spent a considerable amount of time reviewing the cars near Angel's truck. Watched each one park. It's crazy that Wal-Mart happened four days ago, and now Psycho is comfortable enough to walk up to my frigging door. Shithead."

I glanced toward my front door to make sure I had thrown the bolt. Checking, checking, re-checking. I was developing OCD. The little green light from my new alarm system and the dogs' state of sleepy-calm helped me keep my blood pressure down. And Dave was here with his Glock in his shoulder holster. My Ruger was strapped to my ankle under my yoga pants.

"Did you pick up anything from reviewing cars?" Dave asked.

"Mothers opened car doors for their kids. An older couple with their canes. A teenager dressed in skintight pants—none of those people had the right clothes or build. I only saw one car drive onto the lot, at the same time I did, which didn't park or let someone out—a blue Honda Civic. I'd bet good money that's his."

"Show me," Dave said, and I went to get my laptop.

9

At six in the morning, the rattle and bang of a construction truck jerked me out of bed. I ran to my window, ordering Beetle and Bella to calm down. Two men in work uniforms unloaded another debris container onto Manny's side yard. Ah, the never-ending parade of debris containers. Heaving a sigh, I slogged my way into the bathroom for a shower. As I stood under the stream of hot water, I realized how crazy it was to clean myself up before going over to Hoarder Hell—but just the thought of the place made me feel like lice and bed bugs crawled over my scalp and bored into my skin.

Today, for the first time, I had to go in. Two weeks. I'd spent two whole weeks getting the trash out of his yard and power washing the exterior. The neighborhood looked a thousand percent better, though. My house became instantly more valuable with that eyesore gone.

I pulled on jeans, laced up my tennis shoes, and stood at the mirror to braid my hair back. Now for the inside. I'd be safer. Less exposed. So far, my security cameras seemed to be working. Psycho hadn't shown up at my house in two weeks—didn't even leave a letter on my car up until last night. The shit-head. I strapped on my belly holster and checked to make sure a bullet was chambered in my Ruger.

Dave said if Psycho tried to attack me in all that mess, he'd probably get crushed by an avalanche of boxes. I didn't doubt it. Maybe I should be a little worried *I* would end up buried in the crap. Note to self—carry the phone at all times. I'd stick it in my bra with my knife.

I jogged down the stairs to see who was banging on my front door. Squinting through the peephole, I found Manny leaning against the jam, chewing the end of a pen like a cigar.

"Roofers coming this morning." He grinned.

I glanced past him over to his house. "Are you going to supervise my projects as well as you're supervising your place?" I gestured to the men climbing back in their truck.

"Absolutely. You getting started inside?" Manny asked.

"Yup. I do this my way, right?" I turned away from him—I needed coffee.

"You're the chief." He slammed the door shut and followed me into the kitchen.

I fixed a steaming mug for Manny, heavy on the sugar and milk, thinking this all seemed *bizarre*. It was as if this whole escapade with the poker-financed house construction, ancient garbage mounds, and crazy death threats were part of some hallucinatory acid trip.

I looked Manny over. His jeans and sweatshirt were a size too small; he probably shrank them in the dryer. "Don't you work?" I asked, handing him the mug.

"I do this and that right now." Manny gave me a wink. "I'm an entrepreneur."

"Okay." I was still more than a little nervous about our

bargain. Would the workers slack because this was a poker debt? "But you're keeping an eye on the outcome here?"

"Sure am. And, by the way, some guy's gonna come over around lunchtime to talk to you about the new heating and air conditioning unit."

"Holy cow. This seems too easy—a new roof going on, new air systems coming. You'll be done with your share of the barter by the end of the week, and I'm just up to your front door."

"Yeah, well, don't get too excited. I happened on a few suckers and some pretty good cards. It's usually feast or famine, yah know? Can't depend on anything with Lady Luck. I'm gonna try hard to get your house done about the same times you finish up with mine." He gulped his coffee. "I'm thinking six, seven, maybe eight months over here. I've got to find the dupes, then things have to be ordered in, permits need filing, inspectors need to show up." He nodded at me. "You have a plan in your head about how long it's gonna take you?"

I wrinkled my nose. "I have a plan. But in my head, every-thing is much easier and much cleaner."

"I hear you." He clunked his empty mug onto the counter.

I grabbed my jacket and headed across the street. Beetle and Bella sprawled beside me on Manny's porch on-guard. I cast vigilant glances up and down the road, and Boomer had focused one of the cameras on Manny's house. Once inside, Psycho could only get to me in one direction, unless he teleported through garbage heaps.

For the first time, I pulled open Manny's front door, then promptly regurgitated. Oh, dear god. The stench brought my elbow protectively over my nose, and I reflexively coughed to rid my lungs of the foul air. I stood there incredulous, wondering how anyone even got in. The stacks made columns from floor to ceiling of boxes, and plastic bags jammed one on top of the other. Everywhere. As Manny crossed back over the road from my house, sadness for his grandparents, and now for him, overwhelmed me.

"Manny." I flung my arms in the air. "How?"

He offered up an indifferent shrug. "This is the way Nana and Pop's house has always been. I guess someone who's never been in before would find this pretty awful."

I stood, wide-eyed, not sure how to respond.

"Hey," Manny said. "I'm gonna keep tabs on the crew over at your place today while I build a new fence in my back yard. I've got a guy coming over to give me a hand. Have you met Justin?" Manny asked. "He lives next door. Your across the street neighbor." Manny pointed at the guy with a tight-hipped gait, sauntering up the sidewalk with a big grin on his face. He stood about five-eleven, with a lean muscled body, comfortably clad in ripped jeans.

"Yeah, Justin and I have met. Hey there," I said, reaching out to shake his hand. As usual, I registered his callouses, abrasions across his knuckles, grease permanently stained at the cuticle line. They looked like my dad's hands used to. Mechanics hands.

Justin made a sweeping gesture to take in the block. "It's amazing how much things have improved with the junk cleaned up out of Manny's yard," he said. "On behalf of the neighborhood, thank you."

I was offering up a wan smile when I caught sight of Dave coming down his steps. Dave raised his hand in a salute.

"Hey," he called over. "I got your message about the list you wanted to give me. Can I swing by this evening? I'm running late for a meeting."

"Fine," I yelled back. "But I have two things for you now." I raised my hand, showing two fingers to punctuate my sentence.

"Two?" Dave's stance tightened.

"Last night at the hairdresser's. It can wait for later."

Dave took a step toward me when his cell phone rang. He peered down at the screen, waved, then jumped in his car and roared off.

Justin glanced past me with a comically-exaggerated grimace. "You start inside today?"

I blew out a breath, gesturing toward the door. "If you don't see my house lights on tonight, send in a search party, will you?"

Justin laughed. "Yeah. Good luck."

I pulled the first box out onto the porch, and I pawed through. It was crammed full of food labels. When Manny said his grandparents weren't right in the head, he wasn't kidding. "Hey, Manny," I said without looking up. "Could you get a poker game together with a kitchen person?" I walked to the rail, pitched the trash in the bin, then stood in front of him, swiping dirt off my hands and onto my jeans. "My fridge doesn't cool, and my oven only works on broil."

"I'll see what can be arranged," Manny said as he headed around back with Justin.

I missed not having my own kitchen since the fire. It had been sad, sad, sad to me that the kitchen in Angel's and my house didn't even come close to functioning. I *loved* to cook. It served as therapy for me. So much of my unschooling education had happened around the stove, under the watchful eyes of my Kitchen Grandmothers—I missed the warmth and goodness, and connectedness.

Master Wang's wife, Snow Bird, was the one who decided I needed the Kitchen Grandmothers. She worried my lack of "women's skills" would make it hard for me to find an honorable husband. She knew my mother's illness—that had left her bedridden since I was twelve—kept Mom from teaching me what Snow Bird thought of as a "lady's education."

Snow Bird grew up in a traditional Chinese home. In her mind, those wife skills were not culturally suited to the American man. And while she wanted to teach me some things—like sewing and cooking—she thought I would benefit from a broader spectrum of knowledge. Snow Bird chose, amongst her friends at the apartment building, five grandmothers, who were willing to take me under their wings. I'd help them with their day-to-day tasks, and in return, I'd learn from them as I went along.

Each grandmother chose a day of the workweek, and on her day, she would teach me everything she thought I should know. Angel's Great-Aunt Rosa was one of my Kitchen Grandmothers. That was how I met Angel the night of the apartment fire.

Abuela Rosa chose Friday nights as my night to work with her. There, I learned Spanish and how to dance. I remembered how naughty I felt when I first tried to move that way, tempting the boys with swaying hips and coquettish eyes.

On Thursdays, I spoke kitchen-Italian with Nona Sophia. While her pots were bubbling and steaming, Nona would take out the art books. We'd sit at the table talking about paintings and artists. Nona cherished art from all over the world, but the pieces of her beloved Tuscany brought tears to her eyes.

My Kitchen Grandmothers gave me a cornucopia of culture and language—spice and ability. And while the whole concept of "wifely skills" was old-fashioned to the point of medieval, I enjoyed learning about all the different cultures and ways of being and doing. And Mom was thrilled.

"This will give your life such wonderful flavor," Mom had said.

She was right. I adored my Kitchen Grandmothers. I loved how they enfolded me into their family life—sharing their skills and knowledge. I had been cooking that way from the time I turned twelve until the fire. I wanted my traditions back.

Thoughts of Abuela Rosa and Angel bubbled up homesick, bereft feelings. Instead of walking down a sentimental path, what I needed to do was stay focused on my next move to capture Psycho, which today meant thinking over the two things I meant to hand over to Dave this evening. One of these was last night's poem. I paused with a box balanced in my hand, getting a better grip, then I threw it over the railing and into the bin. The poem was same old, same old. It actually made me a little worried that I would come to think of this pervasive dread as my natural state. Get another poem, hand it off to Dave. Get complacent. Become a statistic. I hadn't come up with a strategy for the best way to balance my panic and anxiety with the need to get on with life.

I walked back to the next bag. This one held pinecones. DIY project? I slung it over the rail, pausing to scan the street—black cat. Red Toyota turning left, woman driver. Wind-blown soda can.

The second thing I *might* hand over was the Iniquus list. But should I? Even thinking about it made me feel disloyal to Spyder. Almost traitorous. The list—all the players I could recall from the Iniquus files I worked on with Spyder. Classified files. High-security files. Three years of files.

Though I started training with Spyder when I turned thirteen, I didn't actually puzzle a real case or go out in the field until I reached seventeen. That's when my code name, Alex, showed up in the paperwork. I closed my last file in September. Then Spyder left, and I was done with files.

Should I hand it over? Dave wasn't going to ask questions about the crimes. He wanted to run names through the system to see if he could get locations. Who was in jail? Who was West Coast? Could we narrow any of these down and find a suspect? I was worried. Too many computer pings might just flag us with an agency—though sure, the Iniquus clients came from all branches of government. I worked with the FBI, CIA, ATF, Treasury—lots of clients. Mostly government. A few private. Maybe because they spread over multiple agencies, no one would get curious.

I looked in the next box. Old newspapers. I dragged it down the porch.

Should I give him the list? We had nothing else.

Pause to scan—same black cat, different location. Blue minivan parking, one block down, an elderly man exiting. Kid on a bike. Wind gust making the bare limbs dance.

No headway at the Police Station, Dave kept moving the circumference of his searches wider and wider. I knew it frustrated him, infuriated him, not to be able to stop this for me.

I couldn't keep living this way, always on high alert. It was sucking all of my energy. I needed to find a way to make it all stop.

10

Evening came. After using up all my hot water in the shower, I pulled on clean clothes and sat on my front porch under the protective watch of my security cameras and my dogs. I was eating a sandwich for dinner, waiting for Dave. Beetle and Bella hung out, watching the neighborhood activity—kids jumping rope, people coming home from work, a sporadic jogger. Sarah, who lived to the right of Manny's house, paced along with her five-month-old daughter, Ruby, patiently patting her back and cooing to comfort her. Red-faced Ruby, with her baby fists balled tight, was arched backward and screaming at the top of her little lungs. By the third pass, I called Sarah over.

"Sarah, you look worn out. Here, let me hold Ruby for a few minutes while you sit down."

Frazzled, she handed me her baby and sank down on my stairs. "This darned colic. Her screaming's driving my whole family up the wall. Everyone's angry and yelling."

I laid Ruby face-up on my lap and placed my palms on her stomach. Ruby blinked up at me, startled, but then her eyes softened. Her crying stopped. Ruby and I held eye contact while I spoke in soft, soothing tones to her. "Relax, little one. Let my hands heal you. You'll sleep so well tonight and give your poor mommy a break." Soon, Ruby fell asleep.

I picked her up and cuddled her close, breathing in the honey smell of her wispy copper hair. I loved the baby sweetness of her.

"What in the world just happened?" Sarah's eyes stretched wide.

"Reiki. It's a healing energy thing. Just something I learned to help my mom when she was in hospice. I can't really explain the mechanics, but—"

Sarah put her hand up in a stop sign and shook her head. "I don't care how it works. Look at Ruby. She's not in pain. She's asleep." Fatigue slacked the muscles on Sarah's face, pulling down the corners of her mouth.

We sat quietly. Sarah breathed deeply, letting go of her stress, while I cuddled sleeping, Ruby.

"You know," Sarah said after a long while. "When you bought this house from her, Mrs. Nelson was caught in a bad financial spot." Sarah raked a hand through her strawberry-blond hair. "She was having some health problems, and the meds she needed took up all her money. My husband, Bob, and I weren't sure she ate regularly." Sarah shifted a foot under her hip. "She refused to talk it over with me." After a few minutes of silence, she added, "I didn't push her, though. I feel guilty now. I told myself I was busy with my own family and all." She curled her lips in and pulled them flat in a wry kind of smile. "That's not really the truth. The truth is, we all sort of coexist in this neighborhood. I mean, we wave at each other and everything, but that's about it."

I didn't say anything, just cozied Ruby closer to me. After

a few minutes, Sarah leaned forward to catch my eye, "You seem to have a different way of doing things. You've reached out to everyone since you got here. Where are you from originally?"

"Not far. I'm from DC, too." I leaned my head back against the post. "I grew up in a small apartment building. We were twenty families in all, and we definitely had the 'it-takes-a-village' mentality. We were always in each other's lives and apartments—just a big extended family." I smiled. "Well, mostly. A few apartments preferred to keep to themselves."

"That sounds ideal."

I laughed. "Until I did something naughty as a child, and then I had a dozen moms instead of just my one."

The car driving by beeped then parked down the street. Sarah pointed at the woman climbing out. "Have you met Alice and Andy yet?"

I nodded my head and jostled Ruby a little to ease her back to sleep after the horn had startled her.

"They're coming over for spaghetti tomorrow night. We wanted to watch a couple of videos. Why don't you come and hang out?"

"Tomorrow? Oh, I'd like to, but I can't. I have rescue squad duty." Beetle whined and inched her nose closer to the baby, her nostrils working out the scent. I reached over and scratched under her whiskery chin.

"You're an EMT? How'd you get involved in that?"

"My mom. She was sick for a long time. Toward the end, I had to call 911 a lot. I thought it might be good to know what the EMTs did to help her, maybe get some equipment on hand to make Mom feel better—well, to make me feel better." I pushed Beetle back; her nose was getting too curious. "I checked into it, and the Rescue Squad said they'd pay for my training and certification if I volunteered for them for two years. Sounded like a deal to me, so I signed on."

"Do you like going out on calls?" she asked.

I paused for a minute. Did I like it? What a curious question. I didn't volunteer because I liked it—I did it because people needed help. "It's been a good thing," I said.

Sarah tipped her head to the side. "Can I ask how old you are? You look like a teenager."

"I turned twenty March third."

"That's too young," she said authoritatively. "I mean, with your story, I would say you had to be at least twenty-five." Sarah squinted. "It seems unreasonable that you've accomplished what you have at such an early age." She drew her brows together and offered me a contrite frown. "I hope you don't mind my saying that."

"That's all right. I homeschooled." I waved at Justin, getting into his car across the way. "If I'm talking to another homeschooler, then my bag of tricks is no big deal. I think it's all about, you know, where a family puts their focus. Growing up, I never had to study for an exam or write a term paper. I had all day to just explore and learn things I thought were interesting, from computers and mechanics to magic, languages, physical fitness. Whatever came up."

"Cooking, EMT, healing arts," Sarah added. "Bob and I may have to sit you down to talk to us about how that all worked so we can consider it for our kids."

"Sometimes, when I talk about my education, it's hard for someone who grew up in the linear culture of traditional schooling to understand. There are pros and cons to the way I learned. But it did give me a bunch of life skills I would have missed if I went to regular school."

Sarah nodded, turning her focus to her house. "Speaking of

my kids, I guess I'd better get back and make sure my son hasn't set anything on fire." She turned toward me. "We'll do the dinner thing another time when Andy's in town, and you aren't on duty." She reached down and scooped up her baby. "I can't tell you how much I appreciate your helping Ruby. Thank you so much. Reiki, you called it?"

"Yeah."

I watched Sarah cross the street. *Reiki.* I slapped myself on the forehead. Miriam Laugherty. I bet *she* could pick up a better psychic impression on Psycho. Why didn't I think of her before? I blew out a huff of air. Miriam. Shit. Bands of stress ratcheted across my ribs. That was not the road I had intended to take e*ver* again.

I curled up like a cat on Miriam's living room couch with a cup of hibiscus tea steeping on the table beside me. Miriam was on the phone with the police, jotting notes about a case they wanted her to work for them. Someone's Great Dane came home this morning with a human skull in his mouth. The detective needed a jump-start—some information to get going with while the skull waited its turn on the forensics lab shelf.

Miriam was an Extrasensory Criminal Investigator. Who knew such a thing actually existed? The law enforcement world didn't like to talk about her or her stellar closed-file rate because —well, probably because the concept boggled the mind, or maybe because it threw their rational methodology out the window. I understood all that. When I first talked to Miriam, I thought she was full of hooey, too.

Miriam swiped her hand through the spill of blond curls

cascading down her back and hung up with a little apologetic smile. "Sorry."

I pulled the tea bag from my cup. "How's Kim?" I asked. Kim had been my mom's nurse. She was the one who taught me Reiki and healing arts during Mom's long fight to stick around and see me turn eighteen, and she was Miriam's wife.

"Kim's fine. I'll tell her you asked after her." Miriam's eyes filled with concern. "You, on the other hand, look terrible."

I raised an eyebrow. Miriam always was direct.

"I mean, you're lovely as usual." She flourished long-fingers with the grace of a ballerina. "What I should say is you don't *feel* good to me—your energy's all over the place."

I swallowed, unsure where to start.

"The beginning is usually best." Miriam's laugh jingled; a grin lit up her pixie face.

I shook my head with pursed lips. Being here and seeing Miriam was harder than it should be. The last time we talked had been—

"Right now, you're thinking about our last case together— and it's stopping you from telling me the real reason for your visit. Let's start there, okay?" Her eyes darkened.

My breath caught.

"You saved her life. You understand that." Miriam leaned forward, asserting her conviction.

I focused out the window at a beautiful bare-limbed willow.

"Have you been practicing your ESP?" she asked.

"No, ma'am." I shifted my gaze to my fingers knotted in my lap, then back into Miriam's cyan eyes. "Well, I haven't walked behind the Veil—that is, I haven't tried to leave my body or do remote searches since I stopped training with you. But things bubble up like they have all my life. Knowings. Pictures. Scents."

"Scents?" She cocked her head to the side. "That's new."

I rubbed my nose and sniffed audibly. The pervasive ooze emitted its mephitis. Could she smell it, too?

"I'm glad you're not playing around unsupported." Tension stiffened Miriam's features, especially behind her eyes. "I've never seen anyone make such a profound connection before." She rested her hand on my arm. "I blame myself that you were hurt. I didn't realize it was possible to share the pain and injuries of someone when linked in the ether. I've done some research since then—your abilities are rare. But there are other documented cases."

I reached for my cup, purposely breaking our connection. My mouth had gone dry. My lips stuck to my teeth. The night I worked that case for her had been a hell ride. A young woman, caught on a cell phone video by a passer-by, got dragged from her car at the mall. Responding officers I.D.'d the abductor as a known predator—the detective, fearful for the victim's life, called Miriam in on the case.

When Miriam couldn't pick up on anything, she handed me the woman's photo, hoping I'd get something helpful. As soon as I put the picture in my fingers, I flew out of my body and got the crap beaten out of me. Physically, I was in my apartment, and the woman was in an alley—but we were one. And what happened to her happened to me.

Thank god, I was able to keep one foot on this side of the Veil—part of me stayed on this plane—and I could tell Miriam the name of the restaurant I read off their emergency exit door. The police arrived in time. The victim lived. After three days of unconsciousness, I gathered myself back together and recovered. I never, *ever*, ever! Wanted to do that again. I pulled my gaze from the inside of my cup up to Miriam's concerned eyes.

"You never have to, Lexi. You will always have the choice.

That's how it works." Miriam tucked a leg under her and cradled her teacup in her lap. "Let's talk about the smell." She took a sip, watching me over the rim.

"Can I ask what you're picking up first, before I give you any of my information?"

"Men," she said simply.

"Plural?" My heart stumbled.

"Three," she replied. "Three men in three layers. I'll start with the oldest layer. The first mmn—a beloved teacher with a father-daughter like connection to you. You would describe him as 'exotic.' He's painted midnight blue-black with incredibly long thin arms and legs. This man keeps his head shaved and wears dark, nondescript clothes. When you conjure up his image, you think of the African Anansi tales and his laugh—like thunder rolling up from his belly. Hmm. Very poetic. I believe I recognize him from seeing him at your apartment. This must be your friend Spyder McGraw."

"I'm so worried about him. I haven't heard anything since September."

"He loves you. He misses you. He's working hard on a case. It's of vital importance—he's far away. It will be a long time yet until he can come home."

I let out the breath I hadn't realized I was holding. "Thank you."

"Number two. This man is more recent. There is little here. He seems very new to your life. Hmm... Latino. A soldier—a very good one. He has glittering black eyes, silky dark brown hair, and tanned skin. When you think of him, you focus on his smiles—white teeth and dimples. This man loves you too. This is a joined love." Miriam paused with her eyes closed, swaying slightly back and forth in concentration. "You're married?" Miriam's eyes sprang open with incredulity and grabbed my left hand where my rings glittered. A grin spread across her cheeks. "Congratulations! Oh, I like his energy."

"He's okay, then? He'll come home safe?"

A cloud crossed over Miriam's face. "I can't predict the future, sweetie. Let's see what I can tell you." We sat in silence for a minute before she continued. "He loves his job. He's following his dream—it's all working out well. He thinks he'll be promoted soon. He misses you, though. The hardest part for him is you can't be together." She looked at me sharply. "And if he knew you couldn't sleep because you're having nightmares nearly every night about IEDs, he'd be sick. You need to stop. It serves no purpose. Seriously." Her voice was sharp, then her eyes softened as she shifted her attention. "Hmmn. Maybe this makes sense to you. He thinks he's failed as a man. He let you down. Something about him asking you to follow family traditions… marriage. He's ashamed." Miriam's eyes focused again, and she looked at me with what I could only interpret as disbelief. "You're a virgin?"

The heat rose in the room. Ugh. She *would* pick up on something so personal. "Uh, well, his family is Catholic, and he asked me to wait. And then our wedding night got interrupted. He deployed the next morning. So that left me…" My gaze went everywhere but on her. The room became unbearably stuffy. I pulled off my sweater.

"Oh, Lexi, I'm sorry." She blushed along with me. "Yeah, I'm not even sure what's the right thing to say here. Please don't be embarrassed, honey. Life takes all kinds of strange twists and turns—and from the images, I got from him," she laughed conspiratorially, "he plans to set everything right the minute he sees you." Miriam patted my knee with a wink.

Miriam's dog barked at the door, and she went over to let him out. I was glad for an opportunity to regain my equilibrium.

As Miriam started back into the room, she looked over at me and gasped. "Oh, Lexi! No!" Her face filled with horror. Eyes wide, lips bloodless, she rushed toward me. "Who is this man? The third one?" She grabbed my upper arms in a vice grip and gave me a little shake.

"He's the reason I came to talk to you," I managed to stutter out.

Miriam's extrasensory skills allowed her to pick up impressions from the past. Things that have been. People who have been. Working in the present wasn't part of her skill set, and I knew that coming in. Still, I had hoped for a tidbit—a morsel pointing to a crumb trail for me to follow.

Miriam moved her head back and forth like she was trying to find the sweet spot where she could pick up the right vibrations. "I sense him; the sickness of the man's brain... He feeds gluttonously on fear. He's evil. Mentally ill and off his medications." She moaned softly, her lashes brushed against her cheeks as her closed lids fluttered. "He's killed before. He's hungry to do it again, but he's holding himself back. He wants to drag out the game like foreplay."

I rubbed sweating palms slowly down my jeans, trying not to distract Miriam from her connection.

"He thinks of the final kill as an orgasmic release of tension," Miriam said. "Heightened by the months, he spends teasing his targets. 'Teasing' that's his word for the fear he likes to create. Victims. Their energies are hovering near him. I can't count."

"Why the poems?" I whispered.

She shook her head. "I...I'm not sure. The only thing I'm getting is he didn't write them. It was someone else."

This wasn't new information; they were adulterations of well-known poets.

"Why me? How'd I get caught up in all this?"

Miriam's fingers lay slack on her lap. "He believes he's helping you. He's moving you toward your destiny. He thinks you like this as much as he does." Miriam opened her eyes. "What poems, Lexi?"

I handed the photocopies to her, and she read them with tears in her eyes.

"Miriam," I whispered. "I know how horrible it is connecting to evil. I'm so sorry to ask you to do this for me."

She never had an emotional reaction when she worked with the past impressions she lifted from the evidence handed to her by the various government agencies. Her attempts to get information for me came at a deeply personal cost to her. I could easily sense the price she was paying. I knew, from firsthand experience.

"No, sweetie." She swiped her napkin over her eyes. "You were right to come to me. Right to ask for help. I just can't grab hold of anything—not a single clue to offer you. It's as if his plans aren't in his head. He must be too mentally ill. Surely, you know more. Surely, you're homing in on who this is."

"The only thing I have, apart from these notes, is that he's a six-foot-tall-ish man. Possibly a car description. The police have no corresponding M.O.s. That's why I came here. I needed a bread crumb."

"And I gave you nothing." She frowned.

"Not true. I know that he's out to kill me. I won't try to keep reassuring myself that the letters are the only thing that will happen. I always took this seriously, but I also hoped this was kind of it. But it's not."

"No," she said. "His intention is most emphatically to kill you."

I had to let that sit for a moment. Give it a second to sink in. To catch my breath. To be able to speak. "You said he has other victims. I know the detective on my case has been looking for connections, but he hasn't come up with anything yet. If there were others that he stalked, and they were subsequently killed, you'd think the police would know about it. The FBI? Someone? Wouldn't you?"

11

Giving Beetle a scratch behind the ears, we motored down Silver Lake toward home. The girls and I had been playing Frisbee at the park, celebrating the flower-filled late-spring day. It had been a while since my last poem, and I was trying my darndest to do what I wanted to do, when I wanted to do it. What if the things I chose to do were around a lot of people and included my dogs? It was better than barricading myself in my house, letting the walls squeeze me in.

I was trying to be normal.

Trying.

Time was doing funny things in my head. My house was constantly shifting its appearance. The exterior paint and a new porch, the kitchen, and triple-pane windows. I was getting closer to my goal of making this a comfortable home for Angel and me to nest in. Manny's house was improving, too. Whole rooms had emerged from under the garbage. He could cook in his kitchen, walk to a useable bathroom, and take a shower.

I was glad that I'd taken on his project. It sucked, to be sure. But it helped me see that time was passing, good things were happening, and it helped me make a family out of my neighbors. Not quite like my neighbors at the apartment building, but those relationships had taken time, too. I could be patient.

Waiting for Angel to get home stretched out in front of me. It reminded me of a painting of the colonial woman I once saw. She paced on her widow's walk, searching the horizon for a ship's sail. Hopeful. Expectant. And trepidatious. Waiting for Angel was the background color of my canvas and the reason I had nightmares almost every night, though Miriam had told me to stop.

How could I stop?

Then, there were bright slashes of color across my canvas— unexpected and violent—disrupting the otherwise subtle hues of my life. Psycho. It was funny to me, not in a ha-ha way but in an "isn't that surprising?" way that a letter could feel so vicious. So uprooting and destructive. I think part of the power was in the pace Psycho meted them out to me. I'd start to calm my anxiety, and BOOM! Two in a row, one a week later, nothing for almost two months. I never knew. Was he watching me? Was he calculating? Would he ever make a mistake and leave a clue? Could I ever wash him out of my thoughts? Wash his stench from my hair?

That's what my mind was churning over when I turned into my neighborhood. A "knowing" hit me with a solid blow to the diaphragm. I was pushed against the back of my seat as if driving through an invisible force field. "Exposed" flashed in oscillating red. I slowed my car to scan. Nothing seemed amiss. Beetle and Bella had their heads out the window, dangling their pink tongues. Calm.

I pulled up to the curb, set the parking brake, and stuffed my purse under the seat to free up my hands. Carefully opening the door, I spiked my keys between the fingers of my left hand. My right hand gripped the Ruger in my belly holster. Movement coming from across the street had me ducking behind the opened door. I tilted my head to peek through the glass. Dave. He jogged around the side of Manny's house.

"Lexi, Thank god! Come quick!" He hailed me with an urgent wide arcing arm.

With the girls at my heels, I took off at a run, following Dave around to the backyard where Justin clutched his wrist and cussed. Manny stood with his mouth hanging open, staring at him.

"He's burned." Dave filled in the blank. "Can you do the brush thing with your hand like you did when Fletcher pulled the boiling water off the stove?"

I grabbed at Justin's arm. "Justin, stand still! Justin! Stand still! I can't help you when you're doing that."

Dave clamped a vice-like grip onto Justin's wrist to hold his arm out for me. A mean red streak ran from his inner elbow all the way down to his palm. I reached out and brushed the air above his wound. "How'd this happen?" I asked.

"Fucking Manny doesn't know fucking shit about grilling. That's how the hell this happened," Justin spat through gritted teeth, slitting his eyes and bouncing on his toes.

"They were arguing about how to stack the charcoals. Manny squirted lighter fluid on the already lit coals, and the flame followed the stream. Justin was standing in the line of fire—literally," Dave said.

Exposed could it mean this burn? Exposed to the fire? That didn't seem right. I didn't get a sense of relief telling me I understood correctly. I scanned the back yard, across the top of the retaining wall, nothing.

I continued to brush the air above the burn. "I'm so sorry, Justin. I think I can take this away, though. Just give me a minute." The doubt written on his face wasn't surprising. When Mom's nurse Kim taught me this technique to deal with Mom's radiation burns, I was dubious too, until I realized how well it worked. Soon, Justin stood flat-footed and panting; some of the strain left his jaw.

"How does that feel?" I asked.

Justin looked down at his skin, then back to me. "That's the craziest damned thing I think has ever happened to me."

I giggled at his comical expression—his eyes wide, his eyebrows nearly to his hairline.

"Is that like some sort of magic trick? What the heck did you just do?" Justin examined the spot closely.

"Magic tricks are illusions. This is a simple Healing Touch technique anyone can learn," I said.

"Like for Ruby?" Justin walked over to a lawn chair and plopped down, still examining his skin.

"Yeah. Well, similar."

"Huh," Justin grunted as the three of us grabbed chairs too. I placed mine with my back to the house, and I had the widest view possible. Beetle and Bella flanked me. My hand rested on my stomach, ready to grab my gun.

We sat in silence until Justin said, "Yankees are playing tonight. You guys coming over after we eat?"

I glanced over at the grill. The coals had turned gray along the edges, still a ways to go before they'd be ready for cooking. "I can't, thanks." I reached down and rubbed behind Beetle's ears.

"You don't watch baseball?" Justin asked.

"Sometimes, but tonight I'm going to do a set over at Star-Light. Management wants to see how people like me. I thought it might be good to have a little pocket money. Do you guys know the place?"

"It's nice," Dave said. "Kind of neighborhood-y. Cathy and me go up every now and then when we have someone to babysit the kids."

"You sing?" Justin stretched his legs out in front of him and slouched down in his chair.

"Mmhm and play guitar."

"Is there anything you can't do?" Justin asked.

"Yeah, I don't do geometry or pop culture." The last of the sun's rays warmed my face. I'd need to go get ready soon.

Dave snorted. "Lexi can build a rocket ship and fly to the moon, but she doesn't know the Pythagorean Theorem. Lexi was weird-schooled."

"Weird-schooled, Dave?" I gave him a little kick.

"Yeah. What's the capital of South Dakota?"

"No clue." I scowled at him. I didn't like being teased.

"I went to a normal school, and I don't know the capital of South Dakota, neither." Manny rested a beer on his rounded stomach.

"I was unschooled," I said.

Dave grinned. "And that's weird."

"It's not. Lots of famous people were unschooled."

"Yeah? Like who?" asked Dave.

"George Washington, Thomas Jefferson, Abraham Lincoln, Theodore Roosevelt." I ticked off on my fingers.

"They don't count. They're dead."

"They do too." I sounded testy even to my own ears.

"Hey, Sarah was telling me that's how you were brought up. But I thought she said homeschooled. What's un-schooled?" Justin asked.

"It means I got my education from reading tons of books and from hanging out with people. So, for example, I speak Spanish from talking to Angel's great aunt, Abuela Rosa. I never sat in a class or studied verb conjugations. But after eight years of hanging out in her kitchen, I picked it up. My parents saw formal schooling as a waste of time."

"What's the strangest thing you've ever learned?" Justin leaned forward, obviously intrigued by all this.

"I don't know." I thought for a minute. "We had this neighbor once who worked at the National Zoo." I shielded my eyes with my hand as a cloud moved, and the sudden bright light stung me. I jostled around to get the best visual field again. "I went to work with her all the time. They were having trouble with the monkeys because people were throwing things into their area, and the monkeys ate the debris. The zoo was trying to come up with a better way of protecting the monkeys, so I went through their poop and cataloged stuff that didn't belong there." I shifted my chair to take advantage of the shade cast by the house. "I'd call that a little odd, I guess. I had fun, though. Mostly, I learned normal kinds of things—like I was telling Sarah, my goals were centered on acquiring a variety of skills. Playing the guitar and singing being one of those things."

"And fighting?" Manny asked.

How'd he hear about me fighting?

"Yeah, fighting stuff, that's the best," Dave said before I had a chance to bat that away.

Justin had his chair rocked back onto two legs, with his fingers laced behind his head, looking very relaxed. A one-eighty from the way I found him a few minutes ago. He turned toward Dave. "Fighting?"

Dave ignored my etheric scream to "Shut up!"

"Martial arts," he said. "One day, my buddy Stan and me had her up to the training academy. We were going to teach her to shoot." Dave smirked. "Stan looks over at me and gives me a hard time because I got promoted to detective. He says, 'They had to promote you. You're a liability on the beat. You're so weak you couldn't win against a baby. Not even Baby Girl there." Dave gestured back at me. "I knew she'd been trained in some stuff." He turned to me. "You started when you were what, four? Five years old?" He turned to the other men. "Baby Girl had eleven years of daily one-on-one Kung Fu practice with Master Wang at the dry cleaners across the street from her apartment building."

I glowered in his direction, not sure how to shift this conversation in such a way that it would be easily forgotten. I needed to think of something less personal. This was dangerous territory. Dave trusted these guys, but knowledge was a tricky thing. I couldn't warn my neighbors not to talk about me to lurking stalkers. I tried to come up with something, but the only word my brain would offer up was "exposed."

"But so what, right?" Dave continued the story. "She was a kid. Stan said, 'Come on, let's put you two on the mats.' I thought we were joking."

My dogs sensed my agitation and their bodies grew rigid with concentration. I just needed an interrupting story—topic, something to stop Dave.

"I went out there and reached to grab her wrist—next thing I knew, I'd done a face plant. She had me in some kind of Kung Fu hold, and I couldn't get up." Dave was sitting at the end of his chair, leaning forward, using big gestures, getting into his story. "Now I gotta bruised ego, and I was gonna show her who was boss."

"What?" Justin asked, swinging his gaze toward me, seeing me with different eyes.

"He's pulling your leg," I said with a grimace and a shake of my head.

"Lexi handed me my butt on a plate," Dave insisted. "I tried to get her down. I was sucking-wind, dog-tired, sweating like a pig, bruised head to toe. Still, she tossed me like a garden salad." Dave leaned back with satisfaction, taking a swig from his bottle. "Sergeant Christophe—he's in charge of training recruits—was laughing his head off and says Lexi's gonna be his secret weapon with the new classes coming through."

"You do that, Lexi? Beat up the recruits?" Justin grinned broadly and twisted open another bottle.

I pressed my lips together and checked my watch. Light and fluffy, innocent and cute, sweet little girl-next-door. Dave was blowing my disguise. If someone knew I could fight—*Psycho*—then he'd be prepared. Keeping my skills a secret protected me. Kept me safer.

"Your parents weren't your only teachers?"

"Exactly, everyone has something to teach. You just have to listen and show interest. Most of the people, like my Kitchen Grandmothers, lived in my apartment building. But some, like Dave, are family friends."

And Spyder.

Spyder had known my parents since before I was born. When I was thirteen, Spyder sat in our garage, telling Dad a story about a case he'd just wrapped up. I listened intently, then said it reminded me of the Aesop's Fable about the Ant and Chrysalis.

"How so," Spyder asked, curiosity wrinkling his brow.

"Looks can be deceiving. The ant didn't realize the butterfly would escape the cocoon and fly off, but it seems to me—" I never finished my sentence. Spyder leaped to his feet, grabbed his keys from Dad, and roared up the street. I stood there in shock. I had no clue what I said that made Spyder react that way. A few hours later, he came to our apartment and offered to mentor me. It was a barter deal. He would teach me. In exchange, I'd help our neighbor Mrs. Agnew with her children. I never knew the connection between Spyder and Mrs. Agnew. It was classified—another Spyder mystery.

When Spyder made the offer, Mom and Dad thought the exchange was a great opportunity for me and accepted happily. I was beyond ecstatic. What I got from Spyder was brain training. I used the computer a lot to start, and then we would apply my skills to practical situations. I played the role of a modern-day Nancy Drew, which I wanted to be—more than anything else in the world—ever since I picked up *The Demon of River Heights* at age six. I remembered how I walked around all day, wearing Playtex gloves and carrying a lunchbox with my magnifying glass and plastic "evidence bags."

When I was sixteen, Spyder's training changed; he thought I'd make an excellent Intelligence Officer. I studied and worked in that direction. Spyder insisted my innocent, girl-next-door looks would disarm people. Like Mr. Miller said, Spyder thought I'd be the last person the bad guy would expect, and they'd lower their guard. Spyder drilled into me the importance of maintaining my soft look, not to have the eyes or body stance of a soldier. If I did, I'd become a target. So, I walked around and practiced looking happy, approachable, and carefree all the time. Acting like a piece-of-fluff created my best disguise.

But as fluffy as I tried to seem now, it wasn't helping. I still had an enemy on my trail.

"What an awesome way to learn." Justin's voice whipped me back to Manny's side yard.

"Mostly, it was." I reached for my bag. "Exposed" pulsed in my mind. So not Justin's burn. I needed to get out of there. I stood and tapped my leg; my dogs moved to either side of me. I was balancing from one foot to the other. It felt like a million eyes stared me down. But weirdly, no heebie-jeebies told me to run the hell away. Dave focused on me with tense muscles. He hadn't missed my weird behavior.

"Hey, enjoy your dinners." I managed to keep my tone calm. "I need to scoot." I waved and headed toward my house. Dave grabbed at my elbow as we moved together across the lawn, my girls beside us.

"What?" His voice sounded strained.

"Something's tickling at the edge of my consciousness. Sometimes picking up stuff on the ESP-network is static-y at best."

I unlocked the door, turned off the alarm, and gave Dave a hug. "I'll see you tomorrow."

Dave stood on the porch, looking like he wanted to beat the shit out of someone. "Over at Justin's, you felt the shit-head close by, didn't you?"

"Yeah. But I don't know what to do with that. Until he drops me a better clue—"

"We're clueless," Dave said.

12

I kicked off the blankets with a groan. Exhaustion made my muscles ache. I needed to get some sleep. But the house creaked and moaned all night, and adrenaline rallied me for a fight at every sound. I woke up a dozen times, sitting straight up in bed, my 9mm trained at the door, trying to echo-locate the noise and identify it as safe. To reassure myself that Psycho wasn't lurking in the shadows. Beetle and Bella must have thought I'd gone crazy.

I pulled on a sweatsuit, slid my Ruger into my belly holster, my knife into my sports bra, and laced my feet into cross-trainers. Everything seemed so messed up.

Loneliness sucked. I wanted Angel home.

"Beetle, Bella." I rubbed my girls' heads. "Come on. Let's get some breakfast and go for a run. Maybe I can snap myself out of this darned funk."

A change of scenery might help. Hopefully, a jog by the river will do the trick, I thought as I got us ready then headed toward the garage.

I pulled open the truck door to load the girls in and immediately saw the envelope propped on the driver's seat.

My mind stuttered over the details. I had locked the garage last night. I had locked the truck. I just unlocked them both. No, wait. Did I lock the truck last night? Or did Psycho lock it after he put the envelope in the cab? I don't... I was sure I locked the garage.

Breathing hard, skin prickling, I crouched by the garage door, checking for signs someone had pried or picked or forced the doors, but saw none. Thank goodness Beetle and Bella sat right beside me, acting normal, or I would have jumped right out of my skin.

He got in. He got in? How could he have possibly gotten in? If he could get into my garage, could he get into my house? Past my security? Surely not with Beetle and Bella around. If he were inside when we got home, my girls would tear him to pieces. Unless... A tiny voice whispered in the back of my head that he might hurt my girls—incapacitate them. I couldn't listen to the voice. It made me too vulnerable, too horrified. I couldn't lose Beetle and Bella. I couldn't let anything happen to them. They were my family.

I employed Master Wang's technique for steadying nerves. I acknowledged the fear and vulnerability. I thanked these emotions. Soon they calmed enough that I could function. I called Dave, waited for him to arrive, then we opened the envelope:

The burn on thy neighbor lay,
I were na far away,
But waited for the break o' day
To tell you of my view...

. . .

We sat across from each other at my kitchen table.

"He's watching you, Lexi." Dave's eyes didn't raise from the cream-colored stationery. "Your stalker saw you help Justin yesterday. Now he's taunting you. Calling you out." He shook the paper at me, then reached around to get a plastic bag from my drawer. "We should Google this. I actually think I memorized it in fourth-grade for Mrs. Pate. Had to stand in front of the class to recite it, nearly pissed myself, too. If I'm right, it's Robert Burns' 'Bannockburn.'"

"Robert Burns? *Burns*? Are you kidding me? Maybe this guy has a sense of humor." I laughed. Okay, so I sounded a little hysterical. I didn't want Psycho calling me out. I was supposed to be a suburban housewife, planting vegetables and making meatloaf. Darn it!

The coffee pot light turned green, and I put the carafe on a trivet between us.

"So, how many Xanax are you popping each day?" Dave gingerly set his smiley face mug on the table.

"That would be a fair indicator of how badly this guy's getting to me. Right now? None."

"Nerves of steel?" He was in professional mode, eyes scanning me, assessing. It felt intrusive.

I lowered my lashes for privacy. "Hardly. I'm trying to stay busy, so when I fall into bed, I'm too exhausted to let the tap-dancing in my stomach keep me awake."

"Zantac, not Xanax, keeps you together?"

I focused on the mug I slid back and forth in front of me. "I guess."

Dave reached out a hand to still my cup. "I'm not making light of this. I really want to know how you're handling everything. There aren't any signs, other than your ant-like behavior that you have a care in the world."

"It's spooky, Dave. His lurking—his watching where I go. I'm beginning to unravel."

"You seem pretty pulled together."

"You're not looking close enough. I'm a freaking melodrama." I clunked my head down on the table. My stomach churned. My skin felt flushed and feverish. PSycho was making me physically ill.

He was the black plague.

He was plaguing me.

I sat up and gave a reflexive shiver. I tried to steady myself and refocus on where I was at that moment. I was here, safe in my kitchen, talking to a friend, safe. I took a sip of my coffee, set the mug out of the way, and cleared my throat. "My coping strategy is to distance myself emotionally," I said, lacing my fingers and looking directly at Dave. "I've been trying to think of this as a case I'm working on like I'm puzzling something at my old job. Psycho's always there, though, you know? Like a pot simmering on the back of the stove that I can smell cooking. I keep sniffing the air trying to tell if things are starting to smoke and burn. It's hard to pretend I'm not involved."

"I'm sure it's impossible. Do you need me to get Victim's Services to give you a call? They could probably get you in to see someone."

"A psychiatrist? No, thanks. I'm not going to take any medications that might slow my mind or my reflexes. I can't talk my way through this. It's not over." I got up and poured my coffee into the sink

Dave followed me over with his mug. "Nothing's on the security tapes?"

"I don't have any cameras trained on the garage. I'll call Boomer today and get that taken care of. Run the alarm back there, too. He thinks I'm out of my mind with all this security." I leaned back, arms crossed, lips pursed.

The hardest thing about this for me was that I had been trained for action. Everything with Spyder had been about strategy. Find the target, learn the game, understand the rules, and then manipulate the rules to win. Psycho's game didn't seem to have rules. Like a book without a plot. I knew from Miriam that Psycho's end goal was killing me. Staying in the game meant staying alive. I'd win if I caught him and he was taken out of my equation—prison, death, I didn't care, as long as I didn't get any of these darned letters anymore.

I'd studied the poems for clues. I plotted the dates, the times, the locations when they arrived. The messages—I assessed and reassessed, and all I got was a migraine. But I didn't give up. He'd have to make a mistake. I just needed him to make it before the whistle blew, calling an end to the game.

He had to make a mistake while I still had a chance to survive. *Had* to.

And that was the confusing part for me. The more contact we had, the more opportunities for mistakes. I wanted every opportunity I could get. And yet, having him near, his leaving the notes, and my finding them, reading them? It was hell.

I tipped my head. "Any pings from that list of names I gave you?"

Dave sent me a frown. "I've crossed off a bunch. What can you tell me about Mason Pile?"

"I can't *tell* you anything about anyone on the list. You don't have clearance. I've probably broken five-hundred laws handing you the names in the first place. And you've probably broken a few by accepting the list and running searches." I glared at him pointedly. "Don't get into trouble because of me."

"I can handle myself. I have no idea where the list came from, anyway. Showed up in my personal e-mail one day with the message, 'This information might help in the India Sobado case.'" He checked the screen on his phone, sent a quick text, then stuck it back on his belt. "One of the names, this Mason Pile guy, popped up with a long history, including domestic violence and rape."

"I'm aware."

"He didn't raise any flags with you?" Dave asked.

"Not really." I posted my elbows on the table. "I think he's been a busy boy, too busy to spend time stalking me. I honestly can't see how this poetry-shit could be tied into Iniquus since no one knew about me. Not the company. Not the clients. Certainly not our tags. The people on the list? How would they link back to me?"

Dave scratched at his neck. "Why'd you break five-hundred laws to give me those names?"

"Because no one knew *me*, but they knew Spyder. And there is the thin possibility someone with a grudge against Spyder followed him to me. I have no idea who could be on Spyder's list. It's got to be a mile long, but at least this was a start."

Dave nodded.

"So nothing," I said.

"Nothing worth pursuing. I'll keep working on it. In the meantime," Dave looked at me, pointedly. "I want you to go to Iniquus."

I sat there soberly for a minute, weighing the possibility, then shook my head. "No. I'd just be some chicklet showing up with a sob story and Spyder's name. I'm no one to them. They don't know me from Adam."

"You mean they don't know you from Alex?"

"Shhh!" My hand shot out, and I grabbed Dave's arm. "Don't

say that out loud—ever! And no, they don't. I'm sorry you found out—no one should know what Spyder called me." When Dave winced, I realized I was digging my nails into his skin. I rubbed over the spot with my palm as if to erase the injury. "You know —here's an interesting little point. I was listed in New York with my maiden name on my credit card. India Alexis Rueben. But those flowers came to India Alexis Sobado—they had the right room number on the envelope."

"India—like the ink? Rueben—like the painter?" he asked. It was an old family joke, but there was no mirth in his voice.

"No. India—like the country. Rueben—like the sandwich," I replied.

"He didn't find you by calling hotels."

"Nope. I still can't figure out how he did that other than his having some kind of tracking device on my vehicles. That would explain a lot… I've looked, but I couldn't find anything." I struggled to keep my voice detached and professionally thoughtful, but I was so over this! I felt like my eyes could burn holes through asbestos, like I could kill Psycho with my bare hands around his throat. I itched to get my hands around his throat. I hated that anyone would make me feel this way, make me want to mirror his crazy.

Dave edged away from me, giving my emotions enough physical space to brew.

Finally, I tampered down my emotions enough to continue. "Miriam Laugherty says this is his idea of foreplay. The orgasm of it is me being dead. She didn't say how the dead had happened for his other victims."

"You know her?" Dave pulled his brows together, his voice bright with surprise. After a pause. "Foreplay, huh? When did you go talk to her?" He worked his jaw back and forth.

"Right after New York. She didn't have anything concrete to

tell me, or I would have shared it with you. No names. No numbers. No geography." I watched Dave drum his fingers as he processed. "Okay," I said, "let's think this through. If Psycho came nearby last night, Beetle and Bella would have known it and alerted. The dogs were calm. I didn't get the heebie-jeebies. This guy must have watched remotely during the whole burn scene and put the letter in the truck while I was singing at Star-Light. I took my car."

Dave raised a questioning brow. "Do you always rely on the heebie-jeebies to signal danger?"

My lips quirked into a lopsided grin. "Yup. I've found my heebie-jeebies meter to be a pretty reliable early warning system and accurate threat sensor. It's saved my butt on more than one occasion. When I feel the prickle flow up my spine into my scalp, and my legs want to run, I let them." My smile dropped. "I got nothing and no one last night."

"Have you felt the heebie-jeebies when you found any of your letters?"

"I wasn't around when he delivered any of the letters. I've always been somewhere where I was protected. And for sure, he hasn't been caught on my cameras. He must know they got installed, or he would have slipped up by now. Come on." I reached for my jacket. "Let's take a look at Manny's yard. I want to see the lines of sight for the grill. See if there's any equipment in place."

Dave cast his gaze out the window toward my garage. "I'll dust for fingerprints when we get back."

We trudged to Manny's backyard and looked around.

"This grill's in a bad place to be seen from any kind of distance." Dave stuck his hands on his hips.

"What about from across the way?" A sound barrier rose up behind the houses on the south side of Silver Lake Road. It made for a private backyard, and the highway below gave off a low rumbling white noise. Across the highway, a hill swelled above the other sound barrier wall where a little patch of woods grew. Dave and I climbed into my car with the dogs, and we headed over to the opposite side of the highway.

When we got to the area, I held the envelope for my girls to sniff then let them out of the car. Noses on the ground, they trotted over to the tree close to Dave and howled—their signal they had a hit. Whoever touched the envelope had stood on this spot long enough to leave a scent mark. With the time lag and the wind from the highway, he must have been there for quite a while, or the girls wouldn't have been able to find that mark. I moved over next to the dogs and inhaled deeply. "Can you smell that, Dave?" I asked.

He raised his nose in the air and sniffed. "All I get is car exhaust and pine trees. Is this the scent you mentioned, ESP-wise, the first day you brought me this case that you're talking about? Do you smell it here?"

I shrugged by way of an answer—I haven't stopped smelling Psycho's evil since the first letter slid under my door.

But, yes. Here it was worse. Here it smelled hungry.

Training my binoculars toward Manny's grill, I said, "One mystery solved."

And so freaking what? How did this get me any closer to solving the puzzle and getting this nutcase out of my life? We scanned the area for clues—a piece of trash that fell out of his pocket, a shoe print. My girls snuffled the ground. Nothing.

Absolutely nothing but the damned putrid smell and the creepy hair-raising, spine-chilling feeling that came with knowing someone had had me in his sights.

13

Summer's end blazed hot and humid, but I was comfortable in my house. There were always projects going, things were always a mess, but my air conditioning worked like a charm. Progress was happening.

My fall classes had started up already. This was my last semester before I applied to Georgetown University. I'd have my associates degree by the time Angel got home.

The days I'd marked off my calendar meant Angel, and I were past the halfway mark. More than halfway to him being home with me. *Home.* That word still had magic to it.

The one place where I was at a standstill was Psycho.

I hadn't gotten a letter in a damned long time. I imagined Psycho in the hospital, the prison, a ditch somewhere facedown and moldering. I wished for those things. Prayed for those things. But they didn't seem reasonable. In my life experience, bad things happened to good people. The bad people? They seem to hold the winning hands.

Through my front window, I saw Manny standing in the

middle of the road, stroking his thumb over his chin, staring at my house.

"Hey," I called, walking out onto my porch. "What's up? You look upset."

"I need a stripper," Manny called back. "I thought they'd have a stripper last night, but no. You know how hard it is to find a stripper? Hard. I've had everyone trying to find one for months now, and finally, we have a live one, and she don't show."

I walked down my steps to stand near him. "Manny, perhaps you shouldn't yell about strippers in the middle of the neighborhood. The children are out playing."

"What?" He threw back his head with a full-throated laugh. "No," he sputtered. "Not the girl who takes off her clothes. The girl who comes to get your crapola wallpaper off your walls."

"Oh! A paper stripper. Yeah, we really need that kind. So what happened when she didn't show? Did you just go home?"

"I played anyway. Some nerd from the suburbs showed up dressed like a mob-wannabe. I couldn't walk away from such an easy mark."

"And?"

"We finally threw him out. Stupid cry-baby. But I got a job off him first."

"Doing what?" I asked.

"Chimneys. He owes a lot of money, too. He's gonna come in and clean the chimneys, re-point them, reline them, and put in gas logs with blowers. He's gonna do you, Mrs. Nelson, Justin, and me."

"You?" My voice squeaked out two octaves too high.

"Yeah." He quirked a confused brow.

"Manny!" I stabbed my hands on my hips. "I spent a whole day steam-cleaning your carpets and furniture. The curtains are done!" Messing up my rags-to-riches house didn't upset me. My living room and dining room were still in the trashed stages, and I could easily get them straightened up. But I didn't want to do Manny's downstairs again.

"Not to worry. They put plastic everywhere and clean up after themselves. Hey, I also got a guy coming out for your basement. They're gonna wash everything down, paint, put in some retractable walls around your laundry area, that sort of thing. The guy's supposed to show up tomorrow to get your ideas and sign the contract."

"Those are all good things."

"Good enough, but they sure as hell aren't a stripper. And it's a stripper I need."

"I hear you, brother." Justin walked over with a grin on his face. "Are you trying to convince Lexi to take up more duties at your house? In my experience, the direct approach doesn't really work. Flowers and candlelight, a mixed cocktail, maybe."

"Cute. But we're talking about wallpaper." I gave him a playful shove. "Okay." I looked over at Manny's house. "I need to head in and make some more progress."

"Yeah, me too. Things have kinda stalled over at your place. You've been real patient with the whole situation. I'm trying for a bunch of stuff, landscaping, some gym equipment. It's been a poker dry season for me. If I could just get my hands on a damned stripper."

Justin chuckled under his breath.

The itsy bitsy spider went up the waterspout. I listed to the side. Agh!

"Hey. Hey. Are you okay?" Justin grabbed my arm.

I squinted up at him. The "knowing" clouded my vision as words illuminated and oscillated before my eyes.

Manny drew his wooly caterpillar brows together. "You're white as a ghost."

"I'm fine. I forgot to eat this morning, though. I think I'll go back in and grab something before I work over at your house." I offered him a wan smile.

Down came the rain and washed the spider out!

Holy hell. Spyder! My lungs refused to expand. I tingled from head to foot. "I'll see you guys later." The warble in my voice bellied the nonchalance I tried to project. I pulled free from Justin's steadying grip and moved toward my house.

Up came the sun. And dried up all the rain.

As soon as I was behind my closed door and the alarm was re-engaged, I whipped my phone out of my pocket and pushed the button for my contacts.

And the itsy-bitsy spider went up the spout again.

"Iniquus. How may I help you?" Came the smoothly professional voice of the operator.

I pressed END and slumped to the floor. With my back against the wall, I took a deep breath to quiet my knee-jerk reflexive actions. I should think methodically. Leaping to conclusions would mean making mistakes. It would be better to stop and puzzle this through. First of all, if Iniquus had any information about Spyder—if he were hurt or sick—they would have contacted me. Spyder listed me as next of kin in his file. True, I hadn't updated my new address information with their personnel department, but they still had the correct cell phone number. It would be easy enough to find me. They were operators, after all, and I wasn't hiding.

Did this "knowing" have to do with *my* Spyder? Miriam said he was fine. That was a while ago. Anything could have happened. I held up my phone and punched in the numbers to call her. No. Miriam said she had headed out to South Carolina to investigate a site. She wasn't even in town.

Should I just call Iniquus? Who would I even talk to? Human resources? They wouldn't necessarily be updated on Spyder's status. Command? What would I even say?

I could ask for Striker, introduce myself. I ran the conversation through my mind. *"Hello, Striker? My name is Lexi, and I have a children's rhyme running through my head, making me anxious about Spyder McGraw's safety. Spyder? Well, no, he's not blood kin, but he's like a second-dad to me. Could you help me find out if he's okay?"* God, I sounded stupid. Beyond stupid. Insane.

Striker didn't show up at the paintball war at the Millers' – his team either. I didn't recognize any of the Iniquus players this time. I wondered if Striker headed downrange on the same case with Spyder.

I drifted into the kitchen and made myself a cup of tea. Sitting at my little table, I tried to shove all of my worst-case-scenario thoughts out of the way. So…the list of possibilities. The "knowing" could be about Spyder McGraw. It could mean he was hurt but would recover. What if "crawled up the water spout" meant that he was on the way home? There was no joy in the thought because that would mean something would wipe him out.

Those possibilities felt like dead-ends, anyway. My body still ached: my joints too big, my blood too slow, my bones hollowed. No relief came from those ideas. I put a great big fat X over those thoughts.

A different track. Maybe "Spider" was coincidental and just the first thought that flew into my mind?

For me, "knowings"—that weren't literal like the "Ring of Rosies" crap up in New York—were based on strong associations. How about this? I was the spider. What if I made my way up the spout? My spout could be me setting up a new life, my house, my husband, my schooling, working hard every day, taking steps toward my plan, then BOOM! I got wiped out. The Psycho attacked me. The force didn't destroy me or my path; I just had to wait for the sun to come out, and then I could make my way forward again.

Hmm. Mildly better. My bones had more solidity. Other ideas?

Surely, the spider served as a metaphor. What other associations did spiders have for me? That was easy enough. As a little girl, a black widow spider bit me while I played in the woods. I must have been three- maybe four-years-old, and I remembered being in the hospital for days. I nearly died.

My blood flowed smoothly again. My joints no longer felt bulbous. The itsy bitsy-spider was coming to kill me. A near fatality then an intercession?

I already knew someone had targeted me, so what new information could I be picking up here? *Down came the rain.* Something would stop the spider from reaching his goal. *And washed the spider out.* Some force came into play. Something the spider wasn't expecting or prepared for. Car accident? Atom bomb? Zombie insurrection? *…The itsy-bitsy spider crawled up the spout again.* Well, whatever it was, the Universe set into motion to ward off this nut-case wouldn't last forever. He'd be back.

What do I take away from this? Well, I hated the idea of Spyder, my mentor, and "itsy-bitsy" sharing the same noun. They should share nothing. One represented love and light and the other the dark, dank, sewage-iness of humanity.

Where was Spyder? When would he come home?

Argh. The takeaway. The takeaway. I guessed it meant don't let my guard down. A respite wouldn't mean the story was over. I sat back and thought about it. I let the words, "Don't let your guard down," play through my mind. Serenity blanketed me. It was the feeling I got when I had figured things out correctly—

sort of, the "message received, 10-4 good-buddy" of my ESP world.

It would have been better if the Psycho as Humpty Dumpty played through my brain today... All the King's horses and all the King's men couldn't put Humpty together again. Yup. That would have been nice. I liked the thought of Psycho lying crushed and broken on the ground, never able to function again.

I laid my head on the table. No clues. No clues. Not a single thing to work with—just a looming threat. Day after day. Week after week. Month after month. The constancy of fear. I was Sisyphus. And pushing this hard for so long exhausted me. Weakened me.

I wearily pushed to standing and went to make myself another cup of tea.

14

The next morning, Beetle and Bella's ferocious barking pulled me from under the covers. Slinging my blanket to the side, I grabbed up my gun and bolted down the stairs. After disengaging the alarm system, I swung the door open to find Sarah in front of my porch screaming. Dave and Justin ran toward my house, both in sock feet. Justin got to Sarah first. She collapsed against him, pointing to my front steps. He pulled her away and walked her home, saying something soothing. Other neighbors stood in their open doorways, looking over to see what was causing the commotion.

Dave waved them back inside. "No problem. Everything's okay. Go on to bed." Since the clock read five in the morning, everyone complied. There, on the porch, lay the entrails of a large animal. They spread down the stairway. Blood dripped and pooled.

I was numb, in shock.

What happened? How did he get here?

On my welcome mat, I spotted the cream envelope. I slipped

it into my waistband and moved up to my doorway, away from the gore.

Dave climbed up beside me on the porch, punching the number for headquarters into his phone, his hand clamped on my shoulder as I swayed. The crime lab folks showed up; one of them puked in the bushes. I didn't blame him; it seemed like the right response. I almost joined him. I was sucking air. As the techs took pictures, Dave went inside with me to open the letter. I pulled on latex gloves this time. I had been careful to touch only the corner when I retrieved it. I didn't think the guy would suddenly get stupid and leave prints, but why take chances?

"He got me, Dave." I shifted my focus away from the paper. My face was wet with tears. "He's stabbed me through the soul. I know this poem. He only changed a few words. The real poem I learned by heart. It's 'To Flush My Dog' by Elizabeth Barrett Browning."

Dave took the page from my hand, his lips moving as he read it over.

"It reminds me of Spyder's dogs, so gentle next to my mom on the last day of her life. I brought them in from the Millers' farm because Mom wanted them with her. She loved this poem." I looked up to catch Dave's eye. "Could he know?"

A sob escaped, though I tried hard to dam it back. My emotions swung wildly out of control, overpowering me. "Could he be so…" I flailed around searching for the right word, "*intimate* with me that he knew about this poem, and the dogs, and my mom's death? How is this possible? I don't want this to be. I don't want monsters here in the neighborhood." Shock had protected me for a short time. But now that I was thawing, I more fully realized the pain that filled me full. I curled up, burying my head behind my knees as if becoming smaller would make my emotions smaller, containable.

Dave sat still. Watching me. Giving me the space I needed—and I appreciated the distance. I think if he tried to placate me, I'd turn into a howling mess. I jerked myself up, stumbled to my little half bath, blew my nose, and splashed cold water on my eyes. I glowered in the mirror. *Damn him!*

I had to get hold of myself.

I went into the kitchen and spooned some grounds into the percolator. Something normal, habitual, and sane.

A knock sounded at the door. Dave opened the screen to the officers. They took in my swollen face.

"I have a fresh pot of coffee. May I offer you some?" I hiccoughed—yeah, it was too hard to conjure up a believable fluffy-bunny mask, so I dropped the charade. Here I was in all my red-raccoon-eyed, angst-filled glory. Deal.

"Yes, please, ma'am," they said in unison.

Dave patted my shoulder and went out to hose everything down before the neighborhood came to life. I plopped down at the table with the officers who drank their coffees in silence. When Dave strode in and took a seat, they excused themselves and left.

"Dave, I should move." Misery colored my words. My muscles ached. My heart ached. I was willing to tap out; I just wanted this to end. And end now. I never felt defeated this way before—the mere act of sitting sucked at the last of my emotional strength. I had no more energy to give to this man. I wanted to be who I used to be. Capable. Invincible, even.

"What are you talking about? Why would you even consider leaving?" Dave's voice dragged my focus back to him.

I pushed my damp hair out of my face and blew my nose loudly into a paper napkin. "I'm endangering the neighborhood. The kids! I need to leave."

"And go where?"

I shrugged. Something made me want to keep my plan a secret.

Dave's eyes narrowed to slits. "He'd follow you."

"Even so, I should be someplace away from here and everyone."

"You're always gonna be near someone. Someone could always be impacted by this nut case."

"I don't know what to do. Dave, what should I do?" This morning's events left me dazed. I couldn't seem to bring myself around to make my mind sharp enough for cogent thought.

"Stay here at your house, where you're safest. You have excellent security here. People who love you—who are watching out—around you. I think that your stalker might be trying to flush you out. That was the title of the poem you said, right?"

"Yeah, 'To Flush My Dog.'"

"What if that's what he wants? Maybe you're too protected here, so he wants you somewhere he can get to you easier. Did you check the cameras yet?"

"Big ass guy. Head down. Hoody up. Gloves. Boots. Opened a black plastic trash bag. Fifteen seconds of not much information. I'll copy it for forensics."

Dave followed me into my living room as I paced the floor, slamming my fist into my palm.

"I wish I could just go ahead with the confrontation and end it." My voice had turned hard and menacing. The weakness was falling away, and it left me feral. Rabid. I wanted to attack like an animal. Nothing fluid and beautiful like my Kung Fu practice—I wanted it to be about teeth and claws. Hair, skin, and blood. Primal—that was where I was. Ferocious with survival instinct.

Dave got a crazy look in his eye. "Tell me you're kidding!" He stabbed a rigid finger into my shoulder. "Are you going out looking for this guy? Are you putting yourself in danger trying to get this guy to act?"

"No." I saw that my loose words were jacking Dave's blood pressure, so I outwardly switched directions. My voice softened. I ran a soothing hand down his arm. "I'm being safe and practical. I've put in a lot of time at the range, and I got to beat up the new recruits." I quirked a smile for Dave's benefit.

Dave shifted gears, too. Pushing his hands into his pockets. "I heard. I love it when you do that."

"Yeah, I fought one, a guy named Parker? He took a rather bad tumble. Do you know if he'll be okay?"

"His body's fine. The ego-bruising, on the other hand, will take a while to heal up."

Dave stopped talking and shook his head. "I sure wish I could make this stop for you, Baby Girl." It was the same sentence he'd been using for months now.

"Hey, guess what?" I went to sit down, still reaching for a sense of normalcy, trying to weaken the hold this morning's turmoil had on me. "I heard from Angel." That brought a true smile to my lips. "He called."

"He did? What'd he say?"

"They're heading back up into the mountains. He sounded happy about it, though. The assignment he's working on is a good challenge, and his team is making progress. He's so upbeat about everything, even the heat." I curled up at the end of the couch. "He's used to it, being from Puerto Rico. The guy from North Dakota isn't fairing so well." I patted my chest. "I'm missing him something awful. Hearing from him only helps a little."

"I bet." Dave leaned a shoulder into the wall.

"Yeah, well, he's on a mission with no contact." I focused out the window where a gull hung in the air, lost, hovering for a moment, then flying off. "They should be back in a month if all goes well. If they run into problems, it could be as much as three months before I get word." I turned my focus back to Dave. "This'll be the longest time we've had to go with no communication."

"Then can he come home?"

"No. End of February at the earliest—that's the one-year mark. They're extending some of the special ops out to eighteen months." I sighed and crossed my fingers for good ju-ju.

"Will the army stay in touch with the wives?"

I shook my head. "He said 'no news is good news.' So, that's my mantra for a while."

Hearing from Angel was like manna from Heaven—food for my soul. Angel loved his job; I signed on as a soldier's wife. I'd made my choice, so I'd better live up to my expectations of myself. I didn't want to burden Angel when he called or got through online. I'd just suck it up until he came home.

Knuckles wrapped at the glass storm door. Justin. I signaled him in.

"Hey, I didn't want to interrupt while the police were here. Jeezus! You look like hell. Were you hurt?" He strode over to where I sat.

"No. Not hurt. Coffee?"

He looked toward the kitchen, where I pointed then back at me, hands on his hips. "So, what was that about? Why the hell were there guts on your porch?" He slid onto a chair.

Dave leaned forward. "What we're telling everyone, especially Sarah, is that a dog was hit by a car, and came to Lexi's porch and died. That's the official story, got it?"

"Yeah—I'm not sure anyone's going to buy it what with the police out front, not to mention the fact that it was just the inside of an animal and not a whole body."

"We'll take a swing at it. Try to put some conviction behind your eyes when you tell people, hear?"

Justin had pulled a chair from the dining room and sat with his hands spread wide on his knees, pushing down like he was going to launch himself. "Got it—so that's the official story. Now, what's the unofficial story?"

Dave looked over at me, we held eye contact for a minute, and I gave him a slight nod.

"Lexi has a stalker who's been leaving her bizarre notes and little gifts since around the time she moved in. This is absolutely privileged information and goes no further than this room. You understand?"

Justin nodded his agreement and sat with that for a while. "I could move in." He leaned forward, looking at me with serious eyes. "Your house has more security than mine. I could move into the guest bedroom until this gets resolved or Angel gets back. If you were my wife, I wouldn't want you here alone. I wouldn't mind another guy in the house, adding, you know, presence."

"That's so kind. I love that you offered. And I might even take you up on that from time to time if the girls are off at training." I reached down and rubbed a hand over Bella's head. "Right now, I think I can trust Beetle and Bella's instincts. They were certainly making enough racket earlier. And I have a plan."

Justin nodded and stood. He didn't look too pleased. I knew his male instincts wanted him to be front and center to shield me from danger, and here I was not allowing it.

I walked Justin to the door and accepted his supportive hug. Yup. He had my back, but that was small recompense for what I was going through. I slogged back to the sofa and sat next to Dave.

"A plan?" His expression was flinty. "Good! Let's hear it."

I held his gaze, trying to make up my mind whether to tell him or not. Finally, I said, "I'm moving down with Abuela Rosa in Puerto Rico."

Dave looked stunned.

"I think Psycho would follow me anywhere I would go in the contiguous states." I shifted the cups around on the table. "But I don't think he'd follow me to the islands. I hope not, anyway. I'm not going to shut up my house or anything. I'm not even going to pack a bag. I'll just load the girls into the car one day and drive away. Park downtown. Take a taxi to the airport and disappear."

"And the house?"

I shrugged. My house was so far down my priority list right now. "Manny can work over here without me. I'll figure out some way to finish up his place—maybe hire someone to take over my part—there's not too much more. And when Angel gets back from Afghanistan, I'll tell him what's been going on, get a strategy together."

"Can you give me a time frame?"

"Soon. I'm not telling Abuela Rosa why I want to move down with her, and there are some logistical issues on her end. Health things, and she's moving. But she's thrilled to have me come. It won't be long. Maybe a few weeks." I raked my hands through my hair, pulled the elastic band off my wrist, pulling the strands up in a ponytail and off my too hot face. "I'll e-mail you once I'm heading out. Something cryptic, but it will contain her name and Angel's, so you know it's legit and that I'm safe. I won't disappear…that is to say, if I suddenly disappear, it's not the planned trip."

15

I finished up my dinner. Already the sun hung low in the sky, a bright tangerine orb. The nights had turned brisk and came a little earlier each day. I walked out to the street and leaned against the craggy trunk of the oak, taking in the squawk and call of the geese heading south. South, where I meant to be weeks ago.

Even though October has always been my favorite month, I hadn't planned to be here for it this year. By now, I should have been far away, enjoying the ocean, Angel's family, and safety.

I reached down to rest my hand on Bella's head. Things hadn't worked out as quickly as I hoped they would. Issue after issue popped up for Abuela Rosa. Sometimes, I believed the gods themselves were conspiring against me. I had UPSed a box of warm-weather clothes down to her weeks ago. My photo albums and my parents' journals—the only things of real value to me—were stored in the bank security box. A few more days, I mused. Monday, and I'd be gone. Thank god.

Dave meandered toward me, holding Cathy's hand. "You needed to talk to me?" he asked.

The streetlight above me blinked awake. "Yeah, I got another special delivery today." My voice sounded hollow.

Dave's body tensed. "A letter. Anything else?"

"Nope." This was Psycho's first contact with me since the bloody porch. The valleys of time between poems put me on edge as much as finding a new envelope. The unknown hyped my anxieties.

Dave patted Cathy on the shoulder. "I'll be right home. Do you mind?" Cathy gave me a squeeze and walked down the road.

Dave followed me into my house and back to my kitchen, where I picked up the letter laying on the table. "I found this on my door when I got back from errands."

"Your door? He walked up under the cameras?" Dave's eyes blazed triumphantly.

"Don't get excited. There's no footage. He sprayed silly string on the lenses," I said. My whole body felt sore and exhausted like I'd just finished a marathon—but without any of the satisfaction, so I guess that was a bad simile. Okay, like I'd just had the shit beaten out of me, and I was left in a ditch to recover my senses.

Dave moved to my porch to take a look. I followed behind.

"I went ahead and opened the poem. Nothing new. It's curious that no visual aids showed up with this one. It actually has me worried." I rubbed a hand over my eyes. "Dave, I think he's done playing." And done playing meant he'd try to kill me. Would he wait until Monday—when I had my plane ticket for Abuela Rosa's? Maybe he figured out my plans. How was that possible? I had arranged everything through a fake e-mail address on the library computers. How could that be traced?

I checked in with Miriam. Updated her and asked if she picked up anything else for me to work with, any clue at all. She got nothing new. Same level of crazy. Same joy in the games-manship.

But this sounded… A shiver raked down my spine.

Farewell to Love

Since there's no help, to come to your aid, let us kiss and part;
Nay, I am done, you get no more of me;
And I am glad, yea, glad with all my heart,
That thus so cleanly I myself can free;
Now, at your last gasp of love's last breath,
When your pulse failing, passion speechless lies,
When faith is kneeling by your bed of death,
And innocence is closing up your eyes,
From life to death Thou shall not recover.

"You playing at StarLight tonight?"

"From nine to ten-fifteen. Why don't you get a babysitter and bring Cathy up? I'll buy you guys a drink."

"And then I can make sure you get home safely?"

"Yes, please. I don't want any surprises. I think if I have someone around or the pups, I'd be safe. Only a couple more days, and then…" I stared hard at him, passing the information with my eyes—I'd be gone.

Dave nodded his understanding. "I hear you." He squeezed my arm. "I'll show up for your last set and walk you home."

I stretched up to plant a kiss on his cheek. "Thanks, Dave."

My girls and I headed toward Maryland. I tried to figure out how to take them with me to Puerto Rico. Logistically, it was complicated, especially since Abuela Rosa's apartment had an animal-free policy. I thought Beetle and Bella would be happy living with the Millers, again. This wouldn't be forever, I kept reminding myself. Just until Angel got home, and we got a plan together. Less than four months with any luck.

I meant to take them up tomorrow, stay the night, and drive to the airport from Maryland. But Mr. Miller had asked if he could use my girls in a demo for a security firm. I couldn't say no since he was doing me such a huge favor. It was only one extra night—Justin could sleep at my place like he'd offered. If not, I'd go over to Dave's. I wouldn't be alone. It would be fine. I chewed the inside of my cheek.

"Should I stay with you?" I looked back at Beetle and Bella. They lifted their heads and then dropped them noncommittally. "I did promise Justin I'd cook for him tonight. He's having a house full of people for the game." I reached back to rub Bella's head.

I'd wing it. See how I felt as I went. What if Psycho had more hands to play? And this was really just one more letter in my ever-growing pile of letters. Twenty-six freaking letters. It had been eight months of this, after all. Maybe he was growing bored and was offering me his final good-bye. Wishful thinking and I knew it. Every cell in my body crowded and bumped around, getting ready for the fight of my life.

Monday. Forty-eight short hours. This would all be over. I blew out a huff of air.

Over at Justin's, his friends piled up in the living room. Good thing I had made major amounts of food. I tried to relax and settle in, but I couldn't keep still. I was a distraction—was getting on people's nerves.

Dave moved toward me with a bowl full of chili. "This is good stuff, Baby Girl," he said. His tone was light, but he had his detective face on, scrutinizing me. "You okay?" he asked under his breath.

"Not really." I pulled my shirt away from my chest, fluffing air over my heated skin. "I'm claustrophobic. Probably anxious about my next step. I think being in a room full of people is making my nerves worse."

"What do you want to do?" he asked, setting his food on the counter.

"Honestly? I need to go home and try to relax."

"You think that's a good idea? Being alone over there?"

"I'll have the alarm on. You're close enough to hear it if there was a problem. Justin said he'd come over after everyone left. The game's almost over."

Justin ambled over as Dave, and I grabbed our coats. "You're going home?"

"Yeah, I'll see you when you're done here," I said.

Justin pulled on his coat and walked out the door with us, across the street, and up to my porch. Dave scanned the area, so did I.

"Are you okay being alone here right now?" Justin asked nervously, picking up on the stress Dave and I exuded. "You're sure you don't want to hang out and watch the rest of the game?"

"Thanks. It should be fine. I have some schoolwork to get done." And all those people were plucking at my last nerve. I needed to be still and calm so I could focus. I wanted silence so I could hear. My nerves sizzled and snapped. My breathing was shallow and irregular.

"You're sure?" Justin asked again.

I pulled my gun from its holster.

Justin jumped back. Eyes wide.

Nodding at Dave, I opened my door and re-activated the alarm.

Inside, I picked up my Springfield 9mm; it was heavier, more accurate—I'd have a better shot if I needed it. My Ruger nestled as back up in my belly holster. I went through the house and checked my security. Clear. Locked up tight. Absolute silence. Everything as it should have been.

Panic will kill you, Lexicon. It makes you unable in mind and body. Spyder's whispered mantra tickled the far edge of my awareness. I needed to get hold of my nerves. Stress was making me nauseous, and I decided to take a hot shower to calm myself down.

I undressed in the bathroom. Lifting the hamper lid, my peripheral vision caught a dark face reflected in the mirror. I gasped, my brain processing like a camera with an open shutter. Click—tribal tattoos. Click—gas mask. Click—sink on right. Click—white cloth. Click—sweet odor. Click—no alarm. Click —no help.

While my mind snapped perceptions, my body acted from training. I lowered my hips to drop my weight for better balance and leverage. My left leg swung behind his. I bent my knee in a swift, sharp move as I reached over my head, grasping his shirt to put him on the floor.

But the initial fumes I had sucked in made the room watery and undulating, melting my muscles and my instincts into useless puddles. My arms dropped ineffectually to my sides. One of his hands trapped me against him as I dangled, unable to hold my weight up with my legs, while his other hand smashed the cloth tightly over my nose.

Click. Exhale only. Click. Stay awake! Click… Click…

16

I blinked under bright lights. Dave leaned over me. Strain and grief etched themselves into the lines on his face. Turning my aching head to the side, I tried to get some context for this scene —industrial-green tiled walls and a crash cart. Something medical.

"I'm so sorry. I am so, so sorry." Dave collapsed his head onto my bed.

Huh? "What's happening?" My words slurred out from behind thick lips. I fought for consciousness.

"You screamed. We came running. He cut you with a razor. Pistol-whipped you. Lexi, you're in the hospital."

My brows creased painfully together. I struggled to make sense of Dave's muffled drumbeat words. Coming up with words of my own proved even harder. "I'm okay?" I managed.

"You'll be fine, Baby Girl. We're gonna get the guy who did this to you. All this will be over soon."

I sunk beneath the darkness and slept like Rip Van Winkle for days. I was only minutely aware of Dave and the medical staff. Consciousness was ephemeral, though, I grabbed at aware-ness every time it swirled within my grasp. Lying still with my lids closed tightly against the sunlight, I remembered swatches— the white cloth, searing pain, sirens, a doctor explaining that I had a hairline fracture of the skull and swelling in my brain.

When I opened my eyes, terrible vertigo looped my world like a lasso around me, leaving me panting, nauseated, and confused. So damned confused. If only I had my words, then I could form clear thoughts. I would understand.

Mostly I wanted to figure out what was happening to my body. When I was awake, any sudden noise or sight made adren-aline spike through me. The doctors came in to explain this had something to do with my headaches. No. With the fracture…with my brain…it would go away. Oh. *Away*. A word I could cling to. This feeling of imminent death would go *away*.

I was in a hospital. Safe, I told myself. No, that word didn't resonate. If I were safe, why would my body be telling me, "Run! Fight!" I struggled to get up, to move, to escape.

"Hush, now, Lexi. You're experiencing an adrenaline dump. The sensation will pass. Give it a minute. Breathe."

Who was coaching me through this pain? How did they know I'd be okay? Medication like blue velvet slid up my arm and pulled me into outer space.

———

Half the time, I had Nurse Tina. She had kind, firm hands. Her caring spirit showed in the way she made the methodical seem personal.

The other half of my time, I endured the hard hands of Becky Cranky-Pants. They seemed to do a twelve-hour rotation. Cranky must be done with today's shift and headed home. Tina got me up and walked beside me, supporting me as I wobbled on Jello-O legs to the bathroom, where she helped me clean up. Tina had her hands on my back to steady me while I brushed my teeth, then untied my hospital gown so I could change. I stared into the mirror at my naked stomach.

Holy crap!

The doctors had painstakingly bonded my shredded skin back together where Psycho had razored me from clavicle to hip. My torso looked like an Etch-a-Sketch in the hands of a five-year-old. The black lines, formed from dried blood and glue, created a city road map drawn on my fair skin. I didn't recognize myself as the person in the mirror. I couldn't wrap my mind around the reflection in front of me. I stood there dazed and confused, vaguely aware of Tina talking to me in soothing tones, trying to keep me calm, trying to forestall another one of those damned adrenaline dumps.

She walked me back to my room; I climbed into bed and lay as still as possible. The doctors had ordered me to restrict my movements. They warned me if I pulled at my torso skin, I'd come unglued.

Unglued. That was exactly how I felt.

Outside my door, an officer stood sentinel, guarding me around the clock, limiting access to medical personnel and detectives.

This had me curious.

Worried.

Even with Dave, Stan, and my other friends at the police department, this was over the top—what with the budget crunch and all. There must be more to this story. Something they hadn't told me. No one passed me any information, which frustrated the hell out of me. Why didn't Dave barge through my door with a victory whoop and announce they caught the guy, and it was all over?

I reached up to touch the cell phone I had shoved under my pillow—a touchstone of safety.

Dave had come by earlier to tell me the FBI was working the case and to bring me a cell phone. He said he was the only one who had the number, a burner phone. This confused me. Did Dave think my attacker had the capacity to tap phones? Before I could ask, Dave explained how he planned to call me on this line since the main switchboard was blocking calls in and out of my room. By the time he stopped talking, I had lost my train of thought.

I did remember his warning to me not to contact anyone but him on this phone, or I would "corrupt its covert integrity." That was hard. I'd really appreciate a friendly voice right now to help keep me calm and distract me from the flashbacks lighting my nerves on fire.

I slid my hand under the covers as Nurse Cranky-Pants came in to do her thing at the change of shift. She seemed much inconvenienced that I fell under her care, especially when we got into a battle over my meds. I agreed to take all of the anti-inflammatories and antibiotics, but I refused anything that would make me fuzzy, sleepy, or unable to think and react. What if I had to protect myself? If somehow Psycho showed up again, I needed all of my faculties to survive. Nurse Cranky-Pants wanted me sedated.

I wanted Nurse Cranky-Pants sedated. So there.

When Cranky finished poking me with her thermometer and pumping my arm up in the pressure cuff, she put meds into a line. I read each vial and approved it, which made her whole body bristle. What the heck was her problem anyway? She gave me one last glower and left. Thank goodness.

The phone under my head vibrated. I yanked it out and checked the number—Dave. Who else could it be? Pressing send, I put the receiver to my ear. "Hey, there."

17

Dave didn't answer my whisper into the phone. I strained to hear what was going on. I thought I could make out scraping noises like metal chair legs dragging over a terrazzo floor. Dave didn't say anything. Was this a butt dial? Or maybe someone was standing too close, and he was waiting for privacy. I waited silently. Voices mumbled in the distance. Someone sneezed loudly. A man's deep voice introduced himself to Dave. The name sounded like Gavin Something-or-other. Did Dave want me to overhear this conversation? Why didn't he tell me beforehand?

Dave's voice drifted out of my phone, asking the guy for identification. "I have to be careful about this. They only told me your name and organization when they sent me down here for the meeting." He sounded uncharacteristically nervous. I imagined him wiping his palms on his thighs before he extended his hand for a handshake. The guy used my formal name, "India Alexis Sobado." Definitely about me. And I definitely wanted to know what was going on.

Thanks, Dave!

"I understand you've got background on the situation," the Gavin voice said.

"Shit, yeah. I'm not only lead detective on the India Sobado case, I'm a longtime family friend. This is personal."

"Understood. And as a close friend, you've been involved from the beginning—is that accurate?" Gavin had the cadence of a man who was used to barking orders. Used to having them obeyed without question.

"Lexi—we call India 'Lexi'—brought me this problem two days after she got the first letter. I had no idea it would get this crazy. She's a beautiful girl. Innocent. No family. Exactly the kind of girl who would attract unwanted attention. I've seen men follow her around. I knew this time she'd picked up a sicko—but… Shit." I never heard Dave cuss like this before and with a stranger no less. A few expletives itched at my lips, too.

"She got the first poem, and she brought it right to your attention?"

"No. The first poem showed up on her wedding day, a Wednesday. The next day, Thursday, her husband shipped out to Afghanistan. She brought it to me the day after, on a Friday."

"She had no idea who sent it?"

"We had nothing. Nada. Zip. She's a smart girl—good at puzzling things out. She tried. Lord knows we both did. The letters kept coming in. Twenty-six. They pointed nowhere. Had the other cases been in the system, we would have seen the M.O., and I would have intervened. Sealed files, my ass. I need some coffee. You want a mug?"

"Thanks. Black."

The sound of a chair pushing back screeched through my receiver, and then the clinking of ceramic. A siren wailed nearby. They must be in the conference room up at Police Headquarters.

"Tell me about your role in this. What do you need from me?" Dave asked.

"The FBI contracted us to provide Mrs. Sobado with a safe house and guard until the perpetrator is apprehended. We've also been hired to find the guy and do the capture."

"That's big money. They're going out of agency to contract on this?" Dave sounded surprised.

I was surprised—did the FBI do that for stalkers like mine? Seemed improbable.

"As you now know, there are six similar cases still unresolved. All of those other victims had connections to various agencies. FBI doesn't want to feed this guy anything if he happens to be in-house. We've checked your story and alibis, read the witness reports. You've been cleared. It's our task to have limited communication with the law and no contact with media until this is wrapped up."

"The other women, you said they all had law connections? What do you mean exactly?"

"The other victims were either the daughters or the wives of law officials. Seems each victim represented a different agency —CIA, FBI, Treasury, and so on."

"Lexi isn't law, so how does she fit the pattern?"

"Undetermined. Her husband is Special Forces—maybe this guy's branching out to the military now. The last girl was the 28-year-old daughter of Secret Service leadership."

"That's what happened to Arnold Pauly's girl? No wonder there's plenty of money behind this capture."

Keep going, Dave. I wanted this information. Ask him why they sealed the files. Why wasn't this on the news? A story this big? Surely if Director Pauly's daughter had been a target, some journalist would have pounced on it.

"I guess it makes sense why they're taking this away from

the usual players and bringing you guys in," Dave mused. "Before the attack, I never heard of the other cases. Six, huh? All East Coast stuff? And no major media? No heads up at the station? Even if the files were sealed."

Thank you, Dave.

"They're trying to keep these cases quiet for a number of reasons. It wouldn't help to get a copycat going out there."

Dave blew out his breath. "That's the damn truth."

"The alarm was engaged when Mrs. Sobado went out that night?" Gavin asked.

"Yeah, and re-engaged the minute she got home. When we broke in, we set off the alarm system."

"That's curious."

"Tell me about it."

"And besides that, did she take any self-defense courses? Pick up a gun?"

Dave laughed softly. "Lexi is five-foot-six, hundred and thirty pounds, but, man, she can take anyone down."

"I understand she trained for the police? Was she thinking about joining the force?"

"She shoots at the range with Stan and me or one of her other friends. Comes down every once in a while at Christophe's request. They like to spring her martial arts skills on the new recruits. She reminds them to be humble and respectful —never judge a book by its cover."

A machine by my bed beeped, startling me; I steadied my thoughts to try to avert the adrenaline.

"Lexi's friendly with lots of the area cops," Dave was saying as I focused back on his words. "She's got a good reputation. Friendly. Kind. She acts real young, soft, girly—it's like a costume she wears—you'd never guess she's skilled. My captain wants to recruit her once she reaches the age requirement and finishes college. Command thought she'd be good at undercover. But she's not interested."

Dave was being uncharacteristically loquacious. He didn't usually open his kimono like this. It made me feel vulnerable— just like it had when we sat in Justin's yard after his burn when Psycho was watching me through his binoculars, and Dave was waxing poetic about my fighting skills. I don't like people to know anything about me.

"This gets curiouser and curiouser," Gavin said. "Do you think her connections with police training helped make her a target?"

"Not many people know she has any link with the department other than cop friends and the firing range staff. The men who've gone up against her on the mat aren't gonna share those stories around. They're gonna try to live them down."

"I understand you two were together at your house prior to the crime," Gavin said.

"We were all over at Justin Fowler's, across the street from Lexi's. Redskins played Steelers."

"She went home alone?" Gavin asked.

"Lexi couldn't sit still. She was restless. Stir-crazy. She kept looking out the windows and fidgeting around. Finally, she said she had the heebie-jeebies and asked us to watch her walk home. Beetle and Bella were at their trainer's."

"These are her dogs, right?"

My dogs. What would have happened if I hadn't taken Beetle and Bella to the Millers? Would I be here now? Would they be hurt? Or worse? My heart squeezed—a miscalculation. A huge whopper of a mistake to take them. But I had played by Psycho's terms for eight months. This could have gone on for years. Life had to be lived. At least, I had to reach for my goal of normalcy. Huh—what was it Mrs. Miller said to me? I was cut from a more colorful cloth? Right now, my cloth was colored blood-red and head-trauma blue.

"Yeah, her dogs. Me and Justin get up and walk her home. When she unlocked the door, she turned off the alarm. We waited around while we heard her turn the locks and the beeps that told us the alarm was back on. Then we went back to Justin's to finish watching the game."

"Do you know if she had a weapon?"

"Lexi had her Ruger in her hand when she went into her house. I found both her guns on her bedside table after the ambulance left."

"Huh."

Yeah. That was my thought as well. Would it have made a difference if I had my weapons in the bathroom with me? No. I didn't think so. Even if the Springfield had been in my hand, when the cloth came up, I would have dropped the gun to reach for the flip. I wouldn't have shot behind my back.

"What did your reports tell you about what happened?" Dave asked.

"They indicate you found her naked, bound, sliced, and pistol-whipped."

Bound? Yes, I remembered now. My hands. My ankles. Limbs on fire from lack of blood. The gag...suffocating on my snot. *Stop thinking about it. You're going to dump adrenaline, and you won't get this information!*

"Sliced? Shredded is more like it. From what I can figure," Dave said, "he got to her in the bathroom...before she got into the shower. Her clothes were in the laundry hamper, and the tub felt dry when we put her in to get the vinegar off her cuts."

"Go on," Gavin said.

"We documented the things smashed by the sink: a drinking glass, a perfume bottle. We found a damp rag on the floor. Forensics says it had been saturated in high-grade chloroform."

Chloroform. Wait. Chloroform was a controlled substance—not available to the public. Could this guy be a scientist? Academician? How would he get hold of chloroform? He'd need some legitimate channel.

"Where did you find her?" Gavin broke into my thoughts.

"The adjoining bedroom, on the floor. No signs of struggle. She was out when he restrained her." Dave's voice sounded hollow and tight at the recounting. "At some point, she must've started to come around. He had gagged her with the tape, wound it around her head a bunch of times. She worked it loose with her tongue—that's what saved her life. From what we can tell, after he sliced her, the guy poured a bottle of vinegar over her torso, and she screamed. Fucking hell." Dave's voice ratcheted up. "That scream's gonna haunt the shit out of me for the rest of my life—like a goddamned Banshee call."

"At this point, you were still at Justin's?" Gavin's voice sounded counterpoint calm to Dave's turbulence.

My turbulence.

Breathe, Lexi.

"We were just done watching the game. The time between our leaving her and her scream would have been less than thirty minutes. When she screamed, I figure that's when he must've hit her with the gun because her voice ended abruptly. It wasn't like she ran out of air, or it tapered off. It was mid-scream, and then nothing. We raced over. The house was locked up. I elbowed the window to break the glass, and the alarm sounded. We can't figure out how this piece of shit got in or out."

Darn! I hoped Dave would have figured at least this much out and could tell me. How did Psycho get in? How did he get in? How in the hell did he get to me?

"And her medical status?" Gavin asked. "She wasn't raped or sexually molested, correct?" Gavin asked.

"No. Thank god," Dave said. "Her torso's painful. Her head's gonna take a while to heal. When she's up, she sometimes experiences vertigo. Her eyesight gets fuzzy. She's dizzy and nauseated. She can fall down from that, though she's not passing out. I understand the brain swelling is causing her to have these crazy adrenaline dumps."

"And how does that affect her?" Gavin's voice was methodical, running down his laundry list of the required information.

"I haven't seen it happen to her. Lexi described it to me. She gets a feeling she's in danger, and then her heart starts beating really fast. She perspires, which makes salt get into all of those cuts. She says the pain is almost unbearable—like the vinegar."

The screaming agony of my adrenaline dumps *was* unbearable—vinegar on slash marks magnified. The feelings exploded my senses. Every synapse in my body fired all at once, all rational thoughts annihilated, limbic survival mode of hell.

"As the adrenaline works its way out of her system, she shakes and cries. Then she needs to sleep, basically passes out with fatigue," Dave said.

Escaped. I escaped into my exhaustion. Then I'd wake up terrified I would ever feel that way again.

"What are the doctors doing to help her?"

"The nurses apply soft, cool, wet cloths to get the salt off and to stop her from sweating. If it's the nice nurse, she'll hold Lexi's hand and talk to her about everyday stuff until Baby Girl calms down and falls asleep."

"They aren't medicating her? Giving her Valium or something?"

"It's not like they haven't tried. Lexi's refusing the medication."

"She's medically non-compliant?" Gavin's voice tightened perceptibly. He obviously didn't like the idea of non-compliance. Definitely military. And none of his damned business what meds I decided to take or not to take.

"On this, she is," Dave said. "She says she'd rather be in pain and have all of her faculties than fuzzy, and maybe dead."

There was a pause, then, "That's impressive." I could hear respect for my decision in Gavin's voice. "Most people in her position would be begging for relief. I can understand her thought process. She's seen him. She's a threat. Double danger."

"Yeah, but shit! She's being tortured!" Dave all but yelled.

"The doctors don't think these 'adrenaline dumps' are the product of traumatic stress?"

"They're saying it's a physical thing from the head trauma and swelling, not mental health. It should get better as time goes on," Dave said.

"All right, what about enemies in the area? Any grudges you're aware of?"

Cranky walked in, and I didn't get to hear Dave's answer. I wanted more, the whole damned story spelled out like a novel.

And it needed a Grimm's Fairy Tale ending.

There, on the last page, I wanted to read how India Alexis Sobado got to live happily ever after.

18

The cell phone vibrated against my thigh, pulling me from my re-re-hash of the earlier overheard conversation between Dave and mystery-Gavin-guy. I had been massaging every nuance, trying to understand what was going on. Why did Gavin's voice sound so familiar?

"Hey, Baby Girl, did you get everything?"

"Your conversation with Gavin? Most of it. Thanks for including me," I said.

"I only had a few seconds warning, so I threw a Hail Mary when I made the call."

"How'd you like getting raked over the coals?" I pushed the button to raise the head of my bed up higher.

Dave grunted. "It was interesting. He's damned intense. You'll be in good hands, I think. Looks like your days of dealing with Nurse Cranky-Pants are soon over."

"Oh? Did they tell you when they're going to release me?" I combed my fingers through my hair, catching them on a tangle.

"They aren't going to officially release you. A security team's gonna take you to a safe house."

Gavin. The FBI. A safehouse. This was the stuff of movies. Not reality.

"Do you know when this is supposed to happen?" I asked.

"It's up to them. After this call, I'm no longer attached to your case. They want me hands-off to make sure…" Dave let his words recede, and his next thought lap over it like waves on the shore. "They'll slip you out of the hospital whenever they think they're least likely to be seen."

"I should probably expect this to happen tonight, then?" I stared out my window at the sun setting over an enormous elm still brightly dressed in its golden leaves.

"I'd say, or early morning. Their Team Lead will introduce himself when he gets there. His name is Gavin Rheas. I want you to ask him for his I.D. and look it over carefully, okay?"

"I promise to be safe." I used my "I'm a good girl" voice. Rheas. A vibration ran through me. I knew a Rheas. That wasn't a common last name. "What security team did you say?"

"I don't know if you're going to like this or not." Dave coughed, clearly stalling. "It's Iniquus," he said.

Iniquus! Holy moly. How the heck was I supposed to navigate this obstacle course? Spyder was beyond adamant my work for him be secretive and that Iniquus should never realize I existed. Calm down, I told myself. They won't be able to put this together.

When I worked for Spyder, I was Alex. Different name. Different appearance. Different gender. No worries that someone would recognize me like this. Iniquus would still only know me as India Alexis Sobado, even if it turned out Gavin Rheas was… Now wouldn't *that* just complicate everything a thousand-fold? The words *Hell in a Handbasket* vibrated through my system.

"Lexi? Baby Girl? Are you there?"

"Sorry, Dave, my mind wandered for a minute. I'll be sure to check the I.D. for Iniquus, Gavin Rheas."

"You sound worried." Dave paused then said quietly, "Do you know this guy, Gavin? Is this okay?"

"I've never met anyone named Gavin. Iniquus operators use call names in the field, so who knows? Hey, are there any new developments on my case—do you have anything beyond the artist rendering?" My fingers worked the edge of my sheets.

"Like a name?"

"Yeah, that would be nice." I held my breath. A name would humanize Psycho. Was I ready for that?

"No name, but they're distributing the police sketch to the media. I don't think they're handing out any particulars about your case, though. Just warning people this guy is wanted for questioning. He's considered armed and dangerous, and there's a reward for any information leading to his capture. Listen. We repaired your window, and Manny set the alarm. He wants to know if it's okay with you if he gets a crew in to refinish your floors and paint the walls the way you planned."

My brow wrinkled, pulling at my stitches. "Are the police done investigating it as a crime scene?"

"They took the tape down yesterday."

"Good. Yes. Tell Manny thanks for the help. I'd really appreciate coming home and seeing it clean and shiny and new. I don't really want it to look like it did when I left. Bad memories and all. Hey, Abuela Rosa was expecting me. I should have been down in San Juan by now. Can you call her and tell her I'm delayed? But please, please don't tell her what happened."

"I've got it covered."

"Dave, I'm sorry—this pain is a hot knitting needle sticking through my eye." I panted. "I need to hang up. Is there anything else I should know? Are we going to be able to talk once I'm at the safe house?"

"No and no," Dave said. "You're going to disappear, so no one can trace you. It's important. I want you to follow their rules and take real good care of—" Dave broke off.

I filled in the empty space. "Everything's going to be fine." I tried to work conviction into my voice for Dave's sake.

19

I peered out my window, watching the sky fade from black-velvet to indigo. Wide-awake and anxious, I wondered about the Iniquus team. They'd probably show up soon. I'd better go ahead and use the bathroom, so I was ready when they swooped in to bundle me away to god-knows-where. Before I could press my call-button for assistance, a light rap sounded at my door. I straightened my sheet, aiming for modesty.

"Come in," I called.

Two men moved silently into my room. One stood near my door; the other strode over to my bed on long legs and extended his hand to me. My breath caught, and my face grew warm as the color rose in my cheeks.

"Mrs. Sobado, I'm Gavin Rheas from Iniquus."

I placed my hand in his. "Lexi," I said. He stood in the glow of the utility light over my bed as solid and capable as I remembered him—tall, about six-foot-three. His jacket stretched across the broad expanse of his shoulders. He wore his rusty-brown hair cut short. I wasn't going to have to ask this man for I.D. I recognized him the second he walked in.

Yup, here was Striker, in all his glory, sauntering confidently into my drama. The irony wasn't lost on me. How many times had I fantasized about Striker playing my hero? And now he was my real-life knight in shining armor. I was definitely the damsel in distress, though the role felt unnatural to me. I was used to being more Joan of Arc than Guinevere. Under these circumstances, I didn't really have much of a choice about what role I got to play. Well, when I recovered, everything would change. If I had to be a damsel in distress, for the time being, at least I got to do it in the capable hands of Striker Rheas. Spyder would be glad. Striker's the man he would have picked to protect me.

Striker moved to pull a chair to my bed. Graceful. Comfortable in his skin. He was one of those rare guys who could be conspicuously gorgeous and not seem to have any awareness of it.

I got to observe Striker out of uniform, playing spy on a few heaven-sent operations. Men would instinctively become wary when he entered the room, closing their postures or moving away. The women would hold their ground, giving him long speculative glances. I watched them touch their hair and lift their breasts, subtle communications that they were interested in, and his advances would be welcomed and rewarded. Back on those missions, I wanted to do that—lift my breasts and bat my eyes at him to get him to notice me—but Spyder had me insulated in huge, asexual gray sweats.

Striker looked me full in the face. No, he didn't recognize me; I registered.

Hell in a Handbasket now blazoned red and pulsing in my mind. It was a "knowing." My psychic warning system on high alert. Shit. Now what?

Striker swiveled and indicated his partner.

"Mrs. Sobado, this is another member of your team, Jack." I

focused on the giant posted by my door. He wore his ebony hair cut military-tight. His brilliant blue eyes had a hard-focused edge; I bet he used them to cut through any crap and see the truth. I pulled my sheet up, holding it under my chin.

Jack was dressed identically to Striker in black and gray camouflage fatigues, a charcoal-gray, long-sleeved compression shirt, black Vibram soled combat boots and a black windbreaker with the Iniquus symbol on the left breast in silver. Like Striker, Jack had the guise of someone who would take on anyone, anywhere. I recognized Jack from the paintball war but hadn't known his name.

Jack nodded. "Ma'am." He was at my bedside in two strides, extending his hand.

Putting my hand in Jack's massive paw was like a three-year-old holding her dad's hand. I felt small. Helpless. Dependent. I didn't like any of those feelings.

Jack moved to stand sentry at the door again.

Striker sat down, so we were eye-to-eye. "Here's the deal—we've been hired to put you in a safe house while your case is under investigation. A safe house is a choice. We're not holding you against your will. Do you understand?" Striker's focus rested keenly on me. He was trying to gauge me, getting a sense of who I was and how I ticked. His voice sounded different than when he was speaking to Dave. Now, his voice, with its gentle warmth, invited me to have confidence in him and his control over the situation.

My stomach danced. "I understand."

"You're being taken to the safehouse for your protection, and also because you're an eye witness to a crime connected to a series of crimes that are of great concern to various agencies."

My gown slipped down my arm, exposing my shoulder. Striker's eyes shifted from mine, following my hand as I slid the thin fabric back into place. I blushed and wished I had more clothes on in front of these two men.

Striker refocused on my eyes. "You may leave the safehouse at any time, though it would be unwise. We're dealing with a dangerous criminal." He paused.

"I understand."

"We were brought in on your case yesterday morning, and we've had to scramble a bit to get things in place. The agency that hired us asked us to keep you as local as possible. That way, we can bring you in easily if they need you for an I.D."

"Do they know anything more about the guy who did this to me?" I choked on the last word, and Striker's eyes warmed a little from their professional detachment.

"No, ma'am. We'll keep you apprised, though. We have a house in the area that meets our requirements for your safety." Striker glanced down at his watch as he spoke. "We're handling you carefully. I'm lead on this case, and I handpicked each of the other six men on your team. We've had a heads-up the media is trying to get information about these crimes. We want to move you out before anyone gets to you to ask questions about what happened. Right now, your location is undisclosed, but we don't think this window will last much longer because—"Striker stopped.

I had reached up, cupping my hand over the bandage covering the stitches in my head.

He waited.

"I'm okay, go on." I willed myself to focus on his words instead of the pain, shooting burning arrows into my eye.

"We don't want to give anyone, even at Iniquus, any information. Only your teammates will have contact with you or the safehouse. This presents somewhat of a problem. It's safest to move you out now, but I can't assign a guard until four today."

I wrinkled my brow, confused.

"It's not unusual, Mrs. Sobado, to leave a witness unattended in a safehouse for days at a time. This will not be the case with you. You'll have watchdog support."

"Oh? Why am I different?" This was all such freaking blood and dagger novel fodder. "Watchdog support"?

"Because of your medical condition. My only concern about extricating you now is your physical state. How do you feel physically and mentally about making this move to the house, knowing you'll have to spend some hours alone?"

"I don't understand." Alone? I couldn't defend myself in this state. "Wouldn't I be safer staying here under police protection, and you can pull me out tonight?"

"That was our original plan. We can still take that direction if you prefer. It's a coin toss. You're under police guard here, but the medical staff has access. It's not as protected as it might seem."

"But you said your plan was to leave me until later. What changed?"

"After media was given the artist's sketch of your attacker to put over the airwaves, they swarmed police headquarters, trying to find out what "armed and dangerous" meant. It must be a slow news day—or they can smell a bigger story. If the press gets to you or your records, they'll advertise your location."

"And I don't want my location advertised." I inhaled noisily, trying to get my foggy head to make a good decision. "It's a very safe, safe house?" My voice sounded small and child-like in my ears. Years of fluff training rearing its head when I'd much rather be giving off the impression I was capable.

Striker smiled one of his contagious smiles: slow and slightly crooked, beautiful, white, even teeth, the merest hint of dimples at the corners. His smile started in his moss-green eyes, warming them. I found myself smiling back at him.

"It's a very safe, safe house," he said.

"Can I have a gun?"

"I understand you're well-trained, so we'll make sure you're armed while you're alone."

"Okay—I think that will be okay." Vulnerable. My skin tingled with trepidation.

"You're up to this physically? I know you're having problems with your head injury."

"I'll probably lie on the couch and sleep while I'm alone."

"Sounds like a plan." Striker stood. "Your meds are already in the car. We need to get you dressed and make our move." Striker cast his gaze around the room. "Where did they put your clothes?"

"I don't have anything here—other than my toothbrush." I pointed to the bathroom.

"No shoes?"

"Nope. Nothing."

Striker turned to Jack. "We'll need another hospital gown Mrs. Sobado can wear backward. Also, get a blanket from the supply closet and bring back a wheelchair—we can't have her walking barefoot through the hospital."

Jack nodded.

As he walked out, a man with a shaved head and dramatically arched brows seamlessly replaced Jack at the door. This guy had a scar running down the right side of his face like a pirate—a muscular, bold, intimidating pirate. His dark skin looked like satin. He nodded at me when I caught his eye and offered me a formal smile.

"Mrs. Sobado, this is Axel. He's another member of our

team. Deep is in the hall, guarding your door. You'll meet him in a minute."

I lifted a quizzical brow. "Deep?"

"It's a call name, ma'am. When we're on assignment, we don't use our real names for security purposes."

"Okay, but how did Deep come to have that one?" My question caught Striker by surprise.

He stared at me for a full minute. "I'd rather not say."

In that case, I'd probably rather not know! "Well, how would you like me to address you?" I was afraid I'd slip and call him "Striker" before he told me to. Then I'd need to explain.

"By my call name. It's Striker."

"All right, Striker it is. And I'd like for you and your men to call me Lexi, instead of Mrs. Sobado—that is, unless you want to make up a call name for me, too," I said with a smile.

Striker's eyes glittered with amusement. "We'll try to figure something out for you."

Jack came back into the room with a wheelchair and waited while Axel removed my I.V. Jack handed me a folded hospital gown, which I pulled on like a jacket, securing it in the front, and Striker scooped me into his arms to transfer me to the wheelchair.

Hell in a handbasket clanged its warning through my system.

20

Striker and Jack moved out of the room while Axel covered my bare legs with a cotton hospital blanket he'd pulled from a warmer. The heat cloaked me, giving me a sense of security.

"You've done this before." I glanced over my shoulder to see Axel's face.

"Yes, ma'am, everyone on your team is a trained medic."

"That's good, I guess. How are we getting out of here?" I turned forward again to try to still the vertigo. "I thought I had a police officer guarding my door."

Axel's smile was audible as he said, "The guy felt sleepy and needed a little nap. We said we'd take over for a while."

"That easy? Yeah. I definitely don't want to wait to leave until tonight."

Axel released the brakes and rolled me forward.

Striker peeked his head in. "All clear," he said.

Axel angled me out while Striker held the door; it shut soundlessly behind us. Striker stayed on my right, his windbreaker pushed aside, exposing the 9mm automatic at his hip, as Axel quickly wheeled me down the corridor. Jack propped the elevator open with his booted foot, his hand on his weapon. They weren't playing around. Their eyes cast about, sharp and vigilant. In a way, this felt safe; in another, it felt entirely too dangerous. We entered and rode in silence down to the basement. There, elevator doors opened to reveal the fourth member of the Extract-Lexi Team, Deep. He looked Italian with his dark olive skin and raven hair—glossy even in its tight military cut. His eyes glittered with fun. Hmmm. Glad he found this amusing.

"Clear," Deep said.

Jack went out first and jogged down the corridor. This told me the extraction was choreographed and rehearsed. Everyone had a job to do, and they did it with precision.

I looked Deep over as Axel pushed me through the doors. No, Deep's frame didn't have the bulk of his teammates. Olive-toned skin and dark brown hair, he was built like a cyclist or tennis player with long, steely muscles. He definitely had the stance of a ladies' man with a lot of banter practice under his belt. I think I might understand his call name now. He looked dangerous, but not the same kind of dangerous as Axel.

"Mrs. Sobado." I tilted my gaze as Striker indicated Deep with an open palmed hand. "You've probably figured out this is Deep."

The room whirled; my eyes lost their focus. With a moan, I supported my elbows on the arms of the wheelchair and dropped my head into my hands. *Please, god, please don't make me puke in front of these men. Please.*

Striker crouched beside me. "Vertigo?"

"Mmm," I mustered.

Axel pulled my chair into an alcove. Deep and he formed a wall in front of me. Striker's cool fingers on the back of my neck gave me something to focus on other than the bile that tickled my throat. He put a steadying hand on my shoulder; I guessed to keep me from falling out of the chair and splatting on the concrete. I did some deep breathing to center myself. After a minute, I felt well enough to lift my head back up and nod that we could continue, forming actual words still lay outside my scope of possibility.

Axel rolled my chair quickly forward through a maze of corridors—Jack always just ahead, his boots striking a steady cadence. Large cargo doors emptied us onto a loading bay where three charcoal-gray Humvees waited in a disciplined row.

The chill in the air shocked me. When did the weather turn? My nostrils stung with the odor of rotten garbage, making my unsettled stomach slosh. The stench reminded me of the reeking miasma that I smelled when I thought about Psycho. My skin prickled a warning. *Breathe. NO! STOP! Don't breathe. Don't smell it, just get into the damned car without dumping adrenaline.*

The men beeped the cars unlocked with their key fobs; the sound echoed off the cement walls making me jump. Every nerve in my body stood at watchful attention—every sensation seemed amplified. My teeth scraped over my lips as I chewed on my apprehension.

Striker reached down to help me into the back seat of the middle Humvee, tucking my blanket up out of the door as he shut it. He sauntered around the car and climbed in next to me. Jack slid onto the driver's seat. Up ahead, Axel angled into the lead car. I guessed that meant Deep drove the rear. I made up the filling in a protective sandwich.

Reaching for my seatbelt, I pulled it across my lap and tucked the shoulder harness behind me to safeguard my torso. I leaned my forehead against the cool windowpane. I hoped they had a plan for my clothes. Surely, I wasn't the only damsel they hauled to safety, barely dressed, and they had some strategy in place. I blushed what felt like flamingo pink, radiantly aware that I was riding in a car with two men and no underwear.

In the window reflection, I watched Striker signal Jack to go. I turned to ask Striker where we were heading, but he still had the phone to his ear.

"No trace of either Cammy or Lynda," Striker said. "We're at the twenty-four-hour mark. I've already filed a report with the police."

Two women must be missing. I wondered if they were part of my case. Would Psycho target more than one of us at a time? The thought had never occurred to me before. Why wouldn't he? Maybe he attacked them outside of their homes, and now Iniquus can't find them. A shudder sifted through me.

I frantically searched for something else to fill my mind. My gaze fell, thankfully, on a Hispanic man and woman walking toward the hospital, hand in hand. They must be working the next shift. I wondered what Angel was doing now. I had waited so long for any kind of contact from him. Did he try to reach me? Could he be back from his assignment? If he had a single clue what was going on, he would freak out and still have no way to help me. Maybe this long mission helped. Maybe it was the best thing for Angel.

Angel off-grid. Spyder downrange. Now I was no-contact, disappearing from sight like a magic trick. A tremor shook through me. How scary was that?

No pack.

A lone wolf.

Alone.

Lost in my thoughts, I hadn't paid much attention to the direction the car moved. I tried not to look out of the windows. The shifting landscape hurt my eyes. I had the vague sense we'd driven through the city center, onto a highway, and now we exited off into an unfamiliar neighborhood. The houses were small and older. They dotted the neighborhoods like postage stamps on large rectangular lots.

The Humvees turned left and slowly maneuvered into the driveway of the last house on the road. Three sides of woods surrounded a huge open yard. No one would be able to see this house unless they drove down to the end of the cul-de-sac. Anyone from the house had a clear line of sight to approaching vehicles. The trees would mask any lights or activity at the house, and yet the house wasn't so secluded that I couldn't run for help if I needed to. This felt like a safe, safe house. I imagined Spyder picking this place. That thought bolstered my confidence.

The driveway gently curved behind the house to the attached garage. Axel's vehicle parked to the left of the opening. Jack pulled ours right into the garage and lowered the doors with a button on the dash.

I slid down from the car seat, supported by Jack's massive hand. When my foot touched the freezing cold cement floor, it sent a stab of pain up my calf. I carefully wrapped my blanket around me, toga style, and walked through the door into the house-proper, glad for the carpeting.

I went directly over to the sofa, where Jack had already spread a sheet for me. Thankful to stretch out horizontally and put my head on a pillow, I lay there, child-like, as giant-Jack spread the blankets over me. My head pounded rhythmically.

"Would you like something to eat, Lexi?" Striker asked from the end of the couch. I shook my head no; I had my arms crossed over my closed eyes. The men moved around the room quietly— water poured at the sink. I peeked past my arm as Jack placed a small table beside me. Striker laid a pitcher of water, a glass, and my bottles and tubes of meds on the table.

Jack tucked a small cooler underneath. "These are sandwiches and fruit for when you get hungry," he said.

Striker crouched down, so we were eye-to-eye. "I can't tell you how sorry I am that I have to leave you right now." His voice sounded earnest.

I nodded by way of reply.

"Deep and Axel will be here at four o'clock. The rest of the team is scheduled to arrive at six. We'll bring dinner with us. I'll call in to ask what you want to eat, okay?"

"Thanks."

He held up a Glock. "I know you shoot a Ruger. Are you familiar with this gun?"

"I've shot one." Numb. My brain, my limbs, my emotions. It was as if I turned the volume down too low.

"It's got an extended magazine." He slid the magazine in place, chambered a bullet, and put the gun in its holster on the table beside me. He reached into his pocket and pulled out a necklace with a large white circle pendant. "This is a communication device like they have for the elderly who live alone—you've seen the commercials, 'I've fallen, and I can't get up?'"

"Yes." I was monosyllabic. My tongue and lips couldn't seem to collaborate on the task of communication.

"This is the same type of thing. In an emergency, you push this button, and a two-way transmission will open between you and Iniquus. You talk right out loud as if we were in the same room. There are speakers that will pick up your voice. I think you have something similar at your house."

"Yes." Come on, Lexi, maybe just one full sentence?

Striker slipped the cord around my neck and the device settled between my breasts. "You have help if you need it," he said and checked his watch. "We have to go now." He gave me one last questioning look. I guessed he was trying to decide if leaving me was a good decision or not. What he saw in my eyes seemed to satisfy him. He covered my hand with his. His callused palm felt very capable.

"You're going to be okay," he said, and I almost believed him.

Jack handed me the remote for the TV. He laid a cold, damp cloth over my forehead. It offered me some relief.

I rolled my eyes up to get Jack in view. "Thank you so much."

"Yes, ma'am."

Then they left. And I lay there. Alone in the safe (?) safe house.

21

The wide sofa cushions were comfortable, but I still flopped like a fish in the sun, trying to find a position to fall asleep. I always slept on my belly, curled around a pillow, one knee folded up jack-knife style—obviously not a possibility right now. After a few minutes, I gave it up, picked up the remote, and flipped through the television channels a few times. I hoped something would catch my attention. I desperately needed a distraction.

I flung my covers off and clambered to my feet. Okay. I needed to keep my hands busy. Lying here, listening to my mind whir around the details of my mess, only made my nerve endings spark.

I went to the kitchen, searching for something to make for dinner. The fridge stood completely empty except for two bottles of beer. On the other hand, someone had stocked the freezer with all kinds of meats, frozen vegetables, fruits, some phyllo dough, and an empty Breyers ice cream box. Huh. I pulled the box out and threw it in the trash.

The pantry housed a treasure trove of spices and canned goods. Nori sheets, vegemite, shortbread, sauerkraut, dried ancho chilies. It seemed that whoever put together the cupboard was thinking United Nations. The wine rack held various reds and whites.

If I wanted to get something together for dinner, I needed to get the meat defrosting. The deli sandwiches or fast food I imagined would come in with the crew didn't seem at all appetizing. Cooking would be therapeutic; I needed to sense my Kitchen Grandmothers close. This seclusion wasn't going to be as easy as it had sounded when Dave told me the plan.

I rifled through the freezer to see if I could find ingredients for a stew, maybe even a Boeuf Bourguignon, if I were lucky. Focus on cooking. Focus on something wholesome.

I had my head in the freezer; the cold air swirled around my face. It soothed me and seemed to help solidify some of my wobbly thoughts. Okay, my problem—a freaking serial killer was on the loose and on my trail. I needed to think, to systematically go through the information, to work with Iniquus to come up with a plan, and get my attacker chucked into prison.

My other problem, when I thought about that night when I tried to think and puzzle through everything, I had an adrenaline dump. Even the fear of an adrenaline dump was punitive enough to make me want to cringe, hide, throw up my hands in surrender. I couldn't. I just couldn't deal with the physical and emotional pain.

I needed a strategy. How would I deal with my situation? Nothing like this ever came up in my training. I blew out through pursed lips, trying to slow my breathing and contain my anxiety as I dug around in the freezer and came up with some bacon.

Come on, Lexi. Take a step back, don't think specifically about the case. What if you were dealing with someone else…a victim. How would you advise her? What would Spyder do? He'd say trust the experts. Trust your team. I pulled out a bag of pearl onions and put them on the counter. If I were down for the count with medical issues, my Save-Lexi team members would have their eyes on me and not on the ball. If I got medically worse, I'd end up back in a hospital and in more danger. Logically, the best way to move forward was to allow my team to do their job.

My job was to heal as quickly as possible.

What did that mean? It meant focusing everywhere but on that ball. Take my head *out* of the proverbial game. Act counter to my intuition and training and be that damned damsel in distress. I needed to let those knights ride after my dragon…while I sang a song with my fingers stuck in my ears, and my eyes squeezed tightly together, focused on everything but *him*.

Could I do it? Heck, I didn't know. Fluffy was my exterior disguise. I had never tried to disguise my interior thoughts before. It was going to be a challenge, for sure, just like every other damn piece to this whole puzzling situation.

I located stew meat. From what I had seen with the first four Iniquus men, these guys were massive; I'd wager they had appetites to match. We were eight in total. I'd better triple the recipe. I set the beef on the counter in a giant pile.

While the makings defrosted in the oven, I piddled away some time looking through magazines, pacing at the windows, and startling with every little sound. When the ingredients reached the point that they were useable, I sautéed my beef cubes and followed the inner voice of Nana Kate, adding the components to the stew pot, methodically going through Julia Child's exacting steps.

Yes. Focus on Nana Kate. If she were here, she'd have me knitting. "Idle hands are the tools of the Devil," she'd say. My hands weren't the problem, Nana Kate! It was my mind. My idle mind was devilish for sure, dragging me toward my hellish thoughts of pain, and fear of pain… and fear of death.

"Lexi!" I admonished myself out loud. Okay—Nana Kate. Nana Kate, my Kitchen Grandmother from Nebraska, had a good, steady, no-nonsense attitude and a steel-colored bun on the top of her head. On most days, Nana Kate fed her family from the four food groups—good old fashioned, tried and true, patriotic menus. But every once in a while, she got a touch of the mischief in her, and she'd pull out her Julia Child "Mastering the Art of French Cooking" cookbook. Then we'd revel in cassoulet and chocolate mousse, baguette, and tart tatin. And tonight, Boeuf Bourguignon. Thank you, Nana Kate.

Soon, the glorious aromas from the oven replaced the safehouse's stale, unused smell. It would take three hours on a low heat to realize the wonderful, fall-apart-in-your-mouth tenderness of the meat. I was starting to wear down. The anxiety, and the pre-dawn start, were showing up in heavy arms and sagging shoulders.

In the laundry, I found a man's button-down cotton shirt big enough for a giant. Jacks? I didn't think he'd mind me substituting this for my hospital gowns. I took two towels and the shirt into the bathroom with me. I untied the cotton strings, let the cover-ups fall to the ground, lifted off the communications necklace, and set it on the toilet tank for safekeeping.

Kneeling on the floor, I washed my hair under the bathtub faucet with tiny bottles of shampoo and conditioner—leftovers from someone's hotel stay. I climbed into the tub with a little hot water. What I really wanted was a deep, hot bubble bath. Already this was better than the hospital where I had been sponge bathed. How embarrassing was that? I did my best to clean myself off and shave without getting my torso wet.

Suddenly, a bright, metallic clatter sounded downstairs.

I froze.

My heart hammered.

Glancing wild-eyed around the room for a weapon, my gaze landed on my alert necklace. How far away was help? I didn't expect my team until four. I strained for any telltale sounds. To echo-locate. Echo-discriminate. My blood drummed so loudly in my ears, the thrumming drowned out any other noise. Shit, Spyder was right. *Panic will kill you, Lexicon. It makes you unable in mind and body.* I pinched my nose at the bridge to stop my hyperventilation and steeled myself for action.

Crouching low, I crawled out of the tub. I stayed tightly tucked, squatting beside the sink—hyper-protective of my oh-so-vulnerable torso. I didn't know if the doctors could put me as Humpty Dumpty back together again since they had already managed the impossible once, barely. My thoughts sped through my brain, tripping, and tumbling over each other. The last time I had been alone, naked, and vulnerable in a bathroom—*Do not! Do not go there....*

I shut my eyes and tried desperately to suck oxygen into my lungs and transfer it to my veins so my body and mind would respond appropriately.

Reaching out a shaking hand, I pulled the communicator back over my head. My thumb hovered, ready to press the button. I checked the lock on the bathroom door and shoved the doorstop tightly under the crack. Bracing the wedge in place with my heel, I reached for a towel to cover myself.

The bang sounded again—a sharp metallic clatter.

This time, I recognized the clang of pots hitting against each other in the dishwasher. My breath came out in a whoosh. I moved to sit on the toilet seat and waited for the swirling vertigo to still and calm to return.

If I didn't understand before, I certainly realized now that my brain could be my worst enemy. FDR, you weren't perfectly right—there truly was more for me to fear than fear itself. But in this case, the killer didn't need to get to me; I was going to scare myself to death anticipating him.

Once I felt sure I'd avoided an adrenaline dump, I pulled on the shirt—and pulled myself together, more or less. Finally, I braved a glance in the mirror. If nothing else, at least now I was more modest than in the hospital gowns and cleaner too. I dragged my fingers through my wet hair like a comb, then put the elastic band back around my ponytail. I'd love to have a hairdryer and flat iron. There. Not my usual standards. Still, I was clean and warm and much calmer.

Coping.

I moved toward the stairs, cajoling myself to focus on the mundane.

I can do this. And I crossed my fingers to give that thought a little extra juju.

22

At four on the dot, according to the wall clock, the telephone rang in the kitchen, the unexpected noise sprang me from my dreams, like a Jack-in-the-box, all wound up then *BOING!* I gripped my covers and stared at the phone. Supposedly, no one knew I was here, so I decided not to answer. After about ten rings, the caller gave up.

Seconds later, the garage door ground open, and a car motored in. My hand wrapped around the gun. I slid behind the back of the sofa, crouching down for the second time today—but I was pretty sure this was my team coming in. A knock sounded at the door that separates the house from the garage.

A voice called out, "Mrs. Sobado? It's Axel and Deep from this morning, ma'am. May we come in?"

"Yes, hello," I shouted back. I laid the gun down on the table in front of me and stood facing the door, which swung slowly open. The men paused before they moved cautiously into the room—eyes on me.

I raised empty hands and gave them a reassuring smile. "I'm unarmed."

My attention moved to the TV, which droned on about steaming fish in parchment. I pushed the off button on the remote. I had real humans with me now; I didn't need the background noise to give me a pretend sense of safety.

Axel came over and checked my water, medicine, and food. "You haven't eaten anything we left you—did you take your meds on time?" Axel's mouth stretched into a thin, displeased line.

"I had a nervous stomach and couldn't eat." I gestured lamely at the sofa. "I fell asleep before I was due for my next dose."

Axel looked closely at me—hard, scrutinizing eyes. My hands fumbled nervously at my shirt. He reached out for the prescriptions, opened the bottles, and put the pills on my open palm.

Deep's voice came from the kitchen. "Did you make this?" I looked around. Deep was standing in front of the stew pot, lid in one hand, empty spoon in the other, grin across the face.

"Don't taste anything yet. Dinner's not finished," I called over to him. "I thought we all might enjoy something homemade. I didn't know what Striker meant when he said he'd bring food in tonight."

"He didn't mean anything like this, that's for sure." Deep replaced the lid.

Axel made his way into the kitchen, opened the cutlery drawer, and pulled out his own spoon.

"Now come on," I complained. "You can't taste until it's ready."

"Ma'am, we're charged with your safety. I need to make sure the ingredients are okay before I can allow you to eat this." Axel spooned a large bite into his mouth and chewed slowly, looking over at me. "Mrs. Sobado, if you weren't already married, I'd be driving you to the church right now. What is that?"

A grin spread over my face—these guys were too easy if I could get them to fall in love with me over beef stew. Standing over the pot with his spoon in the air, Axel was a little less intimidating—a little.

"French stew," I said.

"And the bread?" Axel asked.

"Beer bread. You didn't have any yeast for a regular loaf." I sat on the sofa with my back pressed against the arm and my feet stretching out under the covers. I tried to keep my stomach as straight as I could and still see the men.

Deep tugged his cell phone from his pocket and pressed a number on his quick dial. He reported to Striker that I was still in one piece and had dinner ready. Deep looked over at me while he listened. "Striker wants to know if there's anything else he can bring in with him."

"Tell him some salad greens would be good, and there's no milk if you guys like that in your coffee. Oh, and I got tired before I made dessert. If you guys want sweets, he should pick up something already made."

Deep spoke into his cell, "Salad greens and milk...Yes, sir." He shoved the phone back in his pocket.

"No dessert?"

"We usually skip the sugar, ma'am," Axel said.

I looked over at them. Their compression shirts displayed ripple-y muscles and six-pack abs. Nope, no love handles from midnight runs to Baskin Robbins.

Deep and Axel had a private discussion in the kitchen, both of them looking at me while they made their plans. They walked lock-step over to the sofa.

"Mrs. Sobado," Deep crouched beside me, "Axel is going shopping for you. What in particular do you need?"

"I really need you all to stop calling me Mrs. Sobado. I'm Lexi. I appreciate you're doing this for me." I looked at Axel; darn, but this was embarrassing. I took a deep breath. "I need some loose-fitting clothes. You know, so they don't pull at my wounds. And some panties." I blushed as I said that—who would have thought I'd ever be asking a strange man to go to the store to pick out my underwear?

Axel didn't blink.

This must be one of those things you learn to do when your job is to pull girls out of their predicaments. "A hairbrush, toothbrush, and stuff, maybe a hairdryer?" And then came the worst part—I wasn't sure how long I'd be here, so I might as well get it over with in the first shopping trip, so I'd be set for the long haul. I took a deep breath and said on the exhale, "And a box of regular Playtex tampons and panty liners." There, I said it. My inner furnace turned up the heat in my face.

Axel ignored my discomfiture. "I'll be back." He turned to look at Deep. "If I miss dinner, you'd better save me some." His tone was playfully threatening.

After Axel took off, Deep asked, "Is there anything I can get you? Or anything I can do to make you more comfortable?"

"I'm fine, thanks." Well, now that you ask, the attacker's head on a platter would go a far piece toward my comfort level.

"There are plenty of books." He gestured over at the floor to ceiling case. "You can use whatever you want in the house, so grab something off the shelf if you don't want to watch TV. Unfortunately, you can't have Internet here. We can't take the chance that you'd make outside contact or that you'd be traced in."

Wow. That kind of isolation was going to be hard.

"I should also explain." He pointed to the telephone on the kitchen wall. "We program the phone system. The only lines that go through are your teammates' cell phones. I'll post the names and numbers. Of course, in an emergency, you push the button on your necklace. You'll have a 24-hour guard now, so there shouldn't be a problem." He waited for me to nod my understanding. "When a man comes to the driveway, he'll call in, so there's no concern about who's coming up to the house. Like we did earlier. We're going to try to avoid any situation that might cause you physical distress. We've been apprised of your injuries."

I offered up a weak smile.

"If you're okay right now, I'm going to go ahead and program your lines of communication and get some research and paper-work done. I'll be your watchdog until the rest of the team comes in at six—except Axel. He'll get here when he can."

I laid there for a few minutes contemplating my situation, watching Deep do his thing, settling in at the table. I wandered over to the bookshelf to take a good look at the titles. Like the pantry, whoever stocked the house had been eclectic. There were novels and non-fictions of all genres ready to entertain anyone marooned in the safehouse. I bet my childhood librarian, Mrs. Shelack, would have loved having the assignment of putting together a collection that held something of interest to whoever ended up here in the little yellow safehouse.

I pulled some books down and read their jackets without enthusiasm. They were probably pretty good, but I didn't think that I could settle myself down to absorb a story. I went over and stood to the side of the window, gazing up the street, assiduously keeping my thoughts neutral, mundane, non-inflammatory. Deep looked up from his laptop screen to see if I had spotted anything. I gave him my reassuring smile—nothing out there—and turned back to the gulls circling the sky. Day one and already I was one great big jittery, jumpy, antsy, claustrophobic mess. I had better get hold of myself, or this was going to turn out to be a nightmare. Going to turn out to be? I shook my head—it already was.

23

At five-thirty, I went to the kitchen to finish the food prep. Deep closed his computer and set the table for eight. Striker came in and put a brown grocery bag on the breakfast bar.

"Thank you for dinner," Striker said.

"You're welcome. Cooking is therapeutic for me. I needed something to do with my hands."

Striker nodded. "You kept pretty busy today. I thought you'd nap on the couch."

"I needed help passing the time and keeping the heebie-jeebies at bay."

"Were you frightened being here by yourself?" He stood close, his voice pitched low, the question for me only. His tone made me want to be truthful instead of polite.

"A little." I veiled my eyes behind my lashes, too embarrassed to admit how scared I had really been. As I glanced up, the room spun wildly. I lost my balance, and Striker lowered me to the floor. He crouched beside me with his hand on the back of my neck. The whirling sensation soon passed.

"Come and sit at the table, Lexi. My men tell me you haven't eaten all day." He put a supportive hand under my arm.

"Nervous stomach," I said.

The phone on the wall rang; Deep lifted the receiver to listen.

"Roger." He turned to me. "Our car is coming up the drive."

"Yes. Thank you."

The other members of my Save-Lexi Team packed the room: Jack followed in Blaze, Gator, and Randy, I learned, after quick introductions. They gathered around the table, and with playful banter and clattering spoons, noisily filled their bowls, passing the bread and salad around. As they shoveled up their first taste, the table fell silent, and they fixed their gaze on me.

"Woo-wee. That sure is some kind of good." Gator stuffed another bite in his mouth. The men grinned, nodded their agreement, and worked on eating in earnest. A blush crawled up from my neckline.

When the men's appetites were sated—and I kept a close eye on the pot to make sure Axel wouldn't go hungry—I started around the table, making sure I had the names straight. "Okay, you all go by your call names." I began with Striker. "You got yours on assignment in Africa." Striker's face turned hard-edged and questioning—whoops! I wasn't supposed to know that.

Better be careful and hold those cards up until you're ready for everyone to see. I shifted my attention to Jack. "If Jack's not your real name, what does it mean?"

Deep bent over the table, pointing his spoon at me. "If you mess with my man, he's gonna jack you up." They hooted over this and high-fived.

I looked at Blaze. He had intensely blue eyes like corn-flowers—though I'd never say that out loud—and bright copper hair curling disobediently, even in his tight military cut.

"And, you're Blaze because of your hair?"

"No, ma'am. I'm Blaze for my motto, 'If I'm going out, it's

going to be in a blaze of glory.'"

"Ah, I see. And you, Gator?"

"Well, ma'am," Gator eased into his story with a slow southern drawl like a ladle of spicy gumbo, "I used to be in the Marines. I spent a right good amount of time mucking around in them swamps. One morning, I were out there on maneuvers, and I had a ten-foot 'gator sneak up behind me. Before I could blink, he had me in a death roll."

"You're obviously here and in one piece, so there must be a happy ending to this story."

"For me, there is, ma'am." He gave me a wink. I had the impression Gator used this yarn to pick up women in bars. "I had my knife on me. Not so much so for the 'gator, though. He got spit-roasted on our fire come nightfall." Gator's sun-bleached hair, sable-brown eyes, and scattering of freckles across his nose gave him a boyish look, which was incongruous with his gladiator physique. I watched him as he spoke—a little hyperbolic maybe, but he told the truth.

"I hear they taste like chicken," I said. The guys guffawed and slapped Gator's back.

"And you're Randy, and you are Deep." I turned my head toward the other two men.

"Yes, ma'am," Randy cleared his throat. "I got my name—" He stopped when I held up my hand.

"That's okay. I think your names can stay private." More laughing and elbow jostling.

Jack leaned toward Striker and asked quietly, "Any news on Lynda and Cammy?"

Those names had my full attention. Striker's posture took on a rigidity; his face turned stony. I could tell he was worried about the women. Very worried. I wondered if these were two separate cases or if somehow Lynda and Cammy were linked.

"Nada," Striker said. He glanced my way, and I quickly took a sip of water to cover my eavesdropping.

Striker lifted his spoon toward his mouth and paused, focusing in on Randy and Blaze. "Deep and Axel completed their assignment this morning before coming in to guard Lexi. How about you two? I understand you made your capture. Did you get the flash drive?" He finished his bite.

Blaze straightened his back and tucked his chin—back in military mode. Commander Striker Rheas was reviewing his troops. I wondered what kind of assignment the men had on the table, and I got a twinge of nostalgia—the fun of unraveling a crime.

"Yes, sir. We made the capture. We had eyes on her throughout the operation. We followed her to the apartment building, where she entered her address for five minutes and exited. When she got curb-side, we made the arrest. We searched her person, bag, and car—nothing there."

"You posted someone at the apartment?"

"Thorn stayed back on guard duty while we delivered the prisoner to our client and signed her into their custody. They conducted a more thorough personal search and weren't able to find the flash drive, either. We went back to the apartment and shook it down, but we can't find where she hid it. We're hoping they'll be able to get her to cooperate in questioning."

I grinned, looking down into my stew. Striker caught my grin and considered me. "You know where she put it, don't you." It was a statement, not a question.

I looked up and held his eye for a minute, the smile lighting my face. "She probably stuck it the same place I would if two macho guys were on my trail." Everyone turned to me and waited expectantly.

I looked from face to face and then back to Striker. "I'd put it in the place every girl knows a man would overlook—the bottom of her tampon box." I spooned more stew into my mouth. Striker looked over at Randy and Blaze. They wiped their mouths and pushed their chairs back, heading back out the door.

After dinner, Jack cleared the table. I turned on the coffee maker I prepped earlier with grounds and water. While the coffee percolated, I heated water for Striker's tea. I made a generous tray for Axel, for when he got back, and set it in the oven on warm. Deep took care of the dishes and wiped down the kitchen.

At the table, the men pulled out their computers. Jack asked if I wanted coffee, and I shook my head. He brought five mugs to the table with the stainless steel carafe. I poured boiling water into another mug, dunked a peppermint tea bag in, and set it in front of Striker. Striker looked down at the tea, sniffed, and looked back at me.

I remembered from one of our meetings back in my Alex days, Striker never drank coffee at night; he liked peppermint tea. I was amusing myself, playing with his mind a little bit.

"Not what you wanted?" My mouth quirked into a smile.

He narrowed his eyes, cocking his head slightly to the side, looking at me from a different angle. "No, this is fine, thank you."

With dinner over, the mood shifted back to work mode. All the men seemed to have a military background. Clean, precise, and honorable. They were all "yes, ma'am; no, sir." Though I wouldn't say American as apple pie. Nothing light and flaky about their exteriors; nothing obviously warm and sweet about them, either. These men were hard and controlled. Even at the dinner table, where they seemed to be more themselves, joking with each other, they still had the quality of parade rest—a tightness about their muscles and alertness in their eyes, a readiness to spring into action.

They were reviewing open cases; it was inappropriate for me to listen. I roamed into the living room and folded up my bed linens, putting them on the end of the sofa to make room in case the men wanted to relax. Picking up the remote control, I muted the sound while I surfed through the channels, looking for something to distract me from my thoughts.

With my hip leaning into the arm of the sofa, wondering when Axel might get back with some underwear for me, I flipped past the local news. There on the screen hung the rendering of my attacker. The life-like drawing stunned me. With my eyes fixed on the picture, my heart staggered around my ribs like a drunkard. Panic twisted my lungs. The attacker leered at me, a big man of mixed racial background with almond-shaped eyes and a flat nose over a wide full mouth. Two scars disfigured the left side of his face—one ran from his nose to the corner of his lip, and another ran from his eye to his chin. On the right side, he adorned himself with a tribal tattoo showing black against his light brown skin. Horror transfixed me as memories of that night flooded my brain. My skin stung like a hive of wasps from the perspiration's salt. I fell to the ground on all fours, panting for air, tears and saliva dripping onto the carpet, moans crawling up my throat as I rocked back and forth.

Striker barked orders at his men. Firm hands gripped my shoulders. Striker supported my weight as Jack pulled my ankle out straight, and they rolled me onto my back. Randy stood ready with a blanket, which he threw over my legs, allowing Striker to unbutton the bottom part of my shirt and still keep me covered. Though modesty had zero importance to me in the moment.

Help me! Make this stop! My brain shrieked.

Striker carefully reached up under the top button, gently patting my chest, my breasts, my stomach, dipping the cloth frequently into the water and wringing it almost dry. I threw my arms over my face, biting at my sleeve to keep from screaming. Strangled sounds gurgled from my throat. Adrenaline filled my glands and made me stink like an animal fighting for its life. I wanted to battle—to claw and bite to escape the pain. I wrestled those emotions down. The tiny slice of my rational mind still functioning realized laying still would get me relief sooner. It was a hard-fought internal struggle.

Soon, the cool cloth lowered my temperature, and I stopped sweating. The water washed away the salt.

The men had gathered around, staring down at the cross hatches covering my torso like the blackened stitch lines on a crazy quilt. The mood in the room fell deadly silent. The men's fists balling and jaws clenched.

Right away, I swung from boiling to freezing. My teeth chattered together so fast and hard my head clanged. My tongue tasted metallic. Striker squatted beside me and slid one arm under my knees and another around my back. Jack steadied us as Striker pushed to standing and carried me up the stairs with Jack close behind him. I draped in Striker's arms like a rag doll, barely able to keep my cheek pressed into his chest. I felt like Striker had pulled me from the washing machine after banging around then being spun almost dry.

Jack opened a bedroom door and clicked on a lamp that dimly lit the room, then went over to the bed and turned down the covers. Striker moved toward the La-z-Boy and sat down with me in his lap.

Jack brought a thick blanket, draping it over me, and Striker adjusted his arms, so he could hold the cover in place. After a nod from Striker, Jack went back downstairs, closing my door softly behind him.

24

I cowered into Striker's chest and sobbed until exhaustion overtook me. Striker smoothed my hair back behind my ear to get it out of the tears staining my face.

"How are you doing?" Striker's voice sounded like velvet.

"I'm done in," I whispered up at him. "I'm better now," I added. "Thank you for helping me." Striker pulled me a little tighter to him, in a supportive hug; he shifted under me as he lifted me to the bed.

He tucked the covers under my chin, then he sat down on the edge of the mattress and looked me in the eye.

"Detective Murphy said your brain injury causes your problems with vertigo and adrenaline. I was unprepared for the severity. Is this what happens every time?"

I nodded.

"He said you're refusing medications because you're concerned they might prevent you from being able to react sufficiently if you needed to defend yourself. Is that true?"

"Yes."

Striker rubbed his thumb and index finger over his forehead.

"You were in a lot of pain. To be honest, I've never seen anything like what happened to you during the attack. I can't imagine what you endured then or now. Is it possible you're comfortable enough here with us, you'd reconsider taking the medication? Give yourself a break, at least from the adrenaline?"

"No," I said resolutely.

Striker nodded.

We looked at each other for a long moment.

"Thank you, though," I said. "You seemed to know just what to do." I shifted my gaze down to my hands and twisted my wedding ring back and forth.

Striker chuckled. "I got caught off guard for a second, then I realized what was going on. One minute you're standing there with the TV remote, and the next, you're on the floor on all fours, groaning and grinding like a high-priced porn star. You should have seen the shock on my men's faces."

I guessed I should have been scandalized by his ribald joke. In my experience, Striker normally acted like the perfect gentleman. But I had been out on enough assignments with him to know that after a tense undertaking, Striker often threw out some completely off-the-wall comment. Something that took us by surprise. The shock usually served to shift the mood to laughter and teasing. I've never seen him do this with a crime victim, though. When he talked with a civilian, his word choices were always meticulously appropriate. I wondered what made me different? Why was he treating me like he did when I was on the team as Alex? Could he have made the connection? Did he recognize me after all?

It didn't really matter; I had fallen for his shenanigans and grinned back at him. "So, they thought I had succumbed to all of the testosterone in the room? I couldn't handle it anymore, and I dropped into a spontaneous orgasm?" I smirked.

"Yeah, something along those lines." Wariness crept into his voice—I bet he second-guessed his comment and wanted to take it back.

I laughed to reassure him the remark hadn't bothered me. "Hah! Well, you didn't."

"I had a heads-up from Detective Murphy, and I saw the guy's picture on the TV screen." He narrowed his eyes with his assessing look. "Be honest, are you okay?" he asked softly.

"I'm okay. I need to sleep a little now." My eyelids drooped heavily with the weight of my fatigue.

"I'll be in the room on your right tonight if you need anything," Striker stood, smoothed the sheets and blankets over me, and clicked off the light.

He leaned carefully over me and whispered in my ear, "How did you know I drink mint tea?" I didn't bother opening my eyes but let a small, slow smile play across my lips as I drifted off to sleep.

It hadn't been late when Striker tucked me into bed. My stay at the hospital, with the nightly poking and prodding, definitely messed up my sleep cycle. Now here it was, one in the morning, and I fidgeted with the soft satin edge of my blanket, trying not to squirm around and pull at my scabs. It was crazy-making how much my torso itched!

If I were at home, I might take a melatonin to help me get back to my regular schedule. I doubted they had anything like that here. I eased out of my bed and wandered into the bathroom to look in the medical cabinet on the off chance they had something. In between the bottles of Pepto and Tums, I discovered some antihistamines; they should do the trick. I tipped two pills out of the bottle and used my hands to cup some water from the faucet to wash them down.

I climbed back into bed to wait for sleep to drift over me. The clock ticking by my head made me acutely aware of how slowly time paced. The more I lay there, the more my mind wandered. The more my mind wandered, the more I freaked myself out over every little creak and groan that belonged to an older house. I found myself listening anxiously for someone moving around in the garage or climbing the staircase. I had revved myself into a state, and I didn't want to repeat my earlier crisis.

I couldn't stand it anymore.

I flung my covers to the side and snuck out of my room. A night-light in the bathroom lit the hallway. Striker's door stood slightly ajar. My hand rested on his doorknob. *What are you doing, Lexi?* My subconscious stilled my forward momentum. I glanced back at my door.

Which was scarier—the heebie-jeebies and an adrenaline spike? Or this plan?

I took a minute to breathe. Here was the problem—I couldn't handle the adrenaline. Or even the idea of adrenaline. And my mind was getting the best of me. Scared out of my wits, I needed some respite—an island of safety. But was going through this door safe? *Hell in a Handbasket,* my inner knowing reminded me. Whatever that meant.

I didn't really have a good grasp on Striker. He was largely a figment of my imagination—my teenaged hormones run amuck, I reminded myself as I chewed on my bottom lip. My brows knit together.

Past tense.

Very past.

Angel was my reality. I deeply loved my husband. So, was

there really a problem? Did I think going through this door equaled disloyalty to Angel in some way? Unfaithfulness? No. I couldn't. I wouldn't be disloyal.

My Striker emotions were simply mirages and memories messing with my brain. And quite frankly, anything about those feelings that made me awkward or nervous around him—they were nothing compared to the security I experienced when he was near. Striker Rheas was the embodiment of safety.

"Lexi?" Striker's voice rasped thickly with sleep.

I cracked Striker's door open wide enough to fit through, tip-toed over to his bed, and crawled under his covers, facing him.

"I have the heebie-jeebies," I whispered.

He chuckled softly. "Don't you think it's dangerous to climb into a strange man's bed?"

"More dangerous than the heebie-jeebies? No, I don't think so. What would I be afraid of in your bed, exactly?"

"I don't know. Maybe you should worry about my moral fortitude?"

"I'm not even the teeniest bit worried about that," I whispered into the dark. "Maybe if I were any other woman, but I'm convinced I'm completely safe here in your bed, both from any advances from you and from the boogie man."

"And why are you safer here than any other woman?" Striker whispered back to me. I could hear his smile.

"Firstly, I'm a shredded mess, and in no way can that be appealing. Second, you were special ops, serving overseas. You get what that is, and Dave told you my husband's over there right now. The last thing you'd do with a fellow soldier's wife is to lose sight of your moral fortitude."

"That's what you've deduced?"

I nodded against the pillow.

"You're pretty good. Who told you I worked special ops? Have my men been chatting with you?"

"Nope," I said.

Striker waited for me to expound. I still wasn't altogether sure how to play this hand—what Spyder would want him to know. I decided that tucking the pillow under my head and cozying in to sleep was the best way to go.

"Hey." Striker climbed over me and got a pair of sweat pants from his drawer. He tossed them to me. "You at least have to put something on your bottom half. I *am* only human."

25

The sky hung gray and heavy when Striker maneuvered out of bed, holding the blankets to keep the shock of cold air off me—probably trying not to wake me up. I lay with my eyes closed, playing possum. He moved quietly, gathering some clothes from the drawers and his Dopp kit from off the bureau. He headed to the bathroom and turned on the shower. Snuggled under the covers, warm and a little sluggish, I wondered if Axel had brought clothes in for me last night. I hadn't heard anyone coming up the stairs. Under Striker's protection, I had slept very well.

I wandered to my bedroom, and sure enough, I found bags piled on the floor next to the chair. I opened the first one from Victoria's Secret. It held a month's worth of panties—different colors, fabrics, styles. I guessed Axel didn't want to choose what would be comfortable to me, so he told the sales lady he wanted one of everything. I searched the tag for the size. He'd gotten that right, and they were all the same. Hmm, confident, I thought. No bras—good, I couldn't wear them anyway, which I'm sure he understood.

Pulling off Striker's oversized sweats, I put on a pair of white cotton low-rise bikinis. Funny how secure I felt right away.

I opened a bag from a shop unfamiliar to me. Inside were lounge pants and t-shirts of the softest material imaginable. One hundred percent bamboo, the label read. I had heard of bamboo material but never worn it before. I rubbed it against my cheek. Yum! This was beyond luxurious; it felt like an emotion—like kindness. I stepped into a pair of blue and green striped pants. They sat low on my hip below the scabs. I pulled out a shirt that matched the blue stripes, tore off the tag, and pulled it carefully over my head. The cloth settled against my skin. It didn't bind, nor was it so loose that it rubbed. It slid over my crusty torso and didn't catch on the glue and dried blood. Wonderful, Axel. The fabric was thick enough for modesty, even though the girls were going unsupported.

In the bag from Sally's Beauty Supply, I found a mani-cure/pedicure kit, hair styling products, and appliances. The first CVS bag held tampons and panty liners (such a good man), Midol, and a bag of Dove's chocolate. I laughed. Axel must have a wife or a serious girlfriend. Someone had trained him well. The second CVS bag had hygiene products and some basic make-up items: black mascara, tinted lip gloss, and translucent powder— ah, and a new purple toothbrush. When I peeked in the last bag, a pair of fuzzy pink bunny slippers poked out its ears. Too funny. Axel seemed to hit all the bases; I was pretty darned impressed with his selections.

When I got up this morning, I made the conscious decision to keep my thoughts light. Fluffy interior, fluffy exterior. I wouldn't process any of my challenges. My thoughts went to the Buddhist monks who practiced mindfulness and would sit blankly for hours at a time. Blank was beyond me, but maybe I could manage the mundane.

My goal? An adrenaline-free day.

I made my bed while waiting for Striker to finish up in the bathroom. When his bedroom door shut, I slipped in to brush my teeth and use the potty. I brushed my hair back in a loose braid, swiped on some mascara, and used a little gloss. With a critical look in the mirror, I examined my forehead, where the wound over my right brow had turned greenish-yellow and purple. I had a large gash with twelve black stitches. The plastic surgeon said the slight scar would blend into my hairline and become unnoticeable with time as long as I stayed out of the sun. Easy enough, no sun shines in the safehouse. After I'd done the best I could with my appearance, I went back to my room for the bunny slippers and hopped myself down the stairs for some breakfast.

Striker, dressed in his Iniquus uniform, leaned against the kitchen counter with a mug of coffee, his long legs stretched out in front of him. He glanced up when I came into the room. His eyes took me in from head to toe. "Morning, Lexi."

"Morning." I returned his smile shyly. I had just slept next to this man. How was I supposed to act now? I took my cue from Striker and moved on.

Food had appeared in the fridge overnight—probably Axel's doing, as well.

Randy looked over at me from the stove, where he was scrambling eggs. "Breakfast will be done in a minute, ma'am. Can I pour you a cup of coffee?"

"I would love some, but the doctors tell me it's a no-no until I have my head screwed back on right. I think I'll have some tea, though." I went to the cabinet and reached for a mug. My darned head started to spin. Striker caught me from behind and supported me as he moved me toward the table.

"Why don't you let Randy take care of that this morning?" he asked.

"Thanks." I laid my cheek on the cool surface of the polished wood. Striker glanced down at my feet with a grin. "Nice bunny slippers."

I lifted my foot with the huge pink ears and googly eyes. "Mmm. I think Axel was having some fun." I wondered if Axel knew how appropriate these were. I'd use them as visual reminders that I was mindfully practicing being a fluffy adrenaline-free bunny.

Deep and Jack showed up at seven, everyone gathered for breakfast. Randy brought me a cup of Orange Zinger tea. There were scrambled eggs and salsa to wrap in whole-wheat tortillas. A fruit salad of berries, kiwi, and papaya filled a bowl on the table. It all tasted good, fresh, and wholesome. After the green Jell-O hospital diet, I was ravenous.

I caught Striker's eye. "Did the guys find the flash drive last night?"

"Right where you said it would be." He smiled back at me.

"Do I win a prize?"

That brought up a flicker of a memory. Striker stared hard at me; I could see him flipping through his mental files. How did I know how he got his call name? How did I know he was special ops? How did I know he drank peppermint tea after dinner? Where had he heard a voice saying a similar phrase? He was coming up with nothing. He shook his head. "Do you know me?"

"How would I know you?" I used a Spyder technique. If you

answer a question with a deflecting question or statement, you didn't have to give an actual answer.

"Detective Murphy said you were psychic, and I think I'm beginning to believe him. Yes, you've won yourself a prize." He reached into the buffet and pulled out my laptop.

"Thank you." I smiled as he brought it over to me.

"You already know we can't allow you to have an Internet connection—I've disabled your computer. But I thought there might be something on here to help pass the time."

"Yes. I have some papers to write for school, and when I'm done with that, I'm working on a project about my Kitchen Grandmothers."

"Okay, I'll bite. What's a Kitchen Grandmother?" Striker asked, lacing his fingers behind his head.

"These six beautiful older women lived in my apartment building during my teens. They took me under their wings at the end of my mom's terminal illness. Each grandmother came from a different culture, and they shared their families, their talents, and their recipes with me. I was surrounded with so much kindness and wisdom, I really wanted to capture that somewhere. You know, my favorite recipes and their stories. Maybe I can turn it into a book someday."

"Now I understand what you meant yesterday when you said you cook Mediterranean on Monday."

"Yes, Jadda taught me on Mondays. 'Jadda' is what her grandchildren call her. She's Turkish and married to a Moroccan man. They speak Arabic in their home."

"Then I'll look forward to dinner tonight. Randy's your watchdog." Striker stood and stretched, his muscles flexing under his Iniquus compression shirt. "It can get pretty boring here in the house. Let me know if you can think of anything we can bring in to help you stay occupied. Make a list. Don't worry about inconveniencing us. If you're busy, the confinement is easier on everyone. Cabin fever is never pretty."

I nodded. "Axel brought me some nail stuff. I think I'll give myself a manicure this morning and cook—if that's all right."

"If you make a list of ingredients you want on hand, we'll make sure to get those for you. I'll call in before I come back to see if you need me to bring anything for dinner tonight."

The other men were in the kitchen cleaning up. I leaned over to Striker. "Hey," I whispered, "last night when I hit the ground, I was only wearing the button-down shirt. Did anyone, you know, see anything?" I blushed so hard the roots of my hair prickled.

Striker suppressed a smile. "The shirt was pretty big."

Well, that wasn't an answer!

I spent the morning giving myself a thorough and careful manicure and pedicure with Sally Hansen's pink metallic polish. The TV played nothing in particular. I focused on not focusing, not letting my mind meander down dark alleys. So far, so good. But I was starting to get bored.

Once Randy finished up on the computer, he sat in front of the box Axel brought in this morning. He unloaded the contents: a huge photo album, mail, a checkbook, a passport, and a cell phone.

I walked over to peek at the pile. "What's this stuff for?" I asked nonchalantly.

"We have a missing suspect. This is our goody trail to find him." Randy seemed a little disheartened.

"It's not much." I wanted him to feed me some more information. This puzzle was a much more enticing way to pass the time, a thousand percent better than manicures and TV shows.

Randy rifled through the stack. "I hope it's enough." He picked up the photo album and flipped through while I leaned over his shoulder. It seemed like a normal family album documenting good times with friends. He put it down and started in on the mail. I wondered if he'd let me look through the stuff, too? How could I ask and just seem bored and curious? Since Randy was actively working with the contents, I decided to bide my time. I wandered into the kitchen to figure out what to do for dinner.

I had my head stuck in the freezer and called over, "Hey, Randy, do we have a grill out back? Can we do kabobs?"

"No, ma'am. The smell might attract attention. We like to play it low-profile when possible at the safehouses. We can't risk calling any attention to this place. It's imperative no one figures out you're here."

26

After a lunch of falafels, tabbouleh, and hummus, I studied the books on the bookshelf. I stared out the windows. I considered doing my manicure again with a different color. What I really wanted to do was exercise. I sighed. If only the attack—Nope. Not going there. Fluffy bunny, non-scary thoughts only. I wandered over to the table and asked Randy if he'd mind my taking a look at the photo album.

"Help yourself." He pushed it over to me.

Sitting on the sofa, I did a quick scan from front to back to get a sense of the timeline, and then I started from the back to the front to try to pick up clues.

When Mom taught me how to draw as a little girl, she would encourage me to try to reproduce images from magazines and art books. In order to train my eye to take in the line and the detail of the shape and not try to draw a whole image at once, she would turn the image upside down, and I had to try to draw it as I saw it. I could only turn it right-side-up when I thought I was done.

I applied this technique to some of the puzzles Spyder had

given to me, too. Often, I'd pick up on the clue that cracked the mystery when I wasn't looking at the situation straight on. Sort of like gazing at stars through a telescope. Sometimes, if I shifted my eye's focus slightly to the side of a star, I could see a star's color and form more clearly. I had a feeling if I were to glean something from these photos, the "upside-down" or "soft focus" techniques were probably the ones that would work.

That's curious. I squinted at the last picture in the album. Moving over to the little desk, sitting near the bookshelves, I pulled out the magnifying glass I had seen earlier and re-examined the photo through the lens. *Very curious.*

Flipping the pages back and forth, putting my ideas together, hours passed, though it seemed mere minutes. I was pretty darned excited about what I thought I was seeing.

The clock on the wall behind Randy read four; I shuffled my bunny feet into the kitchen to put dinner together, making quick work of it. As soon as everything was ready and warming in the oven, I was headed back to the couch to triple-check those photos when my peripheral vision caught a flash of color heading toward the porch. I made out a man's green windbreaker —that wasn't an Iniquus uniform! My heartbeat took off at a sprint. I forgot all about Randy as adrenaline flash-flooded my body. The next thing I realized, I was crouched behind the kitchen counter with a gun in my hand, sweating and swearing. Peeking around the corner, I watched Randy standing at the window with his cell phone in his hand.

"Striker, we have a situation, sir. A guy is outside on the porch trying to get in…Yes, sir. I would like to, sir, but Lexi has my gun and belt in the kitchen… Yes, sir, locked and loaded… Sir, she sounds like she's in a lot of pain, like last night. She's not responding to my directives. It's probably not the best idea for me to go around and relieve her of the weapon right now."

Time passed.

Striker called from the garage, "Lexi, we've secured the perimeter. We're coming into the house. When the door opens, it will be Jack and me. We're coming to help you." By this point, the sweating had passed, and I was on to the shivering part of the cycle. Striker needn't worry that I'd shoot him; I couldn't hold the gun steady enough to aim.

Striker came into the kitchen slowly, crouched low. He stared at me until I held his eye contact. Gradually, he reached out his hand and took the gun from me and passed it back to Jack.

Striker laid me down on the floor and replayed last night's ministrations. Striker used warm water to dab away the salt.

"Thank you so much." My voice sounded like a jackhammer as my words stuttered past my chattering teeth. Randy held a blanket open to wrap around me. He helped Striker lift me over to the couch, where, once again, I shook and sobbed against Striker's broad shoulder. His arms wrapped supportively around me. I blew my nose and wiped my eyes on the Kleenexes Striker handed me. My eyelids sank shut as I listened to the murmur of conversation between Randy and Striker.

"Who's got the guy?" Randy asked.

"Gator and Axel," Striker said.

"What did he want?"

"Drunk and lost. He thought this might've been his house, but the key wasn't working for him." Jack snorted.

"And now?" Randy asked.

"Gator and Axel are tucking him into his bed—they have an address from his wallet. They wanted to make sure his vehicle ended up in the right driveway. Now, more interesting, how did Lexi get hold of your gun?" Striker reached over to pull the blanket up around my shoulders.

"Shit, sir, I'm not sure. My gun belt sat beside me on the

table. Lexi was on the other side of the living room, standing over there, and then something moved near me. I turned to see what was happening, and Lexi dove for the kitchen and pulled the gun from the holster lightning fast. She crouched down there." Randy pointed over to the kitchen. "Peeking around at the front door. I slid around the outside of the room to stay out of her range. When I got to the window, I saw the guy in a green jacket. At that point, I guess Lexi was dumping adrenaline. That's when I called you."

"Sorry." I yawned. "Instinct."

"No. Training. I can't imagine anyone *ever* getting a gun away from Randy. You must have had a pretty good teacher," Striker said.

"Stan, my dad's friend at the police department, Master Wang from the dry cleaner." I'd just keep mum about Spyder McGraw.

27

Striker crouched beside me, carefully picking up a strand of hair caught in my stitches. I blinked my eyes open. Banging and clattering in the kitchen punctuated the low conversation between the men.

"Hey, are you up to dinner?" Striker asked.

I pulled myself to sitting. "It's all in the oven. I need to get the fruit and tea together." I felt like I'd been performing in the center ring of a circus all day. It took just that one misstep to tumble me down from my high wire act. Thankfully, I had an Iniquus safety net under me; I watched my team moving easily around.

"The guys will take care of everything. Come on, let's get some food in you." Striker placed a steadying hand under my arm, walked me to the dining room, pulled out my chair, and tucked me under the table. Two chairs sat empty when everyone had gathered round; I did a quick inventory.

"Where are Deep and Blaze?" I asked.

"They're finishing up a capture. We're working overtime to

get our cases cleared up so we can concentrate on you." Striker wiped his mouth.

Focus on capturing the killer. I blinked as I struggled to push away the horrific thoughts bombarding my brain-space. I shoved them back into the recesses of my gray matter and slammed a barricade into place. I would not think about my case. Not yet. One adrenaline dump was enough for the day. I concentrated on chewing and swallowing. Mundane. Banal. Pedestrian thoughts. What was on TV? What should I cook tomorrow? Was I ready for another manicure?

We ate with little conversation until Striker considered Randy speculatively. "It was a quiet day until the excitement?"

"Nothing to report, sir," Randy replied.

"Did you make progress on our man?"

"I don't have anything taking me in any one direction, sir. I have a list of leads that need some eyes on. I'll show it to you after dinner."

"He can't have left the country. We have his passport. Did the phone records indicate anything?"

"Nada," Randy said.

I sat at the end of the table, pinching my lower lip to keep from smiling. The conversation stopped, and I lifted my head.

Striker was thrust back in his seat, arms crossed over his chest, eyes narrowed. "Lexi, what do you know about this?"

"Is your guy's name Dennis Peterson?" I asked in my sweet-young-thing voice and batted my eyelashes.

Striker raised a questioning brow at Randy, who shook his head ever so slightly at Striker—he hadn't given me the name. Striker turned back to me and cleared his throat. "Yes, it is. And do you know where I can find Mr. Peterson?"

"Not for sure, but I know where I'd start."

"Tampon box?" He smirked.

My lips raised in a sardonic bow. "I think he's at his boyfriend's vacation house."

"Peterson has a boyfriend?" Striker leaned forward.

"I believe so." I nodded.

"How do you know this guy?"

"I don't." I took a bite of fruit.

Striker balanced his elbows on the table and laced his fingers. His eyes narrowed slightly; I wondered what he was thinking. He was very closed off. Not a lot of "tells" to give me a hint.

"How about a name and address for the boyfriend?" he asked.

"His name is Jason Clemmons. His lake house address is 3564 North Shore Drive." I rubbed my palms down my pants. Gah! I hoped I was right about this.

Striker whipped out his cell phone. "It's Striker. I need you to check an address for me. I need the owners of 3564 North Shore Drive. And a quick search on a Jason Clemmons." He caught my eye. "Any middle name?"

I shrugged.

After Striker hung up, I gave him a playful smile. "If I'm right, do I get another prize?"

The cell phone rang before he could answer me; Striker held up a finger for me to wait while he listened to the other end and then tapped it back off.

"A Catherine and Jason Clemmons own that address, Lexi. If this guy is in the house, you will definitely get a prize. How'd you come up with this information?"

"Randy told me it would be okay if I peeked at the photo album—I got it from the pictures."

Striker reached over to the buffet, where the album jutted out from the brown box, and flipped through the photos. I shuffled back to the living room and picked up the remote to turn on Comedy Central—something ridiculous and light.

I found if I put up the TV volume a little higher than comfortable, it helped to drown out my inner dialogue. The men must have thought I had a hearing deficit because ever since I started using this technique, they gesticulated a lot, miming stuff out for me. Maybe they thought it had something to do with my head injury. Didn't matter. Truth be told, it was pretty comical.

After a few minutes, Striker came and sat beside me, album in hand. "Can I get you to go through this with me?" His voice rose over the Daily Show.

"Sure." I remoted the TV off and curled up beside him, pulling half of the album into my lap. Sitting this close, I could smell Striker's cologne, spicy and warm on his skin; the steel of his thigh muscles felt solid beside me. Somehow this seemed more intimate than sleeping with him had. I needed to make sure I wasn't sending him the wrong signals. I twisted my wedding rings back and forth on my finger and jostled around until we weren't touching anymore.

"Lexi, I don't understand how you got the names, the relationship, or the address from these photos." He settled into the cushion and crossed an ankle over his knee to support the opened album.

Holy crap, what had I done? Now I was going to have to walk Striker through my thought process. Would he think I was just observant? Chalk up the information I gave him to a bored analytic mind? I cleared my throat. "Uh, maybe that's because you're looking at the pictures from front to back. I started with the photos from back to front. See?" I flipped the album forward and pointed at the last picture. "This is where I began to understand."

Striker leaned closer to the photograph of two men standing

in front of a nighttime campfire, near arms around each other's shoulders, outer arms outstretched with beers in their hands, both grinning broadly at the camera. The angle of the photo made me think the camera was propped on something low. A rock? I was pretty sure the men had set the photo timer and were alone. But I decided to keep those kinds of details to myself. Since I was diving in, I should be careful it was a surface dive—too many ways to get hurt if I went in too deep.

Striker put his finger on Jason's image. "And you think these guys are boyfriends?"

"Not at first," I said. "But then I asked Randy."

"Asked him what?" Striker glanced back to where Randy leaned against the kitchen counter.

"I said, 'Randy, let's say you and your buddy were standing side-by-side drinking beers. Out of the blue, a high-priced porn star fell down on all fours in front of you, moaning, and grinding.'" I stopped to grin up at Striker; I was teasing him by repeating last night's ribald joke back to him. He pursed his lips and shook his head at me. Okay, maybe I wasn't funny. I knew he regretted saying that to me. What had made him lower his guard last night? The question still bothered me.

I gave Striker a half-smile, then finished my story. "I said, 'let's pretend this was erotic to you, and you got an erection. Would you drape your arm around your buddy's shoulders and enjoy the moment?'"

The men in the kitchen snorted. Striker seemed to be biting down hard for control.

"And?" he finally managed.

"And, he—" I started.

"I said, 'I'd rather burn in hell, ma'am,'" Randy cut in while the other men hooted with laughter.

Striker stared down at the picture, and this time I handed

Striker the magnifying glass and traced my finger over the man's hard-on.

Striker bent over the picture, studying it closely, then nodded. "Okay, go on."

"I decided I should figure out who these two men are, or if they had other photo connections besides this one." I motioned toward the photo. "If you flip through the pages, you'll notice these two men never show up in the same photo at any other time. Only here in the last picture. But there are other photos connecting them."

Striker's brows came together. Studious. Serious. His eyes shone keen and intelligent. He tapped at his lower lip, a body-language "tell" that he was excited about what he was hearing.

I itched to know what this guy did to have an agency hire Iniquus to do the capture. He looked like he belonged in an L.L. Bean catalog—just a sportsman who loved the outdoors in some pictures, a corporate executive schmoozing and living the good life in others. His face was open and friendly, his body stance confident. Maybe some kind of Ponzi scheme? Or insider trading? Shit, for all I knew, he trafficked child-porn.

"Go on." Striker's voice refocused me.

"I came by their names through this series of photos from the cruise. Look at these two women. This woman in the green dress's nametag says Catherine Clemmons. Look at her rings. Do you see the pattern?" I handed back the magnifying glass.

Striker pulled the album further into his lap and stared down at the eight-by-ten picture from the cruise ship cocktail hour. He wasn't focused on Catherine, though. His gaze was glued to the other woman. She was a tall, curvaceous Latina with a curtain of silky black hair, hanging nearly to her waist. Her little white dress accented her tan and her white teeth as she laughed, a martini gracefully held in her left hand. On her dress, the name tag read, "Lynda."

Striker knew this woman. I'd bet almost anything this was the Lynda who had gone missing. Striker wore that same braced posture he affected every time she came up in conversation—the one screaming that he was personally invested. His wife? His girlfriend? Striker was law enforcement, did Psycho target someone for Iniquus as well as the agencies they served?

When I knew Striker back in my Alex days, he wasn't in a meaningful relationship. That could have changed; it was a long time ago. Could someone have become significant enough for the killer to set his sights on her? That just didn't seem right to me. Besides, there was a man, standing just out of the camera frame, who's hand rested intimately on her low-back—the guy was too short to be Striker—and Striker didn't seem jealous of him.

The more I tried to sense a tie between the killer and Lynda, the more I realized that was completely wrong. This must be a different case—nothing to do with PSycho. When I reached my conclusion, relief washed over me. Thinking that what had happened to me might have happened to two other women—and they could hurt be and bleeding with no support, or worse—had been weighing heavily on me. I let those images go. Thank god. But if this was Lynda, who was Cammy?

Striker moved the book back to rest between our two laps. "Okay, go on," he said.

I decided not to push for information. Yet. "Now, turn the page to this one. Do you recognize him?" I was having trouble repositioning myself where I could be comfortable and see the album but not touch Striker. Striker shot me a funny kind of questioning expression then shifted to a different angle, solving the problem. "He's the guy on the left of the beer photo," I said. "You can make out this man's tag and the Jaso— I assume 'Jason.' Here in this other photo, we see him again. This time he's holding hands with a woman whose face and body aren't in the picture. Now, here's the ring, and she's standing close to him, the green of her dress is just showing at the edge. Look at the pattern on the ring on his left hand—it's the same."

"That's how you got the boyfriend's name Jason Clemmons."

"I assume this isn't the guy you want because it's not his photo album. The other couple is the main subject in the other photos. I came up with Peterson's name the same way, by putting some photo puzzle pieces together, see?" I flipped through the photos pointing out the clues I used.

Striker smiled. "Amazing. Very clever. I'm impressed."

I shifted around uncomfortably. Too clever? Couldn't any girl—bored out of her mind—sit down and figure this out? *Brush it off, Lexi. Make this seem like child's play.* "Yeah, well, Nancy Drew was an early heroine of mine, and I've always loved picture puzzles."

"How did you come up with the address?" he asked.

I turned the pages back to the picture of the two men. "In this picture, there's a rock with a cleat on it. That told me they were near water large enough and deep enough for boating. Now, let your eye go up. Do you see the tree with a birdhouse?" I flipped back a few pages. "Okay, in this picture of Peterson standing next to the tree, follow the branch with the dead deer hanging from it; here's the birdhouse," I pointed and said, "Now, look at the top left—the little flag with the dogwood and magnolia flowers."

Striker brushed against my shoulder as he leaned over the photo with the magnifying glass. "Yup."

I turned the pages almost to the beginning. "Look at this picture of the golden retriever. See the same flag on the upper right-hand corner? Can you read what's visible on the bottom left?" My finger trailed down to the left-hand corner where a driveway sign stood sentinel. With the magnifying glass, Striker said, "Shore Good to See You! The Clemmons 3465 North Shore Drive."

"I thought to myself, if I were hiding, I'd want to go to a place that felt safe, a place that had little traffic, you know, mostly secluded like this house is. I wouldn't want to stay with any friends or relatives. That would make it too easy to track me down. If this guy is having a secret affair with Jason Clemmons, then hunkering down at his lake house might be the way to go. Anyway, that's my theory."

"It's quite a theory." Striker's cell rang. "Striker." He listened, locking me in place with his eyes. After disconnecting, he said, "It appears the Clemmons are out of the country for a while. Mr. Clemmons works for a German company, and according to the housekeeper, they'll be in Europe while he oversees a project. That would free up their vacation house."

The men listened from the kitchen table. Gator and Axel had come in while I walked Striker through the pictures and were eating in silence.

Striker joined them. "It's a reasonable theory. I think this house deserves a visit, gentlemen."

28

Wrapped in a comforter, I ended up sleeping on the couch. I awoke to frost painted windows, looking like silver feathers. Blaze sat at the table, filling out paper-work, with a coffee mug in front of him.

Striker came in, acknowledged him with a nod, and strode over to me. "Why are you down here?" He squatted beside me. "Is everything okay?"

I gave a noisy yawn and pushed to sitting. "I thought Blaze would be lonely all by himself, so I decided to keep him company." Yeah, really I had come running down the stairs just after midnight, freaked out from a nightmare I couldn't remember once my eyes popped open.

"I see," Striker said.

"So? Did you catch the bad guy?" I gripped Striker's forearm with anticipation. Trepidation. I hoped I was right. Why though? Because I wanted this case off their shelf, so they could go full force after the killer? Or did I want to impress Striker as much as he had always impressed me?

Hell in a Handbasket, my inner-self sent the warning, and I sat contritely.

Chastened.

I pulled my brows together in a scowl. I hadn't done anything, said anything, thought anything wrong. Why should I feel guilty?

"We found our man in bed with a bottle of scotch, a fat cigar, and the Washington Post. He's being fingerprinted as we speak." Striker pushed to standing and reached for my hand to help me up.

"Where's everyone else?" I glanced toward the garage door.

"They went home to catch some shut-eye before we meet later. Which's what I'm going to do, too. I'll be upstairs if you need me. Jack's coming in to relieve Blaze."

I followed along behind him as he walked to the stairs, hoping he'd share some details from the capture. I still wanted to know what the guy had done wrong. Striker stopped with his foot resting on the first tread and turned to me, lowering his voice so only I could hear.

"You're a curious woman, Lexi Sobado. I believe you have a lot of secrets. And I think those secrets might be the key to how you ended up in the middle of this mess." He stared down at me. "I want you to consider your situation and if you're willing to work openly with us or not. That means *full* disclosure. You'll share everything that might help us get this guy." His clipped tone held none of his earlier warmth, commander-mode. "I don't see us being much help to you if you decide to keep things to yourself, and we're left chasing down the wrong intelligence." He crossed his arms authoritatively over his broad chest as he scrutinized me.

I curled my lips in to hold back the words wanting to spring forth. The move felt defiant to me. I didn't like Striker's tone or stance. I wouldn't let him intimidate me.

"Lexi, I can't force you to trust us. I'm just hoping you will." He paused. "I don't think you want to work through this on your own. What do you think?"

I didn't know what to think beyond desperately wanting to talk to Spyder. "I think you owe me a prize." I worked up an innocent fluffy-bunny smile.

Striker wrapped an arm around my neck, gave me a kiss on the top of my forehead, and walked me over to the garage. He cracked the door, reached inside, and pulled out a guitar case.

"Oh!" I said as a grin spread across my face. "How did you know?" I scooped it into my hands.

"I have some sources." Striker chuckled, obviously pleased with my reaction. "I'm gonna hit the rack. I'll be down for lunch. What grandma is Tuesday?" he asked, heading for the stairs.

"Biji—she's from Punjab, India."

I went to the kitchen. "Is it you, me, and Jack for breakfast this morning?" I asked Blaze.

"Gator has to run by Headquarters and pick up a file before he heads back to the field. He'll be here to eat at seven." Blaze shifted the papers around in front of him.

I put a pot of water on to boil while I peeled some potatoes and chopped up onion, ginger, and green chili, making the filling for the aloo prata.

At seven on the dot, the phone rang, announcing the arrival of a team member. Though two cars motored up the drive, Jack and Gator came in together. "Goodness gracious, ma'am. I could smell that all the way outside—sure do smell good."

"I made a traditional breakfast bread from Punjab India."

"I was pretty sure it weren't grits." He pulled out a seat for me. Blaze had already cleared his stuff away and put the food on the table with butter and vegetables pickled with mustard seeds. I spooned yogurt into our bowls.

"Okay, guys. I made what I usually eat on Tuesdays for breakfast. It's going to be different from what you're used to, so I won't be offended if it's not to your liking." I demonstrated how to dollop some butter into the center for dipping and how to take the smallest amount of the intensely flavored pickled vegetables and fold them into the bread.

"Have you got any more puzzles to work on today?" I asked as we ate. I liked the diversion of a good puzzle.

"Not right now," Jack said.

That breakfast was the highlight of my day. Jack put his nose into his work files until Striker woke up. I fixed lunch. We ate it. I strummed at my guitar. I made samosas and Darjeeling tea for three o'clock tea time. I spent some time staring out the window, some time flipping through the TV channels, and some time figuring out how to handle what Striker had said to me about my secrets. But I had to do that in small snippets. When I felt anxiety entwining with my thoughts, I pushed those ideas aside and reached for the safety of anything that would numb my emotions. Day three in my safe house and I still aimed for an adrenaline-free day.

Dinner turned out "okay." Biji would never have served it. Biji had a Tandoor oven; her chicken was always falling-off-the-bone tender—every bite rich with spice. The lentil soup and vegetables tasted good, though. Randy had brought tangerines, and that made a sweet ending to the meal. While we were eating, Deep asked how I learned to cook. I told them about the Kitchen Grandmas.

"Which day belongs to your Italian grandmother?" Deep asked.

"Thursday. Why?"

"Tomorrow's my birthday, and I always miss my Nona's manicotti when my birthday comes around."

"Normally, Wednesday is Nana Kate, and you'd get the all-American fare, but I don't think it's breaking a rule to switch the two. Anything else you'd like me to make other than the manicotti?"

Deep grinned. "Surprise me."

Jack swallowed his food, then said, "Sounds like a lot of work to learn five different cultures. How did you get through your homework?"

I laughed. "Everything I did was homework. I was unschooled."

"Is that like homeschooling?" Deep asked.

"Yeah, just less organized." I stood up and started to clear the table. The men got up around me.

Blaze took the dishes from my hands. "We'll handle the KP, ma'am."

I wandered into the living area. The house was built, I'd guessed, around 1930. Someone had obviously updated the inside. The downstairs was now a great room. Coming in from the garage, you'd find a laundry room to the left and a bathroom to the right. The modest-sized kitchen, with all the surfaces in easy reach, made cooking easy. A raised breakfast bar with stools separated the kitchen from the living room and dining room areas. By taking out the downstairs walls and allowing it all to be one room, it made the small space seem both intimate and spacious. Even with seven large men, I didn't feel like we got under each other's feet.

The furniture fabrics were earth-toned with a lot of auburn and chocolates accented by robin's egg blue. A decidedly Crate and Barrel character defined this room. Good-quality, sturdy furnishings filled the space. Not fancy. Livable. Underfoot, beige carpet stretched from wall to wall in the living room and hall; in the dining room, the designer chose wood.

I shuffled my bunny slippers over to the couch and started picking at my guitar. It surprised me when the men gathered around to join in. I took a few requests. Deep had a beautiful voice, and our voices blended well when we tried a few songs. Randy knew a lot of the songs I had learned at the Sobados'.

Randy came from El Salvador. He had Latino dark coloration. I'd think he would have a name reflecting his culture and not something that sounded like a naughty English school-boy. I bet his call name proved particularly effective. No one would put the two together.

As we sang, and I played, Striker stood aloof off to the side, leaning against the wall, watching. He looked at ease to the casual eye, but he didn't fool me. This man was taking my measure. I wondered what he thought of me. Striker hadn't confronted me again about my secrets. He let me marinate in my anxiety.

After a while, I yawned, stretched, and told the guys I was beat. Taking a book off the shelf—*Pride and Prejudice,* an old friend—I went to clean myself up for bed. I fell into a deep sleep just as Mr. Darcy and Elizabeth Bennett made each other's acquaintance at the ball. My book smooshed into the pillow under my head as my eyes closed. Barely awake, I heard soft footsteps come into my room. Striker pulled the novel from under my head, tucked my covers up to my chin, and turned off my light, perhaps hoping that at least for tonight, the nightmares would be held at bay.

29

Sounds outside my door brought me awake again around two in the morning, dragging me out of my crazy dream. In my dream, a giant blew magical bubbles, trapping me inside. I'd float toward the sun, but then my bubble would pop, and I'd fall back to the ground. Just before I hit down, another bubble caught me up. This had been going on for some time. I was relieved to have woken up. Besides, I had to use the bathroom.

I stumbled out of bed and down the hall, pushing hair out of my half-closed eyes. I opened the door to the bathroom, and there stood Striker, looking like a model for Bowflex. Toothbrush in hand…wet hair, freshly showered. Naked. My eyes traveled down his muscular body and stopped at his family jewels. I felt a little frown line form between my eyes as I focused.

"Lexi, I'll be done in a minute." Striker seemed unabashed.

"Okay."

"Lexi?"

"Oh! I'm sorry to barge in on you…" My voice trailed off as I did some more looking, the door wide open, my hand resting on the knob.

"Lexi, you're staring."

"Yes, it's rude to stare," I stuttered, feeling moronic. Flushing painfully. "It's just, I've never actually seen a real penis before. You know, a man's penis. I've seen lots of little boy penises from changing diapers and babysitting." Shut up! Stop talking!

"You're married." Striker's voice sounded strangled—probably choking back laughter.

This was ridiculous. Why couldn't I move? "Yes, yes. Married," I continued, my words catching in my throat because as I watched, it started to grow! My mouth gaped.

"Lexi?" Striker put his toothbrush away in the holder and reached for a towel.

"Wow!" Who knew they got *so* big? It was a little frightening. In that moment, I feverishly wished I'd seen Angel's penis. Then this would be a non-event. I wouldn't be so shocked. I'd just say, "Excuse me," and shut the damned door. Instead, I stood like an idiot with my eyes held wide and my brows up in my hairline. "You could make a balloon animal with that!" my mouth said before I could stop it.

Striker was out and out laughing at me now as he wrapped a towel around his waist.

I looked at him, startled. I shook my head. "Chablis didn't prepare me. She said white men were smaller." It sounded accusatory like it was his fault he was well-endowed.

Striker took me by the elbow and propelled me out of the bathroom to the hall. He went into his room, removed the towel, pulled on a pair of boxer briefs, arranged himself, and dressed in gray sweats. He came back out and guided me down the stairs to the kitchen. That felt better, safe, and non-sexual. Thank god. I was still a little in shock.

Striker poured milk into a large glass measuring cup. He put it into the microwave and punched the buttons. While the milk heated, he took two green mugs out of the cabinet and emptied hot chocolate packets into each. I perched on a stool, elbows on the counter, head balanced against my clasped hands, looking down at the surface. I was reviewing the bathroom scene. Good god, this felt awkward, especially sitting here in silence under the bright lights.

Striker poured the hot milk into the mugs, pushed mine over to me, and handed me a spoon. All of my attention went to stirring in the powder. When I dared to sneak a peek at Striker's expression, I found bemused assessment. I could almost read the "this is going to be good" thoughts in his head.

Finally, he said, "Okay. Let me try to understand what happened." His tone invited confidence.

My focus went to blowing on the hot cocoa.

"You are married, right?"

I nodded, not trusting my voice.

"To a man?"

I quickly looked up. I saw mirth dancing in his eyes, though the rest of his face remained impassive. I dropped my gaze again. "You know I married Angel Sobado. He's an Army Ranger."

"Reviewing the facts from the beginning. Have you and Angel had sex?"

Ugh. Way, way too personal! But I had compared the man's erection to a balloon animal, so I guessed I did owe him some sort of an explanation. "No, we haven't." My memory flickered back to my conversation with Miriam Laugherty. Angel would correct that as soon as he got home. My face turned what I assumed to be a bright tomato-red.

"Do you want to explain?"

I sighed heavily. "Okay. Here it is in a nutshell. Angel and I only knew each other for three weeks when we got married. We fell in love, pretty much at first sight, and we spent a lot of time holding hands and kissing and stuff. But, his great aunt, my Abuela Rosa, had her eye on us. His family is from Puerto Rico —devout Catholics, or at least the women are. Angel's family wanted him to marry a 'good Catholic girl.'"

"You're Catholic?" Striker stirred his cocoa slowly, his focus never wavering from my face. It was unnerving.

I pursed my lips and shook my head.

"Then you fit the bill because of the 'good' part of that phrase. I'm assuming that means virgin?"

"Uhm."

"Go on," Striker said. "Sorry to interrupt your story."

"I guess I got so involved in life and Mom's illness and everything. I didn't date much. Angel's the first guy I had a real relationship with." I cleared my throat. "We decided to get married before he shipped out again. Because of the paperwork, we couldn't make our vows until the afternoon before he left. We went to the Justice of the Peace in the town he deployed from." I pulled in a deep breath and plunged on. "All of his army buddies from his unit stayed in the area since they would ship out together. The guys found out we planned to get married, and when we came out of the courthouse, we found them gathered to congratulate us. They wanted to take us out for dinner to celebrate. I guess there was some drinking involved for the men— okay, a lot of drinking involved for the men. When they toasted, they all had to drink."

"And Angel got soused?"

"In the end, they had to carry Angel back to our hotel room and help me get him undressed. Only they stopped at his briefs.

We tucked him in, and then in the morning, they came to roust him out so he wouldn't be AWOL."

"I bet that was fun." Striker laughed.

"What? The morning? It included a lot of cussing, wrestling to get Angel into a cold shower, some Advil, and lots of black coffee. Voila, my wedding night."

"You didn't drink?"

"I'm not twenty-one."

"Right. This poor guy went off to war without losing his virginity?" Striker's brow creased. Was that pity for Angel?

"He had sex when he was fourteen. The family didn't care so much about the boys' purity, just the girls'."

"Doesn't seem fair," he said.

I pushed my hair back from my face, tucking the strands behind my ears. Striker was right—that really wasn't at all fair. "Anyway, that's how I came to find myself in the position of being a virgin wife." Phew. I was glad to have the explanation over with.

Striker thought about this for a minute. "Okay, I have a grasp on the never-having-seen-a-man's-penis business. Now, would you please explain Chablis?"

Okay, not completely over with. "Chablis was one of my unschooling teachers at the apartments." I shrugged.

"Chablis was supposed to teach you about men?"

"Chablis was supposed to teach me about sex." I edged a thigh off the stool and leaned my elbow onto the counter. "Chablis worked as a hooker. She lived with her aunt," I explained. "See, her aunt usually took care of Chablis's three kids at night, but her aunt's friend had to have an operation. When her aunt went to help out, Chablis didn't have anyone to watch her kids while she turned tricks. For two weeks, the kids stayed with me."

"And, in return, you got sex lessons? Or sex?" His eyes had widened, his eyebrows lifted.

I wrinkled my nose and pushed my un-tasted cocoa to the side. "I was learning how to be good at sex, so when I had a boyfriend or a husband that, you know." I shrugged. "I'd be able to make him happy."

Striker shook his head and looked at me appalled—or maybe that was disbelief? Hard to tell, shocked, for sure. Huh. I wondered why. As he rubbed his forehead with his fingers, I reached for my mug, took a sip, and burned my tongue.

"Were these lessons theoretical or practical?" Striker finally managed.

"Mostly practical." Did Striker have to look at me like I'd sprouted horns? This wasn't all that strange, was it? Chablis was just an apartment mentor. "She had a black dildo she would demonstrate the things on, and she gave me a purple one, so I could practice the techniques," I said matter-of-factly. Striker put his hands on his knees as he bent over laughing, gasping for air.

"It's not funny!" I looked at him, hurt, mortified.

"And the purple dildo you practiced on," Striker came back upright, "didn't prepare you for the bathroom scene?"

I searched my memory. "It was much smaller and thinner, and there was less…well, anyway, I learned her techniques on something smaller, and now I'm really concerned." I threw my arms up in the air and let them flop back down. "Here, I thought I had prepared for the physical part of married life, and now I'm a little freaked out."

Striker stood there, tears running down his face; his body shook in silent laughter. "Oh, my god," he gulped. "Oh, my god." He came around the counter, wrapped me in an affectionate arm, and planted a kiss on the top of my head. "Chica, you're like a surprise party. I never know what's going to come out of that head of yours next." He dropped his arm. "So, tell me about Chablis. Was that really her name?"

"Her work persona name. She said she picked it because she was so sweet and intoxicating."

30

I snuggled back in my bed. Striker had sat downstairs talking to me until my jangled nerves were sufficiently soothed. That was nice of him. He was a good guy. I had put the earlier bathroom images and the first part of my conversation with Striker to the side. I'd give those thoughts some distance in time and space before I took them out for re-examination. I found the whole scene mortifying.

What was a girl to think about in the middle of the night but all the darned creaking and groaning sounds the house was making? Warm and sleepy was replaced with stiff and edgy. A branch outside my window, one looking all too much like a bony hand, scratched at the glass as the tree swayed in the breeze. My mind conjured up the nightmarish reactions I had after reading a Stephen King novel. I was scaring the bejeezus out of myself. I grabbed my pillow and hot-footed my way into Striker's room, diving under the covers.

Striker rolled toward me. "Heebie-jeebies?"

I peeked up at him. "Skeletal hands of the undead."

"Lexi." He reached out, pulled the pillow from over my

head, and moved it to the side. "I don't know you well. But from what I've learned here at the house, you seem to be a mature and rational person who's seen a lot of life and knows it can be messy." He shifted to lean on an elbow and gazed down at me in the dim moonlight gleaming through his window. He gently tugged the strands of hair caught in my stitches and tucked them behind my ear. "You are crazy-smart, and you have an enormous bag of tricks. Then you climb under my covers, trembling over the monsters under your bed. Putting these two sides of you together is pretty confusing." He scanned my face. "Can you tell me what gives?"

I swallowed audibly. Striker's eyes, warmed with kindness, felt sincere to me, and for some reason, this made tears pool in the corners of my eyes and cling to my lashes. I struggled to find the words to explain myself. My voice came out low-pitched and private like I was sitting in the confessional at St. Edwards. "I'm afraid—really deep down afraid. This is the weakest point of my life." A tear dripped, and Striker brushed it from my cheek with light fingers. I drew in a shaky breath. "A week ago, I thought of myself as strong and powerful. I could defend myself physically and mentally against the big bad wolves, you know? I trained hard to be capable and independent. Then one night—" I gestured in a sweeping motion. "I can't get hold of my head. I don't know when I'll be able to stand on my own two feet or when I'm going to be on my knees begging for relief. I don't know when I can have my own emotions or when adrenaline is going to put me in the throes of terror. I have no control of my brain or my safety. Even with you and your men around me, I feel incredibly alone and vulnerable. I'm scared." My chattering teeth punctuated my words.

Striker was dressed in a big t-shirt and sweat pants. He was close enough now that his breath brushed over my skin. He rubbed his hand up and down my arm soothingly while he took a minute to think. "Lexi, I've never seen anyone, in all my time doing this sort of thing, handle everything with as much grace and courage. Give yourself a break." He paused. "We have a good team here. We're going to get the guy. Your doctors believe this is all going to go away eventually, right?"

"That's what they say. There's just no timeline."

Striker nodded, his lips pressed tightly together. "I think, for right now, if you feel safer sleeping in my bed with me, and this is where you can get a good night's rest, then that's what you should do. We need you healthy."

"You're okay with that?" Huh. Conflict roiled in my head. I guessed being in here—making plans for this to be my bed too— felt immoral. Not that Striker wasn't a perfect gentleman, or I had any thoughts beyond my safety. Still, if anyone knew, they'd judge me harshly. "What about your wife? Or your girlfriend? Wouldn't this cause problems?"

"I'm not married or involved with anyone right now."

I fell silent.

"What?" Striker asked.

"I'm weighing this."

"And?"

"On the one hand, being in here feels safe. It would be a relief for me and my head to get a solid night's rest. I think I could sleep if I stayed with you. On the other hand, I don't want anyone to think I'm a bad wife." There, I'd just lay my thoughts on the line.

"Since I'm the only one who knows what bed you're sleeping in, I wouldn't worry about your reputation. You've already deduced I'm not going to make a move on you."

"Yes, but I've seen you naked!"

Striker chuckled softly. "And I've felt you up twice—I can be mature about this if you can."

I loved planning dinner for that night.

Getting ready to celebrate Deep took up time and brain space. Both good things here at the safehouse. I was still working on my fluffy-bunny plan. Diversion was the key.

Before noon, I made some hoagies up for lunch using Italian meats and cheeses, with pesto and tapenade spread on the rolls. I set them in the fridge, ready for the changing of the guard when Striker and Gator would come in.

Opening the oven, I peeked in to see how the tomatoes were coming for the manicotti sauce, and the aroma filled the house. I pulled a bowl from the cupboard and started in on the birthday cake—a coffee-flavored rum cake.

Striker and Gator walked in as I put lunch on the table, and we all sat down. As we ate, the men talked about the news from Iniquus and some of the files they still had open. The conversation turned to the cake we could now smell baking.

"Which Kitchen Grandma taught you this?" asked Striker.

"The cake recipe belongs to Nona Sophia. The bull's eye decoration I'm working on, I learned from Nana Kate. She's a Wilton cake decorating pro." I took a sip of iced tea. "In my neighborhood, where I'm living now, I loved to make the cakes for the kids' birthdays. I got to design a theme cake and go over and do a few magic tricks to entertain them." I sounded wistful as my mind wandered homeward. Not good. I desperately searched for a safer subject where I could rest my thoughts.

"Detective Murphy said you were good at magic. Would you show us something?" Striker asked.

"Sure." I jumped up from the table, grateful for the distraction. Let me see, something complicated, so it has my full attention. Spyder McGraw taught me to do magic. I learned sleight-of-hand tricks—simple at first, then really cool stuff that made mouths gape, and my audience yammer for an explanation. Spyder needed me to be dexterous with misdirection and sleight of hand so I could use those skills in the field. I practiced in front of Mom all the time. Magic took her mind off her pain. Dad had me do tricks for his friends at work. They'd slap me on the back and tell me I freaked them out. That made me proud.

I asked the men to stand in a circle with me. I turned to Striker. "Do you carry a wallet or identification?"

"Yes."

"May I see?"

They each pulled their IDs from their pockets, so I saw where they were. "Hmm. This doesn't make sense to me." I glanced around at the men, who watched me closely, trying to catch me at whatever I was about to do. I tapped my chin with my index finger as if I were thinking hard.

"Let me get this straight. We have four people in our circle. The names of the people are Lexi, Striker, Axel, and Gator. I think you men are trying to pull the wool over my eyes. You told me your names, but that doesn't work out. I know for a fact the only one in this circle without an I.D. is someone named Lexi." I held out my hand to Axel. "How do you do, Gator?" I shook his hand, then I held out my hand to Striker. "How do you do, Axel?" We shook hands. I turned to Gator on my left and said, "Hi, my name is Striker, and you must be Lexi since you're the only one without I.D." Gator shook my hand. They squinted at me.

"Go ahead, Lexi," I said to Gator, "check your pockets." Gator reached in to find nothing but an empty pocket.

"And you, Gator?" I asked Axel. Axel reached in his left pocket—empty. He reached into his right pocket and found Gator's wallet and I.D.

I turned to Striker. "And you, Axel?" He reached into his left pocket and pulled out Axel's I.D. He reached into his right pocket and pulled out a silver money clip and gold credit card holder. Striker opened the card case to show me his credit cards; they had Axel's correct name on them. I reached into my lounge pants' pockets. The left had an I.D. that read Gavin Rheas, and the right pocket had Axel's silver cardholder; the cards inside were issued to Gavin.

"What?" Gator hollered, jumping backward like he'd been bit by a snake. He scrubbed his hands through his hair. "That's just freaky! Oh, man. I'm all freaked out! How'd you do that? I was watching you the whole time. You're standing three inches from me. I didn't see anything. I didn't feel anything. Freaking insane, man. Oh, my gawd!"

Axel smiled broadly. "How did you do it?"

"Magic." I lifted my hands and wiggled my fingers like an illusionist conjuring a rabbit from a hat, smiling broadly. I *loved* to freak people out.

Striker narrowed his eyes and shook his head slowly from side to side. "At some point, you'll stop surprising me—I'll be ready for any damn thing you say or do."

"Aw. What fun would that be?" I asked.

"None, I guess. Is that from a Kitchen Grandma? Or someone else from your apartment building?"

"Another mentor." The stove dinged. Saved by the birthday cake. I scooted into the kitchen while the men got all of their things back in the right person's pockets.

Striker and Axel headed out for a mission.

I headed back into the kitchen. By the time I popped the

manicotti pan in the oven, the rhythm in my head was beating so hard my temples throbbed under my fingers. I needed to go lie down. I washed my hands and was reaching for a towel when the world tilted. The next thing I knew, Gator was carrying me to the sofa where he lay me gently down.

"Sorry," I murmured, eyes shut.

"You're okay, ma'am. I git a hundred points, now I'm in the lead."

"What?" I peeked at Gator from under my hands. He was squatting by my side, unfolding a blanket.

"We have a little contest going. Different points for different saves when you get vertigo. The most points go to a full catch." He covered me up.

"Does Striker know about this?"

Gator shrugged. "I'm not sure, ma'am."

"Doesn't this game encourage people to wait 'til I'm about to hit the floor?"

Gator shot me a good ol' boy grin. "Nah, we wouldn't let no harm come to you. We like you too much." He waggled a finger at me. "Now, that might not be true if you turned out to be a pain in the rear or your cooking weren't so good."

"Mmm, I'll try to keep that in mind."

31

The whisper of a hushed conversation tickled me awake. All seven of the Save-Lexi Team had assembled in the dining room. Someone had set the table, and they were deep in conversation about Iniquus business. I went upstairs to change my clothes and pull a brush through my hair. Coming back down, I gave a smile and a wave to everyone. I went into the kitchen and removed the antipasto and a platter of melon wedges wrapped in prosciutto from the fridge. Gator came up behind me and lifted the dishes from my hands to take them over to the table.

"Gator, are you helping me with those trays because you're a gentleman? Or are you afraid I'll pass out, and your dinner will roll across the floor?" I teased.

Gator grinned down at me. "Little bit of both, ma'am."

Deep leaned his head back and sniffed the air. "It smells like Mama's kitchen. *Grazie.*"

"*Buon compleano,* Deep."

As we all sat down, the men talked excitedly about a case they just finished. I knew Deep had been following up on the

Psycho leads pouring in from all the news attention. But I didn't ask for details, and he didn't tell me anything, thank god.

Gator, a natural-born storyteller, regaled us with some outrageously tall tales about missions he and Deep had been on together over the years. My eyes were streaming from laughing so hard. I gripped at the stitch in my side. When Gator finished telling a particularly amazing tale of do-or-die, he told the other men. "That weren't nothing compared to what I done seen today."

Everyone grew quiet, attention focused. And Gator told the story of my magic trick. It sounded incredible in the retelling—even I was impressed. The guys loudly demanded that I perform the trick again.

I held my hands up. "Sorry. I only do my tricks once. If you can't figure it out the first time, I'm not going to give you a second shot."

"Okay then," Deep said, "How about a different trick?"

I tipped my head and considered him. I didn't have a setup, so the options at my disposal were pretty slim. Hmm, hmm, hmm. "To celebrate your birthday, I guess I will do a little magic." I went over to the buffet and pulled out a plain white envelope. I went to the bookshelf and pulled out a book, then moved back to my seat. I passed the envelope around the table.

"Plain white envelope. Would everyone agree?"

All the heads nodded.

"Someone, please hand it to the birthday boy. Deep, I'd like you to inspect the envelope one more time, and make sure there's nothing in it and nothing unusual about it. If you agree, I want you to lick the tab and seal it, then put it under your bottom."

Deep followed my instructions.

"Don't let anyone touch the envelope, Deep," I warned.

"You have my word, ma'am."

"Now, I think we should read something to Deep. Sometimes, when I need direction, I like to open a random book, turn to a page haphazardly, and let the mystic unknown direct me to a passage that will give me good counsel. Why don't I give this book to you, Jack, you can do the honors of opening it up and reading a paragraph, so we can all hear some words of wisdom directed toward Deep's upcoming year."

Jack opened the book and read, "The storm rose wildly and pulled from the garden all of the beautifully petaled flowers. Seeing the devastation, strangers, from their goodness, entered the garden, removed the debris, and planted the seeds of a new harvest."

I was dumbstruck. Surely this passage was meant for me. These men were the strangers who come to help. Hope tingled through me. I considered the book title. "Chinese Fortunes." My thoughts went to Snow Bird Wang and how she cast the I Ching for direction. That I had picked this particular book from the shelf seemed like a good omen. Jack's voice jostled me back from my reverie. "Ma'am, are you okay? Do you need to sit down for a minute?"

"No, no." I shook myself back to the present. "Excuse me. Jack, would you read it one more time for me?"

Jack did.

"Will you tell me the page number, please?"

"109, ma'am."

I reached my hand out for the book. "109, 109." I shut the cover and laid it back on the table. "Deep, what a beautiful birthday fortune. I would guess either you'll be the recipient of a good deed, or you will be performing an act of kindness in the near future. Lovely." I wandered around the table toward Deep as I spoke. Once I finished making a circle, I tapped at my chin.

"What else could this mean? Perhaps the garden is a fair maiden for you, Deep. Do you have a girlfriend?"

Laughter bubbled up. "Not any *one* in particular, ma'am," Deep said.

"Maybe this has nothing to do with girls. I thought of girls because usually, it's a female who's represented with the flower metaphor. Hmm. Did it say flower, Jack? Should we be thinking in the direction of a girl? Hey, Randy, grab the book, turn to page 109, and remind me again. Did you say a flower or garden?"

Randy reached over the table and took the book. He sat back in his seat, opened the cover, and flipped through the pages. He rifled the pages more slowly, then glanced around the table and back at me. "There is no page 109, ma'am."

"What? Impossible. Jack read to us from 109. Pass the book to Blaze. Blaze, would you please read the passage at the top of page 109?" I walked around the table again to get over behind Blaze.

"Page 109 has been torn out, ma'am."

"Jack, did you rip the page out when you were reading?"

"No, ma'am. I read it then handed it to you the way you asked." A smile came over his lips. I could tell he was having fun.

"Hmm. Well, the birthday message was meant for Deep. Deep, did you tear the passage out?"

"No, ma'am, I didn't."

"I don't believe you, Deep." I crossed my arms over my chest and raised an accusatory brow. "I think you did, and what's more, I bet you put it in your secret envelope under your bottom so no one else could share in your birthday oracle."

"No, ma'am, I've been sitting on this envelope, and I made sure no one touched it."

"Show me," I said.

"What?"

"I want you to take that envelope out from under you and open it up to prove you don't have anything hidden there."

Deep reached under him and pulled out the envelope, slightly crumpled and creased from his weight. He checked the seal—still intact. He tore the envelope open, reached inside, and pulled out the torn page with the number 109.

All eyes and mouths opened wide.

"Deep," I said, "why don't you hand that back to Jack, so he can make sure we have the right page?"

Deep held the paper out to Jack, who opened the book and matched up the edges.

"It's the correct page, all right!"

The applause was punctuated with some hooting and whooping. I dropped a little curtsey. "Thank you. Thank you, gentlemen, for your kind attention." I glanced around at the men's faces, and my breath caught. I saw acceptance written there, and belonging. I wasn't a lone wolf facing the Psycho on my own. These men weren't just coldly doing their jobs; Gator had said as much when he caught me. "We like you too much," he'd said. And right now, I truly felt it. They had accepted me into their pack, and that made me feel happy. Honored. Safe.

Striker sat at the head of the table. He leaned back in his chair with his hands laced behind his neck; a little smile played across his lips. "When we met, you asked me for a call name. I think we need to call you 'Surprise Party.'"

"Too many syllables," I quipped and went to light the candles on Deep's birthday cake.

32

Thursday, my fourth day at the safehouse, I made my way downstairs to find out who pulled the watchdog-straw.

Striker sat at the table typing. When I slid onto my seat, he saved his work and moved his computer over to the buffet. He looked at his watch. "Good morning."

"Good morning. I slept better than I have in a long time. How are you?"

"Just fine."

I smiled shyly and glanced around. We seemed to be alone. "Who's on today?"

"Me. I need to talk to you. Blaze left you breakfast."

I wandered into the kitchen. A bowl of fruit covered with plastic wrap and a basket of muffins sat on the counter. From the oven, I pulled out a casserole and sniffed—sausage, cheese, eggs, and vegetables. Yummy.

Sitting down at the end of the table, across from Striker, I said a little prayer of thanksgiving to myself. I breathed in. Again, I worked hard on controlling my thoughts. Keeping a tight grip. Almost thirty-six hours had gone by since the last adrenaline spike, and I meant to keep this streak going. So right now, I'd focus on breakfast. Everything looked fresh and wholesome, creating a colorful plate.

Striker studied me. "I like the way you eat."

I peeked up. Striker's green eyes were soft this morning, warmed with affection. I smiled back at him. "How do you mean?" I spooned a cube of melon into my mouth self-consciously.

"It's sensuous. You never eat much, but you really seem to enjoy what you're eating, to take it all in. You look at it, smell it, roll it around your tongue like you're puzzling out each ingredient."

"My Buddhist training with Snow Bird Wang and yogic training with Biji in action. Mindful eating is supposed to be meditative and nourishing to the soul and the body. Mostly it means I can enjoy my food and still fit into size two without running a marathon."

He gave me a nod of understanding. As I popped in my last bite, Striker took my plate to the kitchen. When he came back, he set a mug on the table in front of me. I sniffed—Tension Tamer Tea, uh oh. I stiffened.

Striker moved to the chair beside me. "I need to update you on your case."

My breathing suddenly shifted to shallow staccato puffs.

"We've got a name. Travis Wilson. That do anything for you?"

I shook my head, no. My heart rate escalated.

"Thirty-four-years old, from New York City. The information came in on a tip Deep followed up after the police distributed the sketch to the news."

Striker talked to me in a professional, detached tone. These were just facts. Things we knew. They couldn't hurt me. I rubbed my thumb into my sweaty palm; my stomach heated like a furnace.

"Seems Mr. Wilson has spent time in mental hospitals throughout his life—delusional, paranoid, psychopathic tendencies, high I.Q. His parents took custody of him when his medications seemed to be working. That was three years ago. Wilson stayed at their house for two nights and left without his meds."

Saliva pooled in my mouth. Miriam was right. I gulped before I could speak. "And in those three years…?"

"We believe he attacked six women using the same M.O. as he used on you. He stalked them with love poems, which he'd rewritten in a threatening tone, broke into their homes, sliced their torso with a razor, and poured either vinegar or salt on them. He killed them with blunt force to the head, then he disappeared. He has never left any usable clues. No one was able to describe him before."

"I'm his first mistake." I shifted uncomfortably in my chair, not sure what to do with my hands. They fidgeted with my clothes and my rings.

"In your case, not only was he seen, but he left physical evidence. Not enough time to clean up, I'm guessing, especially since he didn't finish the kill. You got a look at him during the attack, and two eyewitnesses saw the escape. We're further along than we've been in three years. Iniquus got your file because I was already assigned to a task force investigating these crimes."

Dave was right. I should've gone to Iniquus from the beginning—they would have recognized the M.O. and protected me. Stupid. Stupid. Stupid.

Striker stopped to assess me. "You doing okay? Can you handle this?"

I nodded. My eyes stretched wide. I white-knuckled the table.

"Chica, take a few deep breaths, take a sip of tea."

I tried to do as he said, but my body wouldn't cooperate. My hands and feet were tingling and numb. I worked to keep my mind solely focused on Striker's words, not allowing my thoughts to stray to the left or right because that's where the heebie-jeebies lay waiting for me.

"Lexi, all of the other women fit a pattern. They were either the wives or daughters of the governmental agencies associated with stopping criminal activities. They were all twenty-four to thirty years old. You break the mold. You're twenty. Your dad owned a mechanic shop. Your husband serves as an Army Ranger. You got your first letter the day you got married, so you weren't even married to Angel when you became a target."

"Right." I felt hollow now. Weirdly, like a piecrust with no filling. I wondered vaguely why I didn't collapse in on myself.

"I'd like to go through your life story a little bit. Your background is unconventional, and I want to try to figure out how you got caught on this guy's radar, okay?"

"Okay." I brushed my sweat-dampened hair from my face. Striker reached around, picked up an elastic band off the buffet, and held it out to me. I made a haphazard ponytail, grateful to get the heat off my neck.

"Let me start with a part that's been bothering me. Do you know how Wilson got to you?"

"I developed a theory—there's only one way I can piece this together. I hate my idea. It makes the guy not only a psychiatric case but damned professional—someone with trained skills."

"Interesting. Do you want to run your ideas by me?" Striker stood up and took me by the elbow. He steered me toward the couch.

I sat down and hugged a blue pillow into my stomach, ignoring my wounds. I had been working on this theory piecemeal as I could—tiny, safe snippets here and there—ever since the attack. I thought I had puzzled everything out correctly.

"It goes like this," I said. "I secured my house meticulously —state-of-the-art-locks, triple-pane windows, outdoor motion sensor lights in front and back, a two-way communication alarm system monitoring doors and windows, and motion detection on the bottom floor." I ticked these off on my fingers. "I trained Beetle and Bella to bark whenever someone put their foot on my property."

"The dogs weren't around the night Travis got to you."

"Right. The first lapse in my security system was their absence. I planned to leave the contiguous states to go to Puerto Rico and be with Angel's family, so I boarded the pups with their trainer. The night of the attack, I went across the street to bring the guys some food for their game. I stayed for a while, but I was wound-for-sound, and finally just went home."

"Because you were nervous from the last poem?"

"I suspected the Psycho was hiding nearby. I had goose-bumps, and the hair on the back of my neck stood up, thoroughly creeped out. When Justin and Dave walked me home, the outdoor motion sensor lights were off—nothing to indicate someone hiding on my property. The locks were in place. The alarm set."

"How did he get in?" Striker leaned forward, his forearm resting on his knee, his focus intent.

"I think he went into my back yard—while I watched the game across the street—tumbled the lock on my backdoor with a burglar's pick and waited for me to come home."

Striker nodded. "The light would automatically turn off."

"Yup. They're on fifteen-minute timers. Once in place, I figured he quickly slipped inside while I turned the alarm off, shut and locked the door, and re-engaged the alarm without the indoor motion sensor."

"And he'd be able to hear the beeps from outside—letting him know he could safely go in," Striker said.

"Exactly." Okay, being professional helped. I cooled back down. "I think the Psycho slipped in, re-engaged the lock, and hid in the downstairs bathroom. I think this because when I came in, I did a thorough search, including windows, for signs of entry. I looked through my living room, dining room, and kitchen. When they were all clear, I went down to check out my basement."

"You were armed?"

"I had my Springfield 9mm out and my Ruger tucked in my waistband. I think Wilson went upstairs and got into my shower while I searched the basement. Before I went up, I checked in the coat closet and the downstairs guest bathroom—obviously, they were empty."

"Did you re-engage the motion detectors?"

"I did. Right after I checked out the downstairs. There are two levels of sensors. The first has a pet corridor so my dogs can walk around without setting off the alarm; a human would trip the infrared beam if they walked into the room. The second alarm I can engage in covering the rooms from floor to ceiling. I used the full-coverage setting that night."

"Only on the first floor, right? What about getting in on the second level?"

"Other than by parachuting in? No. There is no way to get to the second level without a ladder. Not only would a ladder be evident, but I can tell you from the experience of my contractors, the slopes don't lend well to ladders under the best of circumstances."

"Then what did you do?"

"Went upstairs and tried to calm myself. Being paralyzed with fear seemed like a dangerous way to face this guy. I thought I should be safe in my house with plenty of warning and plenty of support if someone did to try to get in. The guys were right across the street—Dave and Justin." This conversation was giving me an onion-cutting reaction. My eyes stung, and tears dripped down my cheeks; I just wanted to wash off in cold water and be done with this. I swiped absently at the snot dripping from my nose. And yet, my voice sounded like I was passing heart-rate information to an EMT partner. "If the neighbors heard the alarm go off, the guys had a thirty-second response time."

"The alarm didn't go off because Wilson was already inside."

"It's the only way this works out. Like I said, I decided to take a long hot shower to relax. I put my weapons down and went to the bathroom to get undressed. I turned to put my clothes into the hamper, and ..." I took a few jagged breaths before I continued. "I saw a glimpse of his face in the reflection of my bathroom mirror. He caught me completely off guard. I couldn't believe someone had gotten in. His hand came up with a white cloth. He locked the rag over my nose and mouth. I reached to flip him off me. Guess that didn't happen. I came to, lying on my bedroom floor, my hands and feet bound tightly. I'd lost circulation. My body burned and tingled all over. Tape covered my mouth—suffocated me."

"And his face?"

"I only got the quickest second, in the mirror. My room was pitch-black."

"He had the tape wrapping your head securely. How did you get the gag off your mouth?"

"I had been told in training that under such circumstances, it is imperative to get an airway into your tape because it's a suffocation hazard," I said as if reading from an instruction manual.

Striker nodded. "You shouldn't depend on your nose alone for air."

"I gathered saliva in my mouth and used my tongue to work the moisture between the tape and my skin. I loosened the gag to the point where I could breathe easily, but I tried to leave the tape adhered enough that Psycho wouldn't realize what I'd done."

Striker pulled his brows together. "You were doing this while he assaulted you?"

"I was in shock. I never felt the razor slicing into my skin. When he poured the vinegar on me," I sucked a noisy breath in, "that was like walking through a wall of fire, like living hell. I screamed. I guess he shut me up by hitting me in the head. Thank god he did." I realized I had a death grip on Striker's arm. Holding on for dear life. I tried to get my fingers to release, but they didn't seem to be listening to my brain anymore. Striker didn't even wince. He sat stoically, ignoring the bite of my nails.

"Dave and your neighbors heard you and came running."

"That's what I'm told. When I came to the second time, I was in the hospital, with my head on ice and my skin glued in place like a Kurt Schwitters collage, my brain scrambled."

Striker had moved closer to me and soothed over my hands until they released from his right arm. My nails made deep indentations in his skin. He flipped my hand over and rubbed his index finger up and down my pulse point. It was hypnotically soothing. I wondered vaguely where he learned to do that. I hoped he wouldn't stop. My galloping heartbeat slowed. My breathing deepened, and the vibrations in my limbs calmed.

"Do you need to take a break?" he asked.

I shook my head. "After I woke up in the hospital, Dave told me they had broken a front window and climbed in to open the door for the other guys. He said the alarm sounded when they broke the window."

"So how did Wilson get back out?"

"I think he got out the same way he got in. He had to be on the stairs, waiting for the window to break. With the alarm sounding and all the confusion, I think he went out the kitchen door, out the garden gate, up the alley, and that's when the guys spotted him, and he took off running."

"This all makes good sense."

"There are a lot of suppositions in my theory that call for some pretty big leaps. He had to understand my house floor plan and my security system. He had to know I was taking my dogs out of the picture."

"Who knew the dogs would be gone?"

"No one. I asked the trainers to keep it to themselves. They're trustworthy. They wouldn't tell anyone once I asked them not to." I contemplated for a few minutes. Striker sat silently.

"Wilson had to know I'd be gone over to Justin's for the game..." My voice trailed off. I looked out the window at the gray, cloudy sky. "I've thought all of this through, and I've come to the conclusion that he stuck a tracking device on my car, bugged my house, and my landline phone." I studied Striker's eyes. Smart. Caring. Warrior-mode.

"How do you figure he got into your house to plant surveillance? Dave told me you had the alarm from day one."

"I was restoring my house, so there was lots of activity. Lots of coming and going. All Wilson had to do was show up in a uniform and make up some job he was supposed to be doing. I'm sure the other workers would let him in. I parked my car on the street—easy access."

"If that's the case, the bugs are probably still in place."

"Inside, yes. The alarm's been on. I bet he came back and got the one off my car. I'm parked curbside. You might be able to pick something up if you do a sweep."

Striker pulled out his phone and called Jack. While he spoke, Striker had his eyes narrowed, assessing me, his head cocked slightly to the side.

"How are you doing?" he asked as he replaced the phone on his belt.

"Honestly? I don't know up from down these days."

Striker looked at my hands; I was convulsively twisting my rings. "Does your husband know about all of this?" he asked.

"He's on a mission. He went off-grid, and they said he'd be gone a minimum of a month and possibly three before he would be back in contact with me. 'No news will be good news,' they said."

"Did he know about the letters before he left?"

"He has enough to worry about. I didn't want to be a distraction to him. He can't help me, anyway, half-way around the world. I had my cop friends, and I thought I had a handle on this... I wanted Angel's mind to be on his target, not wishing he was home hunting my stalker." I breathed in deeply and exhaled in an audible rush.

"Good call." He nodded his approval. "You're a good wife."

"I'm trying."

By then, my temples pounded fiercely. I needed to lie down. Striker handed me two pain pills, covered me with a warm blanket, and turned off the overhead light. I let the sound of rain pattering against the window lull me to sleep.

Until I woke up screaming from a hellish nightmare.

Striker gathered me up and hugged me to his chest. He rested his cheek against my hair protectively; I clung to him. I felt safe in his arms.

He waited for the better part of my sobs to calm, then he whispered into my ear, "I'm so sorry, Lexi. I'm so sorry I had to have you go through all of that. Please believe me. I'm going to protect you from this guy. We're going to get him. He'll spend the rest of his life in prison and never hurt anyone again. Do you trust me?" I nodded into his shoulder, hiccoughing and trying to catch my breath.

33

"**Hey**," Striker whispered. "You've been out for a long time. I think you should probably wake up now."

I groggily pulled myself to sitting, flipped my hair back out of my face, and adjusted my shirt. "No adrenaline dump, just a nightmare." And I'd take a nightmare any day over the pain of my raging hormonal spikes. I looked up into his green eyes. "I'd say I'm making progress."

"I thought so, too. I have a present for you." Striker reached out his hand and dropped three small gizmos onto my palm. I inspected them—one phone bug and two wall socket remote transmitters.

"Huh. Well, this explains a lot—did Jack find fingerprints?" I handed the bugs back.

Striker shook his head. "Nope, clean. So random nut-job is off the table. We're working with a crazy pro. I hate to do this to you, but I still want to get some information from you. I need to find the link from your case to the other victims."

"Let's do it." I swung my legs around and patted the seat beside me.

"Lexi, all you've had to eat today is breakfast. I'm going to make you a sandwich. Do you want one like yesterday with the olive paste stuff and cold cuts?"

I laughed. "You mean tapenade? That's fine. What time is it? I should get dinner started." I checked the clock—1:20.

"It's fine if you want to cook later, Lexi, but you're going to sit and eat something first, or I'll be picking you up off of the floor, and your food will burn."

"If you catch me before I hit the ground, you'll get a hundred points." I grinned.

"What?" As he stood, I had to crane my neck to keep my eyes on his.

"Apparently, the guys are playing some sort of game. Something to do with not letting me hit the floor when I'm falling over with vertigo."

"Should I talk to them?" His lips pressed together sternly, but his eyes glittered. He was laughing at me!

I narrowed my lids in response. "I wouldn't. So far, it seems to be working."

"Which Kitchen Grandma are we enjoying today?"

Banalities, good. Maybe he'd give me a little break from the stalker crap. I was still emotionally exhausted—even after my sleep. "Normally, Thursday belongs to Nona Sophia. I switched her with Nana Kate because of the birthday thingy. Tonight, I planned Nana Kate's pot roast. That is if the normal kitchen magic happened, and all of the groceries from my list appeared during the night." I plopped down at the table.

"I can pretty much guarantee they did. Sit tight. I'll get you some food."

I sipped my tea and ate the sandwich Striker brought me. It tasted good. As soon as I took my first bite, I realized I was starving. I licked my fingers and wiped them on my napkin.

Striker showed up with a note pad. "Ready?" he asked.

"As I'll ever be." The food had fortified me, and the sooner we got through this, the sooner they could piece things together, get the guy, and I'd go home. Finally, safe and sound.

"Let's go over your education. My take on your life is that you woke up in the morning and went from adventure to adventure, mentor to mentor, all day until you went to sleep at night, usually with someone's children under your wing. Is that fair?"

"Pretty darned close." I swiveled on the cushion. We were face to face. I slid my heel underneath me.

"From the stories you've told us, I know about the Kitchen Grandmas, the hairstylist, the florist, the dry cleaners, the locksmith, someone with a bar, a hooker, a Mrs. Drinkwater, your dad, the mechanic, your mom, the artist, and a cop named Stan. How many others?"

"Lots."

"Okay, since this started for you at the apartment building—"

I shook my head. "It started at the motel. I lived in a motel for five weeks after my apartment building burned down. After three weeks, I got married to Angel, whom I met the night of the fire. The morning of my wedding, I discovered the first note."

"And after Angel left, you moved to Detective Murphy's neighborhood." The point of his pen rested on the paper without taking notes.

"I found my house the day after Angel deployed. It took two weeks for the sale to go through. During which time, I moved from place to place each night, trying to elude the Psycho."

"Were you working?"

"I'm an online student at the community college."

"Okay. Before you motel hopped, at the first place, do you remember any unusual events happening during your stay? Do you think you might have seen Wilson?"

"I'm sure I didn't." I pulled a knee up and hugged it to me. Sharp pain screamed from my cuts, protesting my protective posture, making me grimace.

"How are you sure?" He moved the unused pad aside, set his heel onto the chair rung, and wrapped his knee with his hands, somewhat mirroring my position. I wondered if he did that on purpose to make me more comfortable. Body language 101. It wouldn't matter if he did; there was nothing comfortable about this conversation.

"I've got an excellent memory for faces. If I had seen him once, I would remember him."

"He could have been disguised."

I played with the hem of my shirt. "His face is too marked—the scars and tattoo. I'm not saying he didn't see me at the motel. I'm saying I didn't spot him."

"Let's go a different direction—you have some law enforcement connections, though they're not familial, right?"

"Well, Dave Murphy, of course. My friend Stan—he taught me how to drive and shoot. I use the police range for practice."

"They tried to recruit you?"

"It's not the right environment for me." I ran damp palms down my pants legs.

"Anything else?"

"I flew Civil Air Patrol—I started as a cadet around twelve. We did high-adventure stuff together as well as aviation, sort of like scouting." I found myself doing yoga breathing between sentences—in through the nose out through the mouth—trying to stay calm. "I got my pilot's license and did practice missions quite a bit. More so, when Dad was alive. Every couple of months or so now."

Striker curled his lips in and shook his head. "Nope. Not it."

"Uhm, I train with the search and rescue team with my dogs.

I volunteer for the EMS one weekend a month. I knew a lot of those guys through my mom. They transported her to the hospital fairly frequently at the end. I joined the volunteers while she was in hospice." *Shit. Shit. Shit. I'm going to have to tell him.*

"This isn't doing it for me." He lowered his foot to the ground and leaned forward. "That's all amazing stuff, but it's not getting you into the crosshairs of our maniac."

I took a deep breath—*Here it goes.* "Then maybe it was my connection to Spyder."

I saw a flash of surprise. "You mean Spyder…"

"McGraw." I filled in the blank. My body stiffened with apprehension. God, I hoped I chose the right thing to do. Right now, I was only partially convinced I should pony up this information about Spyder. He had been so insistent on my secrecy.

Striker froze for a heartbeat. "Tell me about your connection."

"Spyder was one of my apartment teachers," I whispered.

"Spyder lived nowhere near you." Striker's voice was tight. Confusion mottled my thoughts. This was the hard-edged, dangerous Striker, the combat-ready Striker. His expression jarred me, especially after…well, after the warmth I felt from him.

"I bartered his mentorship for my help with the Agnew family in my apartment building," I explained.

A long moment stretched out between us. Striker was my protector, but his posture made me feel like I was prey. His rigid stance put me on guard.

"How long did that go on?" he asked tightly.

My voice quivered as I carefully weighed my words. "Spyder's been a family friend since before I was born. Spyder started to mentor me when I turned thirteen, and he went off-grid a month before my mom died. So, about six years of study, give or take."

"What kinds of things did you learn from him?" A glimmer of curiosity shone in his eyes.

How do I answer? Spyder insisted on my training being secretive. How would disclosing this help my case, anyway? "Uhm, at first, he taught me thinking skills: argumentation, logical sequencing. We did mind games to improve my memory and perception. He's the one who showed me how to do magic, taught me about the stars, and stuff." That all sounded benign.

"That's not all. What else?" His voice was accusatory.

More? What more should I give up? "Later, as I grew older, he improved on some of the things my other mentors taught me. Like the driving skills and gun skills I learned from Stan." I tangled and untangled my fingers. "He taught me other computer skills than what I learned from my dad. He put the dots of my experiences together into a complete picture for me and made me better."

Striker stared at me like a microbe on a petri dish he was trying to identify. "We know each other."

"Yes," I said and stared him directly in the eye. My chin held up. Was I challenging him? Ah, this was a dangerous game to play, Lexi. *Hell in a handbasket,* my mind flashed—was this what the psychic knowing warned me about? Should I have kept this hidden away in my closet? I didn't know. I just didn't know.

"Can you remind me how we met?" Striker asked.

"I'd rather not." My answer came out terse and professional. See? I can switch modes just like you, Striker Rheas. Why was I so angry? Probably because I had backed myself into a corner. To figure out who attacked me, I had to reveal myself—it seemed like a sucky deal.

My temples throbbed. I wanted to lie down and bury my

head under the pillow. An unwelcome, angry tear, which had clung valiantly to my eyelashes, lost its hold and dripped down my cheek. Striker reached out to wipe it away. I jerked back, blocking his move as if he meant to hit me. Striker's gaze hardened to alpha dog, and it pissed me off. I stared back at him. He seemed to realize what was going on because he scrubbed a hand over his face. When he looked at me again, his eyes had softened.

"Lexi, I'm sorry. I didn't mean to frighten you or to speak to you that way." He exhaled exasperation. "You're such a mystery. I don't understand what I'm dealing with here."

I didn't reply.

"We're on the same team. We're going to get through this together. I need you to trust me. Do you trust me, Lexi?"

We were on the same team. I was part of the pack. And every pack had an alpha. I shouldn't hold this against him. "I trust you because Spyder trusts you."

"Spyder talked about me?" Striker asked.

"Spyder said if I ever found myself in trouble or needed a job, I should get in contact with you."

"You didn't call me when you got the letters."

"I chose a different route."

"Spyder thought you should work for me if you needed a job?" His brows knit together.

"Is that incredulity I hear in your tone? Remember, I'm the one who found your flash drive and your missing suspect. And I got Randy's gun easily enough." My voice shot out defensively, this side of combative, terse, and pitched low.

Striker changed his tactic. "Spyder was working on a project with me when he went off-grid. Do you have any connections with it?"

"I puzzled a case for him just before he left."

Striker cocked his head to the side. I read this as doubt. Why did he keep doubting me? Maybe because I kept hiding things from him, duh.

"We're talking about the crime ring from Colombia?" I asked.

Striker nodded.

"I remember a web of crazy intrigue. I handed the file back to Spyder the morning he left, solved."

"Solved?" Striker's voice rose in surprise. "I never got it."

"If he left it on his desk, Spyder probably assumed I'd recognize it and get it to the right people, but I was distracted and upset when he went down-range. I packed his things without paying much attention." I paused. "It's been a long time since I worked the case. If you bring me your copy of the file, I'll try to remember what I came up with."

We sat quietly together for a minute.

"So that feels right to me," Striker said. "Wilson targeted you because of Iniquus. He must think your friendship with Spyder, or your involvement with the cases, one or the other fit with his crusade. I think he didn't know you were a functioning operator. He probably saw your close relationship with Spyder and thought you made a good target."

"The whole thing's ironic as hell," I said.

Striker's focus drilled into me. "It's becoming cliché for me to say how surprising you are, Chica."

I didn't waver under his scrutiny, just answered earnestly. "It's a quality I've developed. It's safest for me when no one suspects I'm anything but a newlywed college student. Spyder thought, for me, normalcy and innocence were an excellent cover. He said everyone develops a persona for the world at large. Some of us do it with more deliberation."

"Everyone?"

"Like you. You have an aura of honesty, mental and physical strength, power, and supreme control over yourself and over the situation. I'm sure it serves you well."

"You don't seem to be fazed. Most women get nervous around me. They get all giggly and chatty. I've never heard you giggle. Not part of your cover?" He was teasing me, trying to ease the tension still stirring the air. I wasn't in a teasing mood.

"Look, I want to go home and live my life without the stalker messing with my head—literally and figuratively. I'm not going it alone against a serial killer. I'm physically unable to function, and I haven't a clue, other than what you've told me this morning, how to get to him."

"We'll get him." Striker balled his fist.

"I believe that. You're good at what you do. You've got resources not available to me. And more importantly, Spyder holds you in the utmost esteem." My eyes were sharp on him. "Right now, I need to believe you're stronger than kryptonite."

"That's a lot to live up to."

"Probably."

"So, we were colleagues? And Spyder kept that to himself?"

"Yes, and yes," I said.

"Could you tell me one mission?"

"Tanglesmeere Corp. I'm the one who bugged Tandesco for the takedown."

Striker's mouth dropped open, and I went smiling into the kitchen to start dinner.

34

A knock on my doorjamb turned me away from my clothes-folding chores. Striker leaned against the frame, his arms crossed comfortably in front of him, watching me. We were back to our affable, pre-Spyder-revelation footing, which made me more comfortable.

"India Alexis Sobado, you are a food siren. My men are drawn to the scent of your pots like sailors to a rocky shore," Striker joked.

"Mmmm and I'm luring them to their demise on what? Too much saturated fat?" I laughed.

"On the rocks of unrequited love. They all want to marry you, Chica, so you can fill their mouths with wonderful flavors for the rest of their natural lives."

"Good thing I'm already safely married. No need for a battle to break out over my pot roast. I will tell you, compared to the grandmas, I'm not a very good cook—your men are simply under a food spell."

"You aren't a siren? You're a kitchen witch?"

"Warts and all." I loved playing with Striker—maybe that

wasn't such a good thing given my past feelings for him. "Hey, let me ask you about this 'Chica' business. Chica means 'little girl.' Back in my neighborhood, all of the men followed Dave's example and called me Baby Girl. Do I come off as overly naïve or childish?"

"I'd say you come off as fresh." Striker tilted his head to one side as if to observe me from a different angle.

"Fresh like baked bread or garden salad?" I walked over to stand in front of him, holding the half-folded shirt against my chest.

"More like the early morning of a day filled with possibilities." He smiled, reaching up to brush a piece of hair from my face, tucking the strands behind my ear. The touch felt private. Connected. Intimate. Not sexual. More possessive, maybe?

I reached for casual banter. "Since I usually wake up sluggish and grumpy, I think you need to work on a different simile."

"How about raspberries?" He flashed his infectious grin.

"Okay." A smile tickled the corners of my lips. "I'll take raspberries."

Striker reached out again.

This time I took a step back before he could touch me. "When you say Chica, the way you say it makes me feel pretty. Maybe even a little sexy. I'm not sure those are good feelings to have when I'm around you. It confuses me."

Striker's eyes sparked with curiosity, then a flash as he realized he'd crossed a line; he readjusted to humorous sincerity. "So, I should stick to 'raspberries?'" he teased.

"Sometimes you're a jerk." I pushed past him and headed down the stairs. He laughed as he followed behind me. I grinned despite myself.

Downstairs, the men gathered around the table. I only

counted six. "Where's Jack? Should we stick his plate in the oven to keep warm for him?" I asked.

The kitchen phone rang, and an Iniquus Hummer roared up the drive. Jack strode in with a thick manila envelope in his hands. He moved to hand it to Striker, but Striker shook his head and pointed to me. Jack stilled for a minute, confused, then handed the file over. I got up and put it on the buffet.

"Thanks," I said. "I'll read through after dinner."

I ate a quiet meal of Nana Kate's delicious pot roast recipe, letting the men share their news and stories. My mind slid back to my apartment with all the sticky notes on the wooden floor of my bedroom, running strings from one to the other, trying to get hold of the relationships hiding the secret to this puzzle. I remembered a web of deception. The case was a jumble of confusing players. Most were innocent; the roles they played stayed within the boundaries of the law. It wasn't until... I jumped up, ran over to the file, and flipped through. Striker watched me, eyes sharp as obsidian.

"I remember now," I said.

This got the men's attention. What did I have to do with an Iniquus case? They stared at me, but no one asked the obvious questions. They put their heads down and made a show of eating, finishing their plates in silence.

Evidently, Striker hadn't explained my secret to them yet. Now, I wished he *would* tell them about Spyder. I wanted the men to know I was one of them. We really did play on the same team—we were part of the same pack. Cognitively, I understood they worked hard on my case—were out in the field night and day, following up on leads—but I wanted this to be personal for them. I wanted them fighting for one of their own. Would that change the outcome? Speed things up? Make them more effective? Jeezus, I sounded manipulative. Ugly. I didn't particularly like myself at that moment. Or many of the moments during this whole fiasco. I sighed loudly. All I could do on my end was to keep proving myself worthy of their best efforts and keep my head screwed on as tightly as possible. Having Spyder's case back in my lap would help with both of these goals. Maybe. Hopefully.

Jack and Gator took off on assignment while Randy and Blaze did KP. Deep tapped on his laptop over on the sofa, and Striker and I sat side by side at the table.

"Let me try to reconstruct the web for you, so you can follow. Back in my apartment, I did this with Post-It notes and string. That's the only way I could keep track of all the players."

Striker produced a pen, a pad of sticky notes, and, after looking through the garage, he found a ball of twine. As he handed them to me, Striker's phone vibrated.

He focused tightly on what the other person said. "You have a lead on both? Or just... No...Where? ...Right, we'll wait for the call."

Deep had moved over to stand next to Striker, hands on his hips, looking intent. "Lynda and Cammy?" he asked under his breath.

Striker gave an almost imperceptible nod and glanced at his watch. "Brainiack thinks he had eyes on her. We'll rally with him at twenty-hundred." Striker's voice mirrored Deep's guarded tone. "Things are ratcheting up," he said. "Lots of chatter between the players. Something's gone wrong, and Lynda's got herself caught in the middle, dragging Cammy in. Again."

Striker shot a glance at me, but I was well-practiced in the art of watching from behind veiled eyes. His expression was a mixture of exasperation, anger, and fear. There and gone. A brief moment when his stoicism wavered. Whatever crime he was working on had a personal connection to him. Very personal.

"We'll find them," Deep said.

I hoped they'd confide in me, bring me data to puzzle. I wanted to help find Lynda and Cammy, too. We were teammates, after all, even if Striker was just starting to realize this.

I busied myself flipping through the file, filling out each piece of paper, arranging them on the table, rearranging them on the table, moving the string around, working slowly through the process of trying to remember how this had all fit together. At some point, Striker interrupted to let me know Deep, Randy, and he had to leave for a couple of hours. Blaze would be my watchdog. I nodded my understanding without looking up. For me, working on a puzzle was like meditation. I had no concept of time floating by.

I was startled when the door crashed open—no warning call.

Blaze leaped forward. Gun aimed. Body shielding mine.

Unarmed, I squatted. My eyes went wide in my head as if with more light, I could better grasp the moment. I peered around Blaze's leg and forced my mind to focus and understand. Jack—and behind him, Gator.

Ripped clothes.

Blood.

Gator glowed ghostly white beneath his tan. He gripped his chest and leaned into the wall.

Jack held a hand out toward Blaze as if to ward off the bullet that could fly his way. He swayed and went down on a knee.

Blaze was focused, body taut. He thrust his gun into my hand, grabbed Jack's from his shoulder holster, and raced out, slamming the door shut behind him. I assumed he went to secure the perimeter. *He trusts me to protect the interior,* flashed through my mind. Trust!

Jack looked me straight in the eye. "Ambush," he gasped. "Not Wilson, Lexi. It was NOT Wilson."

Relief cascaded over me like cooling water. I switched gears immediately to EMT mode. I pushed the Glock into my back waistband for easy access. In case... As I rushed forward, my mind registered exposed road abrasions and jagged, raw skin.

Jack's injuries were the most obvious. I laid him on the ground. I turned to Gator and used my hands to scan over his body, using Reiki energy to check his status. Obvious injuries weren't always the most serious injuries. I needed to triage the two to know what to do next.

I lead Gator to a chair in the dining room, helped him cross his arms on the table, and laid his dazed, concussive head down. I was kneeling beside Jack when the door opened. My eyes flew up as I jerked the Glock into position and lined up the site.

Blaze had a phone to his ear, reporting to Striker. I stuck the gun back in my pants and turned my attention to Jack.

A scorch mark covered most of his arm. I brushed the air above the damaged skin. Justin's barbeque burn was nothing compared to this, and I wasn't sure I had the capacity to heal, or even soothe, something this severe. I mumbled a prayer under my breath.

As I brushed, the red and heat left the wound and soon became unperceivable. I tore open the ripped cloth of Jack's camo pants and brushed his thigh and calf. He must have come up against the exhaust on a motorcycle. Nothing else would leave this kind of wound.

Jack gritted his teeth and balled his fists. Stoic. Steely.

"Jack, I can help you," I whispered in his ear. "I'll need you to trust me, open up to me." My hands rested lightly over his eyes; Reiki energy streamed from my palms. I had never experienced the energetic force coming through me this strongly before; it made me dizzy and nauseated. Jack murmured a thank you. My eyes sought out Blaze, who had a first aid kit beside him. He was cleaning the gash on Gator's head.

"Blaze, I need you to cut open Gator's shirt. Be careful not to pull. Gator's ribs are broken on the right-hand side. Wrap the ribs in Ace bandages to give him some relief. Then, clean and dress the gunshot wound on his upper arm using butterfly strips. The bullet didn't penetrate—only grazed him."

"Yes, ma'am." Blaze picked a pair of scissors from the box.

"Blaze, what's your protocol for getting people to the hospital?"

"Ma'am, unless the situation is life or death, we can't have EMS respond here to the house. We'll have to transport them ourselves. I can't leave you alone, and you can't come with me. I alerted the team. They're forty-five minutes away if all the lights and the traffic are with them, and they push the pedal down."

An hour passed before the phone rang, and I heard a motor gunning up the drive. The door burst open; the team strode in. I had my healing hands on Gator by now.

Both of the men had absorbed a ton of energy and were in trances, unaware that the others had arrived. Striker looked at me for a report.

Blaze had explained what I was doing when they checked in over the phone.

As I removed my hands, Gator stirred and opened his eyes. I went to the kitchen and washed with soap and water. I took a minute to center myself and disconnect the energetic link before I spoke.

"Gator needs to go to the hospital. Broken ribs on the right. I tried not to touch them with the Reiki energy. The bones aren't lined up properly. Likewise, I didn't work on the gash on his arm." I pointed over at him. "After they suture him, I can heal it. If I do anything now, the skin wouldn't be as neat—it would leave a bigger scar." I moved toward Jack, who pushed to sitting. "I think I got everything else. Jack sustained injuries mostly from a blow to the head and burns from the engine. He stretched the ligaments in his right knee and ankle. I can't see any swelling or bruising now. You'll want an orthopedist to look at him, anyway."

Striker nodded, his face unreadable. "Can they walk?"

"Give them another minute to come out of their healing states. They need to drink water before they go."

Striker glanced toward Blaze, who went to the kitchen and pulled glasses from the cupboard. I moved to the living room and sat on the rocking chair. My hands lay open in my lap. My head leaned back; my eyes closed. The energy continued to pour out of me. I couldn't seem to shut down the voltage. Weird. This had never happened before. I buzzed like a beehive. It felt like my atomic particles had decompressed, leaving me with wide-open spaces, making me translucent and permeable.

Striker crouched at my feet. He reached out to touch me. When our palms met, my head snapped up. I sucked air, yanking my hands back as if burned. Striker's eyes turned from concerned soft green to black as his pupils dilated. I sensed his body brace protectively against the energy. He lowered himself to kneeling. I never thought I'd see this man on his knees.

As he looked into my eyes, bands constricted my lungs. Impossible to take air in—I was suffocating. My heart pounded so fast, and with such fury, it seemed to work its way out of the protective cage of my ribs and up my throat to choke me. I couldn't survive this.

I tried to jerk my gaze away from his to garner respite, but my eyes fixed on Striker with tunnel vision. Nothing else existed in this world but Striker here in front of me. A vein throbbed at his temple, keeping pace with my galloping pulse. We looked at each other for a long time. Finally, Striker pulled his gaze to the right and broke the spell. He pushed to standing and went to help his men into the Humvee, leaving without another word to me.

As soon as Striker moved through the door, the energy vanished. My heart reseated itself. My breath was freed, and I slumped, limp, and exhausted. This had never happened when I've used Reiki before. How confusing. How frightening.

Blaze walked over with a glass of water for me. He said nothing, which I appreciated. After a while, I got up to repair the twine web I had created on the table, putting it back to its original state—from before I laid Gator down across my papers and string—so I'd be ready to explain the case to Striker when he came back. Blaze watched me moving nervously around the room.

"Ma'am, you did a remarkable thing." He sounded reverent.

I waved my hand in the air as if to erase the notion. "Those were simple techniques—anyone can learn to do them. I studied with a hospice nurse who took care of my mom." I paused. "I have to say, I've never tried it on anything this serious before. I was stunned." My brows knit together as I scowled. "I can't normally do that. I'm not sure how I did it today."

Blaze nodded solemnly.

My hands went to my temples. "Blaze, my head is spinning. I think I need to go lie down and get some sleep."

"I'll walk you upstairs, so we don't have another hospital run."

35

Striker climbed in next to me around three o'clock. I lay awake, with my lights on to keep the boogeyman at bay, having failed miserably at falling asleep. I was anxious about Gator and Jack and more than a little weirded out over the whole event—especially the energetic side.

I rolled over to face him. "How are they?"

"Exactly as you said. Jack's going to be fine. Gator got sixteen stitches in his arm and four broken ribs. The doctors said the damnedest thing. They thought the ribs must have been broken weeks ago. They had already started to knit back together."

"Shoot. I hoped that wouldn't happen—did they need to re-break them in order to set them properly?" I grimaced.

"They got them in place by manipulating him."

My brows shot up to my hairline. "God. I hope they had him sedated."

"They knocked him out. Jack's taking a day to rest tomorrow. He sends you a big thank you. Made me stop and get you some flowers—the only place I found open was a twenty-four-hour grocery. I put them in a vase downstairs." He pulled the cover up over my shoulder. "I hope you like magenta and purple because I didn't have a choice. Gator will be on light duty for the next couple of weeks until he recovers."

"I won't see him?" I frowned.

"You'll see him—I bet he'll be showing up for dinner every night. He may even hang out here, doing computer searches on your case. He won't be charged with your safety, though—not until he's a hundred percent."

Quiet filled the room. I couldn't read Striker's mood. Or my own, for that matter.

"Can you help me understand what happened here tonight?" Striker's voice was strength and warmth.

I cleared the debris from my throat. "I was trained in Healing Energy work, and I'm a Reiki Master. These are both forms of energy healing that I learned to help my mother through the end of her terminal illness." I felt self-protective, formal, a soldier in a debriefing. "When the men came in, I understood it was going to be some time before they could get traditional medical care, so I applied what I knew in order to help them."

"I've seen energy healing done in various ways, in the different countries where the military had us posted. I know, in some cases, it can be effective." Striker seemed like a tourist in a foreign country, taking in the landscape, trying to make out the language, non-judgmental. "My men described their experiences to me. Very interesting. Blaze said you whispered something to each of the men, and they seemed to fall into a trance. Did you use hypnotism? Did they need to be in an altered state for the energy to work?"

"Not at all. I asked them to trust me and to make themselves available for healing. I have to give them kudos. It had to have been a very strange experience. I was putting out enormous amounts of energy."

"Energy from you?" Striker's concern was tangible. "I don't want you to exert or injure yourself to help my men."

"That's not how it works. I don't give them my energy. I channel energy, sort of like an electrical conduit." Well usually. I was still trying to wrap my head around what happened after I stopped doing Reiki. I wished I could talk to Miriam and Kim.

The sensations I experienced sitting in the rocking chair unnerved me. They felt...other-worldly. Like I was connecting to something bigger. Stronger. Something dangerously threatening. But not Wilson. I was sure it had nothing directly to do with Wilson. Though... no, that wasn't entirely true. Wilson shimmered around the edges of my consciousness, and the omnipresent stench was denser—acrid in my nostrils. Two entirely different scenarios played out. Two layers. Which probably explained my confusion. With Wilson, I sensed he was physically closer than any of us would have guessed. With the other... I just didn't know. Something was brewing.

I wondered if I could sweep away the first layer—the thick, heavy one that wrapped around me so tightly when Striker touched my hands—would I pick up more information about Wilson? I didn't like the idea of Wilson being physically close. Had he discovered the safe house?

"Then later, when you sat in the chair?" Though spoken gently, Striker's question snapped me back from my thoughts, jarring me.

"I don't know. I've never experienced anything like that before."

"You weren't able to stop the connection?"

"I wasn't connected to either Jack or Gator. I was still pumping energy—just not the energy I recognized."

"When I touched your hands, my whole body lit up."

I shifted uncomfortably around in the bed. My breathing came in shallow puffs. I sat up, hoping to find more oxygen. To gain more control. "Near as I can figure, when you approached, you were a creative force. You wanted to help me, to make sure I was all right. At the time, I generated an equal force. I think our energies knocked up against each other, like two positive ends of a battery trying to meet." I bumped my fists together to demonstrate the idea. "To me, it felt like sparks, like getting shocked. Had you approached in a receptive way, then my energy would have flowed into you."

Striker gave me a long, appraising look. Finally, he said, "I'd like to try. Can you do it now?"

"Sure." I put my palms over his heart, making the symbol and whispering the mantra to start the flow of energy. When the Reiki stopped, Striker took my hands in his, turned them over, and searched my palms, rubbing them with his thumbs. "Thank you," he said.

"Striker? Did this energy seem different from the energy when I was sitting in the chair?"

"Very different. Why?"

"I'd like to tell you something. It has to be confidential. You can't share this with anyone. Promise?" I whispered.

"This sounds intriguing." An odd tone colored his voice— maybe he was bracing himself for a new Lexi surprise. Maybe he should be.

"You didn't promise."

"Lexi, I'm not sure I can. I'll try to respect your confidentiality. I can't give you anything more."

"Okay. I guess." I crisscrossed my legs and looked down at Striker. "The backstory first. My mom started hospice with our favorite nurse Kim. Kim trained people in Healing Energy and

Reiki. When she saw my interest, Kim taught me how to use both forms of energy work to help Mom."

"This has to do with your healing work?"

"No, not really. Over time, as I became better at using the energy to help, I noticed that sometimes the energy shifted, and I had these strange experiences. They're hard to describe, sort of like standing between two planes. I call it 'going behind the Veil.'"

"Like an out of body experience?"

"Sort of—at least that gives you a frame of reference. At the time, I didn't know what was happening. I asked Kim about it, and Kim introduced me to her wife, Miriam, who is a professional psychic. Miriam worked with me a little to see what I could and couldn't do. Now, Miriam isn't a wannabe. She's a respected authority. Law enforcement up and down the East Coast hires her to help with missing persons and to find clues on cold cases. Dave and Stan both know her."

Striker interrupted me, "Is this Miriam Laugherty we're talking about?"

"You know her, too?"

"I know *of* her. The agents hate to call her in. They don't want to believe she can do what she can, but she's undeniably effective. She has a good track record and an impeccable reputation for professionalism."

"Thank you. Your saying that helps me to tell you this story." I sucked in a long inhale. "Miriam started working with me. It turns out I have a talent for remote searches. I trained with Miriam to build my skills until I could 'go behind the Veil' at will and gather information like Miriam can. Miriam wanted me to help her work on some of her cases—she always has more requests than she can handle. I thought I'd like solving crimes with her."

Striker pulled his brow together. How should I read that? Worried, maybe. "Did Spyder know about this?"

Why would that matter? "Uhm, yes."

"I'm sorry to interrupt. You trained with Miriam…"

"Right, and I started being able to leave my body and retrieve information at will. Miriam did a lot with imprints, that is to say, a crime that happened in the past. I couldn't do much with that at all. My skills were present tense. This would have been good had things worked out better. Miriam would have worked on cold cases, and I'd take the immediate cases."

"Things didn't work out?"

"Not at all," I said emphatically. "One night, Miriam brought me this case—a woman in imminent danger—Miriam wasn't having any luck picking up on her. Long story short, I found her. The process was horrific, and I decided I couldn't use those skills ever again."

"Why? What happened?" Striker asked.

"When I went behind the Veil, the crisis seemed to suck me in. I merged with this woman. I could see what she saw and feel what she felt. I experienced all of it. When I was able to separate myself, I had to sleep for three days to recover. It was physically and emotionally painful." My gaze searched along the seam separating the ceiling from the wall. My fingers worked the soft cotton sheets convulsively. "When I talked to Miriam, she and I agreed that doing psychic police work wasn't going to be the right thing for me. She said I should do what felt comfortable and decline the rest. That was pretty much it. I haven't felt a pull toward the Veil, that is, a pull to leave this plane, since Mom died. I definitely felt it tonight when I sat in the rocking chair."

"Do you think it has something to do with finding Wilson?"

"Not directly. His information is unrelated to the pull."

"What?" He shook his head, his eyes quizzical.

"I felt Wilson, but his energy was kind of coat-tailed on. Like the energy attached peripherally."

"I'm not sure I know how to ask questions about this. Did you get any sense of why you felt this way?"

"I'm pretty sure it had to do with you. It started when you came into the room. When you touched my hands, I felt like I should pull you in to see something, something incredibly important. It was such a demanding sensation. I couldn't wrap my brain around what it meant, though, or what I should do about it. The energy stopped when you left."

"I don't have any answers for you. I'm sorry."

"You're not in any trouble, are you? Any danger?" I reached out to grip at his arm.

"My job is to be in danger. I'm in danger all the time. So far, I've made it through. Talk to me about the Wilson-coat-tail thing you said."

"If I'm right about danger surrounding you, it doesn't come from Wilson's direction. I'd say that because you are invested in finding Wilson, you've picked up on his energy along the way, and I sensed it. He isn't far."

Striker stilled. "We aren't far from the capture? Or he's not physically far away?"

"There was too much. Everything happened too fast... If I had to guess, I'd say both. You're on the trail. He's nearby. What nearby means is relative. It could mean here in the vicinity or broader D.C."

"Right here? In the neighborhood?"

"I don't know. I didn't understand the impression. I definitely picked up on a woman and a child, though."

Striker's eyes dilated, and he pushed up to sitting. "What did you get about the woman and her child?" he asked very quietly, barely moving his jaw.

"Just their vague presence. I'm sorry. I'll tell you if I get anything more."

He nodded.

"You didn't seem surprised by all this," I said.

"That's because, Chica, I'm learning to pace myself. You need to sleep." With that, Striker leaned over and turned off the light. And, as if responding to a command, as soon as my head hit the pillow, I was out for the night.

36

My sheets enveloped me in a damp cocoon as I pushed through the surface of a horrible dream. No, not a dream. An impression. A foreboding. I glanced around my room; I was alone. Well, whatever scary-ass thing that was headed my way would come whether I was ready or not. Might as well face it dressed.

My feet were light on the tread as I scooted down the stairs, hoping to find Striker eating breakfast. In the kitchen, Axel balanced on a stool at the counter, drinking coffee and tapping on his computer.

"Striker's gone already?" My voice sounded breathy like I had just stepped off a treadmill.

"He had an early meeting at Headquarters. Left at six." Axel reflexively glanced at the clock.

"Is he going to be gone all day? Are you my watchdog?"

"I'll be here 'til noon. I expect Striker back then." Axel squinted at me. "Is everything all right? Something I can help you with?"

"I wanted to go over the puzzle with him." I pointed at the string and Post-Its all over the table.

Axel nodded, and I went into the kitchen to get a cup of tea. *I'm unsettled,* I thought, and my stomach sloshed violently in response. I burst into the bathroom, vomiting up my anxiety. When I sheepishly exited, I lay down on the couch for a few minutes with a cold cloth over my eyes, but it didn't help anything.

Heebie-jeebies sparked under my skin and across my scalp— my early warning system. But could I trust it? Before the attack, I experienced this specific prickle—this urgent need to move, run, get out—only when imminent danger hovered close. I'd been having the heebie-jeebies off and on since I'd arrived at the safehouse.

At first, I thought it was a symptom of my brain injury. But when I thought it through, I realized this didn't happen at the hospital—only since I came to the house. Odd. This was day five. Nothing had happened to *me* yet—only poor Jack and Gator. According to Striker, Gator and Jack got caught in the wrong place at the wrong time. Just bad luck.

I tried to meditate and center myself—big flop. I couldn't exercise to burn off this frenzied energy… I ended up looking out the window, pacing the floor and vomiting, again, only to move toward the window and start the cycle over. I was driving poor Axel nuts. He kept peering over his computer at me with scrutinizing intensity.

"Ma'am, are you all right?"

"I feel weird, Axel." I moved one hand over the other like I was peeling off gloves.

"Do you need medical assistance?"

"I'll be fine. A little stir crazy, maybe." I picked up the channel changer and tried to find something on TV to distract my attention away from the despair my sixth-sense was picking up from the woman and her child.

The phone rang. I had been waiting for it with so much tension that I jumped.

Axel gave me a sideways glance and answered it. "Striker's coming up the drive, ma'am." He spoke in a placating voice as if he were trying to coax me off a ledge.

When Striker strode in, he studied me with an arched brow. I stood in the middle of the room, digging my thumb into my palm. He glanced at Axel. "Has she been doing this long?"

"Since she woke up this morning." Axel stood to gather his paperwork. "She hasn't eaten anything either—just tea, and she vomited it back up."

Striker walked into the kitchen and looked around. "Did you make something for lunch, Lexi?" I shook my head. Eyes wide. Panting.

Striker took cold cuts out of the fridge, made me a sandwich and a bowl of fruit, and brought them to the sofa. "Can you try to eat something?" he asked.

I nodded and put the food mechanically in my mouth, not tasting a thing.

"What needs to be done?" Striker's low tone ensured only I would hear.

"I don't know. Trouble. Bad people. A lot of fear. Pain."

"Who?"

"The woman and child I told you about last night—It's a little girl, very little, three-years-old? Men—some good, some bad, then some who are good, but who have done something bad and don't know it."

"Do you recognize them?" he asked.

I hesitated before I said, "I've never met them before." I put the plate on the coffee table and closed my eyes against the storm kicking up under my lungs.

When I blinked my lids back open, Striker seemed to be

holding his breath. A muscle ticked under his left eye. "Do I know them?"

"Yes. Well, some of them, anyway. Certainly, the woman and the child. I think this is the woman you've been looking for, Lynda."

His gaze bore into me. Commander Striker Rheas. "What should I do?"

I spread my hands, palms up, and shook my head. "I can't get hold of anything. I've had fleeting images all day long. The sense of desperation... I get something, and then it drifts out of my reach. The more I grasp at it, the farther away it goes. It's awful. If only I had a photo, I could get some answers." I put my fists to the sides of my head. "This is unbearable."

Striker reached out and held my elbows. "Are they in danger right now?" he asked.

I tried to sense, tried very hard to get an answer for him. "The best I can tell you is that at this moment, things are calmer." Who was this woman to Striker? Obviously, someone important. Then it came to me with clarity. "Your sister Lynda and her child haven't been hurt."

Striker looked at me hard, then nodded. His nod told me I had the name and relationship right, and he believed what I said about their safety. He pulled out his phone, pressed a button, and said, "Anything? ... I have information this might be coming to a head. Put Brainiack in the field with Dagger." Then he hung up.

Striker's expression shifted. He covered over his hard edge with a layer of concern. Concern for me. I lowered my lashes self-consciously.

"Maybe we should distract you." Striker stood. "Do you want to tell me about the craziness on the table?" he asked.

We walked over to the display.

"Spyder McGraw brought me this case a year-and-a-half

ago," I said. "It was difficult to puzzle out. As I told you before, the day I gave him the name of the kingpin, Marcos Sylanos, Spyder went off-grid. I thought he had delivered this information to your team." I launched into my explanation, more than slightly guilty about how glad I was for the distraction.

Striker held up a hand to stop me. "I need to document this," he said.

Striker took pictures of the table, standing on a chair to get the names and words clearly in the shot. Then, Striker videotaped me while Axel took notes on the computer, making a record of the information. I explained each person represented on the papers and their role. Then I went back through and described their connections in the web and their involvement with the crime.

At the end of my description, I listed what evidence they could gather to prove Sylanos' culpability. Wow. It sure looked easy spread out on the table, but this was the result of years of data gathering by various officers, special-agents, and operators and months of puzzling on my part.

"That's amazing, ma'am. How do you know these people?" Axel's arms crossed over his chest as he stood, feet wide and stable, studying me.

"Sorry. I can't tell you that, Axel."

"Yes, ma'am." The phone rang, and Axel went to answer it.

Striker leaned over and whispered softly in my ear. "I'm heading out, unless you need me here. I can stay if you want me to."

"I'm not sure how that would help," I spoke quietly, moving my head so I could see his eyes. They were gleaming bottle green. As sharp as glass. "It might actually be making things worse. I'll call you if I pick up anything I think will help."

Striker's jaw worked back and forth. He seemed to be

298 | FIONA QUINN

weighing the choices. Finally, he gave me a curt nod. "Deep will be with you this afternoon, and Jack will be here after dinner. Don't expect the rest of the men today. They're all out in the field, following up on a Travis Wilson lead."

"There's new information?" My breath caught. I squeezed down hard on my emotions, so the hope wouldn't bloom. Hope made me vulnerable.

"Apparently, Wilson has a little addiction issue—nose candy and PCP. We've got several positive I.D.s."

Striker left Deep in charge of my care. I went on having a day from hell. My body felt like it was the wrong size, and my mind like it wanted to flee the scene. My stomach churned up green bile. *Hell in a Handbasket*, my psychic station played on repeat, volume turned up full blast.

Deep reported periodically to Striker throughout the day. He thought I needed to be under medical supervision. He seemed relieved when Jack showed up with takeout.

I stood blindly at the window. Jack came and led me by my elbow to the table, sat me in the chair, and put a plate in front of me. Crouching beside me, he tried to get me to eat, but I just couldn't. I knew it would come right back up. He took my temperature, my pulse, my blood pressure. With a little penlight, he checked the dilation of my eyes. I wasn't exhibiting any outward signs of a medical crisis, but I sure felt like one.

"Lexi, does your head hurt? Are you dizzy?" He ran through the same list of questions and checks he performed every thirty minutes and then called the results in to Striker, reporting that I seemed to be getting worse.

True. I was. Much worse. But I had no context for the pull and draw like waves trying to drag me out to sea, other than that these sensations had something to do with Striker's sister and possibly with the suspect I helped to find in a photo album. I had no crime. No information. Before, when I was training to go behind the Veil for police searches, I had always initiated the sequence. Not this time. This time, something or someone was manipulating me.

The Veil was a painful, terrifying space. I didn't want to go. Yet I did. For a teammate. For Striker. Gah! If only Miriam were here to support me, this decision would be easier. It was my choice, after all—I reminded myself emphatically—no matter how strong the call.

I heard drums, chanting. At first, they were remote—distant, like a game of hide and seek. My mind ran ahead, but the music followed me, twisted inside me, and entwined me with its... conviction? I wasn't sure what the music tried to comport.

I remembered reading Joseph Campbell's "The Hero with a Thousand Faces." And that was exactly how this felt.... The call to adventure, my refusal to go, and now supernatural aid presenting itself to help me along my path.

I got the impression of a group of women—foreign, distant, indebted to Striker for some act of heroism he had performed. They wanted to intervene in his crisis but needed help—my help. God, this was so damned uncomfortable! Unnerving. I hated this feeling of compulsion, leading me nowhere. Nothing I did relieved the sensation. I panted, trying to work through the commotion to find logical thoughts.

If I hadn't traveled Campbell's hero's path—traveling behind the Veil to save the woman with Miriam—I wouldn't have recognized any of this. I'd be begging for a trip to the hospital and some drugs to make it all go away. I wished this *was* the result of my head trauma because this extrasensory connection made me fear for my sanity. The music. The chanting. The summons.

The next step in a hero's journey was to cross over the

threshold and enter the heart of the story. This meant I'd have to move behind the Veil to understand what was really happening. I didn't want to go yet. Convinced that Striker needed to be here with me, I fought the pull and call. I stood alone in the middle of the room, gasping from the effort to wait.

37

The chime on the clock sounded eight. I brought my head up with a snap. Jack sat on a kitchen stool, watching me like I was an alien from a different galaxy.

"Striker," I muttered.

An engine roared up the drive, then Striker burst through the door without the warning phone call. He gripped a pile of photos in his hand, his eyes intense. Focused.

I pointed at the pile of pictures. "That's them."

"Can you help me?" Warrior Striker stood before me.

I pulled bottles of water from the fridge, set them on the table, then tugged the kitchen trashcan over, as well. I fetched a pad of paper and pen.

"I need a detailed map of the area," I said, grabbing a pillow off the sofa, and sat down on the dining room chair with the pillow in my lap. The Veil sucked and dragged at me. *Now! Now! Now!* It insisted. I slipped right out of my body.

"Listen to me and heed every word." My voice sang out rich and mature, with a slightly foreign accent. It echoed in my head as the words flowed from my mouth in a different woman's tone and pitch. One of the women, the Shaman in their group, was using me as a conduit. I became a container, a vessel. "I hold the fates of your loved ones. Their survival depends on the right action. Obey, or they will suffer, as will I. If you touch me, the rip you would create is a fate worse than death to me. Do not touch! Swear it!" I hissed.

Striker and Jack looked at me with the utmost seriousness; they both stared, unblinking, and said, "I swear."

"Do you understand? No matter what you see or hear, you will *not* touch me. Striker—you will have to leave at some point, and you may come back." I cleared my throat and tried to use my own voice. I didn't like to feel taken over and possessed like the victim in a horror flick. But still, it was the Shaman's voice that said, "Jack, you must not go. And until I can walk out of here on my own two feet, I am not to leave this house." She was reciting her rules. Not the same rules Miriam and I used, but this woman seemed to know what she was doing. Maybe if I stopped struggling against her, it would be easier. Quicker. Over and done. That's what I wanted more than anything, right now. This to be over and done.

Jack stood rigidly in full military persona. "Understood," he said.

While I had explained a little of this to Striker last night, Jack was working in the dark. Hell. I had never experienced the Veil this way myself. I was blind, too. I stepped back from rational thought, deciding to trust and allow the energy to use me.

I felt lives on the cusp.

Despair.

Striker's family was in danger—and I knew all too well what it was like to lose family. I was determined to save them.

My fingers gripped the edge of the table. Staying even partially in the here-and-now was painful. I spoke through gritted teeth. "Make sure everyone else stays away until the connection is severed."

"I swear," Striker said.

I reached for the photos and looked at Striker. "I will tell you things—you will have the team working for you on the outside. They will confirm what I say to you. You will say 'confirmed' or 'refuted.' This is all you are to say unless I ask for something more."

I breathed in jaggedly. My center shifted, and I stood in the middle of an African village. Sharp grass crushed under my feet. There was incredible heat and the smell of decay and dirt. As I looked around, I saw no men, only women. Circular huts stood between a river and the fire pit. The women sat in a circle, flames leaping up in the center. They swayed and chanted. Brilliant white smiles flashed at me, and nodded encouragement as they drummed. These were the women that Striker saved. I relayed this information to the men.

"Confirmed." Striker's voice startled me back to the dining room table and the pictures in my hand.

"These women perform rituals daily and have cast a prayer of protection over you and yours. This ritual is what calls me through the Veil. Striker, your service to these women is being repaid." Ah, I had my voice back.

I spread the photos on the table, picking out one of Lynda. "Your half-sister." With the picture in my hand, my nerves bristled. At first, I was terrified I was having an adrenaline dump, and I would be unable to help. But the fear-sweat drenching my shirt came from Lynda's distress, not mine. Now, almost two weeks past my attack, I was thankful that my cuts had healed together, and the salt no longer tortured me. Still, when I lay the picture aside, I was relieved to get it out of my hands.

The next picture I picked up was of a toddler. "This is your daughter? No, not your daughter. Your niece." This little girl's connection to Striker was confusing; it rumbled around in my head until I caught the meaning. "The biological father never saw the baby, and you have taken on the role of her father financially and emotionally. You are her uncle, but the energy is father-energy." I raised my head for confirmation, Striker stood, fists balled, and lips pressed together, the color drained from his face, leaving him ashen.

"Confirmed," Jack said.

I picked up a picture of a Latino man and woman; I ripped it in half and set the woman's picture away from me. "This man was married to your step-sister." I pointed at the picture of the woman I had pushed to the side. "Your step-sister died years ago. Names?" I saw Striker through cloudy eyes. I tingled electrically. There was no room for *me* here – I was a tool.

"My half-sister is Lynda. My niece is Camille—we call her Cammy. My brother-in-law is Juan. My step-sister, Mercedes—she died in a car accident."

I picked through the photos and pulled out a picture of a house and a photo that had a car in it. I tore the picture so that I held only the car. I found another picture of a man that made me moan. "This is Lynda's boyfriend." I looked at Striker.

"His name is Greg."

I pulled one more photo out of the pile. "And this is the devil."

I gave the rest of the photos to Striker and asked him to take them out of the room. He moved toward the garage. The phone rang; Jack answered. He told the Iniquus man on the line to park at the end of the drive and not approach; they were to contact the team and put them on stand-by. He hung up.

I took the picture of the house. "This is the place where it all began. Lynda, Camille, and Greg lived in this house and drove this car." I pointed to the picture of the green SUV.

"Confirmed," Striker said, returning to my side.

The safehouse dining room oscillated and disappeared. I stood in a kitchen, a sink full of dirty dishes on my left. My slippers were slick from the blood puddled on the linoleum under my feet. A mangled form lay to my right. It was hard to make out many details in this dim windowless room. Mouth gaping as if in mid-scream. Eyes wide and staring. Urine and feces. Dead. This had been Greg.

The Shaman reached for my hand and gently lead me up a stairway, down the hall, to the open door of a child's pink princess bedroom. Cammy's bedroom. I reached up and took hold of a purple lamb sitting on the shelf. I waited to gather impressions. I always found this part difficult. Miriam gleaned the most with shadows, where I got little by way of information. I understood nothing of what happened, just the present moment.

The image wavered in and out, making me dizzy. But the Shaman pet a soothing hand over my head, down my back, and whispered in my ear, "This was a gift but not truly a gift. A curse. The insides hold the answer. Only one person knows about this lamb, Greg's friend, Manuel. Manuel believes that if he reveals the secret, he will die. If he can resist telling, he might live. These are his thoughts, but he is doomed. He will be dead soon."

I nodded my understanding to the Shaman, hopeful that I told the story out loud for Striker and Jack to hear. The Shaman wavered away, and I found myself back in the dining room.

"Get the lamb," I said to Striker. "Bring it here. But warn the men, they'll find Greg's body on the kitchen floor."

I waited while Striker made the call. I sipped water from the bottle; the cold burned as it slid down my throat. I vomited into the trashcan, bringing a modicum of relief from the pressure inside me. When Striker disconnected from his phone call, I began again. I put the car picture in front of the house picture. I placed the photos of the devil, Lynda, and Cammy on top and drew stick figures of three men. Two with guns.

On an inhale, I moved further behind the Veil. My center dragged forward as I merged with Lynda. I stood at the end of a driveway. The house to my right. Woods to my left. Four men. The devil, two thugs, and Manuel. I was shrieking hysterically.

"No, no, no—no, no, no—no!" Lynda's cries burst from my mouth. I sensed Striker and Jack reacting to me. They both took a step back and away, jamming their hands deep into their pockets to keep from interfering.

One of the thugs gripped Cammy tightly against his body as she thrashed in his arms, screaming wildly, biting at his skin, kicking her patent leather Mary-Janes into his legs. The devil stood between us, preparing a syringe. Lynda struggled to get to him, to kick the vial from his hands, to tear out his eyes with her nails, but a thug held her tightly in place. The devil grinned maliciously at Lynda then gave Cammy a shot. Cammy slid to the macadam unconscious.

I stared down with disbelief at her crumpled child, lying at the devil's feet. The world shifted; Lynda's legs buckled. Before she fell to the ground, a violent push thrust her back into the car. Lynda peeked up from behind her cascade of hair, watching as Manuel, with a gun at his temple, was forced in beside us.

One of the goons picked up Cammy and tossed her into the front seat, the devil and his men climbed in, and the car took off.

As they drove down the road, I pulled myself away from Lynda, back into the safehouse dining room. "I said that out loud?" I asked.

"Confirmed," Jack said.

I sat silently for a long time, waiting to see where the car traveled. I sensed Lynda's panic. The galloping rhythm of her heart. Her arms clutched around her belly, whimpering and intermittently gasping for air. Finally, the car slowed. I put my pen on the map at Lynda's place and traced the route to a house about twenty minutes to the south.

I breathed in, returning to Lynda's body. The devil had clamped down on her arm with a steely grip. His fingers dug into her skin as he forced her away from the car, away from Cammy.

Will he kill me know? Lynda wondered. *Will I get to see Cammy again? Oh, God, please! Not like Greg. Quick. One bullet. Please!*

Her legs wobbled underneath us, her breath came in shallow puffs, making me lightheaded. I gripped the table, back in the dining room, to keep from falling over.

The devil spoke to someone, whom I couldn't see because Lynda focused on the tips of brown leather boots. His words were lost to me as Lynda slid into shock. We descended into a basement where a man laid face down, shot execution-style. My world went dark as Lynda passed out.

I woke to a pot of cold water thrown over Lynda. Drenching her and raising goose flesh. The water only worked momentarily. When she focused on the man's body, Lynda fainted again. This time, as she slunk to the floor, I jerked away from her and found myself back at the safehouse.

I caught Striker's eye. "You went through that house looking for your family. Not too many hours ago, confirm?" I said with a gasping breath.

"Confirmed," Striker's one word shot out like a bullet.

I had no personal emotion. Just a channel. Thank god. The Shaman and her music were never far.

"Send someone back," I directed. "You searched the house

before the meeting gathered. The men will find Juan's father's body in the basement."

Striker got on the phone and gave the command.

I swigged more water and vomited into the trash. It came up green and bilious. It made the water taste sweet in comparison. Again, I had to wait. The time that passed was meaningless to me, but I sensed how it took a toll on Striker. Jack stood stoically in the corner of the room, arms across his chest, legs spread wide like a child's superhero action figure waiting to be animated.

38

I held a picture of the car. My pen followed its path on the map, tracing their route. I cleared my throat. "The road ends here. The team needs to find a dirt road on the left. Take the dirt road for three minutes at twenty-five miles per hour. Get out. A hiking trail on the right..."

Striker was on his phone.

Somehow, I hung upside down. I lifted my head and saw one of the thugs in the car with Cammy and Manuel. The big one—the one who reminded me of a grizzly bear—had Lynda slung over his shoulder as he tramped through the autumn leaves to a hunting shack. Lynda—slack and in shock—hung across his shoulder, blood rushing to her head, thrumming in her ears. Inside the shack, the devil moved to the corner and lifted something heavy; I couldn't tell what. Thug set Lynda on her feet and took a step backward. Lynda turned toward the devil just as his fist, wrapped in brass knuckles, slammed into her face.

A bright, blinding light lit my vision; my head snapped back as blood poured from my nose. I buried my face in the throw pillow and screamed for mercy.

Fists and boots slammed into Lynda's body. And pummeled mine.

This was exactly what happened when I tried to save the woman back when Miriam needed me. The pain and injury the woman sustained in the alley battered me as well, though thankfully to a lesser degree. I swore I'd never try remote work again. But this was life-or-death for Striker's family. I made my decision earlier in the day. No turning back now. I tumbled down the damned Hero's Path, the "Road of Trials."

Channeling Lynda's voice, her Hispanic accent came through my mouth. Striker and Jack could hear her begging, screaming. They braced themselves beside me, frantic to intercede. Bruises and gashes graffitied my bare arms and face. Blood streamed from my nostrils. It soaked into the pillow, pooled on the table.

I drank from the bottle and vomited up blood and water, missing the trashcan and covering the floor. I pulled my stunned head from the pillow and whispered, "They had a transmitter. The devil beat Lynda, so Juan could hear and be terrified. She is bleeding to death. They left her in the cabin to die alone. Hurry."

Striker held the phone to his ear, giving directives. As he pressed the button to disconnect, it rang again. He listened for a minute. Striker studied me with a face of stone, his full combat mask in place.

"Confirmation of the assassination in the basement."

Again, the phone rang. "Confirmation of the purple lamb— they're bringing it in. Confirmation of Greg's body in the kitchen."

I drank the water. I used my arm to wipe the blood from my face; my nose continued to trickle. I lifted my shirt and swiped at my lips with it. Blood drip, drip, dripped into my lap. It made me sticky. I shivered uncontrollably, but the Shaman had her hands on my shoulders and blew lightly over my face. I stilled. I could breathe again. I gained enough focus to continue.

I picked up the picture of the car and asked where it was driving. I put pen to map and followed the car to a spot where it stopped. I circled the location on the map.

Since Cammy lay unconscious, I needed a resource for information other than her thoughts and senses. I decided to attach to Manuel. He was stepping away from the car. The hard metal of the devil's gun barrel pressed between his shoulder blades, making me arch backward. Manuel looked back at the car, trying to figure out how to make his escape. The two thugs relaxed in the back seat. Cammy lay crumpled in the front—half on the seat, half on the floor.

With a shove from behind, Manuel walked forward robotically, his knees locked in place to hold himself up. We moved toward an elevator. Manuel peered hopefully around, thinking that someone might show up and pull an alarm, and then he'd have a chance. But there was no one.

On the ninth floor, the doors slid open to the sound of men's deep-throated laughter. A light shone from a doorway. When we walked into their office, and Manuel saw the other men, he knew he was going to die. That was the strangest emotion—nothing to do but wait and die.

The devil made the men kneel. Manuel giggled maniacally. The sound as I reproduced it from my own mouth had Striker and Jack shifting on the balls of their feet. Run, flee, their limbic systems were probably warning them. I certainly wanted to— Manuel, too. But instead, we knelt on the office floor, hands bound behind his back, listening to the devil argue with the other men.

Suddenly a blast jarred the air, an explosion, followed by a second one. The devil had shot the men in their thighs. I watched them thrashing on the floor, screaming. Manuel thought about the animals he used to light on fire; they sounded the same. The devil yelled at the injured men, asking questions they couldn't answer.

"The devil is transmitting this to Juan, so he'll feel more terror," I said. "Oh! Oh! The devil shot the two men in their heads."

Manuel looked at the dark holes in the men's foreheads. Felt the silence. Dead. Yes, must be dead. They were dead. Manuel's mind tried to grasp this simple fact. Darkness closed around him, and I swiftly moved to the devil before Manuel passed out.

The devil kicked Manuel in the gut. Manuel didn't move, and with great indifference, the devil shot him and left, whistling.

I was the sportscaster in this deadly game, offering the listeners a blow-by-blow. No commentary. I had no opinions—only sensation, vision, sound. Well, that wasn't true. I had desire—desire to keep one foot on this plane to offer my perceptions—desire to get back to Cammy and get help to her—desire to walk the Labyrinth, face the monsters, and perform the ordeal, so I could get home and make this a distant nightmare.

I swallowed water and vomited, waiting to see where the devil went next. I struggled to be in a victim's body, to face their fear and pain. But I found it so much harder to be in the perpetrator's body—one with the monster. Evil hungrily sucked at me—trying to attach itself parasitically and live in me. This felt dangerous to my soul. If only Cammy would regain consciousness... But as it was, I'd have to fight the fight here, connected to the devil, in order to save her.

Strands of coagulated blood slid down my throat and choked me. I pulled them from my mouth with my fingers. The bruising on my face made my eyes swell. Tears rolled down my cheeks, mixing with the blood flowing from my nose.

The phone rang. They were bringing the lamb in.

"No," Striker commanded. "I'll meet you in the drive. I need you back out." Striker wrote down the address of the office building and jogged to the door. When he came in, he placed the stuffed toy gingerly on the counter. I rested with my head on the table.

The phone rang; Striker answered and listened. Striker's mood shifted to intense emotion and then back to combat.

He lost his composure for a half-breath.

"Lynda is confirmed. She's alive, en route to the hospital."

In the car, the devil looked down. Cammy stirred on the seat, coming around. He shook his head and pulled the vial of medicine and a hypodermic needle from the pocket of his navy sport coat.

"No! No! No! Cammy, stay asleep!" I shrieked as if she could hear me.

As if that would help.

As if I could stay the devil's hand by the force of will.

I was becoming useless as panic sprung from nowhere and overwhelmed me. A song drifted through the air, washed me in the rhythm of its chanting. It floated me until I recovered myself enough to continue, then the song wafted away.

"The devil has the medication out again; he gave Cammy another dose. It's too big of a dose. Too soon," I croaked.

I slipped into Cammy. Her heart beat with a slow thud. Her breath came in shallow distressed gasps. Not enough oxygen. Not nearly enough. Her cells screamed for more. She needed help, and she needed it now.

I slid into the devil to try and figure out the direction they traveled and how to get someone in the position to save Cammy.

His indifference to her distress stunned me.

He couldn't be human and look down at this beautiful child,

watch her turn blue, and only think what good bait she would make to get her Uncle Juan to talk.

And I knew from what the Shaman said at the first house that Juan wouldn't be able to talk. He didn't know anything about the lamb. Only Manuel knew, and Manuel was dead.

I slipped back toward my own body to track the car. I wasn't doing much better than Cammy. Broken and exhausted, blood continued to drip from my nose and seep from my wounds. Again, I touched my pen to the map and drew the route, then circled the place where they stopped.

Striker had his cell phone up to his ear, whispering into it.

In semi-darkness, Cammy lay at my feet. I was in the body of a man I didn't know. He shoved Cammy out of the way with his booted foot and stalked over to Juan. I flitted from person to person, gathering information. The phrase that glared the brightest was, "Maybe we should open her artery, so you can watch her blood drain, eh? Maybe that will help your recall." I couldn't take in anything more.

The Shaman snapped her fingers, and I found myself panting in the safehouse dining room.

I searched for Striker's eyes. They shone black and unfathomable. I gulped at the air. Striker jerked forward to grasp at me as I slid from my chair, but Jack made a lunging grab and kept him from touching me. My head clunked with a resounding thud against the wooden table before I caught the edge and pulled myself upright in the chair.

Striker spun, his fist balled and chambered for a punch. But quickly, Striker seemed to remember Jack wasn't the enemy. The enemy wasn't here. There was no one to fight. With rigid control, Striker knelt beside me. "Tell me what to do."

"This house holds secrets. You can't go in and rescue your child. It's fortified, and there are too many of the devil's soldiers inside." I took in a jagged breath. Having gathered what intel I could and puzzling through the scene to the best of my ability, I offered a plan.

Picking up the picture of Juan, I said, "You can't save this man. He'll die momentarily. Go and negotiate—Trade, the lamb for the girl. The lamb is stuffed with diamonds and packets of heroin, the cause of all the death and misery. They'll trade. They realize the child's in danger and won't survive the medication much longer. They'll think they've traded the lamb for the child's body, and that will make them laugh."

Striker's energy spiked to razor-sharp points. It hurt to be near him.

"I'll do what I can from here to help her." I struggled within myself; the words tangled my tongue. Enunciating through swollen lips made me sound infantile. I gasped and spat blood.

"After you rescue Cammy, and she's heading to the hospital, come back. Remove her photo from my hands without touching me. Wash it in water, picturing Cammy in my arms and us moving away from each other." I was glad the Shaman sat beside me, telling me what to do; I had no clue on my own.

"After that, I can be touched. I need help." I looked from one man to the other; my focus was fogged and almost unseeing. Even still, I caught fear and apprehension flicker and disappear behind the men's eyes. Then Striker picked up the lamb and ran from the house.

Time passed. I swayed in my chair. Sometimes I vomited. Bile and blood covered me. My nose continued to bleed. At some point, I slipped onto the floor beneath the table. I laid on my side, never releasing the photo. Jack knelt beside me, desperate to help. Blood coagulated and covered my nostrils; I breathed through my mouth, my face down in the bloody vomit-water. In the ether, I felt Striker lifting Cammy. Felt her receiving help, oxygen flowing in her veins. Thank god.

Striker crashed the door open and carefully extracted the picture from my hands. Water ran in the sink as Striker washed away the connection. "Done!" When he yelled, the action began.

Jack lifted the table and threw it out of the way. He pulled the strands of congealed blood from my nostrils. He used his fingers to scoop out my mouth and throat, clearing the blood and mucus that choked me.

Striker checked for a pulse. "Medic!"

39

I sunk into a recuperative trance that held me still and unknowing for a week. Then, one morning, I woke up like nothing had happened. I pulled myself upright and glanced over at the medic. "Good Morning."

He nodded. "Good morning, ma'am."

"Where are Striker and Jack?" I was surprised to be alone with this stranger.

"Jack's eating breakfast, ma'am, and Striker is taking a phone call in his room. He said he'd be right back. The call concerned his sister."

"Okay. Can you unhook me from the equipment, please? I'd like to take a shower."

His hands were practiced and professional.

Unleashed from the sensors, catheter, and IV, I picked up a fresh set of clothes and went to shower and change.

In the bathroom mirror, I traced a finger over the thin, red line where someone removed the stitches from my head. A two-inch scar ran along the side of my forehead; I arranged my hair to hide the mark. The Wilson bruising had faded away. I pulled the man-sized t-shirt over my head. Yes, my stomach had healed as well. All the crusty scabs and glue were gone. In the light, pink scars traced their design like the path of a figure skater over me.

Cleaned and ready, I opened the door to find Striker standing, hands on hips, waiting for me. He gave me one of his long, assessing looks, then gathered me into his arms.

"Oh, thank God," he whispered into my hair. "Thank God."

My cheek pressed against the soft fabric of his shirt. I listened to his heart beating an accelerated tattoo. He was warm, steady, dependable. I breathed him in and felt my solidity returning to me. He held me tightly for a few minutes, then released me, and reached for my hand.

"Someone else needs to see you're okay as much as I did."

We went down the stairs together. The team sat at the table, eating breakfast.

Jack leaned a hip into the kitchen counter, coffee mug in hand. He stood when I came in, his face lined with concern.

The men's moods instantly shifted as tension stirred the air. The team watched Jack closely, focusing angry eyes on him. I immediately understood that they held Jack responsible for my injuries. I figured no one had offered them an explanation; neither Jack nor Striker had confided what had happened the night Lynda and Cammy were rescued. How could they? The men must think Jack allowed me to be hurt somehow.

I reached for the stepstool under the counter and laid it at Jack's feet. Stepping up to bring my eyes level with Jack's, I wrapped my arms tightly around his muscular neck.

"Jack, you are so damned loyal and brave," I said. "I can't imagine what I put you through." My voice hitched as my emotions overwhelmed me. "I will always be grateful. Thank you for everything you did to help me." I hugged him tightly.

Jack nodded against my hair, his hands on my hips to balance me. I gave him a big smacking kiss on the cheek and jumped back down.

I turned to the men. "Long time no see, what's for breakfast?"

When the rapport between Jack and the team had found its way back to even keel, Striker dismissed his men and the medical attendant. Jack, Striker, and I gathered in the living room. I curled comfortably at the end of the couch.

"How are you feeling, Chica?"

"Well, thank you. You guys don't look so hot." And they didn't. They were both clean-shaven and dressed in pressed Iniquus fatigues. But the dark circles under their eyes matched their uniforms. Stress gave them an unhealthy pallor.

"I don't think I've had any shut-eye since you decided to play Sleeping Beauty," Striker said.

"I explained to you how I slept for three days after that one case."

"Yes, but this lasted more than twice as long. You've been out for over a week now. When you told me about the last time you did this, you *never* fully explained what would happen to you." His voice was accusatory, making me feel like an errant child, caught in the act, and shamed.

"I pictured you going behind the Veil more like watching a movie," he said. "And, that you found the effort tiring." Striker stopped and scrubbed a hand over his face. Jack shifted around, looking uncomfortable. They both seemed to be struggling.

Striker shook his head and reached for my hand. "I can't even imagine what was happening for you. I *can* say it was terrifying to watch. I never would have handed you those photos had I even the smallest inkling of what I was going to put you through." Guilt thickened his words. I misread what he said earlier. He wasn't accusing me. He was blaming himself.

"It's a darned good thing you didn't understand what I was saying to you, then. I've got no regrets. You shouldn't either." I shifted my focus back and forth between the two men.

"How are Lynda and Cammy?" I managed after a few minutes.

"Cammy's good, no residual effects from the drug. She's moved in with my dad and step-mom down in Miami. They say her only memory is of a pretty blonde woman who held her the whole time and made her feel safe."

"Wow. Surprising. She saw me? Huh. And your sister?"

"She's alive, and that's saying something. The men found her on this side of dead. It was a close thing." Striker stopped for a minute. I think he needed to regroup. "She has some more surgeries to go and a lot of psychological work and physical rehab in front of her. The doctor said if she sticks with the plan, she'll eventually recover."

"Is Lynda in Miami now, too?" I asked.

"They'll transfer her down when she's made improvements. She'll have lots of support—family and her oldest friends—she'll be able to visit with Cammy."

"Good. I'm so glad she'll get the love and care she needs." I considered Jack. "I walked in on some mighty strong cold-shouldering. Have the men been giving you a hard time?"

Jack shrugged. "Picture it from their point of view. They came in from a mission to find the dining room and kitchen covered in blood. You were gone from sight. Medical support wouldn't talk. Striker and I wouldn't talk. I was the guy on duty. We all think highly of you, ma'am, not like a client at all, more like a team member and friend. We were charged with your safety, and they thought I'd hurt you or allowed you to be hurt."

"They didn't think I fell down with vertigo and cracked my head open?"

"It doesn't matter, ma'am. You were in my charge. If you were falling, I should have caught you. Besides, if you fell, we would say so."

"I'm sorry."

"I'm not. It's a small thing, comparatively speaking."

A distant memory stirred. Something I heard before I went into the trance. "You exploded the devil's mansion?"

"Axel did, as soon as I had Cammy with me," Striker said.

"Any survivors?"

Striker shook his head. "None."

"Good." I sighed and shut my eyes. Again, we fell into silence.

"I need to tell you something." I shifted my weight uncomfortably, wanting to postpone my newest revelation, even if for just a few seconds. I cleared my throat and plunged in. "I get these things I call 'knowings'—pieces of information that seem to come from nowhere."

"More ESP?" Striker's posture stiffened.

"A different channel on my psychic network. Anyway, the thing I was 'knowing,'" I did finger quotes in the air, "quite clearly, as I woke up this morning, was that Travis Wilson figured out where I am. I need to leave immediately, and I need to stay at a high-security building. The place I should move to has a square, white office with a green roof set on a large lawn. The colored roof helps disguise the building from the air. This is part of a complex with other buildings near moving water, and a high rise near some woods." I stopped for a minute to recall the picture I had seen. "The designer situated houses to make it appear to be a small subdivision to outsiders. The houses are not really residences. They're storage units, I think. 'Striker will know what bed I'm to sleep in.'"

I blushed as I said that out loud. For any man to choose my bed for me made me feel like I was betraying Angel's trust. Striker eyed me curiously; he had seen the blush. I wondered what he made of it. I took a deep breath and said on the exhale, "That's what I 'know.' I also 'know' I'm to take seven days to finish healing my head, and then I'm to dangle."

"Sorry?" Striker wrinkled a perplexed brow.

I mimed with my hands. "Like putting a worm on a hook."

"You want to be bait?"

"I do what I'm told. My 'knowings' are never wrong. Just sometimes hard to interpret. This one is very clear."

"We need to leave now?" Jack asked.

"Yes. Do you recognize the white building I'm talking about?"

Striker and Jack looked at each other. "We do," Jack said.

Striker's sharp focus seemed to cut through any crap. "If anyone else had said this, I wouldn't pay the least attention—since it's you, it's the gospel. I'm willing to do this, move you, and dangle you. But no secrets. We're partners all the way. Agreed?"

"Agreed." I nodded my affirmation. I wasn't going to dangle on my own, that's for darned sure.

"Do you know how he found the safe house?" Jack asked me.

"I got the impression he followed us from the hospital the morning I was brought here by a tracking device on one of the Humvees. I'm not sure why he hasn't made a move yet. But it sure explains my heebie-jeebies. He's been nearby all this time."

"Right now?" Striker moved to the window to scan the front of the house.

"Right now."

"Is there a mole at Iniquus? Do you know? I imagine not since that's where you want to go," Striker asked.

"Iniquus is clean—when I woke up, the understanding I had was that this guy has an issue with the government. He wants to be a homegrown terrorist, for people to believe he's a great hero when he finally reveals himself as the mastermind. He had a group he was training with, paramilitary, but he didn't work and play well with others. I'm picking up on a mentor who encouraged him to branch out and do his own thing, a special operation, something like that."

I pulled my hair back and secured the ponytail with an elastic band. "Wilson's goal is to terrorize the agencies. He wants to spread fear through the evening news. He's pissed off because he's not getting the publicity he thinks is his due. Even the picture they showed on TV said 'armed and dangerous, give us information'—they never explained his crime, and boy was he furious. He thrives on fear."

Striker turned toward me from his place by the window. "He has someone working with him, then?"

"He's flying solo now—doesn't trust his mentor anymore. They recently had some kind of falling out. This piece of the puzzle explains how he got not only his training but his equipment. The rest of the images mean nothing to me—I have no context for them. Superfluous data for right now. It isn't much, but it's something. Am I really going to your headquarters?"

"That's what you described. Lexi, do you have anything more on this group?" Striker asked.

I shrugged.

"I guess we'd better make our move. I'll bring in a decoy and an escort. Lexi, Jack's going upstairs with you, gather your things, and load them in the car. Are you ready for this?"

"Yup, I put on my big girl panties when I got up this morning and pulled them all the way up."

Striker and Jack grinned broadly.

"Good to know," Striker said.

40

I stared out my window with excitement as we approached the complex. I'd never been here before. The gates were massive, the lawn manicured. They had easy access to the highway. Woods and water protected them on three sides.

As we bypassed the main building, Striker said, "That's headquarters. Our offices are located there. We're going to the barracks."

He drove over to the apartment building and parked in the underground lot. Striker's name, stenciled in yellow paint, marked his reserved spot right in front, by the elevator bank. He scanned to make sure the coast was clear. As I jumped down to the cement, my team surrounded me, shielding me from anyone who would come in and from the security cameras.

"Even though you said Iniquus is clean, I still want you under wraps. We don't know if one of the other men could be giving out information by mistake," Striker said as they walked me into the elevator. Striker pushed the button for the eleventh floor—the top.

"Who lives here?"

"Iniquus men, ma'am," Jack said.

"No women?"

"Not in these barracks. The women share houses by the water, but there aren't many women in our organization."

"What about wives and girlfriends?"

"These are barracks, ma'am. Visitors and family can't come here. Most of us visit our girlfriends' places or have homes for our wives. They aren't allowed here," Jack said.

"Are any of the Save-Lexi Team married?"

"No." Jack chuckled. "the *Save-Lexi Team* are all on the open market."

Striker inserted his key into the apartment door, and we walked in. He pointed down the hall, and Blaze carried my few shopping bags in that direction.

"This is gorgeous!" I let my eyes take in the room. A floor to ceiling window showing a panorama of Washington on the other side of the river took up one wall in the living room. I bet the view was spectacular at night with the city lights twinkling. A huge, stone, wood-burning fireplace formed another wall. Bookshelves, filled with worn leather and new hardbacks, flanked the chimney. I wandered over to read the titles—lots of histories, sciences, and biographies. The walls were neutral, showcasing gorgeous works of art with vibrant shades of blues, violets, and indigos.

I turned to Striker. "This isn't where you live normally?" There was something intangible missing from this apartment; it felt temporary to me.

"It's where I live when I'm working. My house is on the Bay."

I swallowed a sip of juice that Jack handed me and asked, "Does it look like this? Did you decorate?"

"I didn't decorate; it was done professionally to my specifications."

I cast my gaze around again. "Beautiful. Did you pick out the art?"

"I painted those myself. Painting helps me unwind."

"Striker! They're gorgeous. Breathtaking." I stepped forward and read the signature G. Rheas scrawled across the bottom corner. I knew Striker, the soldier and the operator, not the casual, hang out at home, artistic Striker.

This was weird.

Striker stood behind me. "Surprised?" he asked.

"Stunned."

While I explored the apartment, Striker briefed and dismissed the team, then showed me to my room. He pointed to the door next to mine. "The bathroom is here. My room is the next one down."

"If you can't invite people to the barracks, why are there two bedrooms?"

"Sometimes we work through the night, and we prefer to do it here at my place—if my team members need to rest, they do that in the guest room."

"Oh." The rich teal walls were dramatic against the luxurious ivory comforter and sheets that dressed my bed. The lines of the furniture were clean, a modern styling that was reminiscent of the 1940s. As I took it all in, running my hands over the rich textures, Striker watched me closely. "Okay?"

"Just lovely."

Striker looked at my feet. As he raised his eyes, they settled on my chest. "You need shoes...and bras."

I glanced down at my breasts; yup, it was cold outside.

"Can you call someone who would pack a bag for you?" he asked.

"Yes, please. Alice, my across-the-street neighbor."

Striker handed me his phone, and Alice picked up on the third ring.

"Alice? Lexi here. Did I catch you at a bad time? ...Yes, I'm still in rehab, but doing well, thank you. I'll be home in a week... Oh, okay, thanks so much...Alice, I need a favor. A friend of mine, Jack, is going to go by my house to get me some clothes. All I have are pajamas and slippers, and I'm afraid of what might show up if I send a man to pick out my things." I winked at Jack. Everything would be perfect if I sent him to get my stuff. "Would you mind packing a suitcase for me? ...No, no, casual, comfortable clothes, tennis shoes, bras, and stuff. Thank you so much."

"Okay?" Jack asked from the hallway.

"She said she was so sorry I had a horrific fall down the stairs."

Striker put his hands in his pockets and leaned against the doorjamb. "Detective Murphy told the neighborhood you screamed when you fell down and hit your head. The men rushed over to check on you. They had to break into your house, which set off the alarm. The cops were investigating to make sure it wasn't a crime scene."

I nodded. My memory flew back to that night. Anxiety clawed its way up my throat.

"Murphy told everyone you had a head and back injury, and you went to the hospital, then to physical rehab. The men who were involved were sworn to secrecy in order to protect you, the neighborhood, and the investigation."

"Thank you for telling me. I've felt guilty about bringing this craziness to our neighborhood."

.

41

I spent seven days sequestered in Striker's apartment recouping, practicing my quick draw skills, working out as much as possible, and preparing myself to play chum for Wilson. The night before I was headed home to act like all was right in my world, my nerves were getting the better of me. I paced manically, wringing my hands.

"You don't have to," Striker said, from where he sat on the breakfast barstool, watching me.

He had startled me from my thoughts, which were razor-blade sharp and vinegar-soaked. "I don't have to do what?"

"Go home. Act as bait. Face Wilson."

"I should stay a prisoner?"

Some emotion flickered across his eyes.

"I'm sorry. I don't mean that. You guys have been great. I've never felt imprisoned. I'm not sure why I said that."

"I do." He shifted off the stool and held out his hand. "You need to see the sky."

Laying on a quilt Striker had spread in the middle of the green expanse outside the barracks, I pointed at the plane overhead descending toward Reagan National. "Someday, I'm going to jet away to faraway places and see exotic things."

"You haven't traveled?"

"Unless I was flying a mission for the Civil Air Patrol, the farthest I've been from home is the Millers' farm with Spyder and the dogs. There's a long list of things for me to see—the aurora borealis in Iceland, the fields of tulips blooming in Holland... Have you traveled much?" I rolled on my side, propping myself up on an elbow.

"More than I want in some parts of the world, less than I'd like in others."

I nodded in the dark and flopped on my back. "Spyder loved the stars," I said. "He used to tell me all of the stories. I think it's amazing to stare up into the heavens and know that those stars are portals through time. I'm seeing back hundreds, even thousands of years, the same stars at which Galileo and Copernicus studied. Someday, I'll tell my children the same Greek stories the ancient Greek mothers told their children. Do you see Orion?" I pointed up. Striker angled his head toward mine until we touched. "Yes," he said.

"See the belt? Those two stars are Betelgeuse and Bellatrix— the real names of my dogs, Beetle and Bella. Do you know the story of Orion and Artemis?"

"Why don't you tell me?"

"Well," I started in, "Orion was a mortal, and also gorgeous and sexy and wonderful, and the gods and goddesses had taken note of him. He ran around hunting with Artemis. They were close friends. But she had dedicated herself to virginity, and Orion preferred bedding men, so no hanky-panky was going on between them. One day Apollo shows up and gets all jealous of his sister, Artemis, because he thinks she's broken her vow and done the deed with Orion. And really, Apollo wanted to do the deed with Orion."

"The deed?" he asked.

"*The* deed."

Striker chuckled. "Ah."

"So, later in the day, Orion makes a play for Apollo, and they enjoy a sexual tryst. But Orion makes the mistake of talking about Artemis, and this makes Apollo insanely jealous. In his pique, he tricks Artemis into shooting Orion in the head. When Artemis figures out her brother's duplicity, she tries to get someone to help her bring Orion back to life. No one could, so she flung Orion's body up into the heavens. He continued on as a constellation. She sits over his shoulder."

"That's not happy." Striker sat up and hooked his arms around his bent knees.

"Nope. Those Greek gods weren't kind to mortals, but at least Artemis felt sorry."

"Spyder tell you that story?"

I sat up too, carelessly picking at the grass blades and twirling them around my fingers. "Yup. Spyder loved to tell stories."

Striker quirked a brow. "He ever tell stories about me?"

"All the time. You were one of his favorite story topics."

"You know a lot about me then," he said.

"Well, stuff that you did with Spyder—I don't know much

about your personal life. Like for example, how old are you?" I asked.

Striker smiled. "Twenty-six, today."

I drew up to my knees. "What? Today's your birthday? Why didn't you tell me?"

"Things are a little hectic." He reached out to pull a leaf from my hair. His hand rested there, his thumb gently stroking my cheek. His lips looked soft and full. My body urged me into his arms. The pull felt magnetic. I waited for the familiar 'knowing,' the words of warning and caution: *hell in a Handbasket*. But all I heard was the wind rustling the last of the crisp autumn leaves in the trees. My breath came short and shallow as I struggled with desire. This was wrong—warning or no warning. These were the wrong feelings; Striker was my friend and protector. I was really missing Angel's arms.

I pushed myself to standing and brushed off my sweats. I needed a little space between us.

Striker got up, too, folded the blanket, and tucked it under his arm. Neither of us said a word as we went back to his apartment.

I perched on the edge of the couch across from him. "I'm sorry about…" and I made a vague gesture, "that."

He shook his head. His voice sounded low and serious. "Nothing to be sorry for, Chica."

"This," I gestured back and forth between us, "gets hard for me sometimes. Confusing."

He slowly nodded, eyes unwavering, body taut. "I'm sorry. I don't mean for it to be."

I pursed my lips then stood up with a wobbly smile. "I hope this turns out to be a wonderful year. Happy birthday."

He didn't move a muscle, he just looked at me with his green eyes unreadable, closed to me, and I went to my room. Alone.

I woke up early, packed my bags, and climbed into Striker's car for the trip home. The team had been putting surveillance into place all week. Cameras and audio devices peppered my neighborhood, moving outward to include a five-block radius. The team would watch remotely from three blocks over, monitoring all the comings and goings, and keeping in constant contact with my watchdog.

They told me to stay at my house or in my immediate neighborhood but thought we could speed things up if I hung out on the porch as much as possible. I'd be wearing a Kevlar vest whenever I was exposed, and an escort would accompany me on my errands. So, a little more freedom than at the safehouse.

Walking into my home again felt odd. I loved my refurbished wooden floors. The walls were now painted rich, soothing colors, and, thank god, looked totally different from the night I left in the ambulance. Manny had taken my old furniture down to our neighbor Missy's house and stored Angel's and my few belongings in boxes in the closet.

"Looks Spartan," Striker said.

"Ha! Yeah, the painters just got done. My new furniture and stuff are in storage."

"Give me the info, and I'll get everything taken care of right now before you end up sleeping on a bare floor."

Three hours later, a moving truck pulled up, and Iniquus men started to unload. I had my friend Chantal's interior design sketches in hand. She had helped me pick everything out as part of a project she was doing for her advanced design class up at the university. The men brought the things in, I directed them to the correct rooms. They unwrapped my dishes, hung the new lighting fixtures, and attended to every detail. When they left, my home was both stylish and finished. Striker and I wandered from room to room, taking it all in.

"Nice," he said. "I'd say this suits you, Lexi—artistic, inviting, calm—there's always some interesting thing to catch the eye. Very welcoming. Yes, you belong here."

"Thanks. I think it fits me too. And, those descriptors are all things I like near me. Hey, are you guarding me?"

"Yup."

I walked back to my kitchen to make some tea. "Any news on Lynda?"

"She has another surgery scheduled for today. They're rebuilding her ACL."

"Shit!" I said.

"The doctors are optimistic. This is her last surgery before they move her down to Florida." Striker opened my fridge. "There's no food. We should go shopping." He pulled out his keys.

"Do you know how many I'll be feeding?"

"No way of telling who's going to be in and out. Probably no more than two—you and a watchdog—at any given meal. Gator's volunteered to take on that role most of the time. We want someone in your house around the clock. We have to work this, so no one clues into our being here. Most of the traffic will be over at our satellite where the equipment is set up."

"What about at night?"

"Especially at night. Nights I'll be the watchdog, like at the safehouse." He paused. "You seem relieved."

"I am a little bit, can't tell you why—the other guys are great. It's …"

"Let me guess. You're afraid you'll get the heebie-jeebies, and you want me to be the only one who knows what a coward you truly are. So, you only want to climb shivering and shaking into my bed, not in bed with every guy on the team?" Striker was teasing me.

"Yup—jumping into bed with every Tom, Dick, or Harry or in this case every Jack, Deep, or Gator might come off, not only as lily-livered, but also a little slutty, and think about how many loads of sheets I'd have to run through the wash."

42

The surveillance is going smoothly, I thought as I stood in the street chatting with Manny and Justin, catching up on neighborhood gossip. They didn't bring up my attack. Never asked how I was doing. Where I had gone. Just picked up where we had left off the morning of the football game. Dave said he had briefed them before I got home. If Sarah or Alice suspected that Iniquus watched from the shadows, they never mentioned it. They never looked over their shoulders or stared at the trees and telephone poles camouflaging the equipment.

Now I spent most of my time sitting on my porch working on the last little bits of my class assignments, trying to look accessible and vulnerable. The vulnerable part came easily.

A few days before Halloween, Sarah, Alice, and I decided to throw a party in the empty lot next to Justin's house. My team gave me permission to be out as long as I had a GPS tracker, a wire, and a bulletproof vest under my black witch's dress, and Striker and Jack on either side of me.

Halloween night, a storm brewed overhead. The chilly wind made the hot cider simmering in a large black cauldron on the campfire all the more welcome. Homemade cinnamon apple doughnuts kept warm on the coals. I handed out the refreshments to the adult passers-by and candy to the children.

When we returned to my house, Striker sat down at his computer. I went to bed early with a book, falling almost instantly into a restless sleep. When icy hands closed over my throat to choke me, I sprang up covered in sweat, gasping. That nightmare felt too real.

Like a hound, I lifted my nose and sniffed the air. Wilson, magnified. I jumped from my bed and crept cautiously down the stairs, straining to hear. To see. The smell was too strong to miss. Sewage vapors rising noxiously under a blazing sun. The further I moved down the stairs, the more pungent and unbearable the stench became.

I stood on the bottom tread with my hand clutching the newel post. Crouched. Panting in short, shallow bursts, swinging my head from the front of the house to the back. Which way? Which way would he come in?

Striker leaped to his feet. My face must have been an easy read because he pressed the communicator button on his shoulder. "Blaze, what've you got."

"Crickets," came the response.

"Heads up." Striker released the button. "What's happening?" he asked me. Steady. So steady and solid. Like a boulder. Like a fundamental belief.

"I smell him," I whispered.

Striker didn't answer. He was processing, not understanding, waiting for me to elaborate. I couldn't move—didn't know where to move. How to react. What to do. An explosion sounded in the distance. The electricity slammed off.

"Transformer, four blocks over," came Blaze's voice from the plastic box on Striker's shoulder.

"Send Gator to check it out." Striker's hands rested on my shoulders. The world was painted pitch black. Cloud cover obscured the full moon. No street lights. Nothing. Just darkness and the sound of barking dogs. The wind kicked up to a howl, "eerie" didn't even come close to describing this.

The shiver running through my body garbled my voice. "I have a whole-house generator hooked up outside on the back right, by the wall. Let's get some electricity on." We moved together toward the kitchen door.

"Striker, Code Red. We have night-camera visual of an unsub. He meets Wilson's size. Three blocks, west. Moving fast."

We changed directions. Striker gripped me around the waist, steering me to the basement door. This was the plan. Go down. Lockdown. Let the team handle it. Now that we were in motion, this felt wrong. I wanted to face Wilson. Wanted my fingers around his throat. *Needed* to be the source of incredible pain.

Striker told the team where to find the generator. Silence followed their WILCO. I stood in the basement to the right of the stair, my breath ragged. Listening. Waiting. Striker didn't want me in the fight, but if Wilson came into the house, I was going for him.

"Looks like unsub is using eye drops by the garage. My guess is PCP. Climbing wall. Randy's closing. Gator's two blocks," came Blaze's voice over the communicator.

"Roger. Lexi is secured."

Glass crashed in my kitchen, followed by the tinkling of shards hitting tile. The door banged against the wall. My alarm system sounded. I launched myself toward the stair hoping the black and noise would get me past Striker's reach.

As I leaped forward, Striker's arm circled my ribs. I had no context for up or down. I found myself helplessly rolled by a massive wave. When I landed on my stomach, Striker had my legs pinioned wide. My wrists were crossed and clasped in a vice grip stretched above my head. My cheek pressed into the cold, smooth surface of the painted cement. My head was forced back and stilled against my arm. Striker's thumb pushed up in the soft spot under my chin, effectively gagging me. The only noises I could make were groans and whimpers. Striker's full weight flattened me. His hips stacked with mine. I couldn't get enough air. I struggled.

"Relax," Striker ordered. I pressed my weight into my knees and elbows, trying to raise up and find a way free.

As I fought, a woman's voice came over my two-way house-alarm monitor, asking for identification. Announcing that police were en route. Warning that they were taping everything and holding it for evidence.

"Relax," Striker ordered against my ear. "I'll end up crushing you if you don't relax."

I was out of breath. I had no choice. I rested, motionless, waiting for a chance to escape.

"I'm going to lift off. You're going to lay still."

The hell I am.

Striker shifted his weight to his arms, and when he did, I made my move. Striker's hips dropped on top of mine, trapping me again.

"Stop," he hissed.

His fingers never moved from my chin. I still couldn't make a sound. I focused my attention above me. Randy's voice. Shit, he was by himself in the dark with a cranked-up Wilson. I struggled again, but nothing came of it.

I wanted the fight.

I wanted the blood.

Damn it to hell that Striker was preventing the very thing I had craved since my wedding day. Since the first letter.

I could taste vengeance sweet on my tongue.

Hungered for it.

Strained for it.

A hell of a fight raged above us. Now, I heard Gator in the mix.

A crash.

Silence.

Holy shit…

Sirens wailed in the street.

Blaze came over the communicator. "Perpetrator apprehended. Unconscious. Ambulance and police out front."

Striker let go of my chin, so he could push the communication button. "Gator and Randy?"

I worked my jaw back and forth. Striker pressed his body into mine.

"Minor injuries. Gator's headed for the generator." And as Blaze said that, as if by magic, an engine whirred, and the basement lights blinked on.

I managed to suck in enough air to gasp, "Get off of me."

Striker pushed to standing. He towered over me, arms akimbo, legs wide. I rocked back onto my knees, dragged a deep breath into my lungs, and moved unhindered up the stairs.

My kitchen was destroyed. The window was broken out of my door. Table and chairs in pieces. Blood. Wilson lay on his side, eyes closed as if he were sleeping peacefully. He didn't freaking get to be peaceful. He should be tormented. Terrified. Desperate. I kicked him viciously under the ribs with my booted toe. Kicked the wind out of him. His brain stem fought to make his lungs work. I wasn't sated. Not even close. Gator reached out and pinned my elbows behind my back in a vice grip. I wanted to thrash against his hold, but with Wilson knocked out, my attack was purposeless. Screw Striker for keeping me from the fight.

I wrenched myself free, stormed up the stairs to the bathroom, ripped off my clothes, and submerged myself in a tub of hot water, hoping something would soothe my turbulent emotions. Wash them away.

I could hear the men downstairs talking to the responders. The ambulance left without the siren. That meant Wilson's injuries weren't life-threatening. I slammed my fists through the surface of the water, sending a spray across the bathroom.

When I emerged, wrapped in my terrycloth robe, I found Striker sitting outside the door with his back to the wall, arms resting comfortably on his knees, looking relaxed, which I knew was a lie. He didn't get up or move a muscle as I glowered down at him.

"If I had let you attack him, it would have messed you up in court."

"There wouldn't be a court," I spat at him.

"You planned to kill him?" His question sounded more like a statement. A true, obvious statement.

I sunk down the wall opposite of Striker. "Yes." Simple as that. I hadn't thought this all the way through before. But I didn't have a single doubt that killing Wilson had been my strategy all along. I meant to extract my pound of flesh and then make sure this chapter was finished for good.

"The police would have taken your background into consideration. You would have been charged with manslaughter. You'd be headed to jail," Striker said evenly.

"Screw you," I spat out.

"Yeah. I know. I've been there."

"You exploded the house. You got your revenge."

"Not every time. But yes, I got justice for my sister." Striker stretched out his long legs. "We'll get justice for you."

I glared at him.

"I get it. The look and the feelings behind it. And I'll tell you something else, you're going to have to make friends with it because you'll be living this forever. Lexi, it's how the capture had to go down."

"You made me weak," I practically growled. "You stole my chance. I wouldn't feel this way if you had just—"

"Failed to do my job? Failed to protect you? I'm here for one reason and one reason only—to save you. And somehow, you thought with that genius brain of yours I'd turn my back and let you race into a fight with Wilson on PCP? In what universe are you living?" He waited for my answer. I could sense him wanting my… What? Certainly not my appreciation or my gratitude. Perhaps forgiveness? Understanding? I had nothing to give him that wasn't colored bilious green. He was acting his code. His code was why he was solid. It was his core strength.

Like Spyder.

My core was hollow; all I wanted was…

"For him to get a taste of what you went through—you and the other women." Huh. Maybe Striker had some ESP, too.

I glared at him.

"He wouldn't have, couldn't have, doped like that. What were you going to do? Tie him up and wait the six hours for the PCP to clear his system so he could feel fear or register pain?"

I hated that Striker was being practical.

Pragmatism had no place to land on my swirling emotions.

There was no point in continuing this conversation.

I stood up, went to my room, and slammed my door in Striker's face.

43

The next morning, I sat in my living room, curled into a subdued ball on my sofa, thinking how Iniquus would be out of my life now that the mission was accomplished. It was going to be like losing Spyder again. Like losing family. Again.

The work crew put in my new door. Boomer would be over later to move the alarm system—not that it much mattered anymore. Gator—with a hell of a shiner—carried in chairs for my replacement table. Clean up. Finish up. Move on to the next assignment. I was bereft.

Striker crouched beside me. We were eye to eye. "You look like you're brooding." A touch of wariness shadowed his voice. Probably thought I'd hiss like a tom-cat and scratch at his eyes. But the morning light had brought a fresh perspective, and I didn't have any anger left—not for my team, anyway.

"I know. I am. I am so grateful lunatic-Wilson is in custody, and I can move on with my life. There's always some bad with the good, though, isn't there?"

"I guess. What's bad here?" He cocked his head to the side.

"Well, now I'm going to have to go to trial with this guy. A nightmare for sure."

Striker nodded.

"And, there's Iniquus." I held Striker's gaze.

"What about Iniquus?" he asked.

"I'm going to miss…everybody and doing the puzzles. I had fun figuring out those crimes."

Striker reached out and rubbed his finger lightly over my wrist. "How are your classes coming?"

"All done."

"You should keep busy. Command asked me to offer you a job at Iniquus—part-time if you like. Full-time if you're willing. They think you'd be a great asset."

"Really?" I perked up, wiggling upright. "Wait. Did you tell them about Spyder?" I didn't want to ride in on Spyder's coat-tails. I wanted to earn my own place.

"As little as possible while still getting you credit for your work at the safehouse."

I smiled up at him. "Yes. Thank you. Tell them I accept."

"Good. We'll get you outfitted Wednesday."

"Outfitted?" My lashes flew up. "Do I have to wear camo pants and compression shirts?"

"I meant with your credentials. We'll issue you a service gun."

"In D.C. proper? I can't carry in D.C."

Striker grinned. "You can if you're an Iniquus employee."

Wednesday morning, I got to Iniquus early, so I didn't need to fight through D.C. traffic. Last night, as I headed home from the Millers', after collecting Beetle and Bella, Striker called me to say he needed me at Headquarters by six-thirty. Two Panther Force members were heading in with new intel Striker wanted me to hear. Something about a possible terrorist cell. So far, all the Panther Force leads had dead-ended.

Striker thought I could cobble together an idea of where their squad should head next.

Not wanting to call any attention to myself, I planned to be a fly on the wall in the hopes that someone had seen or heard something they didn't realize was significant. From being an observer rather than a participant, I might have the perspective needed to put the puzzle pieces together—to understand the whole picture.

Gray sound-absorbing material covered the conference room walls. A bank of windows hung on the far side, high up toward the ceiling, letting in light and a view of the crimson leaf-clouds from the maple trees below. Dressed in gun-metal-gray this morning—the closest thing I had in my wardrobe to fit in with the men's camo wear—I stood on the right-hand side of the windows and did my shadow walking routine. My breath slowed. I projected the textured, storm-colored wall out in front of me. As the men came in and found their places, no one glanced my way.

Soon, men clad in Iniquus uniforms filled the seats facing Striker, who stood at the front of the room. Everyone from my Save-Lexi Team was there; lots of faces from my time with Spyder, but a few were outright strangers.

The Panther Force, I thought.

As the meeting began, their energy focused sharply on the data the operators presented. There was no kidding around. The cell activity was picking up. The operators had confirmed a specific and credible threat repeated in three separate conversations by different sources. Known, reliable sources. The operators expected an imminent attack.

As Striker concluded the meeting, the dust from the fabric walls tickled my nose. I sneezed loudly.

Striker stared across the room at me.

I wasn't thinking gray-wall thoughts any more. I was thinking I-need-a-tissue thoughts. I watched Striker flip through his mental file folders as I dug a Kleenex from my bag and wiped my nose.

He pointed a finger at me. "Bingo!" He looked triumphant. "*Unbelievable!*"

"What? That I sneezed?" I asked.

"You're Alex!"

Everyone fell silent. The focus in the room rested on me. First, I'd materialized before their eyes, and now Striker had honed in on some discovery beyond me emerging from the shadows.

"You're Alex. Tell me you are."

"Uhmm, I have been called Alex. My name *is* Alexis."

"Yeah," Striker pushed. "And people usually call you Lexi."

"Or Baby Girl, or Chica, or Raspberries." I laughed lightly, trying to make this a joke and move on.

"Lexi, when did you call yourself Alex?" Striker was using his stern parent voice.

"Well, my dad called me Alex—he always wanted a boy."

"And?" Striker pressed.

Huh. Should I let him reveal this? Do I care? I guess not, since I'm working here now. What does it matter? "And Spyder called me Alex."

The men sucked in audible gasps of breath. They all knew Spyder, but they didn't all know me. They certainly didn't know

Spyder and I had a link. They focused back and forth between Striker and me with curiosity.

Striker didn't let up. "Spyder had you take his part in an intra-agency paintball war at the Millers' a little over two years ago."

"Correct."

"Holy crap!" one of the men, Dagger, said. "You're the Phantom."

"What?" Now I was getting confused. What phantom?

"No one ever found you," Blaze said. "We were shaking hands and teasing you about having to use the pink paint, then poof. Gone."

"Oh man, that's right," Gator said. "Our enemies were out stalking, and the next thing they knew, they got your color splattered all over them. Man, they were some kinda pissed off. Excuse my language, ma'am. They were hollering and accusing us of cheating. They couldn't explain how we were cheating. Their whole damned team dripped pink paint, and all of them was kill shots."

"Well..." This was uncomfortable.

"Then you disappeared before we got to congratulate you," Blaze said. "All due respect, ma'am, you're some kinda fierce."

"Uhm. Thanks." I didn't know where to put my gaze, so I fixed on Striker and rolled my lips in tightly.

Jack stood up, grinning. "Hey, I was at that fight. You can't kill the bad guys all by yourself. It's selfish." He gave me a warm pat on my back. "Way to go, Phantom."

The men gathered their things and moved out of the room.

Striker came over to me, laughing.

"Alex, the paintball superhero, that's marvelous," he said.

I smiled at him and gave him a shrug.

"At any rate, you wanted a call name, and it seems like you already have one—'Phantom.'"

"Phantom?"

"Yeah. What's wrong? Too many syllables?"

"No, I just don't want to be known as an un-dead zombie woman with a melting face and rotting flesh. Gross!"

He offered up a huge grin. "Hard to believe you and Alex are the same person."

"Surprising?"

"That would be an understatement. Who taught you stealth tactics?"

"Master Wang. He called it 'shadow walking.' Seriously, though, you have to make the Phantom thing stop."

"I'll see what I can do. Come on. I need you at my next meeting. Are you wearing your thinking cap today?"

"I stuck it in my purse. I don't like to put it on unless I really need to—it gives me hat hair."

"Oh, a funny girl, huh?" Striker nudged me into another conference room. "You stay visible for this one."

Two men sat at the table with a file in front of them. They stood when we came in.

"Gentlemen, this is Lexi Sobado. I've asked her to come and give us her impressions."

"Thorn." The first man extended his hand.

"Nice to meet you, Thorn." I shook his hand firmly.

"Brainiack," the man standing to Thorn's left said.

We sat down.

Striker pulled the file over, flipped through, then pushed it over to me. Inside I found several eight by ten photographs. Most of them looked like pictures of woods. I scanned the photos in a grid pattern, searching for anything interesting or out of place while I listened to the men.

"Langley's in custody?" Striker asked.

"Yes, sir. We brought him in last night," Thorn said.

Striker tapped his pen on a blank legal pad. "He talking?"

"Silent—waiting for his lawyer to advise him, sir," Brainiack said.

"We need a list of contacts. Any idea where it might have gone? What about the money? The serial numbers on the bills will prove the connection."

"Yes, sir. We—"

I interrupted Thorn's thought, "Hey, Striker, can we pause for a minute? I need a magnifying glass."

Striker picked up the phone and made the request. Someone knocked on the door a few minutes later, handed a large magnifying glass to me, and left without a word.

"Thanks. Go on," I said.

"Yes, ma'am. Sir, we only have the information in the file. We trailed him out

to the area in the photos. He walked around for a long time. He seemed to be hunting for something. Then I think he got spooked because he left. We photographed the area and got the GPS coordinates, so we could find the exact spot again for a search—bring someone from the K-9 team out with us. Then we followed Langley back and waited for him to be alone for the arrest."

When I laid the glass down, I found Striker watching me keenly. "What do you see?" he asked.

"Not sure. Was this guy a history buff?"

The three men focused on me with clear astonishment.

"How did you know?" Striker asked.

"Here, in this one photo," I handed Striker the magnifying glass and pointed, "there are three rocks semi-stacked and a branch leaning on them. There are no rocks in any of the other pictures. This area isn't rocky. The only way for rocks to be here is for someone to have placed them. Also, look at the branch. The leaves are fall-colored. This branch has recently been broken off. Otherwise, the leaves would be dead. We haven't had a storm lately with enough power to break off a branch of this size. This is an oak. These are pine trees. It would take a major gust to move this branch any distance, and if it blew to this location, the heavy part would be on the ground, not sticking up. My conclusion is that someone walking in the woods would miss this, but whoever set the marker up would easily find the location."

"And the history buff thing?" asked Striker.

"In the time when the pioneers went west in covered wagons, they often had problems and had to leave their things behind. These items were precious to a group of people who had little. Many times, they'd bury their belongings in the ground and mark the spot with a gravestone, much like the way this area in the picture was marked."

Striker rubbed his thumb along his chin. "Others would think they found a grave..."

"And leave it alone. The family would recognize it and be able to retrieve their property at a future date. When I saw the stones stacked like they were, I was reminded of the pioneer false graves."

"Well, gentlemen, I suggest you go and investigate why those rocks are piled up. Give me a full report when you get back."

"Yes, sir," both men said as they stood and left.

"Do I get a prize if they find something good buried underneath?"

"We'll figure something out for you."

"What now?" I asked.

"Now, we need to work on a call name for you since you

don't like Phantom." Striker leaned back in his chair and steepled his fingers while he studied me.

"How about Artemis? You told me her story—the goddess of the hunt and hounds."

"No, thanks. She vowed off men forever, and while I've never been with a man, I am married, and quite frankly, the wait is killing me."

Striker quirked a brow.

My face prickled as I turned pink. What had I just said? Shit. "Uh. Artemis won't work. It has three syllables and calls only have one or two."

Jack walked in at the end of my sentence. "Hey, Phantom."

"Stop. I refuse to respond to that, and we won't be friends anymore if you continue to call me the undead."

Striker shook his head, amused. "You need a call name to go out on assignment."

"I'm in the field? What for?"

"We need you to plant a bug," Jack said, looking down at the photos on the table.

"Oh. Is that all? 'Cause you know I don't do those daring deeds of do-or-die."

"Wouldn't think of putting you in danger," Striker said. "So, about your call name—what do you think, Jack?"

"Excel," he said immediately.

"Sounds too close to Axel." Striker dug through his briefcase.

"Houdini?" Jack asked.

"Nah. Too many syllables, right Lexi?" Striker tucked the photos away and clicked the briefcase toggles shut. "How about Stealth?" He raised his brows in my direction.

I shook my head—that was too far over the top, like a character in the *Hunger Games*.

"Cookie...nope, too girly—need to keep her gender a secret." Jack rested a hip on the table and crossed his arms over his chest. "Smoke," he said.

"I like smoke—how about you, Lexi?" Striker asked.

"What? No!" Smoke? Gah!

"Mensa." Jack tried. The two of them going back and forth.

"Magic."

"Panther."

"Lynx," Striker said, and they stopped and looked at each other.

"Beautiful animal, excellent hunter, stealthy and smart," Striker said. "Could mean the animal or could mean the links Lexi puts together to solve our mysteries."

"Not too many syllables, not gender-specific, no one has a rhyming name," Jack said.

Striker turned to me and asked, "Do you like 'Lynx?'"

"It's pretty good." Lynx...huh. And his description... Very flattering. Embarrassing. Cool!

"Done. Now let's take you home to get gussied up for your little adventure." Striker maneuvered me out the door and down the corridor. Jack followed behind.

44

I was dressing for a cocktail party—a black-tie affair. Fancy. I needed to fit in but fly under the radar. While Jack and Striker waited for me on my porch, I showered and did my hair up in hot curlers. I upped my makeup from the everyday, keeping it well below the vamp rating. I wore a little black dress with a knee-length full skirt to cover my thigh holster. The neckline was cut to expose enough cleavage to get me up close and personal, but hopefully not enough to stand out in the target's mind. When I was all fluffed and buffed, I went outside and twirled for inspection in my four-inch satin heels. Both men looked me over with shit-eating grins. Striker let out a wolf whistle.

"Good enough?" I asked.

"Maybe too good. Jack, what do you think? Will she cause a riot?"

"Near thing, Striker. I think it'll get her where she needs to be."

A Lincoln Town Car had appeared at my curb with Brainiack playing chauffeur. Striker rode with me in the back seat. He'd stay with the car. Jack would be positioned in the rear of the building. Striker handed me a photo and gave me the name. Soon, we pulled up in front of the art gallery. Brainiack came around and opened the door for me. I accepted his hand as I got out and walked self-assuredly up to the doors. As others held out identification and their invitations for inspection, security checked them off the list. I went around them confidently and waved at the guards like I belonged, and they nodded me in.

The party shimmered with diamond jewelry—opulent wealth on high display. I understood the high security. I scanned the room, searching out my target. I was hoping he'd already arrived and had time to settle in, maybe even tipped back a few drinks. And, sure enough, I spotted him over at the bar. I edged toward him and pretended to be in line for an order.

"Lewis Romalowski?" I asked the short, balding man with his tuxedo beautifully tailored over his enormous paunch belly.

"Do I know you, sweetheart?" he asked with a strong Brooklyn accent.

"Hi, Lewis, I'm Pamela, we met last summer." I extended my hand with my full-on sweet-girl-next-door smile and a bat of my fake lashes—why not slather it on thick?

He grasped my fingers and bent to kiss my hand. "Pleased to meet you again, Pamela. This was at Domenico's pool party?"

"Probably? I'm not sure. What I do remember is meeting you and being impressed." Keeping my smile in place, I stepped closer to him. This seemed to make him happy. He rubbed his little sausage fingers up my bare arm. *Ew!*

"Well, I'm so glad we did meet, Pamela. May I buy you a drink?" He chuckled and gestured toward the server. An open bar—such a droll wit. A real ladies' man.

"Thanks. I'll have what you're having."

"Scotch straight up? You sure?"

"Oh, that's too strong for me." I giggled. "I'm a real light-weight around alcohol. Maybe a Cosmo?"

This not-being-able-to-hold-my-booze business got his attention. He leaned toward me. Good thing, too. I had the transmitter palmed—if I could just find an empty pocket.

He turned and handed me my cocktail. I raised a finger. "I'm so sorry. Would you excuse me for a minute?" As I pretended to head toward a dowager in a silver gown, another woman moved into the space I had vacated. I didn't think Romalowski was going to miss me. When you had bucks like this guy had, you weren't lonely long.

I put my glass, un-tasted, on a passing waiter's tray and left out the front door, calling Brainiack on my cell as I crossed to the stairs. I kept away from the windows as I waited for the Town Car to roll around. The back door popped open, and I swiveled myself in.

"We're recording, Lynx. Excellent job," Striker said.

"That was a joke, right? A test?" I narrowed my eyes at Striker.

"What do you mean?"

"I mean, his tuxedo jacket pockets were all sewn shut. In his front right pants' pocket, he had a money clip for tips. On his left, he had a car key and fob. He only had one back pocket, and that had his wallet. The inside breast pocket had his glasses. If I had put the transmitter in any of those places, he could easily find it."

"Where did it end up?"

"I replaced his right cuff link." I handed Striker the gold cuff link I had removed from Lewis's shirt.

"Why right?"

"He's left-handed—maybe he won't notice it. Hopefully, his scotch is doing its thing. So, not a joke?"

"Not by a long shot." Striker paused while he looked at the cuff link and put it in his jacket pocket. "While you were flirting with criminal elements, Command called. I have information on Wilson."

I didn't like the tense muscles under his eyes; this wasn't good information. I raised a questioning brow.

"Wilson's stable. In police custody at Suburban. He's being charged with breaking and entering with intent to harm, and possession."

I waited for the rest of the charges.

Striker pursed his lips.

"What about six murders and an attempted murder?" My voice squeaked.

"The D.A. is having trouble putting together a case. The original six were linked to you by the MO. We have no evidence. None. Though they've been working on developing the case since your attack."

"But what about me? I can testify. And the neighbors saw him, too. We confirmed the police sketch. Surely—"

"Subsequent to seeing him, you sustained a traumatic brain injury. The defense can shred your eye-witness report on the witness stand. Same with the neighbors. They were running in the dark. Could be a look-alike. With no prints, no DNA, no motive linking you two, the prosecutors need something more, or they can't make the case."

"Dave?"

"Has nothing. Not his fault. Wilson may be juiced, but he's highly trained, very smart, and obviously effective." Striker waited.

I wasn't sure what he wanted from me by way of response, so I offered up a curt nod.

"Is there anything more from your 'knowings'? Anything more we can work with?"

I shook my head and looked down at my lap, where I twisted Angel's rings. Beyond words. Too deflated for anger. Too depressed to feel regret that Striker didn't let me just kill him and be done with this mess. I turned and looked, unseeing, out the side window. I was glad Gator and Randy didn't kill him, though —with their military background and size, they definitely would end up with legal problems. Even with Iniquus's lawyers and get-out-of-jail-free cards.

I stepped out of the car and walked like a zombie toward my front door. Striker's boots sounded behind me. Without looking around at him, I waved, signaling him to go home.

I moved up the steps with my keys in hand. It wasn't over. It was far from over.

45

The next morning, I walked into the Iniquus lobby, swishing my full skirts with what I hoped was a bright smile lighting my face. Wilson thrived on fear. He'd realize somewhere in his cells—even broken and crushed and lying in a hospital bed—that he was winning. He'd take a stab at beating his court charges. Then he'd take another stab at me—literally and figuratively. Well, today anyway, I wasn't going to play his sick-o game. And I wasn't going to freak out over last night's nightmare about Angel. Instead, I'd play my fluffy-bunny role. Sunny, happy, and calm. I'd focus on my fabulous new job. `

Command didn't require me to wear the Iniquus gray camos like everyone else. The ultra-feminine, ultra-chic, fifties-style dress—a hand-me-down from my friend Celia's closet—in rose and coral got me a lot of attention when I walked through the lobby at headquarters. Iniquus is modern, streamlined, and monochromatic, and I bloomed like a garden flower.

Striker met me at the door with a smile.

"What's on the agenda today?" I asked.

"Two things. First, Nancy Drew, your prize from the 'Grave in the Woods Caper.'"

"Already?"

Striker placed his hand on the small of my back and steered me to the elevator. When we reached the top floor, he pointed toward an office with a sign that read "PUZZLE ROOM."

"Tada." He pushed the door wide with a grand sweep of his arm. "This is yours."

"Wow." Surprised would be a gross understatement. My hand brushed over the stainless steel, rectangular tabletop. One of three big tables standing in the center of the large square room, ready for spreading out clues.

"All this for me?" I asked, taking in the whiteboard with various pens, and an enormous corkboard with pushpins. A bin with colored yarns sat against the wall. I guessed these were for constructing more webs like I had for the Sylanos case. I fiddled with the light switch in the full bath and peaked into the closet across from it in the little hallway at the back of the room.

"Your home away from home." Striker watched me intently.

I nodded. Huh. This was a huge office, right next to Striker's. Could I live up to this clear sign of confidence from Command? Suddenly, I felt a deep level of pressure, anxiety, and self-doubt. I eased past Striker. Releasing my breath in a long exhale, I reached out, clicked on the light of the cosmetologist's magnifier, and peered through the lens at my coral-colored nails. Then bit at a hangnail.

Plopping down in the leather chair, I spun back and forth like a kid, taking everything in—plenty of room for people to come in and mill around while we went over things. The two dog beds beside my chair and two sets of food and water dishes made me smile. Someone put a lot of thought into this room. Mixed emotions. Pride. Yes. Stressed. Yes. Overwhelmed. Double yes.

"This is pretty awesome. I take it you found what you needed in the woods?" I asked.

"In spades. We collected enough evidence to put a bunch of bad people behind bars for a long time. Apparently, our boy thought he had a safety net out there." Striker sat on the edge of a table, stretching out his muscular legs, crossing them at the ankle, his weight resting casually back on his arms. "We got dirt on anyone and everyone he ever did business with. He had plenty of information to blackmail them into the next century. Kudos."

"Kudos accepted." I gestured widely to take in the room. "This didn't happen overnight, though."

"Command started putting it together after I brought them the Sylanos file and mentioned you'd had a hand in the Tandesco coup."

"That seems confident on their part." I scowled. "Presumptuous" was probably a better word.

"Command can be persuasive. I left the SEALs to work here."

"I've often wondered why."

Striker's face went incommunicado. His choice was obviously not up for discussion. I changed the subject. "What's the second thing on the table for today?" I eyed Striker. He wore jeans and a button-down shirt he'd left un-tucked to hide his weapon. He looked relaxed and casual. "You're undercover?" I asked.

"Yeah—don't want to call any attention to myself by wearing a uniform. But then you're dressed like that." His open-handed gesture swept over me from head to toe. "So being inconspicuous is going to be a stretch."

"Should I change?"

He smiled, dimples and all. "No, thank you."

We locked the door and headed back to the elevator bank. "I want to take you by a crime scene and see what you pick up."

"A test?" I asked.

"Why's everything a test with you?" Striker glanced out of the corner of his eye at me as we walked.

"Spyder."

"Ah, well, school's over. You're in the big bad world now. Everything's the real deal." Striker punched the button for the garage level. As we stepped out of the elevator, Striker fobbed his way into a charcoal gray Lexus RX 400 and opened the passenger side door for me.

"This is beautiful. Do you think I could give it a test drive?"

Striker's stance tightened.

"I've been trained by the best: Stan Gillespie and Spyder McGraw. I really don't think I'll hurt your baby." I sent him a pouty face. "Pretty please?"

Amusement shined Striker's eyes as he held out the key.

"So, where are we headed?" I asked as I slid under the steering wheel.

"Get on the highway heading north. I'll direct you from there."

We were driving along, each with our own thoughts when Striker broke into mine. "What's going through your head?"

"I was remembering my dream last night. It was pretty vivid."

Strangely, Striker tensed beside me. "Yeah? Tell me," he said.

I shot him a curious glance before I refocused on the road. "I dreamed about a huge rat. When I caught the rat, I called animal control. I hoped they'd kill it—it was ginormous. But they didn't. They decided to put a tracking collar on the rat and release it to find out where he would go, instead."

"And?"

"And nothing, I woke up."

"Hmm. Okay. Good."

I turned my gaze toward him. The tight muscles at his jaw-line had relaxed. "Good?" I frowned then signaled a lane change.

"I thought you were going to tell me about one of your night-mares. Turn here into the park." He gestured at an entrance on my right.

"You know about my nightmares?"

"Lexi, we've slept in the same bed. How could I not know?"

His words touched a tender spot in my psyche, like a toothache my tongue prodded. And I couldn't leave it alone. No matter how painful. Parking under a patch of towering pine trees, I swiveled to face him.

"Did I wake you often?"

"At least once a night. On bad nights, two or three times." His eyes were so soft. Gold flecks. Moss green. "At first, I thought you were reliving Wilson," he said. "Then I realized you were dreaming about Angel. The nightmares were pretty intense. I couldn't pull you out of them."

"What did you do?" I leaned my head back against the glass.

Striker released his seatbelt and said, "I chanted."

Of all the answers I might have expected, this certainly wasn't one of them. "Chanted?" I laughed nervously. "Chanted what, exactly?"

Striker paused for longer than was comfortable, then he said, "You are *not* alone."

My hands came up to stopper my mouth. One time, when I fought in a match at the Do Jang, my attention went to the door as someone peered through the little window, and my partner roundhouse kicked me just below my ribs. Full force. He knocked every molecule of oxygen from my body. As my diaphragm pushed and pulled, sucking at the atmosphere to start my lungs back in motion, I made a horrible sound. It was that inhuman vibration that crawled out of my throat as I wrenched open the door and tumbled out. Unstable. I was thrown completely off-kilter. Striker's words were viciously painful.

When someone knows your weakness, they hold the power—a Master Wang truism.

I felt exposed. Defenseless. Just four little words. Somehow, Striker had not only seen me—touched me—physically naked. Now he had seen me—touched me—soul naked. I scowled at my rings. Angel—my *husband*—hadn't. Neither. The dynamic spun my head.

Striker was by my side, reaching out for me. I raised protective arms. Warded him off. I skittered into the copse of trees like a wild animal. He stopped moving.

Tipping my head to look up to the sky, shaking, I vividly remembered last night's nightmare. The bombs seemed closer than before. A shimmer framed the scene, the kind of atmospheric oscillation that danced around the words of a "knowing." Unsettled, I had clamped down tightly on those thoughts last night, trying not to give them room to grow.

Striker sat down, leaning back against the rough bark of the pine. "There is no case for us to work on. I brought you out here because I have information."

I nodded and slipped to the ground, resting against a tree, too. The solidity pressed against my back.

"Since I realized why you were having nightmares, I've been contacting my government and military friends, trying to find out more about Angel's mission."

I stopped breathing.

"A call came in this morning. Angel's squad was pinned in an ambush last night. Four wounded, two casualties. Angel is *not* one of them. I thought if you were picking up something with your ESP, you might be pretty frantic. I saw it in your eyes this morning when you walked in—despite your smile."

I shook to the point my teeth rattled. Wanted to launch myself into Striker's arms where I knew it felt safe—but that would be the wrong thing to do. Especially knowing how close it had been for Angel last night. I needed to put distance between Striker and me before I showed him another weakness. I owed him a thank you—a big one.

But instead, I stood up and walked away.

46

I popped two sleeping pills at nine o'clock, ready for the day to be over already. The respite they offered me didn't last. I woke in the middle of the night. Couldn't go back to sleep. Beetle and Bella whined beside my bed and stuck their noses over the mattress, trying to see me, see what was wrong. Finally, I decided to get up and give my mind something to do other than search for the reason I felt isolated from reality. I disentangled myself from the bedsheets, damp with the perspiration of my Angel nightmare. No one to chant, "You are not alone." I was alone.

I showered, then dressed myself in black bra and panties, black stockings and garter belt, black heels, black raw silk suit. No jewelry. No make-up. No perfume. I brushed my hair back into a ponytail, pulling it only halfway through on the last turn of the elastic band to make a bun of sorts. I looked in the mirror; huge pupils in enormous eyes in an austere face stared back at me. Pale. I didn't really recognize the reflection as my own, some vague portrait hanging on a blank wall.

Grasping my big leather bag from beneath the side table in my foyer, I scooped my keys from the bowl. The metal on glass as I lifted the fob seemed to echo through my house. The sound had a hollow feel. I activated the alarm system and twisted to call my dogs, only to find they were already beside me. We went out the door. When I turned to lock up, I registered the cold, damp air on my skin. *I should get my coat.* The thought didn't produce the desired action.

I took a step out onto the porch. The neighborhood was at rest; my neighbors all snuggled warm in their beds, each with their own dreams. Every clack of my high heels on the sidewalk echoed large against the stillness. I opened the back door of my car, my dogs climbed in, and I found my place behind the wheel.

Now, where?

I decided to head to Iniquus—the only place I knew where I could be both alone and surrounded by warm bodies at this time of night. I needed warm bodies right now. I had disconnected; it was like floating to the left of where I should actually be. It felt eerie.

At Iniquus, I headed straight to the Puzzle Room, not wanting to talk to anyone. Shut the door. Sat down. My dogs found their places under the table. After a minute, I jumped up. Panic and claustrophobia tightened over my chest with the door closed. I jerked it back open, so I could stave off the loneliness swelling each of my cells.

I thought maybe work would help ground me—help me shake off whatever was holding me in its grip. I laid out the puzzle pieces for the newest case—clues Gator had gathered from a suspect's house. The team wanted me to find the bad guy's location. I sat in my black leather chair and stared at the wall in front of me.

At some point, one of the men coaxed Beetle and Bella out from under my feet, whispering eat. Good. My dogs weren't suffering. Someone would feed and walk them. Water was poured into their bowls after they returned, moping under my table, warming my legs with their bodies. No one spoke to me. My cheeks were wet from intermittent tears dripping down past my chin and plopping on the blank piece of paper in front of me.

Striker stuck his head in, then left. Murmuring hummed outside my door—concerned voices discussing me.

"She's been like that since three this morning—the dogs too," someone said.

"She didn't say anything at all, to anyone, when she came in?" Striker asked.

"Not a word, sir. She hasn't moved," came the reply.

I guessed Striker wasn't sure if he was welcome since I walked away from him yesterday. He didn't get in my face. He let me be. I just sat, muffled by my body, buffered from the pedestrian comings and goings—the human motions of Iniquus.

A cup of tea was set beside me, and grew cold

By two in the afternoon, my tears flowed in earnest. Striker came back in and rifled through the puzzle pieces of the case laid out before me. They didn't seem to answer his questions. He looked at my still-blank damp paper and the untouched pen. He stood solid and calm. His concern was tangible, and I knew he struggled to do the right thing here, to find the right words for whatever was happening. I was sure I looked like I was in the middle of a mental collapse. Maybe I was.

Striker's cell phone vibrated. He stepped out of my room into the hall. He answered, "Striker." Silence stretched like a rubber band while he listened to the caller, then snapped back as he said, "Send them up." He disconnected.

Striker came silently back into the room, pulled out a side chair, and placed it near mine. Sitting down, he swiveled me to face him. He took my hands from my lap and enfolded them in his. He looked me in the eyes and waited for me to focus on him. This took a minute—I cowered deep within myself.

When I finally met his gaze, he spoke slowly and gently. "Two military officers are on their way up to speak to you." I nodded comprehension. Reality still seemed pretty far away. I felt nothing but numbness. I wanted to stay numb—Deaf, dumb, blind, and numb. I wanted to cast a spell that would relieve me of my senses. Dread's bony claws had clutched at my throat from the moment I woke up this morning. And now, everything I feared since Angel deployed was riding up the elevator to confront me.

As the two uniformed men came into my room, my body rose like a marionette's, manipulated by unseen strings. I observed, as if an optical illusion, a right hand extended from my body and clasp the men's hands in handshakes. My frozen fingers were stiff. My disembodied voice said, "I am Mrs. Angel Miguel Sobado. Thank you, gentlemen, for your service. This must be a hard task."

Their hats twisted back and forth between nervous fingers, contradicting their calm countenance. Someone suggested we sit. Striker reached out and guided my body back down into the chair. Striker pulled his seat even closer. His body pressed to my side, giving me stability, and sharing his warmth.

I watched their mouths move. I knew they were giving me information about Angel's death—my Angel's...

I stood. "Wouldn't you gentlemen like a cup of coffee? I need to excuse myself for a moment." It came out stiff and formal. I walked with rigid legs from the room. Bella and Beetle whined under the table. I heard Striker soothing them and telling them to stay.

I found the hall and stumbled along with my shoulder to the wall. I ran into someone—I have no idea whom. I desperately needed privacy.

"Please help me. I need a soundproof room—there must be something here somewhere," I said. I saw a face look at me and blink, confused. Then the face went military flat.

"Yes, ma'am, this way."

We took the elevator down, past the garage, into a sub-basement where cell-like rooms lined the corridor. I stumbled in and closed the door behind me. The man stood outside; before the door closed all the way, I heard him punching numbers into his cell phone.

He's telling Striker where I'm hiding.

I took off my shoes and laid them on the unmade cot. I disengaged my stockings from the clasps on my garter belt and laid them alongside the belt. Then my suit coat. I walked to the far corner of the room and pushed my face up against the smooth, cool cell wall. I opened my mouth. I was beyond crying. I howled. Like a wild thing, I howled. Like a storm brought in by the ocean, I howled. I howled through tree limbs and uprooted great oaks with my despair. I howled to my husband—that the winds would carry my voice to the heavens, and he would hear my grief.

At one point, the door opened and closed—Striker. I kept up my lament. When Striker returned, he brought in a trash bin, bottles of water, boxes of Kleenex, and a king-sized white sheet. He laid the items near me—but didn't interrupt me as I worked hard at my grief. He opened the sheet and worked a portion of the cloth into my right fist and then my left. "Rip it to shreds," he whispered in my ear, and he left.

Rip it. Rip it—sounded good. I used my teeth to gnaw through the hem and then tore at it. Anger blazed hot and red. Pele anger. Fire anger. I wanted to be the Hindu goddess Kali Ma —the Destroyer. Kali of the wild eyes and bloody sword. I worked at annihilating the sheet—screaming and bellowing out my battle-cry of rage against fate—against the self-pity consuming me. I ripped until I found myself kneeling in a nest of shredded linen and thread.

I collapsed onto the rags, weak and spent, my nose encrusted with mucus, my eyes swollen shut from salty tears.

Exhausted beyond measure, I fell asleep.

After some time, I became aware of hands: gentle, confident, and respectful. Two men untangled me from the fabric that had worked its way around my arms and legs. They pulled my skirt and blouse into place. A cool cloth wiped my face. Striker lifted me to my feet.

He and Jack took me to the barracks and laid me on Striker's bed. A blanket as soft as the dawn covered me. Beetle and Bella snuggled up beside me and lent me their warmth. I lost my awareness as I fell asleep, guarded, and safe. The two men took turns at my side, holding my hand—this was balm. Their vigilance and focus had a healing quality. In many faiths, a little like *Shemira* in Judaism, this attention at a death was sacred. Their attention felt like a prayer—it felt hallowed.

I could hear Master Wang whisper in my ear the words he said as he buried his beloved wife, Snow Bird, "Love is vulnerability."

Master Wang and Spyder had both talked to me often about the great strength it took to be vulnerable, and my vulnerability served as my best weapon in this lifetime. Vulnerable. That word defined me at that moment.

The morning light warmed my face as I blinked my eyes

open. Striker sat in a chair by my side. He reached out and covered my hand with his.

"Better?" he asked.

"Yes." My husky voice felt broken-glass sharp, painful from the strain of yesterday.

"You scared the shit out of my men."

"Mmm, and how exactly did I do that?"

"I opened the cell door, and it sounded like I had opened the gates of hell. My men were suited up in full combat gear, lined up, waiting for orders to kill Beelzebub."

I smiled. If Striker could tease me, then he didn't think of me as shattered beyond repair. Somehow that made me feel stronger, capable of handling this. Though I was sure everything about me was horrific, and none of them had ever had to contend with someone like me before.

"Good call on the sound-proof room," he said, any teasing gone from his voice. He was all concern.

"My throat's on fire."

"I bet. What should I get you? Some of your tea? A stiff drink?"

"Tea, please."

Striker handed me a pair of sweats and a T-shirt that were vaguely my size. He must have had them sent up from the supply room. When he left, I disentangled myself from the blanket. My blouse and skirt had wrapped themselves around and about, straight-jacketing me.

The late November winds howled outside as I made my way to the bathroom with my new clothes and adjusted the temperature on my shower. The water ran hot over my skin as I cleaned myself of the previous day's filth. I stood and let the water sluice over my shoulders and back.

I've dealt with death—battled grief too many times before. I knew the extreme level of emotion I experienced yesterday, the shrieks and the tears were not sustainable. There would be intervals when I would be fine and stretches when I would dissolve in pain. Right now, I floated on the cushion of a respite. I needed to use this time to make plans, and phone calls, to tell people what was going on, while I could. I needed to be gentle with myself when I succumbed to my loss. I knew it would be worse in the beginning, and then my mind would find its way back to normal —or more accurately, to a new normal.

I emerged from the shower, my skin red and warm. I toweled off and dressed. In the medicine cabinet, I found a toothbrush still in its cellophane wrap. I used Striker's comb to untangle my long hair and pulled it back into a wet ponytail. I looked in the mirror. It was still my face, still my reflection. I had seen this same reflection all my life. Experience didn't show up for the world to witness, to know. All of my stories were my secrets to hold or to share as I wished.

A knock sounded at the bathroom door, startling me out of my reverie, back to the here and now. The door pushed slowly open; Striker stuck his head in.

"Hey, you've been in here a really long time. I wanted to make sure you were okay."

I put the comb back in the medicine cabinet and looked at him through his reflection. "I'm okay. My mind wandered."

Striker walked over to me and took my hands. "Come on. I'm going to make you another cup of tea. The last one's cold."

Striker shepherded me to an armchair he'd pulled up to the fireplace. Logs crackled softly. The smell of the wood and smoke warmed me as much as the heat from the flames. Striker tucked a blanket around me and put my cup on a table next to me like I was physically frail, overcoming an illness.

Jack had gone by my house to ask Alice to pack a bag for

me; he brought me my address book. I flipped open to the envelope Angel had taped inside. "In case I don't make it back," was penned in Angel's angular scrawl. I opened the envelope and found four pieces of paper. One had a list of people and phone numbers to call. One had a list of instructions for his funeral. A letter to me that I set aside until I was less fragile. And a letter to his mom. I took a deep breath and started calling.

47

Hard. Hard. I had never done anything so hard as being death's herald, delivering the news to his friends and family. I needed to comfort their shrieks and pain. These were people who had known Angel and loved him all his life. I felt jealous of the time they got with him, gypped by my short time, so grateful I had any time at all.

I made it through the list and went to Striker's room to collapse. He let me sleep until lunch and then insisted I eat.

He had the funeral arrangements in his hand. "Iniquus will handle this and make sure everything is followed to the letter. We have a plane at Dover. Angel's remains come in tomorrow morning. We can make the transfer and leave for Puerto Rico immediately." He paused and stroked his rough hand up and down my arm. It reminded me I had substance.

"Your team has all requested and been granted leave, so they can escort you. Your friends are welcome on the plane, but your neighbors want you to know they'd like to have a memorial service when you get back."

"Thank you."

I looked through the suitcase Striker had brought in. Alice had picked out comfortable black clothing for several days of travel, modest black dresses for the days in Puerto Rico, a simple silk suit for the funeral. That was new—she must have called Celia. On top, she had laid my favorite photo of Angel and me, and a note—it simply said, "We love you."

My team filed in throughout the day to sit with me. We didn't talk much, but their presence helped. They hadn't known Angel. I barely knew Angel. My heart knew him, but I didn't have stores of memories to pull out and relive. I mostly had broken dreams, and they were of no comfort.

Time passed. I sat on an airplane. I was wrapped in Abuela Rosa's arms. I walked down an aisle supported by Jack and Striker. I received a flag and a purple heart. People talked to me. I hugged. I nodded my head. I got back on a plane. Manny brought my dogs to me. I shut the door. I climbed under my covers. Alone.

There were days when I woke up and drove to Iniquus to work. And days when I rolled over and went back to sleep. My team made sure I was eating. They cared for my girls, paid my bills on time, and shoveled the early snowfall off my walk.

Sometimes Sarah would come over and let me hold Ruby. Sometimes Fletcher and Colin showed up with burned cookies they made for me. Sometimes life seemed *almost* normal.

Today started out as a good day. A better day. They were coming more frequently now. I could think, and reason, and puzzle, again. I had just put the finishing touches on a case report and hit print when Bruce Morrison, an Iniquus lawyer, walked in. I flinched when I saw him.

"What's the news?" I asked, holding a file in front of me like a shield.

"Wilson is off his traction and machines. The doctors are going ahead and releasing him to prison." He sat on my table.

"What will that mean?"

"He'll be arraigned today." Morrison glanced down at his watch. I took this to mean that the transfer was in progress as we spoke.

"That's taking longer than usual. I thought arraignments happened in the first 72 hours."

"The doctors had to confirm Wilson's ability to understand proceedings. We were able to get them to hold off until now."

"You did this because…"

"The D.A. understands this is more than what lays on the surface. This isn't a breaking and entering or even a possession crime. Everyone is scrambling to get the murder charges in place. The D.A.'s communicating this—as much as he's legally able to—to the judge. We don't think there will be a problem setting Wilson's bail sky-high, especially with his history of mental instability."

"He goes straight to prison from the courthouse, right?"

"Yup." Morrison pushed to standing. "Thought you'd like to know. I'll give you a call when Wilson's locked in his cell."

I decided to go back to my house, get my girls, and go for a run.

Run away from images of Wilson.

Run away from thoughts of screaming pain, from fear, from the ghosts of the six other women who haunted me—why did I survive when they didn't?

When I opened my front door, Bella and Beetle waited for me, prancing in place. I told them to get their leashes and went to change into sweats and cross-trainers. I snapped the leads to their collars for form's sake, pulled on a thick hat and mittens, and we took off for the park. I sprinted about four miles. Both the cold air and my weeks of recovery left me winded, but not as bad as I'd feared.

As we headed back, I noticed a piece of notebook paper stapled to a telephone pole. I bent down to inspect the child's crayoned drawing of a black cat with a pink collar and bell.

"Pleez help me find sam," the sign said. An adult had printed the address at the bottom.

I cast my mind around—a sixth-sense game I used to play when I was a child and helped find the missing cats and dogs from my apartment complex. Sam wasn't far. I decided to take the girls home and come back to find her. I was sure the poor cat wasn't interested in hanging out with my Dobermans.

Back in the park, I sat down with the letter and willed images to appear. In my mind's eye, a little girl with light brown hair pulled into a curly ponytail, tied with a red ribbon, sat at a table scribbling. The black cat streaked past her and out the door. I heard the child calling Sam's name. The cat was scared and hungry. Up. I definitely sensed "up." I saw a tree and a slide. Sam must be over near the kiddy area in the park; I moved toward the jungle-gym.

Sam wasn't hard to find. She was up a magnolia, looking sorry for herself. Hard to coax down, though. I ended up having to climb to her. Snuggling Sam into my chest, I pulled debris from my hair as I walked toward the side street and Sam's home.

When the front door opened, Sam jumped out of my arms and darted through the living room. A relieved and grateful mom was calling to her child. The little girl walked in, squeezing Sam with tears running down her face.

"Good thing you're such an excellent artist." I handed the

little girl her drawing. "The pink bell helped me the most. As soon as this cat meowed, I knew this must be Sam."

I started home again, happy to have helped, considering how I would spend the rest of the day.

Halfway through the empty park, my scalp prickled with a warning—*the itsy-bitsy spider.*

Danger shivered the air.

Panic fought for brain space.

Crawled up the water spout.

I stopped to get my bearings. Tried to sense the direction and source of my alarm. To plan a retreat.

Down came the rain and washed the spider out.

Nowhere to shadow walk and disappear—I stood exposed.

Up came the sun.

I sniffed the air. Oh, holy hell. There it was again—the putrid rot from the bottom of a swamp. Wilson.

And dried up all the rain.

I hadn't smelled this stench since Halloween when Gator slammed his massive fist into Wilson's temple. *The itsy-bitsy spider crawled up the spout again.* I had let my guard down. And I had been warned not to.

A car swerved around the curve at breakneck speed. My foot lifted as my brain commanded, "Run!" The screech of brakes. I swung my head to scan behind me as I raced forward. Wilson was in my peripheral view. Time slowed like a movie scene. Wilson sprinted beside me. Six-foot-two, two-hundred- twenty pounds of rage. His hand tourniqued my wrist. Every action, every thought was suspended in something thick and heavy, like molten lead running through my veins.

In one motion, Wilson twisted me around. Jerked me toward him, hard. Lifted my arm to dangle me. I was on tiptoes, struggling for equilibrium.

Wilson clutched a huge gutting knife. He slashed down my right side.

The sound of cloth ripping. A sharp pain as the blade nicked my ribs, slicing down toward my hip.

Disoriented. Unable to function. In shock. Suddenly, everything snapped back into place. My mind switched to survival as my training kicked in.

"I'm gonna skin you alive, bitch. You think I'm going to jail for you?"

Hopping to keep my balance, I jerked my Ruger from my fanny-holster. Left-handed. Backward.

"You should be dead. No witnesses. Just pain. You gonna know how it feels to have your skin peeled from your bones, bitch."

His breath was putrid. Rancid in my nostrils. My neurons sucked in every single detail to process, searching for an escape. I flipped my gun up to position the grip in my palm. A bullet already chambered. I fired into Wilson's wrist, suspending my right hand. But Wilson was wholly focused on unzipping my skin. The blade ripped into my flesh at my hip, angling down.

I shot the wrist, slashing me.

His knife fell.

Blood dripped down his now-useless hands. He bellowed like an enraged Kodiak, nostrils flaring, eyes distended. I stumbled backward, blood running down my side. Black swirled my vision.

Down is death flashed through my brain.

With my back against the cold cement, I aimed point-blank at Wilson's chest, emptying my magazine.

Wilson lay motionless near my feet. The air eddied around me and went dim.

My last thought: *He can't survive. He's dead. So am I.*

48

I didn't know how long I lay there. A buzz against my thigh roused me. Mechanically, I pulled out my phone, dragging the receiver to my ear.

"Lynx!" Striker yelled into the phone, "Thank god! Listen. Wilson's parents posted his bail. He's on the street. Where are you?"

"Found me," I whispered. I felt the electricity of Striker's emotions buzzing through the phone. "He's dead," I added.

"And you?"

Me? "Almost dead."

"Tell me where you are." Striker's voice was forced calm.

"Park."

"You were jogging?"

"Yes."

"What can you see?"

"Trees, sky, blood..." my world went black.

I woke up in the hospital *again*.

Striker stood by my side.

Jack stayed by the door on guard.

"I'm alive?" I blinked away the spots dappling my vision.

"Looks that way." Striker eyed me appraisingly.

I touched my right side tentatively.

"A hundred and fifty-two stitches," he said.

"Wilson thought it would be fun to skin me alive." A bag of blood hung from my I.V. stand. "I needed a fill-up?"

"Yeah, you were a few quarts low." Striker leaned over the bed railing until he came into focus. His voice was husky.

"How long do I have to stay here?" I asked.

Striker shook his head. "Not sure. As soon as you're stable, I'm taking you back to the barracks with me." He reached his hand out, running a finger from my elbow down to my wrist, then traced soothing circles on my palm with his thumb.

"You want to play doctor?" I attempted a smile.

"No. I want to play hero," Striker answered. No smile. Serious.

My brows drew together. "What do you mean?"

"You were alone in the park when we found you. There was no body."

"WHAT?" I struggled to sit up. Freezing cold disbelief brushed over my skin, leaving me goose-fleshed. "How? No! What kind of monster is he?"

Striker put firm hands on my shoulders to keep me from jumping up. "Tell me what you remember. Why did you think he was dead?"

I described the attack, the gunshots. "I definitely remember his bloody twisted body on the ground." We sat in silence, contemplating an explanation.

"I bet he was wearing a vest and flying on PCP," Jack said.

"My thoughts exactly. He was stoned out of his mind and couldn't sense pain," Striker said.

"Wait. Wait! How in the world did he get out of jail in the first place? Did you say his parents posted bail? That's not possible!"

"Seems that when Mom and Dad Wilson got the phone call saying Travis was in custody, they hired a lawyer to investigate the charges. They wanted Wilson out of prison and back in a mental hospital." Striker paused as a nurse came in to check my I.V. line and send Striker a flirtatious smile. Striker's eyes were on me, and he missed the show. When she left, he continued. "Bail was as high as it could legally be set. We thought the figure was out of reach. But the Wilsons anteed up."

"Why didn't anyone call me with a warning?" Astonishment colored my words.

"Our lawyer got waylaid at the courthouse—no phones allowed there. When he got out, he called Command. Command contacted Morrison to go tell you in person…"

"Blah, blah, blah, the information passed down the food chain to me—but it was too late."

"He must have headed right for your house."

I blanched. And froze in place. "And he's still running free," I whispered. It wasn't over. I drew a deep breath in and released a shaky exhale. Even though Striker and Jack wouldn't judge me for my display of emotion, I wondered if I could ever develop a stoic exterior like they had.

Striker fixed his curious gaze on mine. "Your first two shots weren't kill-shots. You could have blown his brains out."

I knew Striker was thinking about the night Wilson broke into my house, and I had been dead set on killing the freak-show with my bare hands. I chewed my upper lip. "I thought it over and decided the other families deserved their day in court. To get their questions answered about their loved ones. It was damned selfish of me to want all the control."

Striker nodded. I thought I'd just moved up another rung in his opinion of me.

APB—Travis Wilson. The police alerted all of the area clinics and hospitals. The court revoked his bond.

The next evening, when I left Suburban Hospital, Striker wheeled me to the door and lifted me into a gray Iniquus Hummer. Secured in my protective sandwich with Iniquus in the front and back, we drove through the complex, straight to the barracks, and up to Striker's place.

My injuries were a hot topic—everyone who came by wanted to inspect my stitches. They thought my scars would be impressive. Luckily, since the knife had glanced off my ribs, my muscles sustained little damage.

My team turned their attention to the hunt. No one could figure out how Wilson had driven away without the use of his hands, bleeding at the wrists from jacketed hollow-point bullets. Not to mention the impact of fourteen bullets in his vest at point-blank range. That close, at least some of the bullets should have penetrated. Wilson should have had a chest full of ammo.

Every day the guys went out to search. Every day they came back trying to hide their discouragement. They were tenacious and single-minded.

I'd been sequestered in the complex for twelve days when an uproar erupted in the hall. My team marched home, victorious. They found the blue Honda with a badly decomposed Travis Wilson inside. He drove about twenty miles when he careened off the road into a ravine. The evergreen foliage hid the wreckage. The partially submerged car was invisible from the road.

The team had been standing roadside in the frigid weather for hours waiting for the news as a tow truck pulled the car out, and the Coroner's Investigator confirmed Wilson's identity. For days, they had been walking the highways in the hopes that just such a thing had happened.

"It's over, Chica!" Striker burst into the room.

Joy! Pure golden joy poured through my body like champagne, filling me with bubbling ebullience and light.

———

Two days later, I went back to the surgeon. He examined my wounds and pronounced me healed. The nurses patiently plucked out all those stitches. The doctor said the red scar should become a fine white line, but I had to be patient. It might take a year or two to fade. My battle scars. Or—as the men liked to call them—my "bragging rights." The doctor signed the papers, which would allow me back on full-time duty at Iniquus just in time for the company Christmas party.

The best medicine for my recovery, though, was knowing Wilson was dead and gone. Even if that wasn't the ideal end for the other victims' families. What did I know? Maybe it was. I was just glad to have finished this chapter.

49

Christmas Eve landed on a Saturday. I hosted an open house for my friends. Decorated with simple greens, pine cones, and cinnamon sticks, my house smelled of cedar and spice. In the early evening, the kids ran around on sugar highs and high expectations. I made little gifts magically appear for all of them.

We decorated cookies and ate them before the icing set and watched Santa's progress on the NORAD website. Mrs. Martini got a little drunk on the adult eggnog. She took her teeth out and put them in her lap. It was fun. It was family. It was loud!

Later, when the families with young children had gone home to try to get everyone settled in their beds, my home was filled with adults and a completely different vibe.

Giant Jack was doing the shag with his itty-bitty girlfriend, Suz. They were laughing as Jack tried to make the turns under her arm. Gator sat by the fire and whooped up his tales; his girl, Amy, grinning up at him with adoration.

I had planned this scene for Angel and me. A little taste of bitter sat on my tongue. But I consciously pushed those thoughts to the side to make room for something more cheerful.

I whipped up cocktails to drink with our late buffet. Jazzy music played on the sound system. The happy mood glittered like the icicles on my tree. As people tired, they trickled out onto the sidewalks for last goodbyes and good wishes and went home.

Striker stayed and helped me unroll the rugs and put the furniture back in place from where we had pushed them aside to make a dance floor. I ran the dishwasher, wrapped the leftovers, and stuck them in the fridge.

The morning sky showed periwinkle with a line of butter yellow on the horizon when I cozied on the couch in front of the fire with a cup of gingerbread decaf, talking to Striker. He rubbed my feet, sore from my four-inch heels and too much dancing, and looked at me with his warm green eyes, gentle with affection.

"Tell the truth, besides your feet, how are you doing?" he asked.

"Good. I'm doing good. You know, losing Angel is so different from losing my mom last year. Last Christmas is a painful memory." I angled my head up and looked at the ceiling. "When Dad and Mom died, life really changed for me. Someone whom I interacted with each day had gone. The role they played in my life was over. I kept bumping into and tripping over a whole lot of empty, you know?" I focused back down on Striker. "Everything around me had a memory of my parents attached to it."

"And with Angel?" Striker's hands had stilled on my feet.

"He never saw the things in this house. Angel never even saw the house. I had him for three weeks, almost a year ago, and then I had a lot of hopes and dreams. When I lost my parents, I lost a lot of my past. When I lost Angel, I lost what I planned for my future. I have to say mourning Angel is different."

"What did you do with his truck and motorcycle?" Striker

shifted his weight, sliding further under my legs until I was practically sitting in his lap.

"The truck I gave to his best friend, Carl, who's home from his stint in Iraq. The motorcycle I'm going to keep, so I can go on rides and remember our wonderful time together."

Striker nodded. After a while, he looked at his watch, then said, "I found some university catalogs in your kitchen."

"I've decided I'm going back to school full time in January. I'm going to try to be an average everyday college student."

"You? Average?" Striker snorted. "You can't mean that."

"But I do." I sat up, affronted by his laughter. We were nose to nose, my legs trapped under his warm hand that stroked down my stocking. "I want a traditional, normal, everyday life." I sounded childish and whiny to my own ears.

Striker shifted to his assessing look—the one that made me feel like a cryptic message he needed to work through. "That's not going to save you, Lexi," he said, all humor was gone from his voice. "You can't hide behind banality and hope life will be gentle. It doesn't work that way."

I leaned back into the pillow to gain some distance and crossed my arms over my breasts. "Leave me alone, Striker. If I want banality, then who are you to dissuade me?"

"Chica, it's impossible. You aren't wired that way. You're asking a Ferrari to drive twenty miles an hour to church on Sundays and stay garaged the rest of the week. Why would you want that? Do you think that being average means no more loss? No more pain?"

I shrugged. *Whatever, Striker.*

He leaned over and rested his forehead against mine. "Lexi, you are an extraordinary woman. And you have to live up to that. You have to, or your soul will shrivel." He lifted his head and looked me in the eye.

"That's not pretty—a shriveled soul." A smile bowed my lips slightly. Aw. That was sweet—kind of... if you dropped the shriveled soul bit.

Striker waited.

"Okay, how about a compromise between two extremes? I'll head back to school part-time to get my BS, and I'll still work at Iniquus, but part-time."

"Sorry. But no," Striker said.

"No?" I was stunned.

"You can't work part-time. Your country needs you to serve on a special assignment at the request of a very important person. We'll be on a team with him."

"Mmm, and who exactly is this VIP?"

Striker stood, pulling me up beside him. Toe-to-toe, I had to tip my head back to see his eyes. Striker bent down and whispered in my ear, "Spyder McGraw."

My mouth dropped open.

"Yes, Lexi." A full dimpled grin told me Striker thought he was giving me the best Christmas gift ever.

"You heard from him? And you didn't tell me immediately?" Why didn't Spyder call me himself? Hurt. Relieved. Angry. Happy. A mish-mash of emotions confused my face as the muscles pushed and pulled, trying to find the right expression. I bet I looked possessed.

Striker's grin dropped off, replaced with wariness. "He asked me to keep it a secret. Didn't want to disappoint you if he didn't make it in today."

"Today?" Okay. Joy won out in the emotional battle. I seized Striker by both wrists and jumped up and down like I was riding a pogo stick. Striker chuckled at my antics. Beetle and Bella got up from their sleep and danced around, adding their barks to the din.

"We need to head for the airport, Chica."

I ran toward the kitchen, where I had kicked off my shoes. A contented smile decorated my face as I retraced my path, heading for the closet in search of my coat.

Striker pulled me to him, where he stood under the mistletoe.

Good lord, but he smelled delicious—wood smoke, pine, and spicy aftershave.

"I have something for you," he said. He reached into his pocket and placed a little white present with a red bow onto the palm of my hand. I lifted the top carefully and saw a golden brooch shaped like a gift box laying on sapphire velvet. The box looked like the pressure of all the little jewels exploding out of it was lifting the lid right off.

"It's a surprise party." I smiled up at him.

Striker pulled me into his arms, leaned down, and softly kissed my lips.

I pressed my body into him as I kissed him back.

And it felt like I had found my way *home*.

The End

Readers, I hope you enjoyed getting to know Lexi and her Iniquus team. If you had fun reading Weakest Lynx, I'd appreciate it if you'd help others enjoy it too.

Recommend it: Just a few words to your friends, your book groups, and your social networks would be wonderful.

Review it: Please tell your fellow readers what you liked about my book by reviewing Weakest Lynx. If you do write a review, please send me a note at FionaQuinnBooks@outlook.com so I can thank you with a personal e-mail. Or stop by my website www.FionaQuinnBooks.com to keep up with my news and chat through my contact form.

Please follow Lexi Sobado and the Iniquus family as they continue their fight for the greater good in the next Lynx Series novel, MISSING LYNX.

Turn the page for a sneak peek:

MISSING

Lynx

FIONA QUINN

1

I strained against the seat belt, leaning forward with impatience as if by weight and will, I could get us there faster. My fingers drummed anxiously on the car door. I wanted to be at the airport now; I had waited more than a year to see my mentor, Spyder McGraw, and hear his rolling thunder laugh.

Striker slid his eyes toward me then refocused on the road. A little smile played across his lips. "You think that screaming like a Hellhound through Washington is going to get Spyder off his plane any faster?"

Striker Rheas took up a lot of space. His silken rusty-brown hair with its tight military cut brushed the roof; his shoulders — powerfully built from his days in Special Ops Forces — spread wide against the seatback. His bearing was always calm and capable — sometimes too much so. And while I obviously amused him right now, he was pissing me off. I answered him with my best withering stare and turned to the window as he drove sedately through the city streets.

The snow outside fell in big fluffy flakes, powdering the trees and cars, making the road shiny and slick. DC traffic was non-existent this morning. Everything had shut down for Christmas.

Striker pulled into Reagan International Airport's parking deck and set the brake. I narrowed my eyes so he would know not to hedge. "At least give me a hint. What kind of assignment are we going to be working on?"

There it was again, the glimmer of amusement. "I've told you everything I've got. I'll be finding out the same time you do."

"Okay, then where's Spyder coming in from?"

Striker released his seatbelt and swiveled toward me. "He flew his last leg from Dallas — DC" He held up his hands. "I swear that's all the information I know."

"This is a little surreal." I pushed a blonde curl behind my ear. "One minute, I'm starting new classes at the University, and the next, you're handing me my gear to take down some bad-guy. I had a plan."

"Plans change. Seems serendipitous — Spyder reappearing just as you wanted to head out the door." He flashed a smile. I loved Striker's smiles — slightly crooked, hint of dimples, straight white teeth. His smiles started in his warm green eyes where the flecks of gold danced. They disarmed me, but I wanted my armor up.

I arched a brow. "I think perhaps you used more bullying and less serendipity to change my heart. Maybe a little bribery?"

"Incentivizing, Lynx. You wouldn't pass up an opportunity to serve your country — and, of course, to work with Spyderman."

I got out of the car. The wind whipped the skirt of my Christmas-red cocktail dress around my legs. I was still dressed from the party last night. After the guests left, Striker surprised me with the news about Spyder coming home. Since my parents had passed away, Spyder took on a bigger role than playing my mentor; he became my other dad. Spyder's homecoming was the best Christmas gift ever. Well, that and the beautiful gold brooch Striker gave me under the mistletoe — along with the kind of kiss that should end every great romance novel. The kind that promises a happily-ever-after.

I sighed.

Ah, if life were only that simple. I didn't need a fairytale ending. Right now, I just wanted to regain my balance. And truth be told, Striker wasn't looking for fairytales, either.

I wasn't sure what he meant by that kiss. Striker was his job. He was a highly effective operator dedicated to protecting national security. Everything was secondary. Everyone was secondary. Would I change that? No. Could I live with it? Hmmm. I tried before with Angel, and that ended about as badly as anything could end. If Striker wanted a relationship with me, he'd want it on his own terms. He hadn't articulated his parameters to me. Probably because he knew I wouldn't like them.

I tightened the belt around my short wool coat as Striker walked over to my side. His eyes caught mine. He tilted his head with that assessing look of his. "That's a curious expression, Lynx. What were you just thinking?"

I smiled up at him. "That the décolleté on this party dress might be a little inappropriate for Christmas morning."

Striker grinned. "You're probably right, but I'm not complaining. I think you're beautiful." He planted a light kiss at my hairline, entwined his fingers with mine, and we walked toward the terminal.

Even in my heels, Striker's six-foot-three frame towered above me. His Irish cable knit sweater and pair of 501s accentuated everything a girl could want to be accentuated. His assets weren't lost on the woman passing us, pulling her carry-on behind her. She turned to give his rear an appreciative glance, clearly enjoying the view. Pretty tactless — the man was holding my hand, and she didn't know we weren't a couple.

In the waiting area, I shed my coat and paced in front of our seats, wringing my hands. Impatience and excitement made me hot and twitchy.

"If you get any warmer, there isn't much left to shed, Lynx." Striker stretched out his long legs and slouched back in the hard plastic chair.

"It's Lexi. I don't use my call name when I'm off the clock."

Striker's eyes moved over my dress. The low cut bodice showed off my full breasts and cinched tight at the waist like a starlet from the fifties. I'd felt flirtatious and sexy when I'd danced at the party. The skirt had ballooned out as I'd spun around, showing off legs toned from years of running and martial arts.

"What if he's late? Did you check and make sure he made his flight?" I pulled my hair back into a ponytail to get it out of my face. "I should take another peek at the board. Maybe there's been a delay."

"That's fine. You go do that."

I focused down the hall where the flight board stood. "I can't." I plopped down beside him. "My feet hurt too badly."

"I will never understand why a woman does that to herself."

"You think my high-heels are sexy, don't you?" I straightened my leg for him to see.

"Definitely."

"And that's why I wear them." I kicked off my shoes. The cold floor eased the ache. I didn't care too much about propriety since we were almost the only people at the airport. "They make my legs long and my butt perky. I like dressing girly and pretty." Actually, looking young, cute, and approachable made my job a whole lot easier. Being discounted as a piece of fluff let me go places and do things that would normally set off alarms.

Striker wrapped his arm around my shoulders, pulling me to him. "I totally agree with the girly and pretty part, Chica," he whispered into my hair.

I pushed Striker off me and jumped to my feet. "Oh God, he needs our help."

"Who does?" Striker rose beside me, his eyes scanning the room for a threat. "What are you talking about?"

I hopped on one foot, cramming my shoe onto the other one. Striker cupped my elbow to hold me steady.

"Spyder. I heard him say it in my head." I tapped my finger to my temple as I came upright.

Striker's body shifted. His muscles tightened, and the laughter left his eyes. "You heard this ESP-wise?"

A disembodied voice over the loudspeaker announced Spyder's flight was deplaning.

I didn't bother answering Striker. Of course, ESP-wise. Why else would I hear voices in my head?

I grabbed up my coat and purse and ran toward the security gate. The passengers coming up looked rumpled and droopy-eyed. I, on the other hand, was chomping at the bit, eagerly searching the crowd.

Normally, Spyder McGraw stood flag-pole tall and thin. The contrast between his white teeth and midnight, blue-black skin was startling, and it was the only distinctive thing about him. He shaved his head and wore non-descript clothes. Spyder liked to blend.

There! The last one off.

His tall frame loomed in the back behind the swarm. His shoulders bowed uncharacteristically as he moved forward zombie-like.

With my focus glued to Spyder's face, I pushed through the crush of travelers leaving the security gate. The guards jumped up from their posts — my actions drawing their attention, but I didn't care. I had to help Spyder. One guard grabbed at my arm. His other hand popped the snap on his holster. Striker brandished his Iniquus ID, and the guards fell back.

I swam forward against the current of travelers until I could reach Spyder. The deadly strong arms, that I knew so well, hung lifelessly by his sides. I pulled him into a hug. Sweat glistened his face, and his body trembled against mine. I reached up and touched his head; the heat wavered off his skin in almost visible pulses.

"I need a wheelchair," I commanded the guards whom I caught in my peripheral vision. They had braced for action mere inches away. My focus never left Spyder's face. "Spyder, you're burning up."

He mouthed, "Malaria," and keeled over.

Striker lunged for him but couldn't get a good hold from over my shoulder. I dropped to the ground to protect Spyder's head from the tile floor.

The guards pushed passengers out of the way.

"Call an ambulance!" I shouted and struggled out from underneath Spyder.

He was conscious, but his eyes were glassy and his pupils unfixed. I patted his face and called his name. He didn't even try to respond or focus on me. Striker loosened Spyder's clothes at the neck and waist.

Grabbing my purse, I upended it, searching frantically through the debris to find the extra diabetic supply kit I carried for when I babysat my neighbor's little girl, Jilly-bean.

With shaking hands, I grasped Spyder's finger. I have done blood checks about a thousand times as a volunteer EMT, but my training whispered from deep in my brain — muffled by the storm clouds of my emotions. Memories of the night my dad and I were in the car accident swamped my mind. I knelt exactly like this, on the side of the road, holding my dad's head and praying the same prayer, "Please be okay, please be okay," even though it was obviously too late for him.

The number on the meter came up low. Way too low. Verge of coma low. "Think," I commanded myself as I reached blindly for the glucose gel from my purse jumble.

"Striker, hold him still." My EMT voice sounded focused and in charge. Where did that come from? I felt everything but professional; I felt gelatinous. "When I give Spyder this glucose, he won't understand what's going on. He'll fight for his life."

Striker fastened down on Spyderman's wrists. Straddling him, Striker used his weight as leverage.

Kneeling, my thighs clamped like a vice by Spyder's ears to restrain him and protect his head. His chest didn't rise or fall. Horror jetted through my veins. I put my cheek toward his face to reassure myself that he was still breathing. Spyder's exhale whispered against my skin. My breath blew as thinly as his. My legs and feet burned and tingled from lack of oxygen. "Breathe deeper!" I ordered as much for Spyder as for myself.

By muscle memory and not from conscious thought, I held Spyder's nose until he unclenched his teeth and parted his lips. I stuck the tube into his mouth and squirted the glucose down his throat. I used all of my leg strength to protect his head and to keep him in place while I squeezed the gungy gel. As he fought, glucose smeared everywhere.

Striker wrestled Spyderman down like they were on the Olympic mats, going for a gold medal. I knew Striker would have to. Once, I watched Spyder lift a man twice his weight and throw him like a rag doll. Spyder had long thin limbs made of steel.

I had tunnel vision. Nothing existed but Striker, me, Spyder, and the red goo. As I worked, I chanted my mantra. Each inhale was a "Please." Each exhale, "Be okay." "Please, be okay." Like the Little Engine-Who-Could, cheerleading itself through the crisis. "Please, be okay."

I startled when the security guard crouched beside me.

"The rescue squad's in the building, ma'am. They'll be here in a minute."

"Grab more gel and pop the top off for me." I pointed at the tube with my chin. The guard put it in my hand and waited for further instructions.

"Hold his legs down."

The security guard looked dubious but did as I said.

I was squirting the second tube of glucose into Spyder's mouth as the paramedics rushed over with a gurney. I knew one of the guys, Chuck; I recognized him from my volunteer-training. The sight of him buoyed me. We had resources now and trained support. I put on a costume of competence. My teeth stopped chattering; my hands stopped shaking.

"What've you got here, Lexi?" Chuck asked, setting his equipment bag beside me.

"Forty-five-year-old male, with no history of heart problems, weak vitals, reporting a recurrence of malaria. High fever. Exhibiting signs of hypoglycemia. I checked with a meter I had. It read 29. I have most of one tube of gel in, and I'm working on the second one. If you've got any more, we could probably use it."

Chuck opened his case, grabbed a tube, and pulled off the plastic top. He laid it beside me and took out his official blood glucose meter. He swabbed Spyderman's finger, with Striker's help.

"22. He's not coming up yet. He's thrashing too much to try to run a line with dextrose. We may want to use a Glucagon shot." Chuck rummaged in his supply kit.

I caught Chuck's eye. "Since he's not unconscious yet, let's see if I can get enough gel in to calm him down, then we can put him on the gurney and strap him down for the IV."

He nodded. "We'll work your plan. Let me get more gels out. He's spitting most of it on you." Chuck pulled a handful of tubes from his kit.

I was covered in gel; Spyder was covered in gel. It took every single tube the paramedics had brought with them to get Spyder stable. While Spyder became lucid, the EMTs wiped him off and loaded him onto the gurney. I sat on the floor and watched — nerves vibrating.

Chuck tapped his pen against the clipboard. "Malaria. How'd you know to check for hypoglycemia, Lex?"

Spyder had contracted malaria when he was in Africa, supporting a DEVGRU operation. It was Striker who carried him out of the jungle to safety. When Spyder returned home to recover, I made sure that I knew everything I could about the disease. I wasn't about to lose another loved one. Not if I could help it. "I don't know," I said. "I must have read something about it along the way. Quinine and hypoglycemia…"

Chuck nodded. "Do you have a name and address?"

"His name is…" And I stopped. I didn't know his name. He was like a father to me, but the only name I've ever associated with him was his call name, Spyder — or as Iniquus baptized him, "Spyderman" since Striker and Spyder sound the same over the airwaves. I had no idea what his legal name was. I searched out Striker's eyes, and he shrugged.

"His name is Mr. McGraw. He's just back in the country. I don't know where he traveled in from. He'll be living with me." I gave Chuck my contact information.

"Are you following us to the hospital?" Chuck placed a kit between Spyder's legs on the gurney. His partner attached the IV bag of dextrose and saline onto a support arm.

"Yes," I said from my place on the floor.

"Okay, he's packaged for transport, so we're going to head on out. We're taking him to Suburban. Dispatch says they have a pathologist on call this morning. I'll catch up with you at Emergency. It's good to see you again, Lexi. Sorry, it's under these circumstances."

I slowly gathered the contents of my purse back together. Striker helped me to my feet and held me steady until I caught my balance.

"You're sticky." He moved his hands out and away so as not to spread the goop any farther.

"Yeah, let's wash up, and then we can go," I said.

The shock my body was processing pushed me beyond exhaustion. I shambled into the ladies' room and stood in front of the mirror. Not girly. Not pretty. Not even approachable. I was one big fat mess. Red slime in my hair, on my dress, up and down my arms. My mascara had run with the tears down my cheeks, leaving black rivulets. I did my best to wash off, took a deep breath, and headed back to the car with Striker. He opened the passenger-side door for me. I sat down but couldn't swing my legs in. I stopped for a minute.

"You okay?" Striker crouched beside me.

"Ha! My legs are shaking from that workout. Spyder fought like a madman."

Striker put his warm hands on my thighs and slowly massaged them up and down. I reached out and grabbed his wrists, his hands caught under my skirt. I swirled with emotions — too many feelings in one big rush; they made my head spin. "Please don't." The last wayward tear slid past my lashes and got stuck beside my nose.

"Lynx, I was trying to help — I wasn't thinking," Striker said earnestly.

"Not your fault. I'm just — it's too much. My emotions have been doing cart-wheels since the party."

"It's been a hell of a morning for you." Striker looked deeply into my eyes. His calm confidence steadied me. "Okay, Chica?"

I nodded.

Striker slowly brushed a stray lock of hair back, kissed the tear from beside my lips, and walked around to the driver's side.

I hauled the door shut with the last of my energy. "I'm exhausted."

Striker slid under the wheel. "It was a hell of a fight for first thing in the morning."

"What I want to know is why Spyder would chance traveling in that condition. You spoke to him — he said nothing about his being on death's door-step?"

"All he said was, 'I'm coming in for Christmas, gear up, I need help beheading the Hydra."

"Wow!"

"My thought exactly." Striker warmed me with a smile, pulled his belt across his chest, and steered down the early morning streets with his normal calm — which, as usual, drove me absolutely crazy.

GRAB YOUR COPY OF MISSING LYNX AND LET'S GO!

MISSING LYNX IS AVAILABLE IN DIGITAL, PRINT, AUDIO & AUDIO CD FORMATS.

THE WORLD of INIQUUS

Chronological Order

Ubicumque, Quoties. Quidquid

Weakest Lynx (Lynx Series)

Missing Lynx (Lynx Series)

Chain Lynx (Lynx Series)

Cuff Lynx (Lynx Series)

WASP (Uncommon Enemies)

In Too DEEP (Strike Force)

Relic (Uncommon Enemies)

Mine (Kate Hamilton Mystery)

Jack Be Quick (Strike Force

Deadlock (Uncommon Enemies)

Instigator (Strike Force)

Yours (Kate Hamilton Mystery)

Gulf Lynx (Lynx Series)

Open Secret (FBI Joint Task Force)

Thorn (Uncommon Enemies)
Ours (Kate Hamilton Mysteries
Cold Red (FBI Joint Task Force)
Even Odds (FBI Joint Task Force)
Survival Instinct - Cerberus Tactical K9
Protective Instinct - Cerberus Tactical K9
Defender's Instinct - Cerberus Tactical K9
Danger Signs - Delta Force Echo
Hyper Lynx - Lynx Series
Danger Zone - Delta Force Echo
Danger Close - Delta Force Echo
Cerberus Tactical K9 Team Bravo
Marriage Lynx - Lynx Series

FOR MORE INFORMATION VISIT
WWW.FIONAQUINNBOOKS.COM

ACKNOWLEDGMENTS

My great appreciation ~

To my editors, Lindsay Smith and Kathleen Payne

To my cover artist, Melody Simmons

To my publicist, Margaret Daly

To my Street Force, who support me and my writing with such enthusiasm.

To my Beta Force, who are always honest and kind at the same time.

To H. Russell for creating the Iniquus Bible—so I can keep all the details correct

To all the wonderful professionals whom I called on to get the details right.

Please note: this is a work of fiction, and while I always try my best to get all the details correct, there are times when it serves the story to go slightly to the left or right of perfection. Please understand that any mistakes or discrepancies are my authorial decision making alone and sit squarely on my shoulders.

Thank you to my family.

I send my love to my husband and my great appreciation. T, you live in my heart. You live in my characters. You are my hero.

And of course, thank YOU for reading my stories. I'm smiling joyfully as I type this. I so appreciate you!

ABOUT THE AUTHOR

Fiona Quinn is a six-time USA Today bestselling author, a Kindle Scout winner, and an Amazon All-Star.

Quinn writes action-adventure in her Iniquus World of books, including Lynx, Strike Force, Uncommon Enemies, Kate Hamilton Mysteries, FBI Joint Task Force, Cerberus Tactical K9, and Delta Force Echo series.

She writes urban fantasy as Fiona Angelica Quinn for her Elemental Witches Series.

And, just for fun, she writes the Badge Bunny Booze Mystery Collection with her dear friend, Tina Glasneck.

Quinn is rooted in the Old Dominion, where she lives with her husband. There, she pops chocolates, devours books, and taps continuously on her laptop.

Visit www.FionaQuinnBooks.com

COPYRIGHT

©2014 Fiona Quinn
All Rights Reserved
ISBN: 978-1-946661-25-8
Chesterfield, VA
Library of Congress Control Number: 2021910707

Cover Design by Melody Simmons from eBookindlecovers
Fonts with permission from Microsoft

CPSIA information can be obtained
at www.ICGtesting.com
Printed in the USA
BVHW070729080223
658054BV00001B/35

9 781946 661258